THE TENTH
PRAYER

THE TENTH PRAYER

A Novel of Israel

Stephen G. Esrati

28-ESRA

This is a work of fiction. Names, characters, places and incidents either are the product of the author's imagination or are used fictitiously, and any resemblance to any actual persons, living or dead, events, or locales is entirely coincidental.

This book was printed in the United States of America.

To order additional copies of this book, contact:
Xlibris Corporation
1-888-7-XLIBRIS
www.Xlibris.com
Orders@Xlibris.com

Sound the great horn for our freedom;
Lift up the ensign to gather our exiles,
And gather us from the four corners of the Earth.
Blessed art Thou, Oh Lord,
Who gatherest the banished ones of Thy people,
Israel.

The Tenth Prayer
From the morning service

SCRAPBOOK I

LETTER TO THE TERRORISTS OF PALESTINE

My Brave Friends:

You may not believe what I write you, for there is a lot of fertilizer in the air at the moment.

But, on my word as an old reporter, what I write is true.

The Jews of America are for you. You are their champions. You are the grin they wear. You are the feather in their hats.

In the past fifteen hundred years every nation in Europe has taken a crack at the Jews.

This time the British are at bat.

You are the first answer that makes sense—to the New World.

Every time you blow up a British arsenal, or wreck a British jail, or send a British railroad train sky high, or rob a British bank or let go with your guns and bombs at the British betrayers and invaders of your homeland, the Jews of America make a little holiday in their hearts.

Not all Jews, of course.

The only time the Jews present a United Front is when they lie piled by the millions in the massacre pits.

I shenk you this front. I like yours better.

Historically, the corpses of the Jews are very impressive as to numbers. But they are not a monument to Jewish valor.

They are a monument only to the brutality of the Europeans who piled them up. The Jews of America are for you because the corpse of an Irgun soldier is a unique and very high class type of Jewish corpse.

The corpse of Dov Gruner hanging from a British gallows is not a monument to the British brutality that strangled him.

It is a monument to the Hebrew valor that fights for a homeland of its own—and for the dignity of all Jews who have a homeland elsewhere.

Jewish Tories, Too!

Brave Friends, I can imagine you wondering. "If the Jews of
America are behind us why don't they help us with their support
and money?"

This is a legitimate curiosity. I'll try to answer it.

It so happens that a small percentage of the Jews of America
are not behind you—yet. (Remember you haven't won yet.)

Unfortunately, this small percentage includes practically all
the rich Jews of America, all the important ones, all the influential
ones, all the heads of nearly all the Jewish organizations whom the
American newspapers call "the Jewish leaders."

They're all against.

Every time you throw a punch at the British betrayers of your
homeland, nearly all these Jews have a collective conniption fit.

They ululate and they deplore.

They rush in waving white handkerchiefs and alibis.

They didn't do it—not they! Respectable people don't fight.
They gabble. This exhibition of weak stomachs, weak minds and
weak spines would be the blackest mark ever pasted on the word
Jew—were it only a Jewish exhibition.

Luckily for the Jews, history lightens their shameful antics.

History tells us (a little sadly) that respectability and wealth
never line up with a revolution—or a fighting minority. The American Revolutionary Army under George Washington went a long
time without shoes, guns or food.

The respectable and wealthy American colonists preferred British admiration to liberty and freedom.

They thought it was bad taste to fight for such things—against
the British, of all people. And they wouldn't kick in a dime.

In fact they proved their respectability by playing informer to
the British.

You can see how little respectability has changed since 1776.

There's another side to Jewish respectability. I'll tell you a story to illustrate it,

I went to see the old Max Schmeling-Max Baer world championship fight with an important Jewish Hollywood tycoon. He sat beside me for nine rounds without raising his head to look at the ring. He couldn't bear the spectacle of a Jew being beaten by a German.

But in the tenth round my Hollywood friend looked in the ring.

He not only looked. He jumped and cheered. He cheered so long and so hard he was hoarse for three days.

Schmeling was on his back and the referee was counting him out. It didn't look good.

Maxie Baer, with the Star of David stitched on his trunks, was upright and grinning in a neutral corner. He looked fine.

Brave Friends, I can promise you that all the respectable and wealthy Jewish personalities will be on their feet cheering for you—in Round Ten.

They'll all be for you when you don't need them.

That's the sad history of respectable people and Nervous Nellies, whatever their nationalities.

Right now all the respectability of the Jews is handsomely engaged in cooing before the Court of Nations.

Let me tell you what the Jews of America, such as myself, think of these capers.

It may give you a chuckle between jail deliveries.

We are aware that the British pulled the U.N. trick because they were frightened of you. They were afraid that your gallant and desperate fight for your homeland would gather for you the sympathy of the world.

It looked as if the cheering sections were for you. So they took their ball out of play by handing it to the referee—who was a personal friend.

The British figured that the sound of Jewish gabble before a world court would drown out the sound of Hebrew guns in Palestine.

Let me assure you, my Brave Friends, that it hasn't and it won't.

True enough, Jewish respectability is making a bit of noise at the moment. Our "Jewish leaders" are pleading for a Jewish sanctuary in fine and measured strophes.

They are not nearly as hot headed about it as were the bird lovers of America who a few years ago pleaded for a sanctuary for the vanishing penguin. But, barring a little steam, they are much alike.

They want a sanctuary where the Jews of Europe can all stand on a rock and eat philanthropy-fish till the Messiah arrives.

These Jewish Penguin Patriots are very proud for the moment because Somebody is listening to them.

Not the British or the Arabs, of course, who stand ready to shoot down Jews whether they turn into Penguins or Dodo birds.

And, thank God, not you.

The fact that you are keeping to your gallant fight against the British invaders is the sanest and healthiest thing that has happened to the battered Hebrew nation in 1500 years.

Not the gabble of respectable Jews, but your fight is the history of tomorrow.

It will be your fight that will win for the Jews of the World what they have never had-the respect of their enemies—and a land more honorable than a bird sanctuary.

Brave Friends, we are working to help you.

We Are Raising Funds For You

We are ringing doorbells and peddling your cause and passing the hat and trying to lift the heads of our Jewish respectables to have a look at the ring—before Round Ten.

It's tough going—even on the fringe of a fight for freedom. So forgive us if our take is a little meager for the time.

The rich Jews are pouring millions into the business of feeding the survivors of German massacre.

But, for a change, the Jews of America hear more than Jewish groans for solace.

We hear Hebrew courage.

We hear a battle cry that rises above the pathetic gabble in Flushing Meadows.

We hear brave men fighting on despite torture, calumny, low supplies and overwhelming odds.

We hear you. We are out to raise millions for you.

And the money is coming in-not from Jews alone but from all Americans.

Because America is not a Fact Finding Committee and a State Department.

America is a dream of freedom in the hearts of its millions and a cheer for all brave men who fight its never ending battle. Hang on, Brave Friends, our money is on its way.

Yours as ever,

/s/ Ben Hecht

BEN HECHT, Co-Chairman
American League for a
Free Palestine

THE PALESTINE FREEDOM APPEAL, INC.
Emanuel Cardozo, Chairman

GENIA I

Yevgenia Maximovna Koganova liked to recall the spring day in 1931 when she was the most important girl in the world.

It was May Day. The great military parade had finished passing through Red Square and the giant popular demonstration was about to begin. Genia and two other girls from her Young Pioneer brigade broke from the head of the Moscow children's delegation and ran up the stairs of the Lenin Mausoleum. A red bow dangled from her pigtail and a red neckerchief was tied around her white sailor blouse.

With the self-assurance that comes at the age of eight, she presented her bouquet of red roses to Comrade Stalin, who picked her up in his arms and held her so she could see the procession in the square below.

Standing a few feet to the left of Stalin was Maxim Koganov, her proud father, who threw her a kiss before resuming his clenched-fist salute.

Comrade Maxim, who had been at the Smolny Institute in Petrograd with Trotsky and Lenin in 1917, did not assume his post atop the tomb for the celebration of the Great October Revolution that year. Near the end of summer, he was arrested and tried on charges of sabotage and counterrevolutionary wrecking. He confessed and was secretly shot.

On the day Maxim Davidovitch Koganov was arrested, Genia's mother and her Uncle Alexei took her to Leningrad to stay with Babushka Koganova. It was a Tuesday. That Friday *Izvestia* published Maxim's confession; Mama and Uncle Alexei were arrested that afternoon as they came out of Babushka's apartment.

Genia, however, was safe with Babushka, an old-fashioned woman who ate by candlelight that evening.

"Why don't we turn on the lights, Babushka?" Genia asked.

"Because we are Jews and today is a Jewish holy day."

"But we were Jews in Moscow, too, and we always had lights. Why can't we have lights here?" Genia insisted.

"Shh, Genushka," the old woman answered, "your life in Moscow came to evil because your father forgot his heritage. But you must never tell anyone that I eat by candlelight on Friday. People must not know. Can we keep it our little secret?"

"Yes, Babushka."

The danger that Genia would share the secret was slight. It had been understood by all that as soon as the first three stars could be seen in the sky on Saturday evening, signifying the end of the Sabbath, Babushka would take Genia to visit relatives in Vilna. This was not easy in Leningrad where the nights were growing shorter and shorter and the white nights were about to begin, but Babushka made a little concession. At seven o'clock, although still bright daylight outside, she determined that if she were living in Jerusalem, the stars would be out and the Sabbath would be over. And then she could travel.

Uncle Alexei had made all the arrangements through Intourist, and Babushka had even been given some Lithuanian litas. Alexei did not tell Intourist that the "relatives" in Vilna were kindred only through their common descent from the Hebrew patriarchs, but Babushka was told where to go for help in Vilna.

Uncle Alexei had realized from the day of Maxim's arrest that his mother was in danger once the protection of Maxim's position no longer shielded her tenacious observance of Judaism, attendance at all Jewish funerals, and oft-expressed contempt for Maxim's apostasy. That's why he had made the arrangements for her to leave Mother Russia.

Babushka did not stop long in Vilna, and for several weeks Genia slept in hotels and rode on trains. Their trek eventually took them to Brindisi, a sunny city next to an ocean. On the way from the railway station to the harbor, they traveled in an open horse carriage along a boulevard lined on both sides with giant palm trees. Suddenly, their driver pulled his jitney to the side as a large group of men and a band came running down the center of the boulevard toward them. All wore black shirts.

"These are Fascists, Genia," Babushka said. "They are also our enemies just like your father's gang."

* * *

Genia and her grandmother stood at the rail as the *Esperia* drew near the coast. "That is Jaffa," Babushka said. "It is an Arab town. Not far from here there are Jewish towns and cities. In one of them, very far away, my third son, your Uncle Moshe lives."

"I have another uncle, Babushka?"

"Yes. He is my youngest son. Such a good boy! He went to Hebrew school even though your father kept making fun of him. He left Russia in 1919 and came here to live."

Moshe was the first to greet them as they clambered out of the long boat that ferried them ashore. He helped Genia out of the boat, then turned to his mother. As soon as they were both on firm land, he hugged and kissed them, speaking in Russian.

Genia smiled, happy to hear Russian.

"Well, little Genia," her new uncle asked, "have you enjoyed your trip?"

"Thank you. I was seasick once, but I was all right later. I learned to play tennis on the boat."

"That's nice," he said, "but I'm afraid you will not be able to play tennis in your new home; we haven't built tennis courts yet."

Turning back to his mother, Moshe asked after their luggage.

"This suitcase is all we have. We left to go to Vilna for only a few days, you understand."

"You left everything?"

"Yes. I found the ransom money in Vilna and bought Genia some lighter clothes in Brindisi. There was not as much money as I thought, but that is not important now that we are safely here."

Genia burst into tears. "I don't want to be here; I want to be back in Moscow with Papa. My Papa knows Comrade Stalin, and he'll bring Papa and Mama back to Moscow, and then I can go home, too."

"No, Genia," Moshe said gently, bending down to cuddle her. "Stalin won't bring anyone to Moscow. From now on, your home is here. You will like it. So stop crying and let's go. We have a long trip before us."

She brightened quickly, asking: "What do they call the place where you live Uncle Moshe?"

"It is called Golania and it is like a *kolkhoz*. Do you know what a *kolkhoz* is, Genushka?"

"Yes. It is a big, big farm where Comrade Stalin has taken the land from the bad *kulaks* and given it to the workers and peasants."

Moshe roared with laughter as his mother made a grimace. "Well," he said, "you have the right idea, but Stalin had nothing to do with it. You'll see."

They took a jitney from the port to Tel Aviv, riding past tan stone buildings along dusty streets, eventually emerging in a neighborhood where the buildings were built of stuccoed concrete, where people walked on the sidewalks and not in the middle of the street, and where everything looked clean and tidy.

The cab dropped them at a bus terminal. Moshe argued with the jitney driver awhile, then paid him with several coins, some of which had holes in the middle.

Grandmother had immediately noticed the change from Jaffa to Tel Aviv, which butted on each other cheek-by-jowl. "Look," she said, "the signs are in Yiddish!"

"No, Mama. They are Hebrew," Moshe corrected her.

On the bus out of Tel Aviv they sat behind two men in flowing Arab headdress.

"Uncle Moshe," Genia said, "why are those men wearing bandages?"

"Those are not bandages, Genia," he told her. "They are *keffiyehs*; they are worn like hats by Arabs."

"What are Arabs?"

"They are our neighbors, but we have not yet learned to live at peace with them or they with us."

It was a long, long ride through lots of little towns. They changed buses at Haifa and Tiberias, and it was dark when they arrived at Golania, two miles northeast of Capernaum, on the northern shore of the Sea of Galilee. The bus stopped at the end of a paved road and turned to go back to the highway. Moshe took the mail and the suitcase and led them down a dirt road to a gateway, the entrance to Golania. A small crowd awaited them there.

Children of Genia's age began to sing as they approached. A girl ran forward and gave Genia a bouquet of flowers, saying something Genia did not understand. Moshe introduced them to a sunburned woman: "This is my wife Shula. Shula cannot speak Russian, so you must learn Hebrew. This is my son, Avner, and this is my baby daughter, Rina."

During the introductions, all in Russian, Genia shook hands solemnly with each member of Moshe's family and gave Shula a kiss on each cheek. Babushka was introduced next, this time in Hebrew. Moshe's children sprang to life and threw their arms around her and called her *sabta*.

"What language do you speak, Shula?" Sabta asked.

Moshe translated.

"Just Hebrew, Sabta."

"Is there no one here with whom Genia can speak?"

"Oh yes," Shula said, "some of the members know Russian. But Hebrew is our language. Fear not; she will learn it."

Moshe and Shula lived in a long wooden house with four rooms. They used only one of the rooms; the other rooms housed two married couples and a pair of bachelors. A covered porch ran past the four doors and had a toilet and a washroom at each end. Flowers decorated the long edge of the porch.

Moshe's room contained beds against three walls. In the middle stood a small table and one chair. Along one wall next to the central door, there was a bookcase, crowded with books and magazines. On top of it, between two brass candlesticks, stood a painting of Shula. Along the other wall stood an open wardrobe with only a few clothes hanging in it and only a few piled up on the open shelves.

Moshe pointed to a bed along the far wall: "That is your bed, Mama. We will be able to move you to a room of your own soon, but meanwhile I hope you will be comfortable here."

"Where do I sleep, Uncle Moshe?"

"For you we have a much finer bed, Genushka. Would you like to see it?"

"Yes, please."

"Avner, take Genia to your house," he told his son, then explained in Russian.

Avner extended his hand to his cousin and led her out. They walked to a concrete building, the only one in the settlement that was not built of wood. Using sign language, Avner pointed to Genia's bed. Over it, the children had put up a banner with Russian lettering.

"Welcome, Yevgenia," Avner said in Hebrew, pointing to the banner.

"Welcome," she repeated.

* * *

The arrival of Genia and her grandmother was celebrated at a late dinner that night in the communal dining room, a large wooden building that also served as a theater and community house. The tables were set up for a celebration to form a large horseshoe. The white cloths that covered the tables usually served as sheets. Flowers were placed next to each table's *kolbo*, the large bowl used for olive pits, chicken bones, eggshells, and other detritus.

Genia was placed at a table with Avner and other children who would be in her class; grandmother sat with Shula and Moshe. Everyone sat on wooden benches. The food was brought in from the kitchen on a metal trolley carrying large dishes to be served family style by a big teen-aged girl in blue shorts that fit tightly around each leg like bloomers.

The children, who only rarely ate in the dining room, wore their Sabbath clothes—khaki shorts or bloomers, blue shirts tied at the neck with a red string—and a woman came and tied a towel around each of them. When she came to Genia, she smiled and said hello. Genia repeated the word, and the children let up a chorus of shouts as each tried the game of getting Genia to say something. The woman quieted them down

After dinner, Moshe got to his feet, holding up his tea glass by its pewter handle. He said something and everyone stopped talking to listen. He went on and on. Then someone else got up, but she had an accordion and began to play. Genia recognized the Communist song, but when everyone began to sing, she realized that only the melody was the same.

But at the end, they all stood while everybody sang the Soviet national anthem. Genia knew the words: "Arise ye prisoners of starvation . . . " But again, everyone else sang different words. Genia looked at Babushka. She was not singing.

After the singing, Moshe and Shula came over to tell Genia it was time for bed. He said he would see her tomorrow because this was his night to put Rina to bed.

"What will I do all day until then?" Genia asked. "I can't talk to anyone, Uncle Moshe."

"You will learn."

"I hope so."

"Good night, Genushka. Your grandmother and Shula will come to see you when you are ready to go to sleep."

The woman who had tied the towels around their necks in the dining room, also wearing shorts that looked like bloomers, watched them get undressed and washed. Their house was the only one in the *meshek*, the entire community, that had its own washrooms and toilets. The sinks were at the height where the children could use them and their toothbrushes were mounted near the sinks in a large rack with Hebrew lettering under each brush. The toothbrushes were the only private property any of the children had. Everything else, including their shoes and clothes, were worn by whoever they fit. They bore no identifying marks and were handed out when they came from the laundry according to the size marked on each item of apparel.

When all the children had gone to bed, the parents began to arrive. After a short visit, the length of which the parents enforced strictly so no child would get more attention than any other, the children were kissed good night.

After Shula and Babushka left, Genia cried herself to sleep.

GENIA II

As the years passed, Genia learned to share everyone's pride in Golania's achievements. When the children's house grew too crowded and a new one had to be built, Genia and her class visited the site regularly to watch the progress and ask the workmen questions. The workmen, of course, were members of Golania. The kibbutz at that time had no workers, paid or unpaid, from outside. It wouldn't even think of such an idea.

In the children's tours of their small world, they fed new-born animals, visited the babies in the nursery, watched the fishermen pull in their nets, planted their own little vegetable gardens, and went out into the fields to watch their parents work the land.

It was not too long before Genia felt the same possessiveness as all the other children. The kibbutz was "theirs."

With the facility of a child, Genia learned Hebrew without difficulty. At first, she was taught reading and writing separately so she could catch up with her third-grade class. They were *Kita "Gimmel"* that year and each summer they moved up one letter in the alphabet.

* * *

Several years after Genia arrived in Golania, her name became the subject of a debate at a general meeting in the dining room. Moshe *"Gimmel,"* the third bearer of the name, got up and said he thought Genia should have a Hebrew name like the rest of Moshe's family.

Moshe HaCohen, who needed no alphabet letter after his name because he was the first in the kibbutz to be called Moshe, asked Moshe *"Gimmel"* if he meant Koganova.

"No," he said. "I mean the whole name: Yevgenia Koganova."

"But you don't understand," Moshe said. "Genia does not yet know that Stalin killed her father and maybe my sister-in-law and my brother. I want her to keep her name so her family can find her. I believe that is a good reason for her to keep her name."

Moshe "*Gimmel*–" apologized and said he would not ask for a vote on the matter.

But Moshe explained it all to Genia on Sabbath morning, when they ate heavy clotted cream and had honey for breakfast along with the vegetables and the hard-boiled eggs. He had asked her to eat with Shula, Sabta, and himself and she sat and watched him spoon the cream over his salad. She wrinkled up her nose.

"It tastes much better if you eat it plain and sprinkle sugar on it, Uncle Moshe. You want to try mine?"

She shoved her plate across the table, and Moshe tried it.

"Good!" he said. "But the cucumbers also taste much better with the cream on them. You want to try?"

Eventually, he got to the point, speaking in Russian so his mother could understand better: "Genia, your father was a great man. He may not have been right in all that he did, but he was still a great man. He will be inscribed into the pages of the history of our people as a man who helped change the world. Unfortunately, your father has been dead now for five years. We did not tell you because we did not want you to lose hope."

"I knew, Uncle Moshe. I figured it out in Vilna."

Sabta put her arm around her granddaughter and hugged her, saying, "I did not tell her, Moshe."

"No, Sabta. I overheard what you told our 'cousins' in Vilna. But my Mama is still alive, isn't she?"

Moshe answered: "We do not know, Genia. But as long as we do not know, I think you should keep the name my brother gave you, Yevgenia Maximovna Koganova. You should bear his name not only so that your mother may someday find you but also to remind the world that Maxim Koganov lives in you and that you have found the true road to socialism."

* * *

The problem of the name was eventually overshadowed by a problem that was much more personal. Genia. woke up one morning and found that she was wet. She stayed in bed, ashamed to get out.

When Yudit, their teacher and mother surrogate, came in, Genia whispered her secret in Yudit's ear: "I am in heat, Yudit."

"You mean you are having your first period, Genia. You need not be ashamed of that. Come, let us go into the washroom together."

"No, they'll see."

"Don't you think it was wrong for Adam and Eve to be ashamed all of a sudden? But, if you wish, I'll bring you a washcloth and you can get cleaned up under the blanket. But if we do that, everybody will know. Come, get washed and dressed and we'll go to the dispensary together."

Reluctantly, Genia got out of bed. The boys appeared to pay no attention, but Miriam came over and whispered to Genia that it had also happened to her. Genia lost her sense of embarrassment and took a shower as Yudit quietly explained what was taking place in Genia's body. On the way to the dispensary, they passed the sewing room where Sabta was working, "Sabta," Genia cried out proudly, "now, I am a woman."

* * *

One day when they were all working in the potato field, Avner and Shalom, the two boys who had become Genia's best friends, began to tease Oded and Hava, Golania's.

"Oded," Shalom shouted, "you and Hava are still babies. The other girls have become women. Avner and I have started to grow hair here, but you and Hava are still children."

"I have hair here, too," Hava said, belligerently.

"In girls," Avner expounded with all the wisdom of his twelve years, "that does not count. Girls have to have what Genia and Miriam have, then they become women."

* * *

Sabta, still shocked by the way in which the children lived together, brought up that subject one evening as she sat with Moshe and Shula in the eucalyptus grove, overlooking the Sea of Galilee. By now, Sabta knew Hebrew well enough so that she and Shula had no need for Moshe's translations.

Shula assured Sabta that she need not worry; the children were better off growing up with knowledge and fact than with half truths and smut like city children.

"But Shula," the old woman persisted, "they can't keep on sharing their rooms like this. Who knows what they will start doing soon."

"Sabta, they would do the same things even if they were kept apart. I did. Moshe did. You probably did, too. Isn't that right, Moshe?"

"Yes, Mama, it is. Remember that they are rarely alone. They will not get into trouble. But I want to assure you that the age at which the children are separated by sex is still being discussed in all kibbutzim. Right now, the age varies, but in no case is it done before they leave elementary school. In one of the older kibbutzim, they tried to segregate at thirteen, and the children were unhappy at the sudden separation. I don't know the ideal age, but I suppose we will eventually split them. But we do have to take the twins into consideration. Apparently their development is a bit slower, and we can't do something that would injure them."

The discussion about moving the boys out into a different house arose again that summer when a dozen city children from the party's youth movement came to Golania during their school vacation. They were housed in tents near the houses of Golania's children and spent their days with the Golania children. But there was one big difference. The city children went to the men's and

women's communal showers for their ablutions and used the out-
houses to void. They never went into the children's houses to use
those facilities, even though the old children's house was nearer
and had flush toilets.

Although the city children were the same age as Genia's class,
they were altogether different. The Golania children noticed and
asked questions.

Genia asked Yudit if she, too, could use the adult showers. She
was told that she was free to do as she liked, but Yudit asked her
why she would want to since it was much more convenient to
shower right next to where she slept. Genia accompanied the city
girls to the showers one day after they finished working in the
chicken house. She noticed that the city girls wore bras, and also
noticed how they hid when they changed or voided. She remembered that the city children had laughed at her a few days ago
when she had gone to void in the field because they could all see
Genia.

The problem was not new in kibbutzim. The mothers of
Golania were divided about any change because of the twins. The
saying at any meeting that took up the matter was: "We cannot
separate Hava and Oded from each other."

But a compromise was reached. Walls were put up inside the
children's shower room and in the middle of their four toilets.
This "solution" was completely ignored by the children, who went
to whichever commode was available and wouldn't think of ending a conversation just because they were headed for the shower.
But the parents were happy.

The children called the partitions "wailing walls."

* * *

The following summer, Genia had her first romantic experience. A
city boy was extra special. He was good looking and said he would
join Golania when he grew up. They were sitting on his blanket at
a campfire and had sung themselves hoarse. As the fire burned

down, they lay back, looking at the stars. He kissed her and began to touch her. She let him, but soon made him stop when she started to feel uncomfortable.

"Genia, did you ever kiss a boy?"

"Not like just now, Natan."

"Did you like it?"

"Yes and no."

"Why no?"

"I don't know. It made me feel funny inside."

"Me too. I kissed a girl here last summer, but I didn't feel anything. I guess I'm growing up."

Later, they went to the older children's house to start dancing. They began with folk dances that they all knew, but the city children soon started to dance differently with each other, as one of them played American "hits" on the harmonica. Natan tried to dance with Genia, but she did not know how.

That night, Avner reached over and banged Genia's foot.

"Go away, Avner."

"Do you know what I did tonight?" he whispered.

She clambered down to the foot of her bed to hear him.

"I did it tonight, Genia."

"What do you mean? You mean you did it?"

"Yes, with Ahuva."

"Was it good?"

"Yes."

"Did she let you?"

"She showed me how. Would you like me to show you how."

"No. I have time."

"Hurry. You're missing something very good. Good night."

" 'Night, Avner."

The next morning Genia worked near Ahuva in the tomatoes. She looked at her clinically to see if she could detect any change. Finally, her curiosity getting the best of her, she asked point-blank to tell her how she had done "it."

"Did what?"

"What you did with Avner last night."

"Did you see us?"

"No, he told me"

"Stupid donkey!"

Ahuva ran off, furious. Genia did not understand why she was so annoyed. Natan came over to see what was going on.

"What's the matter with her, Genia?"

"I don't know."

"Why did she run off like that?"

"I just asked her a question. I don't know why she is angry."

"What did you ask?"

"Well, I, uh, I asked her how she did it."

"Did what?"

"You know, what men and women do."

"Oh. Why did you ask?"

"She did it last night with Avner."

"Oh."

"He told me."

"Oh."

"Why do you suppose, Natan, that she ran away?"

"If you do that, you don't tell."

"Why not?"

"You just don't, that's all."

"I don't understand. Everyone in Golania knows when we take the cows to the bull."

"That's different. If you and I did it tonight, would you tell Avner?"

"Why not? We have no secrets, except once when I first became a woman."

"Why did you have secrets then?"

"I was being very childish. Yudit told me that when grownups do it, all the other grown-ups know because they come to the dispensary to get things."

"You mean these?" Natan said, pulling a package of condoms from his pocket.

"What are they?" she asked.

"They prevent babies. I got these in Haifa because I would be too ashamed to ask for them at the dispensary."

"Oh, go away, Natan. I don't understand you and your shames. You'd be ashamed of everything."

That night, Avner crawled into her bed and started another whispered conversation. He could not understand why Ahuva had been angry, either. They decided that city children were crazy.

* * *

As Genia turned into young womanhood, Golania had to spend more and more of its energies on defense. When the Arab riots broke out in 1936, their area was relatively peaceful. But in 1937, Fawzi el-Ka'ukji, supported by Haj Amin el-Husseini, the Grand Mufti of Jerusalem, and by Italian agents, led his first invasion into Palestine. The British refused to allow Jews to arm themselves.

Moshe took charge of the defense of Golania. *Slicks*, special hiding places for weapons, were built all over the *meshek*. The members took turns standing guard, and the silo, built on a tel in the middle of Golania, became the command post. Up on top, guards watched for Arabs, down underneath, there was a bomb shelter and a telephone connected to Rosh Pina's general store.

Happily, there was no fighting near Golania that year. In a change of policy, the British had decided to chase the invaders out of Palestine. They even gave the Jews limited permission to acquire weapons, provided each bullet was accounted for to the British district commissioner in Tiberias.

When Britain decided in 1939 to fight Hitler, Moshe and eight other members of Golania left for the British army. The month he left, Genia's class finished school and started their apprenticeships. In 1942, they were all elected members of Golania. Genia had just turned eighteen.

* * *

In the summer of 1945, the Jewish Agency in Jerusalem received a questionnaire from a field worker in Germany seeking the whereabouts of Moshe HaCohen. His sister-in-law had been found.

Sabta came to the room Genia shared with Miriam to deliver the good news.

Genia, who had come to accept Moshe and Shula as her own parents, was dumbfounded. Avner and Shalom came in with Hava and Miriam, big smiles on their faces. Avner picked Genia up and spun her around and passed her to Shalom. The room filled; everyone was happy for Genia.

Genia was on the edge of tears.

She walked out of the room with Sabta, who was still trying to explain: "Think of it. Your mother is alive. I am going to Jerusalem to arrange for her to come here. With you in the country, she will have preference for a certificate."

"Where is she?"

"In Germany."

"How did she get there?"

"I don't know. Come, I am writing her a letter. You write something, too."

"Oh, Sabta, I don't know how to write Russian any more."

"That's all right. I'll write what you tell me."

They went to Sabta's room and Genia dictated:

> Dear Mama,
>
> I do not know how to write in Russian, so Sabta is writing for me. It is wonderful to learn that you are not dead like six million of our people.
>
> It was in the hope that you were alive that I have retained the name you gave me, Yevgenia Maximovna Koganova. Now that we have found you, I no longer need to keep such a terrible name. When you come, we shall go to

Tiberias together and ask the district commissioner to give us back our real name: HaCohen.

We live in a kibbutz named Golania, after the Golan Hills which we can see in Syria. Moshe and his wife, Shula, have two children. Avner was in my class; Rina is younger and is still in school. Sabta—that's what we call babushkas in Hebrew—lives with us, too. She does not need to work because she is over the age, but she always wants to, so she sews clothes for the members. She is very good.

Moshe is in the British army. He is a major in the Jewish Brigade which fought in Italy. Before he went into the army, he was secretary of the kibbutz and wrote books.

Shula is an animal breeder and veterinary helper. Thanks to her, we have won many prizes with our sheep and our hens.

I worked in the vegetables a long time. Then, we tried to start a vineyard, but it is too hot here. We are two hundred meters below sea level. So, we plowed the vineyard under and I now work with a class of children, two years of age. I shall work with them for sixteen more years and then get a new class.

I hope you come to join us soon. It is such a lovely place.

From your loving daughter.

"Let me sign my name, Sabta. I know how."

* * *

Sabta returned from Jerusalem several days later. The Jewish Agency could do nothing to speed Natasha's journey. However, one of the people with whom grandmother spoke had a good idea, and Sabta wanted to know if Genia and Shula approved.

"For God's sake, Sabta," Shula said impatiently, "come out with it already. What is the secret idea?"

"It will not meet with your approval. You are Socialists, though Jewish ones. You will say no."

"Oh for heaven's sake, Sabta," Shula implored. "Haven't we made you understand that socialism as Maxim saw it and socialism as we live it are different? Not even after all these years?"

"All socialism," Sabta said quietly, "denies freedom to the person, Shula. You celebrate the Jewish holy days like pagans, you do not teach your children about God, you even allow the eating of pork, which is against God's law. But let us not argue, Shula. The man's idea was good. He took me to an American, who said he could make arrangements."

"American?" they both asked.

"Yes. Natasha will tell her story to an American magazine. Trotsky's widow did. If we tell Natasha to see a man in Munich, he will be able to write her story for her. The money she makes will make it possible for her to come here as a tourist, without needing a certificate. After she is here, perhaps we can arrange for her to stay."

"Why, that's wonderful, Sabta," Shula said. "What made you think we would disapprove?"

"They want the story to hurt Stalin."

"Why should we object?" Genia asked.

"But you are Socialists!"

JACK I

Two days after the 88th Infantry Division sent the first American units into Rome, Jack Frumkin went AWOL from the 313th Field Hospital for what was to be a private victory parade through Rome's Arch of Titus.

Since Hebrew school, Jack had known that the arch was built to celebrate the fall of Jerusalem and that for two millennia no Jew had walked through it; but he would do it, a blue-and-white banner of David held high, to mark the fall of Rome to the Allies.

If he lived to reach Berlin, he would climb the Funkturm and hoist his flag to the top, the flag of vengeance and victory.

Beyond Rome, the 88th Division ran into the nemesis it was to meet all the way to the River Po, all the way to the Brenner Pass—the Hermann Göring Division of the SS, which had knocked the 88th out of the front line shortly after the fall of Rome. That's when Jack had been wounded.

Jack thought the arch was at ground level across some broad avenue. He was wrong. It cannot be marched through. Its central passage near the Colosseum is high above the excavated terrain of the Roman Forum. Jack had to devise a different way to celebrate.

He scrounged some sheets, ropes, camouflage paint, and rocks that he wrapped in rags. Tying the ropes to the sheets, he threw the rocks over the arch and hoisted the sheets over the front and rear entablatures. Finally, he unfurled the flag and attached it to the side of the arch.

When he was finished, the inscription on the arch—IUDEA CAPTA—was replaced by his signs: ROMA CAPTA! IUDEA RESURRECTA!

Jack backed up. He came to attention, saluted and started to sing. It must have been an odd sight, a five-foot-ten technical sergeant in his torn and dirty fatigues, liberated from the hospital, standing in the Foro Romano and singing in Hebrew.

"In blood and fire, Judea fell. In blood and fire, Judea shall rise, shall rise."

His usual clear tenor voice, was impaired by the choking that came with tears of joy.

But the carving, which had proclaimed its message for nearly two thousand years, was covered by Jack's sheet for, at most, fifteen minutes. MPs arrested him and he concealed that he was AWOL from the hospital. He was taken back to his unit, Fox Company of the 351st Infantry Regiment with a recommendation that he be court-martialed for desecrating a protected historic monument. His company commander tore up the recommendation and sent him back to the hospital.

* * *

For Technical Sergeant Jacob Frumkin this was not God's war or Roosevelt's war, or America's war. It was his war. He was the avenger. He would take eye for eye, tooth for tooth. Not for him any Christian love-thine-enemy preachments, nor any diminution of his naked, burning hatred, the fierce hate that was kindled even before the Frumkins left Germany for the safety of America.

As a child, Jack saw the brown SA marching through the streets singing about the Jewish blood that was to spurt from their daggers. He saw SA men standing guard before Jewish stores with signs calling on Germans to prevent disease by not shopping in them. And, in the first grade he was forced to change schools because Jews could no longer attend public school in Berlin.

Jack could remember the tear-filled good-byes as he and his parents left his grandparents in Berlin. He remembered the day when his grandmother Jenny sent her first letter to Boston bearing a return address from "Sara" Apfelbaum. But, most of all, he remembered the deaths of his parents.

Dr. Hans Frumkin had gone back to Germany late in 1938 as a brand-new American citizen to try to obtain American visas for his parents and his mother-in-law. It was in November—November 9, the night of the broken glass, the night that will forever be remembered as *Kristallnacht*. Nazi hoodlums coursed through the streets breaking windows, torching synagogues, humiliating any Jews they encountered. One group of Nazis, led by a former patient of Dr. Frumkin, ran into him as he returned from a futile visit to the U.S. consulate. He was left in the gutter in a pool of his own blood. The American consul wrote to Boston that Dr. Frumkin had died in a "traffic accident," as he had been informed by the police.

Just before the outbreak of the war, Klara Frumkin and her husband Alwin left Germany with a French transit visa and American assurances that their visa application would be transferred to the consulate in Paris. At the fall of France, still without U.S. visas, the aged couple trekked into unoccupied France.

Finally, the visas were issued by the consulate in Vichy, and they crossed to Morocco to board a freighter. Three days before reaching New York, their ship was torpedoed by a U-boat. There were no survivors.

Late in 1943, a postcard arrived from the International Committee of the Red Cross in Geneva. "Sara" Apfelbaum was dead. She had succumbed to a kidney disease in Theresienstadt. But to Jews, Theresienstadt was already known—as were Dachau and Buchenwald.

(In 1991, when Nazi records held by the bankrupt German Democratic Republic were made public, it was learned that Oma Apfelbaum had actually died of starvation seven months after being shipped to Theresienstadt. She was 59 years old.)

Anna Frumkin took the news of the death of her mother as a traditional Jewess. She placed the house in mourning. The mirrors were covered; she wore torn clothes and went barefoot at home. A twenty-four-hour memorial candle burned on the mantelpiece. But it fell to Jack to mourn in the synagogue for he was the last male of the line. Each day he huddled with nine other men in the age-old service for the departed at Roxbury's beautiful Temple Mishkan Tefillah, facing Franklin Park.

The Frumkins mourned in the custom of their people because they knew no other way. It was not that they were deeply observant in their religion; they were not. Nor was it because they kept a kosher home or observed the Sabbath; they did not. But how else does one mourn? One lights candles, and says *kaddish* and sits *shiva*, and one tries not to weep.

One morning, when Jack arrived at the Mishkan Tefillah, he found three boys painting swastikas on the doors. Jack leaped on one of them and was, in turn, jumped by the other two. The fight was stopped by Patrolman Francis Xavier Dooley, the cop on the beat. Dooley grabbed Jack and, pinning him in one arm, began to hit him over the head with his night stick.

"Ya little Christkiller bastard," Dooley yelled as he brought his club down on Jack's skull, "I'll learn ya to hit a white man." The noise brought the prayer circle, the *minyan*, out of the synagogue. Jack was taken to Beth Israel Hospital with a fractured skull.

When Anna was told what had happened, the news was more than she could stand. "First the Nazis beat my husband to death," she said, "and now they beat my son." Then she collapsed with the telephone still in her hand.

Jack had to fight hospital rules to win permission to visit her room. A reporter and a photographer witnessed the reunion.

"Jackie," she said, "I'm glad they let you come. I have things to tell you before I die. . . . No, Jackie, let me talk, I haven't much time left. You are the last of us. You must promise you will bring back the dead. Name your children after your grandparents and don't allow our families to die out. Have many children and replenish the earth."

"Cut it out, Mom," Jack pleaded, stroking her hair. "Don't talk like that."

"Don't argue, Jackie. Listen to me. Your grandfather's name

was Alwin Frumkin and Oma Frumkin was Klara. My father was Adolf, but that name you better not use. My mother you know. Will you remember?"

"Sure, Mom, but you'll be able to tell me all that when the time comes. Now I'll leave you and let you have some rest. I'll visit you again later."

A flash bulb went off as Jack, his head swathed in bandages, kissed Anna. The picture was on the front page of the next morning's *Globe*. Anna had waited to give her final instructions to her son before her heart gave out. The newspapers made much of the death and the funeral. Prominent persons, Jews and gentiles, attended the service to expiate community guilt. The *Globe* even did a Sunday feature on the extermination of the family, including a German newsphoto of the sinking of the freighter with the Frumkins aboard and an oval portrait of Dr. Frumkin in his World War I German army uniform, his Iron Cross proudly displayed on the tunic.

A few days later, Dooley was given a reprimand for using excessive force.

Jack enlisted in the army and the Public Latin School awarded him his diploma. He asked to be assigned to the infantry, even though the Army offered to make him a chaplain's assistant when it was noted that he had attended Boston's Hebrew Teachers College.

"Hell, no," Jack said. "I want a rifle, not a prayer book. I've got scores to settle."

* * *

At the end of the war, Jack became an interrogator at the 88th Infantry Division's large POW cage in Brescia. The point system was instituted and eighty-five points earned GIs a trip home. Jack had more than enough, but still hoping to get to Berlin to put his flag on the Funkturm, he signed a waiver and requested a transfer to Germany.

Eventually, Fox Company was moved to the prewar border

where Italy, Austria, and Yugoslavia meet. Jack was billeted in former Italian army barracks near Fusine Laghi. Over the entrance to one of the buildings was an Italian inscription: "The border is sacred and must be defended!—Mussolini." Over the mess-hall door was: "If I advance, follow me; if I retreat, shoot me." A wag had scribbled "Done as requested" under it, in English.

But Jack was most impressed by the inscription running along the top of the mess hall wall. A Hebrew frieze had been painted there. When the acting company commander, First Lieutenant Martyn Lynch, ordered the mess hall whitewashed, Jack asked permission to contact the division's Jewish chaplain before the Hebrew frieze was painted over.

"What for, Frumkin?" Lynch asked.

"Well, Sir, that frieze is in Hebrew and I think the chaplain might want to see it."

"Can you read it?"

"Sure. 'In this place in Iyar 5705,' that's the date this spring in the Hebrew calendar, Sir, 'the Jewish Brigade ended its struggle to erase Hitlerism from upon the face of the Earth. In blood and fire, Judea fell; in blood and fire, Judea shall rise.' "

"Sounds like the Bible."

"Yessir," Jack said. "There was an outfit from Palestine. They passed through here."

"OK. Get in touch with the chaplain. We'll wait with the mess hall."

A few days later Chaplain Morris Goldberg read the frieze and the ledger books that had been found among the rubble in a shed.

Jack looked at one book. It was an inventory. There were entries for *Roveh* Enfield, *Roveh* Sten, *Roveh* Bren, *Mikla* Vickers, Bangalor*im*, and other items he could easily identify by their adjectives.

"Isn't it strange to see the language of the Bible used to describe machine guns and Bangalore torpedoes, Frumkin?"

"I suppose these Palestinians had to improvise quite a few words to use Hebrew in their army, Sir."

"Yes, I suppose that's so, but it's the sort of thing it takes getting used to." He paused, continuing in a lowered voice. "I had another thing I wanted to talk over with you. These inscriptions did not really bring me way up into these mountains. I came here because I need an assistant."

"Nothing doing, Sir. I'm trying to get transferred to Germany."

"What the hell do you want in Germany? I can't imagine any Jew wanting to go to Hitler-land."

"I was born there and I want to go back."

"Well, I'll be goddamned!"

Jack was taken aback to hear the slight, kindly looking rabbi break into such language. "Don't get me wrong. I want to go there for the opposite of what you're thinking. I've still got scores to settle."

The rabbi quickly understood. "It's too late for that. The war is over. No more killing. Above all, no more killing of Germans. We Jews have other enemies to fight."

As he said this, he looked into Jack's eyes with a searching look. Then he put his arm around Jack's waist and began to lead him from the compound of buildings toward a partly destroyed railway station nearby. "Yes, Frumkin, there are other enemies! Those who make our displaced people into hopeless refugees with no place in the world to go to or even to look forward to. Let me tell you why I want you to come and help me."

They sat down on the railroad tracks that used to lead into Yugoslavia. There was not much to explain; the rabbi was helping the Jewish underground smuggle refugees to Palestine and he needed help.

Jack realized he had found a kindred spirit.

"OK, Rabbi. I'm with you. I'll put in for the transfer right away."

"Good. I knew you would. I had heard of your adventure in Rome from my predecessor. But hold your tongue. You're trans-ferring to Division CP only to help me at services. Got it?"

"Check."

* * *

In little more than a week—fast for army paperwork—Jack's orders came through and he left for Division Headquarters in Gorizia.
The six-by-six chow truck on which he had caught a ride pulled
up in front of a modern, cream-colored building from which the
American flag flew. Over the main entrance was a sign "HQ &
HQ CO—88TH INF DIV—LEGION" bordered by the outlines
of chiseled-down fasces. Down the street was the Division Command Post with its sign, flag, and an MP guard.

The rabbi was seated at his desk and Jack saluted and reported
with snap. The rabbi signed with his head and hand not to be silly
and waved Jack into a chair. "Glad you made it so soon, Frumkin.
I'm snowed under and we have a lot to do. There are hardly any
Jews in the division until our peacetime replacements arrive. So,
for the time being, our services are strictly for civilians. Can you
sing?"

"I haven't done it since my bar mitzvah."

"That's all right. I must have some legitimate reason for an
assistant other than that the table of organization calls for one.
You're now my cantor."

He offered Jack a cigarette. "Now, to business. First, let me
straighten you out on military courtesy. When we are alone, I
don't care what you call me, nor will I stand on salutes or chicken.
But outside this office, I'm Chaplain Goldberg and you're going to
open doors for me and snap to. You will of course be my driver,
too."

"OK by me, Rabbi, I can soldier with the best of them, but let
me get some stuff off my chest, if you don't mind. I studied at the
Hebrew Teachers College in Boston under a teacher who convinced
me that most Zionists are bums. I joined Vladimir Jabotinsky's
movement and campaigned for a Jewish army made up of the Jews
of Europe and Palestine. I wanted to destroy the Jewish Diaspora
before the Diaspora destroyed the Jews. And, above all, I wanted a
Jewish state.

"My teacher said a Zionist is a Jew in America who collects money from another Jew in America to send a third, poor Jew to Palestine. He loathed the World Zionist Organization because it practiced selective immigration, distributing the few immigration certificates permitted by the British only to its true believers, Socialists who don't want a Jewish state and who have actually turned over our people to the British. So tell me, Rabbi, which side are you helping here?"

The rabbi leaned back in his chair, put his hands behind his neck, and looked up at the ceiling. "So you are a supporter of the *Irgun*, Frumkin. Or are you perhaps for the Sternists, who just killed Lord Moyne in Cairo?"

"Both, actually. I am in favor of a Jewish state in Palestine, just as Theodor Herzl was. I don't have any use for the Socialist Zionist leaders in Palestine. And from what I've seen since the end of the war, I'm not impressed by the underground in Europe that is smuggling Jews to Palestine. They seem to want to put people through agricultural training in Europe more than they want to get them to Palestine."

"Now just you wait a minute, Frumkin. I am working from morning to night with people from the Joint Distribution Committee and with Palestinians wearing British uniforms who are deserters from the Jewish Brigade. They get the people to Italy; they ship them to Palestine. I don't ask about their politics."

"So you won't help just those who want only Socialist agricultural laborers? You'll send anyone?"

"I don't 'send' anyone. I help those who do. I have no say over who sails. I don't ask the Palestinians which side they belong to. I do what I can. We have a synagogue here in Gorizia that was pretty badly vandalized by the Germans. The synagogue—like the rest of the city—was totally destroyed in the First World War. The synagogue was rebuilt largely with help from the Ascoli family, prominent Gorizia Jews who were violent opponents of Mussolini. They live in the States now. There are only about twenty-five Jews left in town, so we don't have much to do in the way of services. There may be as many as five hundred more in Trieste, but a Jewish Brigade rabbi looks after them. And then there's a DP camp in Udine. Those poor bastards are entirely dependent on charity.

"Our main job is to worry about the new arrivals who are trucked here by the Jewish Brigade. They bring them here, to this American-occupied corner of Italy, because they can cross the border from Austria most easily here. From here, they have to be taken to the ports from which they sail to Palestine. Some are driven directly to our synagogue, and I sometimes don't find out about it until Friday evening services. Others are driven to the big synagogue in Trieste, which the Germans spared because they used it as a warehouse and stable. Those people have to be fed, clothed, given medical attention, and sent on their way."

"Why don't they just go to the DP camp in Udine?"

"Because the people who are being sent here are illegal. They don't exist; they're not even in Italy. They're still in a concentration camp in Germany. The minute they get into a DP camp, the British know they're here."

"Where do I come in?"

"Superficially, you'll be my driver. I've had a rough time since Abrams went home on points. I can't really trust a motor pool driver. We make the rounds every week, looking for the people who have been delivered to us. We distribute what the Joint gives us. Have you ever heard of the 179th Royal Army Service Corps Company."

"No, Sir?"

"It's a trucking outfit in the British Thirteenth Corps, to which this division belongs. There's only one rub. Every man and woman in the 179th RASC is a deserter from the Jewish Brigade. The entire outfit is phony. Let me give you the background.

"When the war ended, the British wanted the Jewish Brigade the hell out of Italy for two reasons. They did not want them anywhere near the coast, lest they fill ships full of DPs bound for Palestine. In addition, there were an awful lot of mysterious disappearances of Nazis in southern Austria and witnesses always reported that 'British military police' had knocked on the door and arrested the missing persons, who were never seen again. The shit really hit the fan when Odilo Globocnik, who was the biggest Jew killer of them all—according to Heinrich Himmler—disappeared from his home. He was wanted for war crimes and real British MPs apparently just missed catching him. Globocnik, by the way, was the top Nazi for this area and lived in the same castle that is now used by Gen. John Harding, commander of Thirteenth Corps.

"So the British put most of the Jewish Brigade in sealed box-cars in Italy and sent them across Germany—sealed boxcars, Frumkin, just like Jews heading for Auschwitz—to Holland. That's where most of the brigade is now. A few are still in Trieste; but a huge number deserted and somehow ended up in the 179th.

"Here's where we come in. The people bringing Jews from Germany are apparently separate and distinct from the 179th. They don't even work together. That is done for security reasons. The people running the operation from Germany are mainly em-issaries from Palestine who work under various covers. When the DPs get to Italy, it's my job to get them out of here on 179th trucks. Many of them get shipped to the area south of Genoa, to ports in Civitavecchia and La Spezia. Those who get to Trieste, don't need me for transport, just for physical help. But those who come to Gorizia and other places around here, I've got to find them and get them hooked up with the 179th. A few weeks ago, about 150 Jews ended up in the division brewery in Tolmezzo and I had to find some way of moving them out of there. It isn't easy, especially because I cannot be obvious about any of it. I believe our army's Counter Intelligence Corps and the British army are looking into all this.

"Anyway, the 179th picks up relief supplies in Leghorn for us—that gives them a legitimate reason to go there. There is noth-ing to stop them from carrying a few passengers on their way there, is there?"

He smiled, but it was a forced smile.

"Is all this against army regulations, too, Sir?"

"You bet. Does that bother you?"

"No, Sir. And forget about what I said about selecting illegal immigrants. This sounds like everybody who comes gets shipped. That's the way it ought to be."

JACK II

Jack wandered around Gorizia toward the International Style villa that housed the American Red Cross. On his left was a hospital, one of the locations described in Ernest Hemingway's *A Farewell to Arms*. On the opposite side of the street stood a Protestant church, which also figured in Hemingway's book.

He turned a corner and went past the public bath house, where GIs and German POWs often found themselves under the same shower. Walking on, he turned another corner and headed back to the main drag, passing the forbidding structure that sprouted a huge, fluted red star and signs proclaiming it as *Dom Narodni Slovenski*—the Slovenian National Home. Because it was the stronghold of the Yugoslav Communists who wanted Gorizia to be part of Yugoslavia, the building was off limits to GIs. But Jack felt a kinship with it because the music pouring out of its loudspeakers were strangely similar to the Palestinian folk songs he had learned at Hebrew Teachers College.

When he got back to his room, a note was pinned to his blanket: "FRUMKING REPORT TO SINAGOG IMMIUTLY."

The synagogue was on a dingy street. Heavy wooden doors opened onto a cobble-stoned courtyard, littered with rubble, saw horses, and lumber. Grass grew between the cobbles. The building was ugly, its stucco cracked and peeling; a bas-relief of two lions holding the tablets of the Law was above the lintel, but the tablets were full of bullet holes. Inside, rough benches surrounded a central platform, showing that this was a Sephardic place of worship.

"Hello, Frumkin," Chaplain Goldberg's voice called from the women's gallery above. "Up here."

Jack found the stairs and climbed to the balcony, which had only two wooden benches behind its latticework screen. Two people in British uniforms sat on one bench, their backs to the screen. The rabbi sat facing them. He got up, put his arm around Jack, and led him toward his friends.

"Frumkin, I want you to meet Major Aron and Sergeant Ben Dror."

The others rose as the rabbi made formal introductions, using the military pecking order: "Major Aron, this is Technical Sergeant Jacob Frumkin, my new assistant. Frumkin, this is Sergeant Ben Dror."

Jack failed to notice that he outranked Sergeant Ben Dror, only that the sergeant was a woman. He shook hands and mumbled, "Pleasedtomeetyou."

Major Aron was English, his rank shown by red crowns on his epaulets. The sergeant's uniform bore no insignia other than her upside-down stripes.

Chaplain Goldberg got straight to the point. "I asked you to come here to find out about your last leave."

"Sir, my last leave was last year at Montecatini Terme," Jack said, remembering his instructions on military courtesy.

"Splendid," the rabbi said. "Then you are entitled to leave, aren't you?"

"Yessir."

"How would you like two weeks in Venice?"

"Why—Sir, I would be delighted, Sir."

"Oh, you can drop the chicken, Frumkin. Sorry I didn't tip you off sooner. You're among friends. As to that leave, you will go to Venice right after Christmas; but let me tell you what it's all about first. Major Aron is with the 56th London Division, which is—like the 88th Division—part of Thirteenth Corps. He is also helping Jews get to Palestine. Naomi is a *sabra* from Jerusalem and was with the Jewish Brigade Group. She is also working on *aliyah*."

"*Aliyah* is immigration, Sergeant," she said.

"I know," Jack said in Hebrew.

"Naomi is going to Venice with you," the rabbi interjected, stopping a discussion on that subject. "Major Aron will explain it to you while I go outside for a smoke."

Aron peered through the screen until the rabbi was out of the building, then faced Jack: "Do not assume, Sergeant Frumkin, that the rabbi is not to be trusted with what I am about to tell you. We try to safeguard information and prefer that those who do not need to know don't know. The rabbi is accustomed to this. I must urge you to exercise the greatest caution about all you will see, hear, and do in connection with our activities. If you wish to beg off, please say so now."

"I won't beg off, but I'd like to know whom you are working for. I will have no part in selective immigration."

Naomi's face broke into a broad grin. "Don't tell me you are one of us."

"That depends," Jack said, "on who 'us' is."

"I belong to the movement of Jabotinsky," she said, being careful. "Do you know who he was?"

"*Tel Hai!*" he replied, in the greeting of the movement. "I am a member of Betar in Boston."

Betar was a militant Jewish youth organization that not only wanted a Jewish state when nobody else did, but had actually planned an invasion of Palestine before World War II to drive the British—and the Arabs—out. In Europe and Palestine, Betar wore brown uniforms that made its enemies compare Betar to Hitler's storm troopers. After the war, Betar gave birth to both the *Irgun Zvai Leumi* and the Sternists and the former head of the Polish Betar, Menachem Begin, commanded the Irgun.

Aron appeared uncomfortable. "It is not my purpose, Frumkin," he said, "to get involved in the politics of the Zionist movement. My sole concern is to get Jews out of Europe and past my country's blockade."

"One moment," Jack said. "Are you Jewish?"

Aron dismissed the question with a wave of his hand; but then thought better of it and said, "I am a Zionist Christian, Church of England at that."

Throughout these exchanges, Jack had been examining the plain and unattractive Naomi. Her uniform was too large for her, making her look fat. Her hair was cut short and she wore no makeup, not even lipstick.

Aron lowered his voice and began his orientation: "We are expecting a ship. It will be the first to leave from the Adriatic coast and we must prepare for it. The people working on the Tyrrhenian coast will assist us; but we shall have to establish some form of organization first and that is what we propose to have Naomi and you do. You, Frumkin, will serve as cashier."

"Cashier?" Jack asked.

"Yes, cashier. Most of our operations are paid for in cigarettes and whisky, as you may well imagine. However, the ship requires money to lay in provisions—in local currency to allay suspicion. A large amount of hard currency will need to be exchanged, more than a freighter would normally carry. I expect you to make these exchanges and to do so at the best black-market rates you can obtain. You will also have to buy whisky for our people in Venice who will need it to bribe my compatriots."

"How do I make contact?"

"That will be made clear presently. You shall have a list of rendezvous and will get precise instructions before your departure. Is that clear?"

"Yessir."

Naomi smiled at Jack and asked, "Well, Sergeant, are you decided?"

"Yes, I am." He was emphatic.

The major rose. "We can begin to leave."

In the courtyard, they found the rabbi sitting on some loose lumber, smoking.

"Good chap you brought us, Goldie," the major said.

"Is that so? Glad you approve, major. He is almost the last Jew

left in the division. I wouldn't know who else I could have provided to you."

"I'd thought of that, Goldie. You would have been a fine choice
yourself."

"I? You're joking. A rabbi would be unable to go on leave with
a young woman. Well, we better break up. You go first, Major."

Aron walked out of the yard. Naomi said she would hitchhike
to her unit in Trieste. "Nothing doing," the rabbi exclaimed. "We'll
make you lovebirds seen."

"Huh?" Jack said.

"Even before you two go to Venice, it would be nice to have
you seen together. Go to the Wagon Wheel and enjoy yourselves.
Later, pick up my jeep, Frumkin, and drive Sergeant Ben Dror
back to her quarters. I'll leave a trip ticket at the motor pool."

"Is that an order, Sir?"

"You bet."

"Now we are lovebirds," Naomi said, laughing. "I met you
just a half hour ago, so we are pretty fast, aren't we? Or is the rabbi
playing at being a *shadchan*, a marriage broker?"

As they approached Gorizia's main square, she pulled his sleeve
and asked: "Why so quiet, Sergeant?"

"I was thinking that you are the first Jewish girl I've ever taken
out. I used to work nights as a kid and with Betar meetings and
all, I never had time for dating. The girls I've met in the army were
either patriotic goody-goodies who kept their phone numbers secret or girls whose phone number everybody knew."

"If I had a phone, Sergeant, I do not know if I would keep the
number secret. Maybe yes; maybe no. But I would tell my friends,
and you are my friend—*chaver* in Hebrew, though it means comrade, too. One does not make secrets from friends in America, no?"

Jack noticed that her impeccable British English had faltered.
He wondered why.

She noticed it, too, and also wondered why. Naomi had had as
many one-night stands in the army as Jack, but she knew that she

had always been in full control of herself. Why was this American who claimed to belong to Betar affecting her so differently?

They walked past the fountain in the square, turned right at the cathedral and headed for the prefab beer garden across the street from the Art Deco post office. Inside, a GI combo played big-band music as several hundred soldiers sat around small tables drinking beer from pitchers and eating sandwiches being prepared at top speed by four German POWs.

They went to the service counter.

"What is a BLT?" Naomi asked, looking at the sign.

"Bacon, lettuce, and tomato. Good," Jack explained, ignoring the Jewish injunction against eating pork.

"I'd like to try one," Naomi said.

"Make it two, Nazi."

"I vass no Nazi, Sergeant," the POW behind the counter said.

"Yes, I know. Hitler killed six million of my people all by himself. Cut the cackle, make the sandwiches."

"Why do you antagonize him?" Naomi asked, in Hebrew.

"I love to hear them all say that they were not Nazis. I've heard that from every Kraut I've ever talked to, even the SS men we captured at a postwar parade in Bolzano while they were giving themselves medals. Did you ever hear one admit it?"

"I must confess, I've never talked to one before."

The POW served their sandwiches and Jack seated Naomi at a table in the middle of the room, just opposite the combo. He wanted to show Naomi off. Then he went to buy a pitcher of beer.

"I'm surprised you eat bacon, Sergeant." she said, when he got back.

"Hey, let's get one thing straight. I'm Jack to you, see?"

"No. I shall call you Ya'akov. And you may call me Naomi, but please say it right: neh-OWE-me."

She watched him take a bite out of his sandwich, and asked again: "Does it not bother you to eat pork?"

"I heard you the first time, Naomi. I do not keep kosher. My Jewishness is strong in its nationalism; but I do not keep *Shabbat*, do not fast on Yom Kippur, and I no longer go to synagogue, although my new job will change that. I was brought up observant and I took a prayer shawl into the army in my *tfillin* bag. Let me ask you something: If there is a God, how could He permit Auschwitz? How could He permit the extermination of my entire family merely because they were Jews? I no longer believe. I no longer observe. Does it bother you?"

In response, she picked up a rasher of her bacon, and put it in her mouth. "I ordered it; I'm eating it. OK?"

"Did you do that for me?"

"No. For my people. You are right. God failed us before the war when Jabotinsky called for the evacuation of the Jews of Europe. God did nothing in 1938 when my brother sailed the *Melk*, an *Irgun* Danube river boat, from Vienna to the Black Sea with 550 people on board and the Zionist leaders would not provide money to feed them. God forgot us when the Germans sent their special killing units to the Baltic countries to wipe out whole Jewish communities. So why not eat some bacon, although I daresay it appears an acquired taste."

"Yup. Anyway, I don't pray anymore," he said.

"Prayer will not bring back the dead. Prayers don't bring the survivors to Palestine. God no longer listens to prayers. 'He only helps those who act for themselves.' "

"You mean, 'He helps those who help themselves.' "

"Exactly. If we Jews would have resisted Hitler more, fewer would have died. Instead, we depended on our Christian 'friends' and prayed. Both were wrong."

They were silent for a few minutes, when Naomi said: "Shall we dance? Do you know how?"

The combo was playing "Rosamunda"—the Italian version of "The Beer-Barrel Polka"—and Jack did know the polka. That was followed by some slow fox-trots when, without warning, the combo went into an almost undanceable Stan Kenton routine, starting with "Eager Beaver." Jack tried to boogie-woogie, but Naomi waved him off and went back to their table.

Later, as he started to pour more from the pitcher, she said: "Perhaps it might be a good idea to head for Trieste. I am not at liberty to stay out past twenty-two hundred hours."

He took a last gulp, got up, and walked around the table to help her to her feet. It was then he noticed, for the first time, that dozens of eyes were watching his every move.

Outside, she said, "It is very odd to be the only woman in such a place."

As soon as they got in the jeep, she started her third-degree on him. "OK, so you were in Betar before going in the army. What does Betar do in America?"

"It's a Zionist youth movement. We teach our thinking to younger children. The older members demonstrated for the creation of a Jewish army starting in 1940, called for boycotts against Germany, tried to instill Jewish nationalism into the Jewish community, and did close-order drill. Just before I enlisted, we obtained some old Springfield Ought-Three rifles . . . "

"What for, to attack the White House?"

"Are you making fun of me?"

"Well, in my country, Betar faces danger defending Jews from British and Arab attack, we smuggle in illegal immigrants, we volunteer for missions of the *Irgun Zvai Leumi*. Every New Year, a Betari blows the *shofar* at the Wailing Wall and is promptly arrested by the British. It seems a little like a children's game to have Betar in a country where Jews are not in danger."

"And you?" he asked. "What have you done?"

"I lost my brother on the *Struma*, a ship the British purposely permitted to sink. I was arrested in December 1939 in a demonstration calling for a Jewish army when I kicked a British policeman in the crotch. I spent two years in jail before being allowed to enlist in the ATS. I served in Egypt and, when the British finally permitted one tiny brigade from Palestine, I was allowed to transfer. I then set up *Irgun* cells in several parts of the Jewish Brigade. But most important—and something I shall never forgive or forget—one day after Britain went to war against Germany, on September second 1939, the first person killed in anger by a British bullet was an *Irgun* soldier on the beach at Tel Aviv who was unloading an *Irgun* boat filled with Jews escaping Hitler. I was there. He died in my arms."

"And what are you in now?" he asked, blandly.

"Well, of course," she said, "I am still in the brigade and am under *Irgun* discipline."

"But the brigade is in Holland," he said. "Are you one of the deserters?"

He had taken her by surprise.

"Some of the people in the brigade stayed behind in Italy as a trucking company. I serve in that."

"So you are a deserter," he said.

She did not answer for a while. After a few minutes of silence, she asked: "How do you know so much?"

"The rabbi told me."

As the jeep entered the western end of Trieste, she directed him past the waterfront to an area close to the demarcation line between the Allied area of Venezia Giulia and the part that was administered by Yugoslavia. The signs outside the barracks looked like any others on British billets. There was no Hebrew, no stars of David, no sign whatever that this was not a British army barracks.

She got out of the jeep, thanked him for the ride, and walked through open gates into an interior courtyard.

* * *

Gradually, the "lovebird" idea grew in Jack, but she resisted. He rented a little house for her to stay in when she was in Gorizia. She treated him politely but stand-offishly. Their meetings were sporadic, except on Fridays when she always came to services; but she always went directly to the women's gallery without letting anyone know she was there.

One evening, as they sat in the American Red Cross club in Trieste, a former fish market along the waterfront, Jack decided to ask what he had been thinking: "Why don't you girls wear lip-stick, Naomi?"

"We are in the army, Ya'akov," she said. This, of course, was no longer true. But Naomi and her fellow deserters continued to act as if they were subject to the King's Regulations, talked as if they were still in the Jewish Brigade, and behaved themselves in such a way so that nothing they did brought even the slightest suspicion.

"Do you mean it's *verboten*?"

"Yes. The British allow a little, but because there are many *chaverot* of *kibbutzim* in the Brigade, we wear none."

"Don't you think you would all look more attractive with lip-stick?"

"Perhaps; but in the army, who cares?"

"Maybe that's why your uniforms look like bags, as well."

"Don't you like our uniforms?"

"Hell, no. You don't look feminine in them."

"How do you want women to look, Ya'akov? Do you want them all to look like Rita Hayworth?"

"I can't expect that, but there is a difference between looking feminine and looking like men in skirts and with long hair. Good God, if they issued you girls kilts, you'd look just like that Scotch outfit here. I'd like to see what you look like in a dress, nylons, high heels, and all the fixings. Why, I haven't got an idea of what your figure looks like. For all I know, it's better than Hayworth's."

"Thank you, but if you think I shall undress to show you, you are quite mistaken."

"What's wrong with you? I was talking about dressing you up. It was you who brought up undressing. But, as long as you brought up the subject, perhaps you can explain this attitude of yours. You've told me you like me, but you won't let me get near you. I've never even been in the house I got you."

Naomi tried to interrupt, then waited for him to finish. She took a sip of her coffee, toyed with her doughnut, and then let loose:

"Ya'akov, now I shall tell you the truth. I do not want another affair. An affair is meaningless and unsatisfying. When it is over, it leaves a void. In the army, all we have is temporary. We are not sure where we shall be the next morning. We are both in—let us call it—the *Bricha*, or Operation Flood, for the flowing out from the killing fields of Europe.

"We are in two armies, the army whose uniform we wear is not as important as the army without uniforms, the army of secrecy. How can you talk or think of love in times like these? How can you ask for permanence under such conditions? You are asking me to 'Sing the songs of the Lord in a strange and foreign land.' "

Her voice had dropped so much that he had to lean across the tiny table to bring his ear as close to her as he could. She stopped, ate some doughnut, and looked around the room. And then her voice rose, almost to a shout: "An affair? No, Ya'akov, I shall not have an affair with you."

Then her voice dropped down again and he realized that she had seen another Palestinian and was being noisy for her benefit.

"I have considered it, Ya'akov. I like you. You are very nice. You and I enjoy ourselves when we are alone; we agree politically, and I can even speak my own language to you. But I am sick and tired of living make-believe. I want something real. It shall not be until I am home and until my country is free. I swore to dedicate my life to a Jewish state on both sides of the Jordan and I shall abide by my oath. I will not 'sing the Lord's song in a strange and foreign land, for I prefer Jerusalem over my chiefest joy.' "

"Monism!" he snorted as she recited Psalms. It was Jabotinsky's word for what she had been saying in biblical phrases. The movement would not even think of what kind of economy or political system a Jewish state should have until the state existed. Thus, it was thought, even a Socialist could be in the movement. The questions of whether the Jewish state would have a king or a president, would be socialist or capitalist, would be pious or secular were simply put off. This, unfortunately was utter nonsense. The Jewish leadership lied about the *Irgun*, about its goals, about its methods. No Socialist ever joined what was usually termed "fascist."

Monism was like a slogan Jack had often seen in a doughnut shop in Boston:

As you wander on through life, brother,
Whatever be your goal
Keep your eye upon the doughnut
And not upon the hole.

Similarly, in Naomi's thinking, one had to put off all personal commitments until the Jewish flag was flying over Government House in Jerusalem.

"Yes, monism. My oath comes first and foremost," she said.

"And what do you think I feel? I have no place to go when I leave the army. I have no family. I've had no mail since I came overseas. Do you think I'm after something temporary, something that will be forgotten tomorrow? I know that the rabbi only play-acted at being our marriage broker and that this whole thing of being lovebirds is a sham, but you are the first woman I've ever met whom I wanted to share my life with. I don't want something temporary, either."

"Ya'akov," she said, putting her hand on his, "I must struggle with my inner self. I am not ready for sharing my life, and that is precisely why I am more cautious with you than I have ever been with anyone else. I am not ready. I must control my feelings because I am not free."

"Do you think the women of a revolutionary army must stop living because of their revolution?"

"No. That's just it. We have not yet begun our revolt against the British, Ya'akov. That's what I mean. Once it starts, we shall win. Then, I can love, marry, raise a family. Now I must serve. There is time for nothing else."

"So you are seeing me only because you are playing lovebird?"

"No. If it were not for the *Bricha*, I might still have been willing to spend time with you. I do like you. But let's not beat around the bush. If it is that you want to go to bed with me, I shall tell you to go to a brothel and get it out of your system."

"That's a hell of a way to talk."

"Why? It's what you want, isn't it?"

"No, goddamn it," he shouted. "I've had that since I landed in North Africa. I can say 'I love you' in Arabic, French, and Italian as well as you can in Hebrew. But I've never said it. That's not for an affair or a one-night stand, and I don't want those, either."

"Very well, then find yourself an Italian girl who will gladly come to America with you. I will not grow fond of you only to see you leave for America. My future is my oath."

She got up and put her hand out to shake hands. "I shall walk back to my quarters, Ya'akov—alone."

* * *

Naomi's house stood on a dirt road that led to the Isonzo River. Jack had chosen it because it was well away from any areas frequented by GIs.

He was sitting on the grass across the street from her house, waiting for her to arrive prior to Sabbath evening services. He heard her whistling before he saw her, got up and ran toward her. The whistling stopped and she flashed a smile—surrounded by brightly painted lips.

"Well," she asked, "does that look more feminine?"

He nodded silently.

She took his arm and guided him toward her house. "Please, Ya'akov, let us not quarrel. If you prefer, I shall stop seeing you after Venice, so that you can forget about me."

He shook off her arm and turned toward her. "That is exactly the opposite of what I want. I want to marry you."

He blurted out the words, and they even surprised him. He looked for a sign in her face, but she gave him no clue.

As she unlocked her front door, she said: "No, you are not serious, Ya'akov. You are lonely and want companionship, but you are not ready to have a wife. If I were to marry, it would need to be a brigade marriage—to make someone legally eligible to enter Palestine—not a marriage to someone who can sail into Palestine whenever he pleases. I would marry someone whom we need in Palestine and who cannot wait for a certificate. You don't need one."

"Boy! You think up some nutty ideas, don't you? You would actually marry someone you don't even know? Did you dream this one up yourself?"

"Oh no," she said. "We have girls who have done it. The *Bricha* needs some of the men in the camps and a marriage gets around the British White Paper to keep Jews out of Palestine and to make it yet another Arab state, guarding the empire's lifeline to India and British Petroleum's oil. But even if that were not the case, Ya'akov, I would not go to America with you. The Diaspora is not for me."

"And if I were to come to Jerusalem with you?"

"You would not. Even though you are in Betar, young Jews from America do not come to stay in Jerusalem. They come only as tourists. Only the rich and the old come from your country to stay. They come to die. With the money they bring, they can live just as they did in America. They live only to die—and they live in luxury. Young Jews only come when someone is chasing them. It will be the same with the Jews of America."

"So you don't think I would stay if I came?"

"Who knows? You yourself do not know what you want."

She put a kettle on the Coleman stove and started fixing tea. He unpacked the cookies and candy he had picked up at the PX and put them in the tiny larder of her one-room house.

"When did you get into the movement, Naomi?"

"When I was seven, in 1929. My brother and I were on an Egged bus to Tel Aviv, when the bus was attacked by Arabs. The driver was very heroic and sped up and raced down the hairpin turn to get away. Fortunately, he was a good driver and we were safe. But then we got stopped by the Palestine Police. The driver complained about the ambush just up the road. The British reaction was: 'Serves you bloody Jews right. You're not wanted in this country, either.' My brother took me to a Betar meeting when we got home."

She poured the water over tea bags into the two canteen cups he had left her. "Unlike you, Ya'akov, I made a positive vow. I do not seek vengeance like you. I want and shall create a Jewish state."

"Don't you think I want a Jewish state?"

"You will show that by your deeds."

"Ahah! So you want me to kill Englishmen instead of Germans."

"No. I do not hate the English; only the English police in my country. The English in England are nice, and I admire them. Would that we were as fortunate as they are. But we have an army of occupation in half our country and a puppet Arab sheikdom in the other. That other half Trans-Jordan, incidentally, is the only place on God's earth that has achieved Hitler's ideal: It is *Judenrein*, free of all Jews."

"Trans-Jordan?"

"That is how they call it."

"What do you call it?"

"Eastern *Eretz Yisrael* or Gilead."

He drank some tea, ate a fig newton, and stared. He was mystified. Here he had just proposed and instead of getting a kiss, he got a lecture on Jewish irredentism. But he suddenly realized what was going on. The flag on the Funkturm would have been just a symbol, as had been his singing at the Arch of Titus. She put it all into perspective.

"Naomi, I am coming to Palestine with you," he said, waving his canteen cup in the air as if in a toast. "I shall become a Jew."

"But Ya'akov, you are a Jew."

"Only by a religion I don't even follow any more. I was an American Jew. Now I want to be a Jewish Jew from Jerusalem."

"So you want to become an *Eretz Yisraeli?*"

"That's it," he said. She had understood.

"Will you visit me in Jerusalem?"

"Naomi, I'm coming to Jerusalem with you. And I shall never leave either of you."

She kissed him. "After the synagogue," she said, "sleep here tonight."

JACK III

Finishing their meal at a *trattoria* near the Venice railway station, Jack and Naomi opened their instructions from Aron.

MONDAY: Register at a civilian hotel. Orient yourselves and find a small shoe shop named Filiberti in the Street of the Clock. Have some snaps made.

TUESDAY: Bring the snaps to Filiberti before 1000. He will direct you to your contact. Sgt. Ben Dror is to go into mufti immediately. All contact with our people by her are to be in civilian attire (exception: Filiberti).

EVERY DAY: At 1130 you are to sit in Cafe Florian in St. Mark's Square. The contact will have your snaps.

PASSWORD: Hey, Joe, you wanna buy girl some mosaics?

COUNTERSIGN: I'm of the Mosaic persuasion.

A second set of instructions was marked "Sgt Ben Dror only." She read hers through quickly. Looking up, she noticed that Jack was straining his eyes to see what she was reading. She handed him the paper, "*Yah, Yakoub*, it won't do you any good. It's in Arabic."

They found a little *pensione* near the Academy and Naomi confided her concerns to Jack: "I did not know I would be required to wear civilian clothing, Ya'akov. I do not have any, you know."

"What's the difference?" he asked. "We'll buy some."

"But Ya'akov, do we have enough money?"

"I have about a hundred dollars and two cartons of Chesterfields. That should do it."

"But I would need more than one dress, and possibly a coat. It does get chilly here, you know."

"We better borrow some money from Filiberti. That should get what you need. You'll need shoes, too."

"But I have shoes."

"Nothing doing, Naomi. You're going to wear nothing but civilian clothes—from the skin out. I'll pay him after we pick up the cash."

They arrived at Filiberti's shop a day ahead of schedule, armed with the photos of themselves taken as they fed pigeons in St. Mark's Square. There were two sales clerks. Naomi approached one and put the pictures on the counter. He looked at the snapshots and smiled. Looking up, he said: "Very nice. Very nice. Very nice Venezia, no?"

The other clerk came over, glanced at the pictures, and asked Jack, in English: "You wanna buy girl some mosaics?"

"No. I'm of the Mosaic persuasion."

"I am Filiberti," the man said as he extended his hand across the counter. "Do not tell me your names, they are not for me to know. But why are you here? I was expecting you tomorrow, Tuesday, when he does not come to work for me."

"Can we talk?" Naomi asked.

"Oh sure, sure. He knows only two words of English. But I do not yet have any informations for you."

"We need money to buy the young lady some clothes," Jack said.

"How much do you need?"

"We don't know. We need everything. I'll pay you back in a few days."

"I am not afraid, my friend," Filiberti said. "You may have what I have. I do not want it back. It is for a good reason. Twenty thousand lire enough?"

"That would be a little less than two hundred dollars," Jack calculated. "It should be enough."

"Shoes, of course, you need not buy. I have many. What would you like, miss?"

Naomi went outside to look in the shop window. She pointed at a pair of plain black sandals. Jack shook his head at Filiberti and pointed toward his choice, black pumps.

"But, Ya'akov, I could not walk in those. They have such high heels."

"You'll learn. If you're going to wear civvies, you're going to wear nothing except the most feminine civvies we can find."

Filiberti measured her feet for size and she tried on the pumps, then limped back and forth in them. "It's impossible, Ya'akov. I cannot walk in them. I've never worn such heels before. I do not know how."

"Aw, come on, Naomi. You can at least try. Other women do it; you can, too."

She gamely walked around the store, improving her gait as she gained confidence. After a bit, she stopped in front of a floor mirror and posed herself. A smile crossed her face, turning into a victorious grin as she said, "All right, Signor Filiberti, I'll have these."

"But then you must also have a pair for walking, miss," he answered tactfully.

"The sandals?"

"Very well. You must try them on."

She put on the sandals, smiled agreement, and put her army shoes back on.

"Signor Filiberti," Jack said, "thank you very much. About the money, though; I shall repay you, including the price of the shoes. You have been most kind."

"Please, my friend, when a Jew gives to Zion, he wants no thanks; take and be well. May God help you in your work."

After another round of thanks, they left, carrying the new shoes in their hands because Filiberti had no wrapping paper.

* * *

Slowly, they built up a wardrobe for Naomi. She chose a simple black frock, figure-clinging but not tight, of Italian silk. She tried it on and came out of the changing cubicle to let Jack see. He whistled.

"You don't like it, Ya'akov?"

"When an American whistles, he likes it. I love it."

"Good. I want it."

At a lingerie shop, where Jack wanted to buy a diaphanous chemise he saw in the window, he had to pull the salesgirl out into the street to show her what he had in mind. With mischief in her heart, she pretended not to understand and he pointed and exclaimed to the delight of a small crowd that gathered to watch the fun. When the girl had finally satisfied her whimsy and pointed to the desired article, the crowd cheered and Jack turned crimson.

"You want to make Rita Hayworth out of me?"

"Nope, I just want you to look pretty. We're buying you makeup next."

"And the money, Ya'akov?"

"It's holding out quite well. I won't be satisfied until you look like the best-dressed, most beautiful Palestinian in the world."

"You are expecting far too much, Ya'akov. I am plain. I hope I am not ugly; but I know I am not beautiful."

"You are to me. Anyway, how can you tell? You've been in uniform since you got out of prison five years ago. You've never had a chance to look like anything since you became a woman. But next, we've got to get you to a beauty parlor to get your hair done. That straight short hair may be OK at roll call, but it doesn't go with your new duds."

"Very well, Sergeant. Your wish is my command. I shall obey my lord and master."

He smiled and gave her a light punch on the chin. He knew she was only putting up token resistance because no amount of cajoling could have changed her mind if she had been in earnest.

* * *

That evening they toured the city. It was full of Polish soldiers, veterans of the Second Army, which had stormed Monte Cassino. More than half the Poles did not want to return to Poland as long as it was governed by Poles who had spent the war in Moscow; the rest wanted to go home no matter what. The two sides were at each others' throats all over Venice. British MPs, working with the *carabinieri,* pulled several bodies out of the canals every week.

Jack and Naomi rode a *vaporetto,* visited a coffee bar, walked in and out of expensive but empty tourist hotels, window shopped the congested route from the Rialto Bridge to St. Mark's Square, and ate in a *trattoria* near their *pensione.* At every stop, Jack tried to learn what he could about going rates on the black market. Finally, they returned to their room.

During the evening, Jack had been extremely solicitous in helping her remove her raincoat. The simple dress had been embellished by a string of paste pearls. He glowed in her beauty and was proud to be seen with her.

Jack got under Naomi's skin with repetitive allusions to her beauty, telling her that she had the dimensions of a Varga girl in *Esquire.* When they got to the room, he wanted to see her in the chemise he knew her to be wearing.

"Did you see the dirty looks I got in the coffee shop from the Italians?" he asked.

"I hadn't noticed."

"They hate to see their girls with foreign troops, for which I can't really blame them; especially when the girl is a looker."

"A looker?"

"You know: *yaffa, bella, schön, magnifique.*"

She laughed and began removing her clothes. He watched, and she knew he was watching. As she began to remove her slip, she turned her back on him, but he hurdled the bed. She gave up her attempt to hide and stood, her arms outstretched, directly in front of his eyes, in the black chemise. When he came to take her in his arms, she stopped him. "You'll rip the silk. Wait until I get it off."

* * *

The next morning they gave Filiberti the pictures.

"Is this the same young lady who was with you yesterday?" he asked.

"Certainly," Naomi said. "Don't you recognize the shoes?"

"You need new photos. No one will recognize you from these."

"Thank you, *signore*," she said, making a little curtsy.

At the appointed time, they sat outdoors in the piazza, shivering from the cold. "Let's go inside, Ya'akov," she pleaded.

He wouldn't hear of it. "We have to wait here for our contact."

A tall blond man with a square jaw and a crew cut eyed them as he passed their table. A gold crucifix on a thin gold necklace showed at the opening of his thick black sweater.

"He does not look very Italian," Naomi said.

"Naw, more like a Boston Irishman," Jack said, as the man approached and asked: "Hey, Joe, you wanna buy girl some mosaics?"

"No thanks, I'm of the Mosaic persuasion."

"Righto, I'm Jim. Mind if I sit down?"

"Not at all," Naomi said, "but let's go inside where it's warmer."

"That crucifix sure had me fooled, Jim. Good idea," Jack said.

"Don't jump to conclusions, friend. The last name is Kelly and the crucifix is not a stage effect."

Jack was embarrassed and hastened to apologize. Kelly interrupted. "Never mind. But how about introducing yourselves. I'm sure you don't realize that I don't know your names; but, then, how would I?"

After the introductions, Naomi said, "Let us leave and go somewhere to be alone."

"OK by me," Jack said.

"Not you, Ya'akov," she said. "We two must he alone. I shall meet you here in about an hour."

Long after the hour was up, Naomi returned with a package. "I have your money, Ya'akov. Go to a toilet in one of the hotels to count it. Be sure to look as though you are sitting. I mean, let your pants down."

Amused by her instructions, she laughed heartily.

When he came back, she asked, "What did you do whilst I was with Mr. Kelly, Ya'akov?"

"The waiter brought me some English magazines. Did you know that the Labour Party, now that it is in power, has repudiated its pledges on Palestine. It intends to uphold the White Paper to keep Jews out."

"As we expected," she said. "We never expected that our Socialist leaders would win anything from Britain just because they knew the words to *The Internationale*. How did you do with the money?"

"Eight thousand dollars," he said. "It's going to be rough. They were smart to make the bills small, but it's an awful lot of money to change."

"What will you do?"

"The Poles will sell whisky at a hundred dollars a case. That's twelve bottles. I can get twenty dollars a carton for American cigarettes. If I can sell the whisky at ten dollars a bottle, we make twenty dollars a case. Out of that profit, I should be able to buy butts at twenty-one or twenty-two. On the other hand, the best exchange I can get on the money is a hundred fifteen lire to the dollar, which is lousy. I can get almost two hundred in Gorizia. Because of the rotten exchange rate, I'm gonna have to go into the whisky-and-cigarette business. But that takes time and some Italian help."

"No good," she said. "The ship will need lire."

"I know. You did not follow my thinking. I buy cigarettes and hooch with American money; I sell the stuff for lire. That way, I set the exchange rate. The Poles won't even look at lire. They want hard currency to take out of Italy with them. Oh, by the way, have you any idea how much money the ship will actually need?"

"Mr. Kelly does not know. They have never bought supplies in Italy before. They don't know prices and, to add to their woes, they do not yet know for how many people he must lay in stores."

"I see."

"Oh, I almost forgot to mention that Mr. Kelly needs some lire tomorrow."

"What's the hurry?"

"He did not explain. Can you get him a thousand dollars in lire?"

"I'll try."

She walked away from the Florian, toward the three flagpoles in front of the cathedral. Jack ordered another coffee and tried to make order out of the chaos. When he returned to the *pensione*, he tucked all but two thousand dollars into as many hiding places as he could, hoping they would escape the eyes of the *padrone*'s wife. Then he went in search of the black market. It was not difficult. He accompanied the first man who bought his cigarettes to a coffee house in Zattere. He had more coffee with the man who brought him there, watching the door and the brass espresso machine. A man in a meticulously tailored, double-breasted suit came out of a rear room and signaled to Jack as he passed him on his way out of the coffee shop. Jack walked along the embankment with him in the direction of San Giorgio.

After protracted haggling, they came to terms. Jack changed one thousand dollars directly into lire and agreed to buy a thousand dollars' worth of cigarettes, a total of fifty cartons. Transferring the cigarettes to Filiberti's store ten cartons at a time took him the rest of the afternoon. On his last trip, Filiberti asked Jack to leave ten cases of whisky for his own use.

He asked Naomi about that, wanting to clear it with Jim Kelly. But Naomi reassured him: "Don't be silly. That money is for all the ship's needs. Filiberti needs the whisky for bribes, and the ship will need the friends whom the bribes will buy. Mr. Kelly understands that some of the money will be used on shore. But we have time for the whisky. Where did you leave the lire?"

"With Filiberti."

"OK," she said. "Go get the lire and meet me at seventeen hundred hours at the Academia landing."

"Will Kelly be there?"

"No. We shall go to the ship. It arrived on the morning tide and we are invited for dinner."

"What do you make of Kelly, Naomi?"

"I knew you'd ask that sooner or later. I suspect he is a member of the Irish Republican Army who is helping us fight England. But I am not sure."

"Strange ally," Jack mumbled.

"Not so strange at all. Have you ever heard of Adolf Eichmann?"

"Vaguely. He was some sort of big shot in the German program to kill Jews. Right?"

"He was much more than that. He was the man who created the 'Final Solution to the Jewish Problem.' He ran the extermination squads, the moving of Jews to extermination camps, he was the man who—more than anyone else—was responsible for the slaughter of our people. But at one time, he helped us."

"Huh?"

"This is not generally known. When my brother was ordered to Vienna after the Germans annexed Austria, the Germans immediately spread their policies into Austria. One thing they did was to humiliate the Jews by making them clean the streets with toothbrushes while the Viennese stood by and laughed. But the policy of extermination had not yet been decided. Eichmann's belief then was that it was his job to rid Austria of Jews by shipping them out. So he chartered the *Melk* for the *Irgun* and provided funds to feed the 350 Jews we got out of Austria.

"But the Zionist leaders would not pick up the tab after we got them to the Black Sea. They had not chosen these immigrants. They were afraid that they might vote wrong once they got to Palestine. Eichmann was quick to notice. He stopped helping us. Then he recommended that his boss, Reinhard Heydrich, persuade Hitler to make the bet that brought on the Evian conference. Hitler said he would let the Jews leave Germany if he could find countries that would take them. At Evian, only one country, Trujillo's Dominican Republic, opened its doors. And that's why Jabotinsky said Evian was spelled backwards, it was the 'naive' conference."

"Jesus! Won't the Zionist leadership make hay with that one!"

"They already have. They knew that Betar had a naval school in Civitavecchia, approved by Mussolini. That was to train seamen for our rescue ships. They knew that the fascist Polish government provided Betar with training and weapons for the invasion of Palestine. So the official Zionists call us fascists. But they never lifted their fingers for getting the Jews out of Europe before Hitler killed them all. To be quite exact, they brought fewer than 400 people to Palestine in violation of the White Paper. But they collected huge amounts of money to do so. We collected nothing, and brought out all we could."

* * *

The *Gloria* did not inspire confidence in her seaworthiness. Rust showed through the peeling and flaking paint, the decks were filthy, and the hatches were secured by sloppily tied tarpaulins. On her fantail, her home port was given as Monrovia and she flew the Liberian flag.

The only clean area was the freshly painted wardroom, where they met Kelly. He greeted them in Hebrew. "Welcome to *Gloria*. I assume you are wondering how I fit into all this."

Jack, now sure he was looking at an Irish Republican, readily agreed, "Even more so now that I see you speak Hebrew."

"It's really quite simple. I was in the British army in Palestine before the war and I married a Jewish girl. In any event, you wouldn't expect an Irishman like me to lose any love on Britain, would you?"

"No," Jack said.

Naomi interrupted to ask, "Which of you converted?"

She asked because the British had not instituted civil marriage in mandatory Palestine, which still followed Ottoman *irades* assigning all matters of personal status—marriage, divorce, and inheritance—to the major religions. No intermarriage was possible.

"I did," Kelly said. "Officially I'm Jewish, all done quite properly by the religious court in Tel Aviv. But I still attend mass and I still do not eat meat on Fridays. But, please, allow me to introduce my shipmates."

Naomi realized—although Jack did not—that Kelly had just admitted that he gone through a mock conversion to be able to marry in Palestine. She wanted desperately to ask Kelly what he considered himself, a Jew or a Christian.

Two of the crew were Palestinians, one was American. A German non-Jew, who had captained the first Palestine-registry ship, the *Tel Aviv*, which had flown the blue-white ensign in 1935, was captain of the *Gloria*. He termed himself a "would-be *sabra*."

The captain said the passengers would help sail *Gloria*, which he referred to as "one of our best vessels to date."

When they sat down to eat, Naomi turned to Kelly in English, and asked the question that was nagging her, reinforced by his wearing of the crucifix and what he had said.

"I am a Jew," he said, "who believes in Jesus Christ. I don't usually talk about it. My wife knows and we are bringing up our children as Jews."

Naomi knew better than to pursue the subject.

* * *

Jack thought their work had been completed except for the whisky-cigarette business, but Naomi showed increasing concern. He sensed that something was wrong, but she kept her own counsel.

A note from Major Aron that was passed to them by Filiberti explained Naomi's worries. Aron urged them to finish their business and leave Venice as fast as possible because British intelligence had found out that Venice was being used as a port.

Both knew that the British were powerless to stop the sailings as long as Italy was unwilling to do so. And so *Gloria* had to take on the appearance of a coastwise tramp steamer, repeatedly displaying herself in various Italian ports with freight.

General Anders' Polish veterans, some of whom would have

gladly helped the Germans in killing the Jews of Poland, were not to be trusted, and the cordial response at Anders' headquarters to British calls for help convinced the *Bricha* that Polish anti-Semitism was more responsible for such willingness to cooperate than any attempt by the Poles to ingratiate themselves with the British so they could sail off to Canada or Australia.

An elaborate plan was worked out to dock *Gloria* at the southern end of the enclosed Venice lagoon, near Chioggia, and to shuttle the passengers from Venice in small boats. As the complexity of the scheme grew, the danger increased that any minor hitch would tip off the British and the Poles. But some members of the British military police and the CID, the Criminal Investigation Department, were amenable to a type of persuasion long exploited by the *Bricha*—whisky. The scotch that Jack obtained delayed some British intelligence reports.

In fact, Jack was able to do better than he expected. Rather than buying the whisky from the Poles at a hundred dollars a case, he found that the off-limits gambling casino on the Lido was a good place to find British officers who had run out of chips and were willing to part with their whisky rations at five or six dollars a bottle.

Jack also sold some whisky to GIs who had been sent to the recreation and rehabilitation center on the Lido. They paid as much as four thousand lire—roughly forty dollars—a bottle.

Soon, Jack had more than doubled the worth of the money he had been given. He teased Naomi about staying in Venice and becoming a millionaire. She stared him into silence.

When Naomi got back into uniform for the return to base, she did not resemble the woman in the tan raincoat who had been running around all over Venice. Nor did she resemble the "British" sergeant who had boarded a train in Udine two weeks earlier. The new hairdo and the makeup only accounted for part of the difference. She herself knew the reason—contentment. The happiness that showed in her face had not been granted her since she was a schoolgirl and it was now enhanced by the satisfaction that she had achieved something all on her own. Self-possessed and independent, she had acted alone for two weeks, making decisions and negotiating policies based solely on her own intellect and conviction. She credited her Betar and her *Irgun* training with giving her the self-reliance to respond to all challenges with confidence. In addition, she marveled at her enhanced femininity, judged by the number of times someone attempted to pick her up.

On the train, she stunned Jack with an announcement: "Ya'akov, I have placed a limit on my monism. I have decided that when we have a Jewish state, I shall become a barrister. And, if I am able, I may start preparing myself for the law even before we have a state. I shall enroll at the Hebrew University when I get home."

JACK IV

While Jack and Naomi were in Venice, the 88th Division was electrified by news of the murder on Christmas Eve of Walter Fujawa, a soldier in the 349th Infantry. *The Blue Devil* said the killing was by "Jugs," the derogatory term for Yugoslavs. Security was tightened. Jack first noticed the changes at the border between Italy proper and the American-occupied area of Venezia-Giulia, where the division commander, Maj. Gen. Thomas Guthrie, had posted an MP checkpoint.

Jack's ride from the railhead in Udine dropped him at the Wagon Wheel and he walked past the command post to his quarters. An MP stood guard before the CP and the two-star flag showed that Gen. Guthrie was in the building.

Jack transferred his pack to his left hand, ready to salute officers.

"Hiya, Jack," the MP greeted him.

Jack did not recognize him.

"Don't you recognize me, Louis Gilman from the Hebrew Teachers College?"

"Well, I'll be damned. Hi Lou. How long have you been in the army?"

"I got drafted in April and came here . . ." He snapped into a salute as a group of officers came out of the building. Jack followed suit.

"I wouldn't want your job, Lou. Is that all you do all day, stand here and salute those ninety-day wonders?"

"That and the flags: gotta take 'em in and put 'em out every time the Old Man comes or goes."

"Have you been to services here?"

"I just got transferred to the MP Platoon last week. I was in the mountains before."

"Come around some time. I'm the cantor."

"OK, Friday night. It's swell to see someone from home, isn't it?"

"You can say that again," he said as he turned to go to his office.

He told the rabbi that the division now had two graduates of Boston's Hebrew Teachers College. The rabbi ignored him and signed to him to close the door.

"How did it go?" the rabbis asked.

"Fine."

"Did you have good weather?"

"Fine."

"Cat got your tongue?"

"Nope. Look, I'm going to have to tell you sooner or later, so I better tell you now."

"What's up?"

"I want out. I'm going to cancel my waiver and take my discharge here. I'm going to Palestine with Naomi when she gets out. Can you help me?"

"I won't be helping anyone around here any more, Frumkin. Take a look at this." He pulled some mimeographed papers out of a manila envelope and handed them across the desk. Jack glanced at them briefly, immediately grasping their meaning. The rabbi had been ordered home.

"What happened?" Jack asked.

"I dunno."

"Your time isn't up, is it?"

"No, I signed my last waiver after you came to Gorizia."

"Yeah, I remember. When did these come?"

"In this morning's distribution, but the funny thing is that they did not come from the division chaplain. They came straight from the adjutant general. I'm pretty upset."

"Let me snoop around a little. Major Aron warned us in Venice that British intelligence was watching us."

"Go ahead, but be careful. Don't give away anything. I have a few hunches and they all point to that English sergeant major who has been attending services. I saw him coming out of a private apartment house on the Corso the other day. Later, I went back and looked in the lobby. The mailboxes and bells don't say anything, but the whole second floor is a British headquarters of some sort that they are keeping under wraps."

Jack did not need to go far to get the news. Okie Anderson, the assistant to the division chaplain, called him aside to tell him about the rumors he had heard.

"Can you keep it under your hat, Frumkin?"

"Sure, Scout's oath."

"They've discovered that Chaplain Goldberg is involved in a big black market operation. They don't want to create a scandal about it so they are easing him out with a minimum of fuss. It appears that your boss has been selling relief supplies. I overheard the G-2 talking to Chaplain Metcalfe and it seems British intelligence had a hand in uncovering it. Rumor has it that they'll throw the book at him when he gets Stateside. Meanwhile, you have to see Chaplain Metcalfe this afternoon. He wants you to run the services until a new rabbi arrives. I didn't know a layman could run a Jewish service, Frumkin, but I was told I was wrong. Can you do it?"

"Yeah, Okie, any adult can, only I'm not keen on the idea."

"Well, maybe Chaplain Metcalfe can work something out for you."

Jack rushed out of Headquarters Company to get back to the CP to talk to Louis, but he had already been relieved. Jack found him inside.

"Do you have some time, Lou?"

"I'm off until 4 p.m., when I do another four hours."

"OK. Let's go to a cafe and grab some coffee."

"We're not supposed to eat anything in town, Jack."

"Yeah, but coffee's OK."

Jack steered him to a café on the Corso where they could watch the apartment house the rabbi had mentioned. After difficult conversation about their few mutual friends—because Jack was three years older than Louis—they saw a small British staff car stop across the street. A civilian got out, entered the building, and reappeared a few minutes later in a British noncom's uniform.

"Got any idea what goes on across the street, Lou?" Jack asked, not expecting the rookie to know.

"Sure," Louis answered. "I've been there a couple of times for training. It's the office of the FSS. Boy, you should see the crime lab they've got. They showed us all about fingerprints and powder marks and stuff. They're looking for escaped war criminals."

"FFS?" Jack asked.

"No, FSS—Field Security Service. It's like our Counter Intelligence Corps and Criminal Investigation Detachment all rolled into one."

Jack saw that he was in luck and returned to the rabbi as soon as he could drop Louis.

"You're back soon," the rabbi said. "Learn anything?"

"Plenty," Jack replied, lowering his voice to a whisper. "You've had it, Rabbi. They've got you for black marketing Joint supplies. The G-2 got his info from a British outfit called the Field Security Service in that apartment house you spotted. They may court-martial you when you return to the States."

"So that's it, is it? Strange, isn't it, that when they want to go after me for smuggling Jews to Palestine they accuse me of being a stereotyped 'Jewish businessman,' I'm sure that there is some anti-Semitism involved in this 'black market' charge. Find out anything else?"

"That's all I've been able to dig up. What do you do now?"

"There isn't much I can do. If I defend myself, I may expose the whole show. It's probably just as well that they think it's black market."

"Don't you think the British may be wise to the truth?"

"They may very well be, but they certainly would get better

cooperation from our people if they make it look criminal rather than moral."

"That's how I doped it out, too. They may know plenty and are keeping it quiet. From their point of view, the goal is to crack the *Bricha*. They probably don't care how they do it. Anyway, when the new rabbi arrives, I'll try to hook him into the *Bricha*, too."

"Fine, at least as long as you're still here. How long is your present waiver?"

"I signed for a year in Bolzano, so about the beginning of June."

"Gives you five more months. Meanwhile, I hope you think over the idea of going to Palestine. I'm all in favor of taking the surviving remnant of the Jews of Europe to Palestine; but I'm dead set against Americans going there. The United States is our country."

"Yes, Rabbi. That's what my family thought about Germany, too. My father had an Iron Cross and he was really proud of it. But they left him dead in a Berlin gutter."

"I suppose I better start getting myself ready to ship out," the rabbi said, ignoring the dig. "Can you get my laundry? It's with those washerwomen at the MP Platoon. Bring it to the bachelor officers' quarters. And go over to G-1 to find out when I'm supposed to report in at the repple-depple, will you?"

* * *

After retreat, he called Naomi from the rabbi's office. He told her in Hebrew what had taken place.

"Very well," she said, "I shall inform our people. I am sorry for the little rabbi. It would have been better had it happened to a stronger person."

"Please go to my house tonight and ask the rabbi to join you. If I am not there by midnight, I shall not come."

They played chess at Naomi's with the carved set she had

given him for Chanukah. The rabbi had Jack in a precarious knight fork when Jack was rescued by the entry of Naomi with Major Aron and a corporal.

"I am so glad to see you here," she said. "You know Major Aron, of course, and I should like you to meet Corporal Shlomo Ben Hayyim. Shlomo, this is Rabbi Goldberg and Sergeant Frumkin."

The rabbi shook hands with Ben Hayyim, a dark-haired, rough looking man whose face bore a scar from right temple to mouth. Some of his facial muscles appeared paralyzed and his features were only symmetrical when his face was at rest; when he smiled or spoke, the right side did not move. He half smiled when he took the rabbi's hand, "Good to meet you, Rabbi."

Aron started on the rabbi: "Now then, Goldie, what's this we hear about you?"

"I'm on orders," the rabbi said, boiling it all down to a few words.

"So I had gathered. Do you know any more?"

"Better ask Frumkin to tell you. He tracked it all down this morning."

Jack repeated what he had learned as Ben Hayyim took notes. Naomi gave a brief smile when he mentioned the FSS.

"That's what I feared," Aron said. "The man is known to us. We knew him when he attended his first service to be a former member of the Palestine Police. His name is Diestenbruch and he was once an inspector in Jaffa. Although he is Jewish, he is incorruptible, even on behalf of Jews. Neither we nor the Arabs were ever able to dent his honesty with *baksheesh*."

Jack noticed that Aron had revealed unguarded familiarity with Palestine, leading him to believe that Aron wasn't the Church of England type that he pretended to be, either.

"Now see here, Goldie," Aron continued, "we shall not be able to help you unless you wish to desert and go to Palestine."

The rabbi shook his head vigorously, "No way! My country is the United States."

"You see," Aron continued, "we cannot endanger *Gloria* by making any accusations. We do not want to encourage any inquiries that we can ill afford. But the rabbi's problems are our least concern. Today, we were alerted to start moving the people here. *Gloria* has sailed for Bari with supplies, and as soon as she returns to Venice, we must board the people."

"Isn't that the normal procedure, Major," Naomi asked. "Why the sudden tone of urgency?"

"Haven't you seen what the Americans have done all along the border with Italy?"

"You mean the road blocks?" Jack said.

"Precisely."

"I don't understand," Jack said.

Aron glanced at Ben Hayyim, who nodded. Jack noticed; he guessed that Ben Hayyim was the actual commander of this operation.

Aron continued: "This is contrary to security, Frumkin, but I must explain to you how we move the DPs. As long as they were headed in the direction of Genoa, the lorry company took them there, entirely through Italy, not the Anglo-American zone of Venezia-Giulia.

"We have not brought anyone here for several weeks, because this time we're sailing from Venice. So we are taking DPs from the Udine DP camp, which is also in Italy proper and not in the Anglo-American sector, and sending them on the *Gloria*. The trouble-makers are known to the camp staff, and they stay on to give an appearance of permanence, while, in fact, we will replace a goodly number of people in the camp. We must bring the replacements from the north into Italy and avoid the Anglo-American sector of Venezia Giulia entirely so we don't run afoul of you Yanks."

"Now you have lost me too, Major," Naomi said.

"Have you that map, Corporal?" Aron asked.

Ben Hayyim unfolded a map and smoothed it on Naomi's bed.

Aron pointed to the area where Italy, Austria, and Yugoslavia come together and ran his finger along the Italo-Austrian border.

"See here," he said. "This entire Italian-Austrian border is solely guarded by Italy. The Anglo-American sector, Zone A, begins here at Cave del Predil. There's a 351st Infantry checkpoint there. We don't want to get near it. So we must drive all around Zone A, through Tolmezzo and eventually hit Cividale and Udine without ever passing an American checkpoint."

"Isn't that what you've always done in bringing people to the camp in Udine?" Jack asked.

"No. We crossed from Austria near Tarvisio and got past the Italians without trouble. Then we drove south to Cave del Predil and entered the Anglo-American sector with no controls at all. Now we have a double problem. The Italians are cooperating with my government, which may make Tarvisio troublesome. And we cannot cross at Cave del Predil. So, as I said, we have to drive around Venezia Giulia, but we haven't yet got a way of getting the people out of Austria. And that, Frumkin, is where you come in. We need you to go up into the mountains and see if you can find a way to drive in from Austria without going through any controls. The corporal favors going through Yugoslavia, but I reject that out of hand. I don't know how Tito feels about Jews. We shall also have to overcome British controls in that part of Austria, which is controlled by my country."

Jack agreed to try, but had no idea how he would set about it. When they broke up, Jack walked the rabbi back to the bachelor officers' quarters.

"Who's this Shlomo, Rabbi?"

"He's the boss."

"Above Aron?"

"Oh, yes. Their outward ranks don't have anything to do with their positions in the *Bricha*. Aron ran the show tonight because it is his responsibility."

"Is Aron from Palestine?"

"Lord no. He's English, went to Oxford, and all that. Tonight was the first time I've ever seen him let his guard down. This Diestensomething character must really have him worried."

* * *

After Rabbi Goldberg left for the Replacement Depot in Leghorn, Jack went to see Lieutenant Colonel John Metcalfe, the division's chief chaplain. He sought to make a good impression while gaining an official cover for his reconnaissance on behalf of the *Bricha*. He had become aware through his meeting with Louis that about 5,000 new men had joined the division since September.

"Chaplain Metcalfe, I'd like to go up the Morgan Line and advise the newly arrived Jewish personnel about our facilities and services. Chaplain Goldberg had intended to do this, but since his departure for the repple-depple, I guess that job falls on me. Do you suppose I could obtain locator cards from G-1 and permission from you to go up there?"

"Splendid idea, Frumkin. Ask Anderson to help you with the details. You must take someone along though. I won't have you getting killed by the Jugs."

"I have a friend in the MPs who went to Hebrew Teachers College with me. Could we get him on TDY or DS?" The references were to temporary duty and detached service.

"I'm sure Anderson can arrange that. Ask him."

When he had been given the locator cards, Jack went to G-2 for maps, along with overlays showing where to find the units he wanted to visit. He noticed immediately that there were no American checkpoints whatever between Tarvisio and Cividale, so his main job was finding a way across the Italo-Austrian border.

Before leaving G-2, he was given a map case and instructions by the G-2 himself, a full colonel: "Those maps, as you know, are classified. If you go anywhere near the Morgan Line, Frumkin, the possibility of a fire fight is likely. We have rigged an incendiary grenade to the case; you are to pull the pin even before you return fire. Is that clear?"

"Yessir."

He saluted and started for the colonel's door.

"Just a minute, Frumkin. Close that door, won't you?"

Puzzled, Jack closed it and returned to the front of the colonel's desk, standing stiffly at attention.

"At ease, Frumkin. What do you know about Chaplain Goldberg?"

"Nothing, Sir," Jack replied.

"I understand, and I'm not asking you to squeal. But it may be a good thing for you to know what our allies are up to, so read this, won't you?"

He handed Jack a three-page, single spaced "TOP SECRET" report from "Chief of Staff, Intelligence, XIII Corps (British)." As he read it, Jack realized that the British were wise to the *Bricha*. They knew about the port in Venice; they knew the Palestinians were carrying Jewish civilians in their vehicles, mentioning Chaplain Goldberg as a pivotal figure in this traffic in people. No other names appeared. There was no clue that the Palestinian trucking company was not really part of the British army.

"I'll give it to you square, Frumkin. I'm on your side. I was taught that the Kingdom of Heaven approaches when the people of Israel return to Zion. I would not want to be responsible in any way for acting against God's will. In view of that, you should know that this report has stopped here. There will be no charges brought against Chaplain Goldberg. He was shipped out with a clean record and a good report from Chaplain Metcalfe and General Guthrie. He'll probably be promoted to major Stateside. I was able to persuade G-1 to ship him out before his record could be marked in any way. But I must now warn you to be careful, too, since you are also suspect. I hope your outpost reconnaissance finds a nice hole for your people to drive their trucks through. I would suggest Cave del Predil, but that's only a suggestion. I don't think the 351st Infantry's commander likes taking orders from Thirteenth Corps on how to do his job. As a matter of fact, I can tell you, that Colonel Overmyer up there called me to ask about this, saying,

'George, I thought our mission was to keep peace in this area until there's agreement on whether it goes to Italy or Yugoslavia. I didn't know that we were being made into cops for stuttering King George.' So I told him not to worry about it, and I hardly think that the men at Cave del Predil will worry about your passengers."

"Still no good, Sir," Jack answered, deciding to trust the G-2. "Once we're inside Venezia Giulia, we've got to get out again, and there are Division MP roadblocks all over the place. Thanks for the tip, which I'll pass on, but I think we'll drive through Tolmezzo and Cividale and avoid Venezia Giulia completely."

"You run your show as you deem best, Frumkin; but before I forget, you should know you have an English undercover agent attending your services. He appears to be responsible for blocking your moves in this area."

"Thank you, Sir."

"All right. That's all I have for you. Good-bye."

"Thank you, Colonel. I'll inform my friends of your kindness," Jack said as he came to attention for a salute.

"Just one more thing, Frumkin. I wish to remain anonymous. If you must tell your superiors, as I imagine you must, say 'an American staff officer,' or something of that sort. My usefulness to your cause would be severely curtailed if our allies knew about me. They might decide to avoid channels and go directly to General Guthrie, and that, I fear, would bring the division into action against your effort. General Guthrie does not share my feelings about Jews."

"Thank you, Sir. I'll do that."

He rushed back to his own office and gave the field telephone a tremendous cranking, violent enough to give the Signal Corps man on the switchboard a slight shock: "Legion, this is Legion one five. Get me Major John Aron at the Fourth Queen's Own Hussars in Lucinico. I don't know the routing, but you can get it through corps. I'll wait."

He strummed his fingers on the desk, smoked a cigarette, strummed some more, and then began pacing up and down.

Eventually, the operator called back. "Major Aron, please. . . . Major Aron? This is Sergeant Frumkin at the Jewish chaplain's office in the 88th Division, Sir. . . . Yes. . . . Would you be able to come to the synagogue tonight for *Kaddish*? I am unable to find a *minyan*, or quorum, Sir. One of the civilian members of the congregation has died. . . . Yes? . . . Very good, Sir. . . . Can you bring any other Jewish personnel? . . . Three more? That's excellent. That would complete the quorum. Thank you, Sir. Good-bye."

* * *

Just before sundown, someone entered the courtyard. Jack went out to see who it was and found the gates open. A jeep started its engine in the street and swung into the yard. When the desert-brown vehicle had cleared the gates, Jack swung the gates shut behind it.

Aron and Shlomo Ben Hayyim had come alone. The major lost no time. "What ever is the matter, Frumkin?"

Jack repeated what the G-2 had told him, and outlined the British intelligence report. He said he could not reveal the staff officer's name.

"You most certainly will, Frumkin. Stop futzing around." This was an order from Ben Hayyim.

Aron nodded. "I realize your predicament, Frumkin, but you must realize that intelligence leaks can work both ways. Maybe your source will give the British our information."

"Oh, no, Major," Jack said with emotion. "I think you can trust him. He was absolutely sincere."

"You misunderstood," Aron said. "I mean to have him tell the British what we would like them to know. I shall have an intelligence report prepared for their use that may send them on a wild-goose chase as we load *Gloria*."

"Very well, Sir. He's Colonel George LaChance, the G-2."

They cheered. He was amazed. These two unemotional, unex-

citable men had cheered as if they were at Fenway Park watching
Ted Williams hit one out of the park.

"Where's the map case?" Ben Hayyim asked.

"In the *shul*," Jack said, indicating the synagogue.

They went inside and Jack opened the case and unrolled the
maps on a bench. Then he traced the route through Cave del Predil
that the G-2 had preferred. The major insisted on caution.

"We still have no way to get them in from Austria and you'd
best get up there to see if the Italians have any roadblocks along
the road from Tarvisio to Cividale. Do you think you can find us
clear sailing out of Austria?"

"Not with vehicles, I don't. On foot, I already know a place."

"How?" Ben Hayyim asked, suspiciously.

"I occasionally went hunting from my old outfit at Fusine
Laghi. The Austrian border is wide open east of the Tarvisio crossing point. And there's an unused railroad tunnel through the
mountains that once led from Villach in Austria to Ljubljana in
Yugoslavia."

Jack pointed at the tiny Fusine lakes on the map and traced
the defunct railroad eastward to the Yugoslav border. Then he went
the opposite way and traced its course into the mountains.

"Remember," Ben Hayyim said, "that some of these people
will not be dressed for prolonged exposure in the Alps in the middle
of winter and some may not be capable of walking very far."

"Don't worry," Jack said. "I think this will prove suitable, but
I'll check it to make sure."

"Very good," Aron said. "Have you got the timing? Our
latest word is that *Gloria* is due in Venice on Monday. We
shall move the people south from Udine camp after sundown
on Saturday."

"OK. Where do I bring the information?"

"Naomi's house will do. She will await you," Aron said.

"If anything goes haywire, I'll try to get word to you, Major.
I'll use the same techniques."

"Quite! *Kaddish* is a very convenient excuse. Indicate whom you want me to bring. One short is only me; two short indicates you want Sergeant Ben Dror there, three more adds Corporal Ben Hayyim."

* * *

Jack and Louis drove straight north out of Gorizia, planning to go through Caporetto and Plezzo, both full of GIs of their old regiment. They wore their olive drab overcoats and were absolutely frozen in the open jeep. They borrowed warmer clothes at Louis' former company in Caporetto.

As they drove, Jack began to tell Louis what this was really all about. Louis appeared enthusiastic about taking part in what he termed "rescue."

"Naw," Jack said, "rescue could have taken place way back when, but the Zionist leaders balked at it. We're not rescuing Jews any more. Most of them are dead, and what we're doing now is just moving the survivors around."

They continued on to Tarvisio, a German-speaking town that used to be home to a Wehrmacht rehabilitation hospital now being used as the headquarters of their old regiment. They ate there and then continued east toward Fusine Laghi.

Jack was welcomed by the men he had served with and by Lieutenant Lynch, now a captain. In the orderly room, Jack pulled out his locator cards and asked for a soldier named Nathanson.

When Nathanson reported in, Jack told him about the Sabbath services in Gorizia.

"You gotta be kidding, Sergeant," Nathanson said. "I'm not going to drive three or four hours to Gorizia to come to services."

"I did not mean for you to drive. I meant for you to hitch a ride with the ration truck when it returns to Gorizia."

But Jack's heart was not in the discussion; he wanted to get to the railroad tunnel. They went to the supply room and signed out packs, canteens, blankets, and shelter halves. Then they left Fox Company and started back toward Tarvisio. Louis strapped the map case to Jack's pack in such a way that if it were torn off with a jerk, the grenade pin would be pulled.

"I hope you've got a good throwing arm, Lou," Jack said, realizing that the grenade would get him, too.

Rifles slung over their shoulders, they drove the jeep off the road until they came to an open stretch leading north through the woods where the single railroad track was covered by snow. Jack put the jeep in four-wheel drive and they bumped their way north along the track and found the tunnel. When they emerged on the Austrian side, they were just south of the River Gailitz near the town of Goggau. They hid their weapons in the tunnel, wrapped in the shelter halves and Jack's poncho, and walked toward the little town, where they went to a ski store and bought ski suits, knit ski masks, visored caps, and walking sticks. Jack paid with American money he had been given in Venice for such purposes, although possessing dollars violated army regulations. When they changed into civvies, they were committing a second violation. But merely being in Austria in an army jeep was subject to court-martial, so "desertion" only added to the possible charges.

They took their uniforms back to the tunnel and buried them in the blankets and Louis' poncho. Then, they headed for Arnoldstein, a town in which they saw quite a few British soldiers. Nobody paid any attention to them or to their jeep, its bumpers clearly painted with "88XX DIV HQ CO."

At Villach, they found a British roadblock along the road leading east to Klagenfurt and south toward Italy. They were waved through.

They asked the concierge at the Park Hotel in Villach about local train service. Speaking British English, he told them that the tracks to Italy were used only to bring supplies from Trieste to British troops in Austria.

When they got back to the tunnel, they dug up their clothes and their rifles, emptied the jerry can into the gas tank, stashed their civvies under the shelter halves, and started south.

* * *

Friday evening, Jack conducted his first service, with about ten
civilians and two dozen GIs scattered around the central platform.
Diestenbruch was in uniform and seated as close to the entrance as
he could get.

From where Jack stood on the central platform he was no longer
facing the entry.

He had been watching, waiting for a glimpse of Naomi as she
came in and headed for the stairs to the women's gallery in the
balcony. She had not come to Gorizia since he got back from Austria and he was upset that nobody seemed to care about what he
had learned.

After the service, Jack and Louis shook hands with a few people
in the courtyard. Jack had left the jeep a few blocks away from the
synagogue so he would not shock anyone by driving on the Sabbath. As soon as he had closed the gates, he rushed to the jeep and
drove to Naomi's house. It was empty.

He waited up some time, then curled up on her bed and went
to sleep.

A knock on the door woke him; it could not be Naomi for she
would have used her key. He went to the door and opened it a
crack, a stick of fire wood in his hand. Seeing a British soldier, he
motioned for him to enter.

"*Shabat shalom,*" he said. "I am sent by Sergeant Ben Dror.
Here is the key she gave me. May I bring in my things?"

"*Shabat shalom,*" Jack answered. "Make yourself at home."

The soldier, obviously a Palestinian, although his uniform did
not disclose that, brought in a wooden packing case and then another. From their markings, Jack discerned that they contained
communications radios. After the third crate had been brought in,
Naomi entered with a woman soldier.

"Ya'akov, this is Aviva. I suppose you have met Avik."

"As a matter of fact," he replied, showing his annoyance, "I
have not. He has been unpacking a ten-ton truck into our room."

Jack gave Aviva the once over. From the neck down, Aviva was fairly nice looking, but her hair looked much like Naomi's before he got her to a beauty parlor, and, of course, she wore no makeup.

"Stop exaggerating, Ya'akov. He had only three boxes."

"Where in Sam Hill have you been, Naomi?" he asked.

"Stealing radios," she said cheerfully. "We got these at Thirteenth Corps Signals."

"Huh?"

"I drove Avik to the Royal Signal Works. He went in with a request that the *Bricha* printed. Ten minutes later, three Englishmen put the crates into our trailer. Very ordinary."

Avik pried open the crates, then set up the radios by stringing wires around the room. He sat on the floor, wearing earphones, and twirled knobs.

"Ya'akov," Naomi said. "Where is your friend, Louis?"

"He went to the Verdi Theater to see the U.S.O. show."

"Are you meeting him later?"

"I told him that if I'm not at the Wagon Wheel, I'll be here."

"Good. Let's all go to the Wagon Wheel."

"Wait," said Aviva, "I must change."

Naomi hit Avik on the shoulder to get his attention and led the two men out, leaving Aviva in the room to undress. When Aviva came to the door, dressed as a civilian, Naomi said, "Very good, let us go eat."

"No, thank you," Avik said. "I must finish. Can you bring me back something?"

"Sandwich and some coffee?" Jack asked.

"Make it two sandwiches, if you please," Avik said, patting his stomach. "I'm starved."

Taking each woman by the arm, Jack guided them downhill toward the enlisted men's club. Naomi explained that Aviva was moving into their house to run the radios. Jack said nothing, wondering how that could work. Finally, Naomi reported that the convoys had entered Austria just before the Sabbath.

"How come nobody wanted to know what I learned up there, Naomi?"

"We have been playing cat and mouse. The English caught one of our convoys in Germany, even though it was in the U.S. zone. We had to send another by way of the CSR."

"Where?"

"Czechoslovakia. It stopped in the French Zone of Austria. We shall direct it in on by radio. We intend to come through Villach and then along whatever route you suggest. You will be asked about that later."

Louis joined them at the Wagon Wheel, and walked back to Naomi's with Aviva on his arm. Naomi carried food for Avik and the others, but when they got to her place, the jeep and trailer were gone. She opened the paper bags and set out the sandwiches— cold hamburgers to avoid any questions about bacon—and paper coffee cups. As they began to eat, Aviva kept peering at her watch. At ten minutes to nine, she squatted in front of the radio and began listening and turning dials slowly back and forth. Suddenly, she pulled the earphone jack out of the set. Crackling filled the room. No one spoke. At precisely nine o'clock, a British voice called, "Baker Oboe Queen, this is Baker Oboe Victor. Over."

Aviva pushed her microphone button and said calmly, in English that did have a pronounced accent: "Baker Oboe Victor, this is Baker Oboe Queen. Over."

"Baker Oboe Queen, I have a message for you. Procedure Victor Easy. Message follows: TO: Figures wun six too RASC—I spell— Roger Able Sugar Charlie. FROM: Figures wun six too RASC—I spell—Roger Able Sugar Charlie, Mobile Thuree. Ack. Over."

Jack and Louis sat and watched, surprised to see the standard radio procedure of the U.S. army being used.

The message being sent took less time than the acknowledgment procedure. It was: "Estimated time of departure figures wun eight owe owe Central European Time. Signed: Charlie Oboe, Mobile Thuree."

That was from the commander of the third convoy.

Aviva kept exchanging more and more "Over" and "Out" messages, then shut off the radio. "They are leaving on schedule, Naomi," she said in Hebrew.

Naomi turned to the men: "Will you be able to join us tomorrow at six?"

"To do what?" Louis asked.

"Visit Austria. You two know where to cross."

"I was wondering when you would ask," Jack said.

Jack tried to turn on his little radio to get music from Munich. It had been unplugged.

"Hey, Aviva, is it all right if I plug my radio in again?"

"Yes, until ten minutes before midnight," she said, "Unless Avik comes back first."

He got the AFRN station in Munich and started dancing with Naomi. Louis sat on the divan with Aviva.

"Where are we going to sleep tonight, Naomi?" Jack whispered.

"In our bed. She will sleep on the divan."

"Isn't that going to embarrass you?"

"No, silly. Anyway, it will be only for tonight. Aviva will find a place of her own."

"Isn't she in the army or the *Bricha* any more?"

"Tonight, you saw her desert for the second time. She has fallen out with the *Bricha*."

"What does that mean?"

"I shall explain, but not now."

Avik burst into the house, speaking rapid-fire Hebrew: "Did you get a message, Aviva?"

"Yes," she said, "Six o'clock our time tomorrow."

"I'm sorry, Naomi," he said. "I must turn off your radio. I must transmit."

Avik squatted before the transmitter and changed the settings. He did likewise to the receiver. Then, he began talking: "*Qui parla la stazione maritima di Trieste. Tutto è in ordine. Fa buon tempo. La temperatura è quindici. Il vento è meridionale a venti-cinque chilometri. La condizione è rossa. Fino della nostra trasmissione.*"

"What was that all about?" Louis asked in utter amazement.

"Italian weather report," Jack answered.

"Quiet," Avik ordered.

The radio spoke. "*Qui la stazione maritima di Pola. Nostra trasmissione in lingua italiana. Fa buon tempo. La temperatura fa tredici. Condizione è rossa. Smrt fasizmu. Zivel Tito. Govarit Pula. . . .*"

Avik shut off the radio. "Please allow me to explain. That was not Pola; that was *Gloria* on a prearranged frequency. The prearranged nonsense confirms that we are bringing the people at the previously arranged time. Now, perhaps, I should introduce myself. I am Avraham Loewenstein. Unofficially I call myself Avik Evenari. I am in charge of communications. As you see from my sleeve, I was a corporal in the Jewish Brigade. I have deserted. This station will not be used again for some time. Aviva will receive instructions when she is to reopen the station. And, before I forget, our Bedfords will cross the South Bridge across the Isonzo at 1800 tomorrow. They will pick up anyone hailing them with 'Hey *Yecke!*' I leave you now. *Shalom.*"

He took the sandwiches and the coffee with him.

"It must be hard to eat regularly when you are in nobody's army," Jack said.

"Very much," Aviva said. "Whilst in uniform we cannot eat in Italian restaurants because Thirteenth Corps has banned eating the food brought in for civilians. And some messes are distinctly unfriendly in allowing transients to eat there. Avik may not have eaten all day."

* * *

They had been asleep perhaps an hour when there were loud knocks on the door. Jack pulled on his trousers and went to the door. "Who is it?"

"Ben Hayyim, open up!"

Shlomo came in with a manila envelope which, without apology or introduction, he ordered Jack to get to Colonel LaChance, the 88th Division G-2, immediately.

"In the middle of the night, Shlomo?"

"Immediately. It is most urgent. Do not open it; do not leave it with the charge of quarters; you must hand it to him in person. The charge of quarters should know where he lives. Then you must watch exactly what he does and report back here to me. Understood?"

Jack dressed, studying the envelope with the hope of discerning a clue to its contents. It was a regular U.S. Army envelope bearing a neatly stamped return address that said "CIC Det, APO 88, NY, NY." Inside was a stack of papers. Paper clips and staples could be felt through the envelope.

Jack walked directly to the bachelor officers' quarters. The duty officer directed him to a requisitioned villa on the outskirts of Gorizia. He double-timed to the motor pool and took out his jeep, promising the guard that he would bring in a trip ticket signed by Chaplain Metcalfe in the morning. Twenty-five minutes after receiving the envelope, he was knocking at LaChance's door.

A pudgy maid in a chenille housecoat opened the door and led him in. The colonel was still in his pink trousers, but had taken off his shirt disclosing a white undershirt that was against army regulations.

When Jack handed him the envelope, a hint of a smile crossed the colonel's face. He led Jack into the book-lined study—containing the owner's Italian and French books—and bade him to sit down.

"This is strange, Frumkin. Where would you be getting a top secret CIC report?"

Jack decided to play it straight: "From my superiors, Sir."

"Uhh, I see. Your people are trying to have me help them with a little black propaganda, it seems. Smart! This looks totally authentic, and, I suspect they'd like me to send a copy to my opposite number in Thirteenth Corps. You may as well read one, too."

CIC DETACHMENT
APO 88
New York, N.Y.

TOP SECRET   TOP SECRET
TO: AC/S, G-2, 88th Inf Div
SUBJECT: Jewish underground activity in 88th Div area

(1) This report was prepared in accordance with instructions from AC/S, G-2, 88th Inf Div, regarding revelation of participation by Capt (Ch) Morris Goldberg in illicit traffic in Jewish civilian personnel from DP Camp, Udine, to points unknown.

   a. Capt Goldberg has been relieved from assignment and transferred to ZI. Until replacement arrives, his functions are being performed by T/Sgt Jacob Frumkin, chaplains asst.

   b. On or about 2 Feb 46, T/Sgt Frumkin, with concurrence of Div Chaplain, Lt Col John F Metcalfe, made a tour of 88th Inf Div outposts along Morgan Line. At or near Caporetto, T/Sgt Frumkin illegally and without authority did cross the Morgan Line into Zone B, presently occupied by the Jugoslav army, to make arrangements with foreign military personnel—officers and men of the Jugoslav army—for purpose of assuring transit of Jews from Jugoslavia into 88th Div area.

                          SOURCE-civilian contact C-47-i

   c. On or about 4 Feb 46, T/Sgt Frumkin was reported to be illegally and without authority and in violation of directives of the Theater Commander in civilian clothes in the city of Ljubljana, located in the Federated Republic of Jugoslavia.

                          SOURCE-civilian contact J-382-B

d. At 2100Z, 4 Feb 46, monitoring station, 88th Sig Co reported following intercepted message on a clear band which CIC had asked to be placed under surveillance: "CVQ this is ERL. CVQ I have a message for you. Message follows: To MG (CIC note: initials of Capt Goldberg) from ERL. Body of message follows. Leaving Ljubljana 0430 GMT 8 Feb. Estimated arrival Kobarid (CIC note: Slovenian for Caporetto) 0730."

(2)   CONCLUSIONS: Reasonable evidence exists for conclusion that Jewish underground movement exists in 88th Div area. T/Sgt Frumkin; his girl friend, Sgt Naomi Ben Dror, 179th RASC, XIII (Brit) Corps; and Capt Goldberg appear to be at hub of such activity.

(3)   TACTICAL COUNTER-MEASURES: On Feb 6 units of 351st Inf Reg will be placed on two-day practice alert in vicinity of Caporetto. 2d Bn will conduct mock attack on and along road leading from Caporetto to Jugoslav-occupied VG. 3d Bn will be brought into exercise at 0001 7 Feb.

FOR THE AGENT-IN-CHARGE:

OFFICIAL

Top secret, auth MTOUSA ltr dated 18 Nov 45

John W Svetic

Agent CIC

Jack read his copy slowly. He was angry at being named in the document. He looked at some of the attachments, and found them to be copies of the alleged radio transmissions and the originals of the civilians' reports.

"Looks as though your people do not hesitate to expose you to prosecution, Frumkin," the colonel said.

"Yessir, only it isn't true and I can prove it."

"Well, let me see how much of this checks out. I'm calling the 351st." He went to the field telephone, cranked it, and said: "Legion, this is Legion Two calling from home. Get me Lesson Two. Call me back."

The call went through immediately. The colonel listened as the charge of quarters reported. "This is Colonel LaChance at Division G-2, Corporal. Are your second and third battalions doing anything in the vicinity of Caporetto tomorrow and Sunday?"

There was a pause. "Thank you, Corporal. Do you know who ordered them out? . . . Yes? . . . I see. Thank you, Corporal. Good night." He turned the crank. "Legion, I'm finished."

He turned to Jack. "They're very thorough. I don't know how they did it, but the second battalion is already on alert. The third is moving up. They were ordered out by me."

"And you didn't?"

"Nothing of the sort. I'll bet the 351st was called out by teletype, because they wouldn't have been able to imitate my voice. Where and when they tapped our TTY circuits should be easy for Signal Company to track down."

"Do you think these really are from CIC?"

"Absolutely. The reason for sending them to me through you in the middle of the night is to make sure I don't screw up the alert in Caporetto."

"Then you think the whole thing is on the up and up?"

"This report, Frumkin, is correct in every particular. I'm sure it has been sent through normal channels to everyone indicated in the distribution, including my office. It should cause our allies to come up with some countermeasures of their own. However, it is quite fraudulent in all its major details—this Caporetto thing, for example. You must know the route better than I and you are coming through Cave del Predil, aren't you?"

"Nossir. We're avoiding Venezia Giulia and going from Tarvisio to Cividale by way of Tolmezzo."

"So that leaves your alleged trip to Yugoslavia, which is cut from the whole cloth. Right?"

"Yessir."

"Well, I have nothing but admiration for this. It is a wonder-

ful piece of counterintelligence work. I don't know how they feed
their false reports to CIC, how they got these copies for me, or
how they intend to rescue you from the hot water they've thrown
you into. If I may advise you, you should apply for immediate
discharge so I can stall any investigation. If you wait too long, one
of these copies to higher headquarters may end up bringing you
up on charges."

"Thank you, Sir. I had figured that out for myself."

"Good. For my part," the colonel said, lighting his pipe, "I
promise to do nothing about Caporetto. Nor will I send this report up through channels."

"I hope that is what was expected of you, Sir."

"If not, I don't know what they want, Frumkin. Well, let's get
some sleep. Good night."

"Good night, Sir."

* * *

When Jack returned to the room, Aviva was gone.

"Where's Aviva?" he asked.

Avik answered: "We had to get Aviva back to our unit. The FSS
is going to arrest her for desertion and they can't very well if she's
in uniform and on duty."

"Aren't they wise to the whole business with the 179th RASC?
That it is not part of the British army?"

"Not yet. But they are wise to Aviva. They've learned she's a
Sternist and they would turn nasty if they could arrest her."

"This does not make any sense," Jack said. "Why would they
arrest her for desertion and not all the rest of you? And why not
arrest her for the real reason, instead of because she is a Sternist?
None of this makes sense."

Avik gave Naomi a pleading look and shrugged his shoulders.

Naomi took over. "The FSS is in political counterintelligence.
They don't care if Field Marshal Montgomery deserts, but they
would care if he joined the Communist Party. They care about

Aviva because she follows Avraham Stern. That makes her an FSS target. But they do not want to arrest her for being a Sternist, because they would have to prove that in a court-martial held under the King's Regulations. How do they prove it? But desertion is easy. If she is in civilian attire and not in her unit, that they can prove."

"How did you guys find all this out?" Jack asked.

"We have some telephones tapped," Avik said. "They are raiding your synagogue in the morning to arrest her. Now that the Sternists have finally started working with us, we do not want to lose her. She's a good radio operator. It has taken too long to get the Sternists to cooperate. Naomi here has been working with us despite the fact that her high command would have objected before today."

"You lost me again," Jack said.

"All three movements," Avik said, "*Haganah*, *Irgun Zvai Leumi*, and the Stern group have come together into *Tnuat Hameri*—the United Resistance Movement."

Ben Hayyim came back and said, "I got Aviva back in time. Did the colonel tell you what was in the report, Ya'akov?"

"He let me read it. Then he called the 351st to verify it. He won't screw us up about Caporetto and told me to get discharged on the double. I did tell him the route we were driving from Austria."

"I concur with him," Ben Hayyim said. "I hope you are out of the army before they make things difficult for you. Can you prove you were not in Yugoslavia?"

"Sure."

"Then ask for that discharge Monday morning. You would be of no further use to us unless you do."

"The colonel also said the report was a good piece of counter-intelligence. He could not imagine how you got hold of it."

"After Svetic went home," Avik said, "our contact in his office brought them to us. She is a professional spy. She will do anything for anyone for a price."

JACK V

Trucks from the 162nd RASC came to the Goggau tunnel from the Austrian side and discharged their passengers, who were told to walk south through the tunnel. The 162nd, like the 179th, was completely phony. It worked out of Milan and worked with other British units as if it were part of the British army. It serviced their vehicles, supplied their messes, hauled their supplies, and drew from army warehouses.

After unloading the people at the Austrian end of the tunnel, the empty trucks headed west toward the Villach–Tarvisio road and past the Italian border controls without a hitch. The trucks arrived at the southern end of the tunnel only fifteen or so minutes after the first refugees did.

They loaded the trucks again and drove along the route Jack had recommended. It all went without a hitch, and the people were delivered to a compound of the 179th near the railway line in Udine. The 162nd then drove back to Milan—or wherever it had come from—and the 179th proceeded to substitute the new-comers for the people it had moved out of the DP camp.

Jack and Naomi returned to Gorizia with Avik and Aviva. At the MP roadblock on the Italo—Venezia Giulia border, they were stopped and the three Palestinians were asked to show their iden-tification cards.

"Good that we did not come through Venezia Giulia," Avik said.

As soon as they got to Naomi's house, Aviva again changed into civilian clothes while the others stood outside.

"I'm dressed," she said after a while, opening the door to the others.

They started telling each other what they had done, and Jack was describing the problems with some of the old people who had difficulty walking through the tunnel.

" . . . so these two boys were carrying this old man by linking their arms into a fireman's carry. And the old guy was singing at the top of his voice. I have no idea what he was singing, but some of the other people started clapping in time with his song. It was like a picnic at the Jewish Home for the Aged, but without food. When they got to the end of the stream bed and on the highway, the boys put the old man down and joined a circle that was dancing the *hora*. I asked someone why they were so happy. They told me: 'We're out of the Land of Death. Nobody speaks German here.' "

Aron and Ben Hayyim came in and Aron raised his hand: "Let me have your attention, please. The lorries have returned from Chioggia without incident and the people are safely aboard. We do not yet know if *Gloria* got out of the lagoon safely. I suggest you turn on the wireless and stay on *Gloria*'s frequencies."

Aviva did as she was told, and Aron pulled Jack aside, urging him to be speedy about being discharged. "We have found you a job, which will let you prove to the Americans that you can support yourself in Italy. The job is quite fictitious, but the Americans will hardly know that. You will open a Venice office for the Joint Distribution Committee, although you will not be working for that organization. Start on your discharge tomorrow morning. If you are asked why you are in such a hurry, tell them you want to accept this position. And, while I'm about it, I must tell you that Aviva will remain with you and Naomi because she is now unable to move freely. You must feed her and take her to the local bath house. She will move to Venice with you."

Ben Hayyim turned to the women: "Burn your uniforms."

Naomi took off hers and threw it on the sofa next to Aviva's, saying, "I hope we'll be able to do likewise with yours, Ya'akov."

"I'm being discharged," he said. "I don't have to burn mine, Naomi."

* * *

Gloria's eleven-day voyage to Palestine was uneventful but awful. The four hundred passengers were crowded; the stench was overpowering. And—even in winter—the holds became unbearably hot. Minor violence erupted when someone tried to get to the front of the food line. The passengers were not allowed up on deck, and the ship maintained radio silence.

Naomi and Aviva kept listening, but heard nothing.

When the ship came within sight of Palestine, curiosity could not be restrained and the passengers surged onto the decks to find vantage points, even climbing the mast. It might have caused tragedy, but the ship appeared to be undetected by the Royal Navy.

She sailed toward Kibbutz Shefayim just north of Tel Aviv, running toward the shore on a southwesterly tack. The people of the kibbutz came out in small boats to bring the illegals ashore.

Gloria had been renamed *Moledet*, or Native Land, just before landfall. The Jewish flag was run up the mast and on the fantail. She rode high in the water as the small boats ferried people into the surf, dropped them ashore, and turned around. That's when two frigates out of Jaffa sailed toward her on her seaward side while another tried to get between *Moledet* and the shore. *Moledet's* captain sensed the danger and signaled full speed ahead on the ship's telegraph, turning his vessel's prow toward the beach. He brought her up hard on a sand bank, allowing everyone to get on the beach and scatter. It was not, however, all that easy. The British surrounded Shefayim with infantry, armor, and police. Soldiers raced along the beach grabbing all civilians with more violence than needed.

To make it more difficult for the troops to tell *kibbutzniks* from illegals, some of the new arrivals had changed into shorts just like the ones worn by the *kibbutzniks*. Everyone had been instructed how to answer questions.

> Q. Where are you from?
> A. Here.
> Q. How long have you been here?

A. Always. (or: Since the days of our teacher, Moses.)
Q. What is your name?
A. Israel, David (if a man); Israel, Hannah, (if a woman).

The *kibbutzniks* answered the same way. No one had any identification. All had the same name. No one had any other address than Shefayim. But the pallor of the illegals and their tattooed concentration camp numbers made it easy for the British to make a "selection," a term used by the illegals to recall its use by the Germans in choosing those who would go to the gas chambers and those who would become slave laborers.

Those arrested were put into cages on trucks and driven to the Athlit detention camp.

Among the prisoners in Athlit was one David Israel on whose chest hung a crucifix and in whose pocket rosary beads were fingered silently. This David Israel was pale and weary, for Jim Kelly had suffered from diarrhea since the ship passed Bari. Having made no effort to identify himself as a legal resident of Palestine, he was herded away with the others. Had he been found out as one of the crew, he would have faced jail, so Kelly preferred to take his chances as an illegal.

It was through Kelly that the cell in Gorizia finally learned that the ship had been detected. Each illegal was permitted one postcard and Kelly sent a postcard to:

Jewish Chaplain
88th Infantry Division (USA)
Gorizia, Italy

It was delivered by the Venezia Giulia mailman to Headquarters Company and bore this message:

David Israel #132
Athlit Camp #3
Athlit, Palestine
The 132nd holder of this name sends Passover greetings to
Naomi.
    With a little whisky, this place would not be half bad.
Of course, Scotch would be the wrong kind.

Kindest regards, David Israel #132

* * *

Jack was told that his request for immediate discharge could take
three months. Meanwhile, life went on in Naomi's little house.
They could soon live there without any need to go out except to
bathe, and in Gorizia's municipal bathhouse, the women's side
was usually empty in the morning. Jack shopped for groceries, and
the women went on a nearly vegetarian diet since the house lacked
any means of keeping food cold. Since they were both Palestinians,
this was no burden; they were used to eating vegetables, even for
breakfast.

    Kelly's postcard brought mixed feelings. Naomi, whose move-
ment had advocated illegal immigration before the war but did
not now make it a big priority, was angry that the people would
now have legal certificates doled out to them by the Zionist leadership. That meant that the boat full of people would not affect
the total that would be allowed to come into Palestine.

    Aviva took a more militant stand. "I thought *Tnuat Hameri*
blew up all the radar stations to keep the Royal Navy from finding
our ships! What went wrong?"

    "They still do have the Royal Air Force and the Royal Navy,
Aviva," Jack said, trying to soothe her.

    "We should prevent the capture of our ships," Aviva went on,
"by engaging the enemy. We should sink their ships in harbor,
fight their police, bomb their army barracks. Keeping them busy

fighting against our forces of liberation, would end these humilia-tions at sea! I realize that *Lechi* is tiny, that *Etzel* is not much larger, but *Haganah* is strong and if it would only start to fight, we would win. They are still observing *havlaga*, self-restraint."

Jack knew that *Etzel* was the Hebrew contraction for *Irgun Zvai Leumi*, but he had never heard of *Lechi*. So he asked.

"We are *Lochamei Herut Yisrael*, Fighters for the Freedom of Israel—and we do not want to be called the Stern 'gang,' " Aviva said.

Ben Hayyim was present during this exchange and let loose with the official view from the top levels of the Jewish Agency: "You're wrong, Aviva. If your challenge to Britain were taken seri-ously by the British, how long do you suppose we would last. We are half a million Jews surrounded by Arabs taking on an empire that stretches around the world. If they were to recognize your 'declaration of war,' they would bomb our cities, deport many of us to the Indian Ocean, destroy our economy. Our leaders are wise to insist on *havlaga*."

Jack, who had heard all these arguments back in Hebrew Teach-ers College, said, "Same old *havlaga* talk, but I never expected to hear it from a ranking officer in the *Bricha*."

Aviva stuck to her guns: "Even though we do not believe in illegal immigration as a weapon against England, our high com-mand has ordered us to cooperate with the *Bricha*. We believe only in active measures to rid our country of the English."

But things changed in the ensuing weeks. After formation of *Tnuat Hameri*, the united resistance movement, Haganah blew up the bridges over the Jordan; Etzel raided the RAF base at Lydda and sabotaged the oil pipeline from Mosul in Iraq to Haifa; Haganah attacked the remaining coastal radar stations; Lechi robbed two British-owned banks; a Haganah ship landed safely at Bat Yam, and Lechi blew up a troop train carrying soldiers of the detested 6th Airbourne Division.

The *Bricha* also became more active. Weapons and explosives were bought from stocks that had been hidden by wartime parti-

san units, mostly in Yugoslavia and Czechoslovakia; a first-class
radio network was established all over Europe, and ships larger
than *Gloria* were being purchased.

As Jack shared their secrets, he also heard some of their brag-
ging. Finally he found out how Ben Hayyim had realized—when
the Jewish Brigade was sent to Holland—that it became necessary
to maintain an armed Jewish presence in Italy. Out of this grew
the phony companies, the 179th and 162nd Royal Army Service
Corps companies. Even Ben Hayyim was amazed that the British
had not discovered the subterfuge long ago, but the two companies continued their British army duties while trucking Jews all
over Europe.

Meanwhile, some governments in Europe, particularly Czechoslovakia, were making amends for doing nothing when there was
time to save the Jews—particularly at the Evian conference—by
doing all they could now. The *Bricha* ran "Red Cross" trains, was
given access to diplomatic pouches and intelligence reports, and
was even provided with some military road transport.

* * *

Jack's discharge finally came through in February. The women were
looking forward to getting out of their one-room prison, and Ben
Hayyim came to say good-bye.

"I need not tell you that I do not agree with your politics. You
are dissidents from the policy of our people. But I want you to
know that I will testify the rest of my life to the glorious moment
when the three sides worked together in harmony and, especially,
for what you two have done here."

He shook hands with both, as he helped them load their goods
into a truck from the 179th RASC that would take them to Venice.

Jack left the division in a whimper. There was no ceremony,
only a handshake from the commanding officer of Headquarters
Company. But Jack would not have it that way. As he came out of
that building, he marched to division headquarters where the flags

showed that General Guthrie was not in. He turned to the American flag, saluted, and said to himself.

"I leave you now, but I am grateful. You did allow me to live; you let me fight against the enemies of my people. I shall always respect you for your ideals and for your promise of freedom. I only wish that it had been you after Evian that opened its doors to save the remnant of my people. For saying no, for turning away those who fled to your very shores and were turned away, I shall leave you now. I remain grateful. I remain bitter."

The MP who was watching this private mustering-out ceremony looked on without understanding. When Jack brought his arm down from his salute, the MP asked: "What was that all about, sergeant?"

"Just saying good-bye to the 88th Division, pal. I've been with it since Camp Gruber. My time is up."

* * *

When they arrived in Venice, Filiberti helped them find an apartment and an office. He was no longer needed as a contact with the *Bricha* because they now had the radios, but he came in handy in helping Jack find civilian clothes.

A radio message sent all three of them to Filiberti's one day as he was reopening the store after lunch. They were surprised to see the familiar face of John Aron, now also a civilian.

"Good to see you again," Aron said. "My name is John, and I want you to call me that. I'm back at work as the local agent for World Tours. I'm to reopen our office here. Isn't it nice to see you all in Venice . . . "

Aron's voice petered off and he looked in alarm over Jack's shoulder. Jack whirled and saw another familiar face.

"What's this?" Jack shouted, "old home week? Hiya, Kelly."

"I thought you were in Athlit," Naomi said.

"I was, Naomi. His Britannic Majesty permitted me to immigrate to Palestine as David Israel and my wife insists I should marry an illegal in that capacity. Anyway, I am here to sign on another ship."

Aron whispered to Naomi, and after being reassured by her, said: "I fear you have a long wait, old man. There has been a delay because of typhoid. Our convoy did not make it to Austria. They're all in bloody quarantine in Czechoslovakia. I suggest you try La Spezia."

"No," Kelly answered. "I've just come from there. I tell you the vessel is coming here. It's the *Innocent Voyager* and she flies the Panamanian flag. I've checked with the Italian port authorities, and she is due tomorrow at the Cosulich pier."

"Very well," Aron said, sounding miffed that he had been left uninformed. "Now, Mr. Kelly, were you told to meet us here or were you just calling on Filiberti to say hello?"

"Filiberti asked me to come."

"Then you must be the man I was to meet—only I was given the name of Israel." Aron had apparently not heard all the chatter that greeted Kelly's arrival.

"He and I are one," Kelly said.

Aron led them all out of the shoe store toward the Rialto Bridge. On the other side of the Grand Canal, near the British Consulate General, they entered a villa to which Aron possessed the keys. As soon as they were settled around a mahogany dining table, Aron started with Jack and Naomi:

"We are sending you two to Germany. Aviva will remain here with the radios. You are to report to the DP camp at Landsberg to train immigrants for Palestine."

"Train them for what?" Naomi cried indignantly.

"Oh, you know, agriculture, cattle breeding, chicken farming, that sort of thing."

"You are pretty damned casual about it," she said, her lips taut. "I'll be hanged first. I wouldn't have part in any such thing. I know what you are up to, you're going to select which immigrants to bring to Palestine."

Jack, who had also caught Aron's drift, chimed in: "Count me out, too. We take them all, or I don't play."

"I concede," Aron said, "that we are going to select our illegals. We cannot possibly take them all, so we shall take the best."

"Without me," Naomi said, "I will not take part in such a cruel hoax. First, it accepts England's right to control how many may immigrate; I disagree. Second, it is seeking to create a leftist majority by bringing in agricultural workers only. Ben Gurion's party has a big enough majority. We need fighters for our movement, and you would never find them qualified to sail. Again, I say no! Finally, I must tell you that I am fed up with your concept of resistance. It is very well for you to show the world that the Jewish remnant wants to go to Palestine; it would be better if you got them there. The British do not even take them to Athlit any more. Are we helping to build a Jewish state by settling our people in detention camps on Cyprus? I say we are not. I shall return to my country and fight the British enemy, and when I say fight, I mean fight. Immigration is not enough. We must push England out . . . "

"But . . . " Aron began.

"No buts," she said. "I am resigning from the *Bricha*. I am going home. Come, Ya'akov."

Jack did not budge, and Aron finally got his innings: "Don't be an arse, Naomi. I'm in your movement, too. Though I am not a Jew, I have been a follower of Jabotinsky for years; I am a personal friend of Dr. Rudi Hecht, Hillel Kook, Yitzhak Ben-Ami, and others in your organization. I mention their names to reassure you. But I am also a friend of Pierre van Passen and I recently met Senator Guy Gillette. They are not Jewish either and agree with your viewpoint one hundred percent.

"I can say that I did expect you to react to the orders I am passing just as you did. They are, I admit, orders from the *Bricha*, not from Menachem Begin. But permit me to say a few words before you fly off the handle again."

"What, exactly, do you mean when you say you are in my movement?"

"I am in *Etzel*. I thought you had always realized that. Before the war, when I was working for World Tours in Haifa, I became friendly with Jabotinsky's son Eri, who was beginning to run in illegal ships. This was all before the Jewish leaders in Palestine and abroad had accepted the idea of illegal immigration, when Dr. Weizmann was making statements about bringing in 'pickpockets and prostitutes,' and when Ben Gurion reviled illegal immigration as he now reviles combat. I have known you were in the *Irgun* since you were assigned to my cell in Gorizia. I thought you had been told about me as well. See here, Naomi, you can't just pack it up and go home. You are, after all, a deserter from His Majesty's forces. If you refuse to go to Germany, why don't you sail on one of the ships?"

Kelly took it from there: "That's a great idea, Naomi; why not sail on *Innocent Voyager* with me?"

"Good idea, Kelly," Jack said. "Me, too."

"And me," Aviva said.

"Oh no," Aron said. "You stay here with the radios, Aviva. I'll make sure it is not too long. But for now, the *Bricha* desperately needs you. Trust me. I shall not keep you from the battle."

* * *

That night, Aron got the bad news from Aviva. The typhoid outbreak had interrupted the flow of people and no replacements were ready for Udine camp, which was to give up three hundred people for *Innocent Voyager*. Aviva had heard the 162nd RASC being ordered to bring the three hundred to Venice without replacements.

There was only one problem: *Innocent Voyager* had room for more passengers. Aviva asked Milan for instructions. "Send as is," she was told. "Will direct next move."

Voyager, therefore, sailed out of Chioggia without destination. Of those aboard, only the crew knew of the mixup. But on shore there was apprehension.

Three days out of Venice, as she sailed past Brindisi, *Voyager* was ordered to La Spezia. When she arrived, all hell broke loose.

The British consul visited the Italian port commander and ordered him to detain the vessel. The Italian, a former admiral in Mussolini's navy, flatly refused to take orders from the consul and queried Rome for instructions. Meanwhile, a cruiser and two destroyers of the Royal Navy entered the harbor to blockade *Innocent Voyager*. The *Bricha* commander took matters into his own hands and decided to use *Voyager* to embarrass and humiliate the British. The ship sprouted signs proclaiming the passengers' will to leave the lands of Europe, the lands of death. The port commander allocated a small area at dockside for the use of the ship. And the fences around that zone were quickly made into billboards, too. The gate into the enclosure became *Petah Tikva*, the gate of hope. Townspeople sent gifts of food to the ship. Stevedores, members of Italy's Communist labor federation, donated a day's wages to *Voyager*.

Meanwhile, the Jews who had been brought to La Spezia to board *Voyager*, were passed through the gate by the Italian guards. Among them was Shlomo Ben Hayyim, who immediately took personal command of the vessel.

Rome, under pressure from England, valiantly defended its territorial integrity by refusing to detain *Innocent Voyager*. Reporters from all over the world raced to La Spezia to cover "The Revolt of the Innocent."

The British had miscalculated and the *Bricha* had taken up the challenge with a propaganda victory over England; but *Voyager* stayed in La Spezia. Two Latin American nations offered the passengers entry. Ben Hayyim ordered a vote, then announced the results over the ship's loudspeakers:

"This is *Innocent Voyager*. This is *Innocent Voyager*. The following announcement is the result of the vote taken by the Jews on this ship. To the question, 'Would you accept the offer of the Argentine to settle in Argentina?' Against: seven hundred and ninety-six; in favor: none. To the question, 'Would you be willing to accept the offer of the Dominican Republic to settle in the Dominican Republic?' Against: seven hundred and ninety-six; in favor:

none. The Jews aboard *Innocent Voyager* are determined that they will go nowhere except to their own country. We are announcing to the world that as of midnight tonight, all Jews on *Innocent Voyager* will fast until allowed to leave for Zion. We will die of starvation before returning to the fleshpots of Europe, where we have known only suffering and death. We are descendants of the Jews of Masada, death before slavery."

The port commander, on orders from Rome, ordered the Royal Navy out of his harbor; the British refused. The Italian Foreign Ministry sent an official protest to the British High Commissioner in Caserta, claiming a violation of Italian sovereignty and of the terms of Italy's surrender to the Allies and its subsequent declaration of war against Germany. The Briton replied that until a peace treaty with Italy were signed, His Majesty's Government and the government of the Kingdom of Italy had still not re-established the *status quo ante bellum* and that the presence of the Royal Navy in Italian waters was in accordance with Italy's unconditional surrender.

Italy, shocked by this disregard of her declaration of war against the Axis and of her contribution to Allied victory—including the capture of Mussolini—rejected the British response on the grounds that it violated the Allied concession of February 25, 1945, by which Italy was granted cobelligerent status and again permitted to control its own affairs, except in areas, such as Venezia Giulia, that were to be decided in the peace treaty. The Foreign Ministry sent a full delegation to Caserta to complain to the full Allied Control Commission. The hunger strike, meanwhile, went into its second day.

At Caserta, each commissioner received instructions from his government. It was clear from the beginning that the French and Soviet commissioners would acknowledge Italy's case under the terms of the Allied concession. The result hinged on the vote of the American commissioner. For reasons never made public, he voted to uphold his English-speaking ally.

Ben Hayyim had an argument with Naomi, who wanted to charge the United States State Department with anti-Semitism, being in the pay of the oil cartel, and voting pro-British merely because the Soviet commissioner was on the other side. Ben Hayyim overruled her, wanting to do nothing to offend any power that was a potential ally.

On the third day of the hunger strike, Count Mateo de Santis, the Italian statesman who had endured fascism in exile, spoke over the Italian radio. He reminded England that he had taught at Cambridge for twenty years and was grateful to England for many things, not the least of which was her superb struggle against the forces of repression. Now, his friends had changed into tyrants and he was appalled at the sudden transformation directed against innocent people who, like him, had suffered tyranny under fascism.

The following morning, angry mobs surged into the streets of many cities in Italy, demonstrating their anger against England's behavior. On *Voyager*, a naval burial service, using an empty coffin and the Jewish flag, was held on the quarter deck. As the haunting chant of the mourner's prayer invoked the blessing of the Lord, the British vessels hove anchor.

Innocent Voyager sailed on the morning tide, but during her entire voyage to Palestine, the Royal Navy kept a faithful escort. The Jews, free to come on deck, taunted the British without cease. Ben Hayyim asked Kelly about the protocol of flags on the high seas and learned that the flag of the country of registry was flown on the stem, while the flags of the countries of last stop and next destination were flown on the mast. Up went the flags of Italy and the blue-and-white Jewish flag. But Ben Hayyim had yet another flag and wanted Kelly to tell him where to fly it, a red British naval ensign with a superimposed swastika. Kelly told him to fly it at the bow. Ben Hayyim made a ceremony out of hoisting it; but the British response, from the cruiser, was to shoot at their own flag with small arms.

Within sight of Mount Carmel, a megaphone message drifted across the water: "Ahoy, *Voyager*, we are going to board you. We shall use all necessary force. Stand by for boarding."

Below decks, the *Bricha* had organized resistance. Nuts and bolts were to be hurled from strategic points; hoses were assigned to teams to direct high-pressure streams of water and steam at the boarding parties. The bridge was to be defended by men and boys armed with homemade shields and pieces of iron pipe. Naomi talked herself into this defense point despite the objections of Ben Hayyim. and Jack, both also stationed there.

The fight lasted only a few minutes; tear gas was loosed on the *Voyager* before Royal Marines crossed over. Most of the amateur army was quickly overcome with little injury. But the bridge was the scene of a fierce battle. Naomi shrieked piercing curses as she loosed a skull-cracking attack on the first Marine to approach her. Others, despite the fumes, followed her example. All defenders of the wheelhouse and the bridge had to be carried ashore at Haifa.

The captives were herded into rolling chicken coops, bound temporarily for Athlit where they became fellow inmates with all the leaders of Jewish Palestine, the *Yishuv*. Future prime ministers, generals, and ambassadors had been arrested by the mandatory government in an act of vengeance for the most devastating blow yet dealt by the underground.

The well-guarded and almost inaccessible headquarters of British military might had been blown up in the King David Hotel in Jerusalem by the *Irgun Zvai Leumi*. (It was later learned that Teddy Kolleck, then a Jewish Agency official and later a popular mayor of Jerusalem, had warned the British of the impending attack.) British prestige sank from low to abysmal. No English soldier was safe in Palestine, and the army enclosed itself in barbed-wire enclosures that the Jews reviled as "Bevingrads," named after Britain's Minister for Foreign Affairs, Ernest Bevin.

England had become a blind giant wildly thrashing out at her adversaries, a figure of dissipated strength, a Gulliver with half a million troops tied to the ground by a handful of Jewish Lilliputians.

United States, 1947-48
En route to Palestine, 1948

DAVE I

In the summer of 1940, a formal retreat parade was held at Camp
Betar in Hunter, New York, in honor of the Leader, Ze'ev Ben
Yonah Jabotinsky, called Vladimir outside Palestine, from which
he had been exiled a decade earlier by the British.

Jabotinsky was the visionary, the prophet, the dreamer. For
him, there was but one goal: a Jewish state in the entire territory of
the League of Nations Mandate, or, as his song went: "Jordan banks
are two; one is ours, the other, too."

Dave Gordon, eighteen-year-old head of the first all-American
squad in the New York Brigade, was in the guard of honor. As the
Leader approached, relays of boys and girls garbed in uniforms
emblazoned with seven-branched candelabra, were posted along
the highway from New York City. Although few in number, they
were made to appear many more by being constantly ferried ahead
along the route to cheer again and cheer again.

Jabotinsky was not fooled. In good humor he commented that
the young people seemed so out of breath and, because he felt that
way himself, he excused himself from taking the review to rest in
his tent. Ten minutes later, word spread electrically through the
camp that Jabotinsky was dead.

He was buried in Queens "until the President of a Jewish State
orders my body to be returned to Jerusalem." Madame
Jabotinsky—called the Mother of Betar—stood at the graveside
like a soldier. Nearby was the six-man *Irgun* delegation to the United
States headed by Hillel Kook, son of the Ashkenazi chief rabbi of
Palestine. In America, he called himself Peter Bergson.

It was a small funeral for the man who had created the Jewish Legion in the first World War and who had died while, once again, rallying Jews to arms—to form a Jewish army to fight against the greatest enemy the Jews had ever known.

Dave was in the cemetery in a tight cluster of uniformed Betarim, including Jack Frumkin from Boston and Misha Arens, a future member of the Israeli cabinet, from the Washington Heights squad.

* * *

Before the war, Betar in America had been composed mostly of Jews who had first joined Jabotinsky's movement in Europe and who tempered their belief in the return to Zion by suggesting that they were merely improving their lot by being in America as they awaited their call to Zion. They had unpacked their brown Betar uniforms, held meetings, marched behind Zion's banner, and sang nationalistic songs in Hebrew, many of which had been written and composed by Jabotinsky.

But American Jews had not been born into the environment of pogroms and anti-Jewish restrictions that had nurtured Betar in eastern Europe, especially in Poland where Betar had more than ten thousand members. American Jews did not need a self-defense organization and shared with their non-Jewish neighbors a repugnance toward uniforms and militarism. Some ridiculed the "fascists" in their midst and compared Betar in its brown uniforms to the German-American Bund.

Nevertheless, Betar began to attract native American Jews, who were brought to Betar by their abhorrence of the German-American Bund and Gerald L.K. Smith's Silver Shirts. The movement took root, albeit slowly. When war broke out in Europe, Betar took up and propagated the call for establishment of a Jewish fighting force in the British army. Dave Gordon joined the United States Army Air Corps shortly before Pearl Harbor and was trained to become a bombardier. The other men and older boys of Betar thronged to enlist as well—turning Betar into a band of girls knitting socks for their men in uniform.

On V-E Day, Dave was a major with seven oak leaf clusters on his Air Medal, two Purple Hearts, a French croix-de-guerre, and several lesser medals. A Distinguished Service Cross had been awarded to him by General Eisenhower for successfully evading captivity after being shot down near Ploesti.

But discharge for Dave meant only a change in uniforms. His last months in Europe had rekindled the flame of Betar as he saw the victims of Bergen Belsen being bulldozed into mass graves. He attended the first postwar congress of world Betar in the Landsberg concentration camp. In uniforms fashioned from whatever they could find, Betar men and women marched to the songs of Jabotinsky. Commander Yossef Katzin called on the assembled Zionists to learn their lesson:

"Have we Jews no pride? Are we to be terrorized, victimized, gassed, cremated, hounded, and pushed into exile forever? Are we never to awaken to our national destiny? Are we never to return to Zion?

"My answer to you is no. We shall be free. We shall have a homeland: a Jewish state on both sides of the Jordan.

"To any power that stands in the way of our national redemption, I can but repeat the words of the ghetto fighters' song: 'Make way; we are coming; we are here!' "

Dave followed Katzin to the platform. In broken Yiddish, he uttered his life's vow: "Comrades, I stood at the graveside of the Leader of Betar on the day of his unhappy burial on alien soil. He was the man to whom many of you here owe your existence today. Had he not taught you the art of war, you would also have perished in Auschwitz and those other unspeakable places where our people quietly walked to their doom. Had he not taught you to fight back, you would not have been with the partisans; you would have been among the tattooed victims of the 'Final Solution of the Jewish Problem.' But our Leader also taught the final solution of the Jewish problem. He taught it simply: 'A Jewish state on both sides of the Jordan.' That, comrades, is the one, the only solution to Jewish exile, to Jewish victimization, to Jewish extermination. Thus, let me tell you the vow I took at the graveside of Ze'ev Ben Yonah Jabotinsky: 'I shall make it my life's work to bury you in honor on Mt. Zion. To do so, I shall fight—and die if necessary—for the creation of a Jewish state on both sides of the Jordan. Tel Hai!"

That greeting, which sounded so much like the "Sieg Heil" of the Nazis, was one of the facets of Betar that made it totally unacceptable to most Jews, but it was a repeated recall of the first great Zionist martyr, Josef Trumpeldor, the one-armed former captain in the Czar's army who led the Zion Mule Corps at Gallipoli in the first World War and who died defending the settlement of Tel Hai in the Upper Galilee against a French-inspired Arab attack in 1920. It was also a reminder that although four Jabotinsky followers had fallen alongside Trumpeldor, the leaders of Jewish Palestine would not even put their names on the monument at Tel Hai. After all, they were just "Jewish fascists." Yet every year, the young Jews of Palestine make a pilgrimage to Tel Hai—but only to honor Trumpeldor.

* * *

When he returned to New York, Dave went to work reorganizing the movement. He contacted veterans returning from the war, rented office space with the adult Revisionist Party, spoke at youth centers, agitated on campuses, and climbed soap boxes on street comers, many of them in Brooklyn. He took his "52—20" money, twenty dollars for fifty-two weeks, while he was an "unemployed" veteran and worked eighty hours a week for Betar.

Then a popular cause was found, the revolt of the *Irgun Zvai Leumi*. Excitement hung in the air, members were easier to find and keep, and, in the summer of 1946, Dave had sufficient strength to stage a mass rally at Manhattan Center to protest the treatment of *Innocent Voyager*, the *Haganah* ship that the Royal Navy had bottled up in La Spezia.

It was a heady time. Hillel Kook's people had recruited Ben Hecht, and full-page ads appeared in newspapers backing the *Irgun*. The illustrations for these ads were drawn by Arthur Szyk, the famed miniaturist. Famed actors, including Paul Muni and Stella Adler, joined the movement and performed in Hecht's spectacular "A Flag Is Born." Support came from non-Jewish labor leaders, and Senators Dennis Chavez and Guy Gillette spoke in the Senate for a Hebrew state and attacked British perfidy in keeping Jews out of Palestine. They had the support of former California Congressman Will Rogers, Jr., and a handful of prominent movie stars.

The veterans, including Dave, took advantage of the GI Bill of Rights and set out for distant colleges and universities, spreading Betar beyond New York, Boston and Philadelphia for the first time. Nests were founded in San Francisco, Toronto, Chicago, Cleveland, and Detroit. They planned their studies with a purposeful ideal, how best to serve the Jewish state they were going to create. Dave chose aeronautical engineering at the Massachusetts Institute of Technology. Losing no time in finding the Boston Betar, he found the five members of the Boston nest: Sophie Gurevitch, formerly of Betar in Tientsin; Yehezkel "Zeke" Rapoport, a Harvard freshman from Tel Aviv; Murray Blatnik, a fifteen-year-old student at Hebrew Teachers College and the Public Latin School; Billy Stone, a student at the Massachusetts Institute of Art, and Joe Sachs, a car salesman just discharged from the army.

Dave was curious as to what had attracted the last three. Billy was quite frank; she joined to meet a boy. She had watched Betar at a street-corner meeting and the boys had looked nice. After she joined, they made her secretary and she was still waiting for any of the boys to pay attention to her.

"My only privilege is that Sophie and I go up the ladder last so no one can look under our skirts," she said, "but my luck may have changed, Dave. You better look out 'cause you're real sweet and I think I'm falling in love with you. If you want me, just whistle."

Dave smiled. He had seen that movie.

Joe Sachs had been in the Betar parade in Landsberg concentration camp. When he reached home, he found the group by calling Dr. Tscherney at Hebrew Teachers College. The old man told him to contact Murray, who, in turn, had been spurred by Tscherney's avowal of Betar and love for Jabotinsky.

These five became Dave's executive committee during the expansion of the Boston nest. They met regularly in a loft over an abandoned coach house in Roxbury. The unused garage below was their drill hall. The walls of their headquarters were covered with slogans and pictures.

Under a sign that proclaimed "IT IS GOOD TO DIE FOR OUR COUNTRY" (the last words of Shlomo Ben Yossef, the first *Irgun* soldier hanged by the British) hung portraits of their heroes: Jabotinsky, David Raziel, the first commander of the *Irgun* who died while carrying out a secret British mission against the pro-Nazi regime in Iraq; Ben Yossef, who had been a Betari, and a laurel-wreathed question mark where there should have been a picture of Menachem Begin, commander of the *Irgun*. Nobody knew what he looked like.

Each meeting began and ended with a military formation. The Betar hymn was sung at the first, *Hatikva*, the national anthem, at the last.

Their chief activity was to raise funds for the *Irgun*, but they worked long and hard at other tasks, such as learning Hebrew. They launched a boycott of Britain with stickers saying "OYCOTT LOODY RITAIN' flowing out of a large letter "B." Joining them in the boycott were members of the Irish Republican Army, who hid their Irish connection by calling the campaign a drive sponsored by the Sons of Liberty.

"Action night" was Saturday. As soon as the Sabbath was over, they met in front of the G and G Deli on Blue Hill Avenue in Dorchester with collection boxes. They followed a pattern that had proven effective in which a Betaria mounted the milk box and started a sing-song plea.

"Who'll help make a Jewish state? Who'll help me make a *yiddishe medine*? Just help me buy the bullets. Six cents buys a bullet to kill an Englishman in Palestine—in *Eretz Yisrael*. Six cents buys a bullet. Who'll gimme six cents? Who'll gimme six cents? Just six cents by six cents by six cents and you have a rifle. Six cents buys a bullet. Who'll gimme six cents? . . . "

They went beyond street-corner solicitation, picketing the British consulate on numerous occasions. Once, they even occupied the consulate to hold a memorial service for Dov Gruner and his companions on the gallows. Zeke Rapoport led the *kaddish* standing on a consular desk.

In May of 1947, the nest had a solid core of twenty members who could always be counted on to make door-to-door appeals, to picket British movies, and to heckle meetings of the "pseudo-Revisionists" of the American League for a Free Palestine, not aware that Hillel Kook and his *Irgun* colleagues had set up this highly successful non-Jewish propaganda and fund-raising organization. The argument was not about whether they were not both helping the *Irgun*, it was over definition of the word "Jew."

The League, which had set up an "embassy" in Washington for the Hebrew Committee of National Liberation, held that a Jew was someone who practiced a particular religion. This applied to American Jews or Jews in other countries where Jews had become citizens. This meant that there were American Jews and French Jews and so on. But in Palestine and in the DP camps, the committee termed the Jewish people Hebrews. Its embassy issued "Hebrew" passports.

Betar rejected such a concept because, it said, the Jewish people was indivisible and all of its adherents owed allegiance to the totality, as Betar did.

At its 1947 summer camp in Ellenville, New York, Betar conducted instruction in street fighting and house-to-house combat as well as infantry tactics and weapons training. It obtained rifles from the federal government under a program sponsored by the National Rifle Association to teach Americans to shoot. For this purpose, Betar was a rifle club. One of those learning how to shoot was a thin Brooklyn boy with curly black hair, Me'ir Kahane, whom everyone called simply "Kahany."

Leading that summer's school were four members of the *Irgun* who had escaped from British detention in a camp at Asmara, Eritrea. They approached each Betari separately and invited him or her to become members of the *Irgun*. All were sworn to secrecy. When the Bostonians returned home, the three cells found that each of them was commanded by Dave, who was now also an officer in the *Irgun*. No cell knew of the existence of the others.

When the United Nations voted in November 1947 to partition Palestine, Betarim had their first ideological split. A few joined with the rest of Boston's Jewish community for a big celebration at the Parkman bandstand on the Boston Common. Dave ordered black mourning armbands to be put on the uniforms and in his role as a member of the New England Zionist Emergency Council spoke from the bandstand along with Boston's Zionist leaders.

"We do not accept partition," Dave said. "In Hebrew, 'partition' is '*chaluka.*' What you are dancing for is *Chalukistan*, not the Jewish state that we deserve, the entire territory promised to us in the Balfour Declaration, the entire territory turned over to England by the League of Nations. That territory, as the words of the Palmach hymn say, is 'From Metulla to the Negev, and from the sea to the desert.'

"Our Socialist friends in the Palmach literally shout that song, never realizing that it calls for a Jewish state on both sides on the River Jordan, a concept that the defeatist Zionist leadership opposes. Yet Metulla is in the north; the Negev is in the south; the sea is in the west, and the desert, damn it is in Gilead, around Rabat Ammon, where a British puppet rules a Judenrein desert sheikdom."

One of the Zionist leaders pulled Dave away from the microphone, saying: "You will not destroy our celebration of the greatest day in Jewish history in two thousand years."

"What are you celebrating?" Dave shot back.

"A Jewish state," he was told.

"That's what you have opposed for the last twenty-five years. Why the sudden change?"

They dragged Dave away from the microphone, and, after a while, the young people around the bandstand broke out in dancing and singing.

* * *

As the winter of 1947–48 came to an end, Dave called a special meeting. Forty-five Betarim lined up as two nests of three squads each. Squad leaders reported to their nest commanders. When Joe Sachs called on the commanders to report, they saluted and barked their total strength. Joe wheeled and reported to Dave: "My Lord Commander, the brigade is formed and is at your command," The Hebrew was crisp and clipped.

"Thank you. Take your post, Sir," Dave replied, returning the salute.

Joe marched to the head of the formation, and Dave ordered "at ease" in Hebrew, then he turned to English: "I have a general order from the headquarters of World Betar."

He unfolded it and started to read:

Sons of Betar and the Revisionist Movement! To the colors!

The great hour approaches. The great hour that has been awaited by seventy generations of our people draws near. It will take place.

Once again, the fate of our people hangs in the balance of history.

We face the alternatives of becoming a free people or of total annihilation.

We have been offered the opportunity of staging the greatest revolution in the life of our people and of giving material shape to the age-old vision of freedom for Zion and independence for Eretz Israel.

"God," Dave thought as he read the clichés, "why didn't they write this in English? And why are they celebrating? I just ordered mourning bands on the uniforms."

In the name of our six million brethren who were ruth-
lessly exterminated in the gas chambers, in the name of the
remnant of our people, in the name of the homeless orphans
and childless widows, in the name of the martyrs of Jewish
history, and in the name of the Betarim now fighting in the
front lines

YOU are called upon to join the ranks of the Jewish
liberation army, the army which will conquer and bring
freedom to our people.

YOU are called to a war of redemption and a struggle
for freedom; to a decisive battle for the integrity of our
fatherland in its historic boundaries.

Betarim, the eyes of the Jewish people turn upon you.
Rise! Join the ranks of the fighters to show your might and
the strength of Jewish arms.

With justice as our cause and with the strength of steel,
we shall conquer. our enemies will be defeated.

Betarim, to the colors! Your brothers await you!

Without an order from Dave, Zeke Rapoport came to attention behind Dave with the flag and brought it in front of Dave.
Then, facing the brigade, he waved it over his head.

"Take your post, Zeke," Dave ordered, annoyed. "The order I
have just read is signed by Menachem Begin on behalf of the Betar
World Executive. Commander Sachs, take charge of the formation. The nests are to come upstairs to fill out enlistment papers.
Take over."

Dave climbed the ladder and sat down at his desk. He wondered how many would sign up. As they started to come up the
ladder, they saluted him and came forward. He offered to help fill
out forms. Six in all, he thought. Lousy response. Then Sophie
and Billy came up the ladder, presumably after Joe had cleared the
boys out of downstairs.

Sophie signed up without a word. Then Billy approached the
desk saluted, and leaned over to whisper at Dave: "Well, Dave?
We're way ahead of them, aren't we?"

"Yes, Billy," he said, "but I'm no longer leaving with you."

She was stunned and stood back up to her full height. "What?"

"I've been ordered to take charge of a group leaving in May. You better go ahead before the State Department invalidates your passport."

"What if they invalidate yours?"

"Orders are orders, Billy. I'll see you after we leave the Grove Hall deli, and I'll explain it all. OK?"

"I guess so."

* * *

Their affair had been kept secret. Dave felt that he had to behave absolutely according to Betar honor so he could maintain discipline. So they never left the deli together and eventually met at a subway station or at Billy's basement apartment in the Back Bay.

It had all begun when Dave complained about his prefabricated wooden barracks at MIT, barracks built during the war for the Navy's V–12 program. There was no privacy and little silence.

Billy gave him a key to her place and he gladly accepted. Her collection of classical long-playing records and her cooking might have been further inducements, but neither was needed. He had come to study, and study he did—at first. Then, slowly taking notice of Billy, study became a little less important.

As he studied, Billy worked at her easel. She made numerous sketches of Dave as he bent over her kitchen table opening and closing his slide rule. Then he brought his drawing table to her place and worked with drawing tools and a T-square. He was not in love with her, although she was with him. He had not even asked her to join the American *Irgun* because he thought her too frivolous. Aware of his detachment, Billy signed up to go to Palestine before the mobilization order just to prove herself to him.

This time, they left the Grove Hall deli about ten minutes apart, but she was waiting for him at the Dudley Street subway station.

"I had planned not to come to your place tonight, Billy," he said, "to give you time to pack."

She took the Allston bus and he took the train downtown. There was no good-bye.

Billy left the United States on the *Ile de France* a week before the United States put the Neutrality Law into effect, barring all citizens from the Middle East. Dave, who already had his passport and a visa to go to Italy, ignored the law. He withdrew from MIT, handed over his command to Joe Sachs, and reported to a secluded house in Poughkeepsie at which Land and Labor for Palestine had set up an embarkation center. The first glance at the place made Dave sick: A flagpole sported the U.S. flag at the top with a Jewish flag and a red flag on halyards that were attached to a cross beam, as on a ship's mast. He knew Land and Labor was a Socialist front organization to which the *Irgun* and Betar had pledged support, but the red flag sickened him.

A week later, three buses unloaded one hundred and fifty young people at the American Export Line's North River pier. Dave was the senior *Irgun* officer among the six American *Irgun* members, all of whom had been sworn into the Palestinian *Irgun* before reporting to Land and Labor. He was aware of more *Irgun* members among the Palestinians who also came to the dock.

Someone at the Jewish Agency had arranged press coverage of their departure. Despite protests from Amiram Ben Cohen, the senior *Haganah* officer, the photographers got their pictures, which ran that afternoon with such captions as "Zionists Sail to Fight in Palestine."

When *Marine Carp* sailed out of New York, its itinerary included Piraeus, Beirut, Haifa, and Alexandria, in that order.

On May the thirteenth, the ship steamed out of Piraeus for Beirut.

DAVE II

The Jews aboard *Marine Carp* were acutely aware of the imminent end of the British mandate in Palestine. Clustered around short-wave radios, they eagerly followed the news. A group of girls sewed pale blue bands and a Star of David into a flag made from a sheet provided by a cabin steward. Dave was watching a poker game in the lounge to relieve the heightening tension.

A Lebanese-American asked him what he would do when the ship arrived in Beirut.

"What should I do? I stay on board and mind my own business," Dave answered.

"Listen, buddy, I've got no ax to grind in this at all. I'm an Arab, but I'm a Maronite Christian. I don't like Moslem Arabs any more than you do. My only concern is for my people in Lebanon. I hope they don't get caught up in the fighting. So, if you weigh all the elements of this coming war, I'd like to be neutral; but if push came to shove, I'd cheer for you guys when nobody is looking."

Dave understood what he was being told because the Maronites in Boston had given five hundred dollars to an *Irgun* emergency appeal for medical supplies and ambulances—in cash.

"Let me give you some advice," the man said. "When the *Carp* pulls into Beirut, the war will have started for real. Don't assume that the Republic of the Great Lebanon is going to wave you people on to Haifa to fight against it. I assure you that the Lebanese consulate in New York saw the pictures that were taken when we sailed. There's going to be trouble when we arrive in Beirut, and if I were you I'd claim I wasn't Jewish."

Dave was disturbed. It had not occurred to him that anything could happen, but the man was obviously right. He found Amiram on the top deck arguing loudly with the first mate.

" . . . I tell you that you must ask your line's permission to change course. You must sail directly to Haifa. We are to dock in Beirut on the very day the mandate is to end, the day a Jewish state is declared. There will be war and there will be trouble in Beirut."

"Listen to reason," the mate said. "This ship belongs to the government of the United States and is on lease by the U.S. Maritime Commission to American Export Line. We are legitimately scheduled for our regular call at Beirut. We carry no contraband. I've been in Beirut a dozen times. They wouldn't dare do anything against the United States of America. I guarantee that nothing can happen."

"Can you at least ask American Export Line?" Amiram pleaded, sure that an Arab government would do exactly as it pleased. The Arabs knew where the oil was and had long since figured out how the State Department behaved.

Dave kept out of it, letting Amiram carry the ball.

One of the girls approached the mate: "Will you fly this flag when we enter Haifa?"

The mate knew. He had been in Haifa, too. But he wasn't having any: "Our instructions are that the port will remain under British rule even after the mandate ends. We will fly the Union Jack as always. That's captain's orders."

The girls looked glum, but turned cheerful when one said, "Well, if you need an *Eretz Israeli* flag, you know where to come."

When the mate left, Dave turned to Amiram to suggest a plan of defense in the event that the protection of the U.S. flag turned out to be illusory. Amiram resisted any such suggestions.

"Above all, David, don't let your people act independently. I know you have weapons aboard. I also know you have radios. I assume the radios will be safe in the hold, but please get rid of the weapons before Beirut. We cannot have any contraband to protect ourselves under the American flag."

THE TENTH PRAYER   133

"No, Amiram, I can't agree with that," Dave said, as his right hand closed into the fist he always made when he was making militant speeches to Betar. "If you will not make plans, I will make them for my people. I'll inform you of the nature of those plans, trusting in your honor not to interfere; but I reserve the right to independent action if any of my personnel are endangered. I know you also have weapons. Will you throw your arms to the fish? Neither will we! If fight we must; fight we shall."

But Dave was talked out of all this by Yossi, one of the Palestinian *Irgun* members who had spent two years in Gilgil prison in Kenya. "A ship lashed to the pier is a poor place for a fire-fight. You cannot take enough of the port area to protect yourself and your people. You may have the strength to do it, but you are unable to make the detailed plans and rehearsals for doing so. First of all as a leader of *Etzel*, you must learn that you must never endanger your command unnecessarily, even in their defense. We learned in guerrilla warfare that our superior strength came from surprise attack and rapid withdrawal. Otherwise, we would not have risked a battle with a superior enemy. You are behind the enemy's lines. You have no route of withdrawal. The United States Marines will not invade Lebanon to rescue you and your people— and Amiram's people will fight you. Remember that they were the ones who turned us over to the British for our vacations in Eritrea and Kenya. Thus, a fight becomes stupid if not self-destructive. Let's hide our arms with the crew and play along with Amiram."

Dissuaded by both Amiram and Yossi, Dave gave in. He ordered his people to bring their weapons to Amiram's cabin. A cabin steward placed them all in a laundry locker.

* * *

As the sun went down, the Jewish passengers gathered in what had been the troop mess hall of the converted troopship. People who had not shaved since New York, appeared beardless. Men who had not worn a shirt since sailing, wore ties and jackets. The women showed up in skirts and nylons. Not one leather jacket was in sight, although almost every Palestinian had bought one in the United States. It looked as though everyone were coming to a wedding.

All the Jews aboard *Carp*, including some from among the crew, were prepared for the ceremony to welcome the Sabbath, but it was for more than a Sabbath service that even the atheists among them had come. When the rabbi, also a passenger, finished the brief service, Amiram came forward, removed his hat, and called for their attention with "*Hakshivu! Hakshivu!*

"We have gathered to celebrate the Sabbath. We are also here to celebrate the birth of the Third Jewish Commonwealth. The state of *Eretz Israel* has been born."

They cheered—at least some of them did. Dave glanced over at Yossi, and saw that his teeth were clenched, his face looking upward, even though his eyes were not open.

"Amiram," Dave thought, "couldn't even bring himself to say the 'Third Jewish State.' Commonwealth indeed!"

Amiram silenced the crowd: "*Hakshivu!* The ship's radio room made a recording of the broadcast of the event. The radio officer will play it over the loudspeakers. Please remain quiet."

After considerable static and a hurried, but inaudible announcement, a *shofar*, a ram's horn used on the high holy days, blew a call for attention like the one on Rosh Hashanah. Then, the voice of David Ben Gurion, unmistakable to the Palestinians, filled the steel-walled hall and reverberated from the bulkheads as he read the Declaration of Independence:

We hereby proclaim the establishment of the Jewish State in Palestine, to be called Medinat Yisrael. "We hereby declare that, as from the termination of the mandate at midnight, the 14th-15th May, 1948, and pending the setting up of duly elected bodies of the State in accordance with a Constitution to be drawn up by the Constituent Assembly not later that the 1st October, 1948, the National Council shall act as the Provisional State Council, and that the National Administration shall constitute the Provisional Government of the Jewish State, which shall be known as Israel."

It was the first time that anyone in the mess hall heard the name of the new nation. There was a murmur, then some applause.

After the reading of the proclamation, *Hatikva*, Israel's national anthem, was sung by the assemblage in the Tel Aviv Museum and by the passengers in the mess hall. There was a pause as both audiences sat down. A new voice came over the loudspeaker, reading the ancient Jewish prayer, *Sheheheyenu*. In turn, the prayer was taken up by the *Carp*'s passengers, "Blessed art Thou, O Lord our God, King of the Universe, Who has kept us in life, and has preserved us, and has enabled us to reach this day."

Ben Gurion's voice was heard again: "I shall now read Ordinance Number One of the Provisional Government of Medinat Yisrael. 'All laws enacted under the British Government's Palestine White Paper of 1939, and all laws deriving from it, are hereby declared null and void.' " With that short statement, it was now legal for Jews to come to Palestine.

The radio room broke in to say that this was the end of the recording. The passengers began to get up, but Amiram put his hat back on and pointed to the rabbi. The rabbi put on his prayer shawl, faced the bow, and said: "Blessed art Thou, O Lord our God, King of the Universe, Who has given us to see this day."

He turned toward his audience. "We do not ordinarily wear our *tallit* at this hour. It is worn, as many of you know, at morning services. This, however, is the morning of a new day for our people. In view of this, I call upon you to say with me the *Shmone Esre*, the eighteen benedictions, from the morning service." He again turned toward the bow.

A few of the passengers, those who performed their religious obligation as part of their daily lives, spoke the prayers with the rabbi. At the tenth prayer, he turned, and spoke slowly, not in Hebrew, but in English: "Sound the great horn for our freedom; lift up the ensign to gather our exiles, and gather us from the four corners of the Earth. Blessed art Thou, O Lord, Who gatherest the banished ones of Thy people, Israel."

When the brief service ended, decorum and solemnity gave way to a celebration. Dave stayed a while, then went out on deck, wondering what the morrow would bring. Miriam, a girl from *Hashomer Hatzair*, a far-to-the-left group, sat down in a deckchair beside him as his thoughts wandered back to the day of Jabotinsky's death. Although Ben Gurion had declared a Jewish state only in part of the homeland, Dave thought, he had declared a state. Would Jabotinsky have joined in the dancing below decks? Or would he have continued the mourning Dave had proclaimed back in Boston about partition.

"David," Miriam whispered, "as much as we hated him, Jabo should have heard our Dovidl tonight. He would have been very happy."

"Funny, I was just wondering about that. I don't believe he would have been happy at all at a half loaf of a half loaf. Anyway, Miriam, I should not think you would be happy. Your party was against any kind of a Jewish state, remember? You guys wanted a binational state with an Arab majority, remember? And only six weeks ago, your guys were still turning our people over to the British as we attempted to liberate Jaffa."

"That's all over now," she said. "Now we must fight not only the British, but the Arabs, too. I am joining *Palmach* when we land, but I no longer believe in political armies. I hope we have a national army soon with no more factions. My stay in America made me realize that our politics are exaggerated. If we are to survive as a state, we must stop living inside our little political states."

"I hope you're not the only one who feels like that. If we all believe it, our state will become strong; if we don't, we'll be fighting each other forever."

"What made you join *Etzel*, David?"

"Through Betar. Better ask me what brought me to Betar."

"All right. What did?"

"The German-American Bund."

"I don't understand."

"Before the war, the Bund had many followers in New York. There were some in my neighborhood in midtown Manhattan. One day I was stopped in the street by some boys bigger than me. They asked, 'Who are you for: Franco or the Communists?' I anticipated them and said, 'Franco.' They asked, 'Who are you for: China or Japan?' This was right after the Japs had shot up the *Panay*, an American gunboat on the Yangtse River. I felt rotten about the first answer, but I couldn't lie again. I said I was for China. It was a moment of truth. They beat the hell out of me, broke my collar bone, and gave me a fractured skull. When I got out of the hospital, I joined the YMHA to learn boxing and jiu jitsu. The instructor was a Betari and I soon joined. Much later I learned that the brown Betar uniforms looked like those worn by the Nazis, so I helped Americanize them. Surprised?"

"No. I saw your people in a demonstration once. They were all quite nice, younger than our Betar in Pales . . . Israel. There were girls there, too. In Tel Aviv, they are almost all men. When I told them I was from Tel Aviv, they welcomed me. That would never have happened at home; they would have asked first what party I belong to. Then I would have been pushed away."

"Really? Are we so terrible?"

"In Tel Aviv, yes. You are fascists. Are you a fascist in American politics, too, David?"

"I am not even a fascist in Zionism, Miriam. As hard as it may be for you to believe, I am mildly socialist, what we term New Deal Democrat in America. I don't know yet what economic policies my party will follow in Israel."

"Aren't you all capitalists, officially?"

"I don't know what 'officially' means, but if you mean what I think you mean, the answer is no. Until now, we have put economic and political philosophy aside until the first goal—the state—was achieved. Jabotinsky used to call it monism. Now, with this pathetic little state, there are going to be splits in our movement, whichever direction we take. But, to tell you the truth, now that the struggle for statehood is over, all Zionist parties—including yours—will split and split again. On top of that, there will be splits between the party members in Israel and those in the Diaspora."

"Why?"

"Don't you see, Miriam, that the so-called Zionists outside Israel are going to appear pathetic fools if they don't pack up and go to the land they have created? Why, they'll be a laughing stock! But, because they hold the purse-strings of the parties in Israel, they will demand that they set policy. No Israeli party will stand for that. And the Orthodox will be the most absurd of all. Imagine, for a few dollars they can obtain a visa to go to Jerusalem. All of them! There will be no need to pray for 'Next year in Jerusalem.' But they'll keep praying, keep begging money, keep paying lip service, but will never get that visa."

"Did Jabotinsky teach you that?"

"No. That's my own prophesy."

She sat up in the deckchair and turned to him. "Are you married, David?"

"No. Are you?"

"No. I asked because I wondered if you were alone. You will be lonesome in Israel. Even though you belong to it, you will not like our Betar. Even though you are in *Etzel*, you will not like the dark-skinned Jews who make up most of its membership. I will give you my address in Tel Aviv and when you are in town and would like a real American date, you can find me."

"Thanks, but didn't you say you were going to the *Palmach* ?"

"I mean after the fighting is over."

"Then I shall return to America to finish school."

"So you are coming only to fight?"

"This time, yes. I'll come back after I finish MIT. I have two years to go."

They never went to bed that night. Their talk, always with a political undertone, went on. Other passengers came on deck with their Zenith Globemasters, hoping to hear Jerusalem Radio with the latest news. Slowly, it got light and a shadowy land could be discerned. A mate hoisted the Lebanese flag. A British flag signaled the next port of call.

"It might not be a good idea to fly our flag here," Miriam said, "but how I hate to see that rag up there."

JACK AND NAOMI I

Before sailing from Italy, Naomi became Naomi Frumkin, a "ghetto" name she despised because it was not Hebrew, like her maiden name. She asked Jack to adopt the name of Ben Dror as his own. Jack refused, but offered to choose a new name.

After long arguments, they agreed on Ben Horin, son of freedom or freeman. In the prison-hospital at Athlit, that was the name they gave to the British.

After their release from Athlit, they became legal immigrants; Naomi wanted to conceal her own identity lest the British send her back to prison to serve out her 1939 sentence. But getting out of Athlit meant entry into the prison that all of Palestine had become.

It was far from quiet in Jerusalem in the summer of 1947 when Jack entered *Etzel*. The British had deported the passengers of *Exodus 1947* to France, which refused them permission to land; the *Palestine Post* was bombed, probably by the Palestine police; the United Nations Special Commission on Palestine (UNSCOP) held open and secret hearings all over Palestine to hear as many viewpoints as possible; Betar was illegal; the British were moving into barbed-wire encircled enclaves-called "Bevingrads" by the Jews, a sarcastic reference to Ernest Bevin, the British foreign secretary; *Etzel's* radio programs went on the air with less than precision timing, starting each transmission with the whistling of the Betar hymn; mimeographed copies of *Etzel* broadcasts were posted all over the country during the night at great risk to those who pasted them up; there were constant raids by the police, the army, and the Criminal Investigation Department.

Jack was introduced to an *Etzel* officer, and was enrolled in a cell led by Shimshon. Arieh was the only other male member, but there were also Tamar and Rachel. Jack gathered from bits of conversation that all had served in the British military during World War II.

All meetings began in a Rehavia cafe and always ended in a closed store to which Shimshon had access. Behind closed metal shutters and with drawn blackout curtains they received their training. First, a briefing on the structure of the *Irgun*—important because they would never meet an *Etzel* member who did not belong to their cell—and then instructions in street fighting, house-to-house combat, fire and maneuver, fields of fire, and enfilade firing. It was all theoretical, based on Shimshon's drawings or military manuals he brought to class. This was done as a safety measure because possession of any weapon called for the death penalty in this British police state; possession of an arms manual carried a sentence of twenty years, and the British were not expected to be around that long.

As Jack was spending his evenings in Rehavia stores, Naomi did a nightly stint of reading *Voice of Fighting Zion* scripts into a tape recorder or an older wire recorder. This usually happened in a fashionable Katamon house with a basement. The finished tapes or spools of wire were then taken to a mobile transmitter and broadcast. The time of the broadcast varied because the truck could not always find a suitable area for broadcasting. The *Voice of Fighting Zion*'s only dependable thing was its frequency, which was always the same. Listeners just had to leave their radios tuned until they heard the *Irgun* whistle. And sometimes the broadcasts stopped in mid-word as the driver hit the switch and moved the truck. Sometimes, the station came back on; sometimes it could not.

Jack found a job working in a lawyer's office preparing briefs in English. He worked under the supervision of a law clerk who was reading law at the Hebrew University. On the next registration day, Jack signed up. Naomi said she would wait because of a "conflict" she could not describe even to Jack.

In August, UNSCOP released its report, backing a partition

of Palestine. The British took the passengers of *Exodus 1947* back
to Germany. When the three floating prisons entered the mouth
of the Elbe River, the *Exodus* passengers saw billboards on both
shores attacking the British. At a Hamburg dockside, the captives
battled against British soldiers in a desperate, clawing, biting, kick-
ing, and screaming savagery meant to show the world, Ernest Bevin,
and the soldiers with whom they struggled their dread of being
returned to Germany, the land of death. In Palestine, *Etzel* prepared to strike.

Jack's cell was a propaganda unit. Shortly after Naomi's broadcast, its members were to drive through the streets of the city in a
jalopy. The girls prepared brush and leaflet, gave them to the boys
who dashed from the car and put up the notices. Sometimes, they
just stenciled the *Etzel* insignia on walls in black: a map of the
original Palestine mandate, including all of Trans-Jordan, an arm
holding a rifle superimposed over the map, and the words "Only
Thus." Above it would be any one of their slogans: "Jordan banks
are two; this is ours, the other, too." Or, "Whip us and be whipped;
hang us and be hanged."

On the day the *Exodus* passengers were staging their
foredoomed fight in Hamburg, the placards taunted the British
army:

> HAIL TO THE HEROES! GLORY TO THE
> CONQUERORS! **FOR SHAME!**
> Not content with keeping the Hebrew people from
> their historic homeland by the massed power of the Royal
> Navy, the once-proud and valiant Royal Air Force, the Royal
> Marines, the famous 6th Airbourne Division and nearly all
> the means and forces of modern technology; not content
> with armed attacks on the unarmed vessels which bring the
> remnant of our people home; not content with deporta-
> tions to Cyprus and exile of our fighting sons to concentra-
> tion camps in Eritrea and Kenya; not content with curfews,
> raids, searches, and the general disruption of our lives

YOU HAVE NOW SOUGHT TO ATTACK OUR DIGNITY

By carrying the passengers of Exodus 1947 back to the land of Hitler's terror, the land where six million of our people were destroyed while your soldiers, sailors, and fliers fought to destroy their destroyer; the land which sent out its air flotillas to wreak havoc on London and Coventry and which unleashed the heinous terror weapons—the buzz bombs and the V–2—on your cities; the land which may have killed YOUR fathers, maimed YOUR mothers, destroyed YOUR homes, and given YOU your proud battle scars

YOU HAVE SUNK TO A NEW LOW

We, the soldiers of the National Military Organisation in Palestine (*Irgun Zvai Leumi B'Eretz Yisrael*) make this vow to you for this cowardly and heinous thing which you have done:

WE SHALL CONTINUE OUR WAR AGAINST YOUR ILLEGAL OCCUPATION ARMY WITH RE-NEWED VIGOUR. WE SHALL PENETRATE YOUR DEFENCE ENCLOSURES AND SEEK YOU OUT. WE SHALL UNLEASH OUR FORCES AGAINST YOU SO THAT YOU WILL QUAKE IN TERROR AT THE MEREST SOUND AND WILL SLEEP THE SLEEP OF THE FRIGHTENED. YOU WILL HAVE NO PEACE.

We keep our word. We are capable of carrying it to you. We penetrated the fortress of Acre which had not been penetrated in all history, not even by Napoleon. We have whipped your soldiers when you whipped ours. We have hanged your soldiers when you hanged ours. We shall now ATTACK YOUR DIGNITY. Your defence enclosures will not protect you.

Headquarters
National Military Organisation in Palestine
Irgun Zvai Leumi B'Eretz Yisrael

* * *

On the night Jack's cell prepared to paste up this placard, a plane hired by the *Lechi*, the Fighters for the Freedom of Israel, took off from Orly Airport near Paris to bomb the houses of Parliament in London. Letter bombs were sent from post offices around the world to high British officials. Two sergeants of the 6th Airbourne Division were found tied up in the streets of Petah Tikva wearing only black lace panties and signs attached to their chests with medical adhesive tape. The signs said: "British dignity."

Jack got home at eleven. The lights were out, but, at first, he thought nothing of it. The door was ajar. He gently pushed it open and reached through it, feeling for the light switch. A hand covered his and snapped a handcuff on his wrist while a flashlight blinded him.

"Who are you?" a voice asked in English.

"Ya'akov Ben Horin."

"Are you the husband of *Irgun* Irma?"

"Never heard of her."

Pieces of radio equipment were lined up on the dresser. Naomi's toilet articles had been thrown on the bed. A tape recorder was on her stool.

The sergeant and his two men returned to the foyer and turned out the lights.

Addressing the others on the floor with him, Jack asked: "Who are you?"

"Quiet!" a soldier ordered, also in Hebrew.

A soldier shined a flashlight, shielding it with his hand. Jack looked up at him and asked: "What's all that junk on my wife's dresser?"

"Want to hear it?"

He played the light on the recorder and pushed a switch. A husky female voice came through the little speaker: "This is *The Voice of Fighting Zion*, broadcasting station of the *Irgun Zvai Leumi B'Eretz Yisrael*, the National Military Organization in Palestine. . . ."

"It's not Naomi," Jack said to himself, with relief.

"Hail to the heroes! Hail to the conquerors! For shame! Not content . . . "

"Turn that bloody bitch off!" the sergeant ordered.

Jack wondered where Naomi was. Was this one of the evenings she would come home late or not at all? That often happened. He hoped she would stay away, so she would not be arrested, too. He wanted to warn her off if she came home.

"OK," he said, this time in English, "so you have a tape recording of the terrorist broadcast. What the hell did you bring it here for?"

"Shut your face, stupid. We didn't bring it. It was here. It's your missus, ain't it?"

"Shut up, Barton. You, too, Ben Horin. Keep quiet."

They sat. They waited. Time dragged and Jack's wrists became raw and red from the manacles.

"All right, on your feet!" the sergeant ordered as the lights went on.

Jack looked at the dresser clock. It had stopped. The three on the floor had one handcuff opened so they could stand up.

They were led out of the building and put into a covered truck. Four paratroopers climbed in with them. Jack tried to figure out which way the truck was going, but couldn't tell because the back flaps were tied down. The echo from buildings decreased, so he figured they were leaving town, but he had no idea in which direction. Eventually, they all fell asleep.

A fusillade of shots woke him. The truck stopped.

"Of all the Limey trucks for our guys shoot up," Jack thought, "they sure picked the wrong one."

The soldiers jumped off and began to fire their Stens. The driver and the sergeant were firing a rifle and a Sten from the front of the vehicle.

"Who are you?" Jack asked his traveling companions.

"Jews."

"What's going on?"

"That was the *Etzel* transmitter in your house. It was raided."

Another man interrupted: "Hey, Ben Horin, you are not chained to us. Drop off. Run. They're busy."

Jack moved to the rear and peeked around the flap. They were stopped on a sharp curve. The road was edged by white stone markers on one side along a deep ravine. The guards had dropped behind the markers and were firing slowly, one shot at a time, up the hillside on the other side of the road. Jack realized they were trying to conserve ammunition.

The driver and the sergeant had crawled under the truck. Jack pulled his head in to tell the others. A grenade went off behind the truck. Fragments hit the canvas top, making a noise like hail on a tent. The men behind the truck increased their rate of fire at shadows on the hill. Volleys of automatic fire were aimed at their muzzle flashes from the hillside.

"They're after our guards," Jack yelled. "They're not shooting at the truck."

"Obviously, dope," one of the others yelled.

A burst of shots came from the front of the truck. Jack leaned around the edge. A figure ran down the hill in what Jack took to be foolhardy white robes. The rifle and the Sten under the truck fired at the zigzagging figure in white, who was taking cover behind rocks, dashing for another rock, and diving down again.

Suddenly, the truck began to roll backward. The wheels stopped against one of the men underneath and he screamed. Several grenades and more automatic fire drowned out his cry. The engine started and the truck sped forward. Now, the rear wheels passed over both men who had sought the protection of the truck. The truck stopped again. Four Arabs ran down the hill and took up positions near the truck, crouching. The decoy in white got up and hurled a final grenade toward the last position of the four paratroopers. Then there was silence.

Two of the Arabs began searching the bodies in the road. Another pair went down into the ravine to try to recover the guns of the dead paratroopers. One of the Arabs came to the back of the truck and gave Jack the key to the handcuffs that he had taken from the sergeant.

The four Arabs climbed into the truck. "*Yakh, habibi*, that was not so hard," one of them said, mostly in Hebrew. The engine started and the truck drove off while Jack and another former prisoner tied the flap from the inside.

The next day, *The Voice of Fighting Zion* came on the air with the following broadcast:

> This is *The Voice of Fighting Zion*, broadcasting station of *Irgun Zvai Leumi b'Eretz Yisrael*, the National Military Organization in Palestine.
>
> We are pleased to announce that we shall continue to broadcast in Hebrew and in English. Yesterday's attempt to put us out of operation has failed. The illegal occupation army can harass us; they cannot stop us. The right will win.
>
> In the past twenty-four hours, soldiers of the *Irgun Zvai Leumi* carried out the following missions against the invader:
>
> — In Tel Aviv, two sergeants of the 6th Airbourne Division, who had been fraternizing with Hebrew women, were stripped of their uniforms and dressed in the undergarments of their treasonable companions. The women, who are the first to suffer this punishment for giving comfort to the Nazo-British occupation army, were stripped and had their heads shaved. Jewish womanhood, cease your association with the enemy.
>
> — Between Sinjil and Sawwiyeh, a lorry carrying four soldiers of *Irgun Zvai Leumi* to Acre Prison was successfully attacked and captured with no losses to our soldiers and the loss of six British soldiers and their weapons. The former prisoners are safe and well. They are Commander Akiva Barzilai, Dov Hazaken, Re'uven Nardi, and Ya'akov Ben Horin.

Jack, Akiva, Dov, and Re'uven heard the broadcast in a mud

hut in an Arab village near Nazareth. All were amazed to hear their names on the air, something that had never been done before.

In historical times, Zippori had been the capital of Galilee and a proud center of Jewish learning. Now, it was called Saffuryah—an Arab hamlet with hostile inhabitants. A cloister, the only building without a mud roof, was run by Christian Arab nuns, and the fugitives were hiding in the hut of the nuns' gardener. The nuns were told to remain out of the garden as the mother superior led the four into their hiding place, clutching her crucifix in front of her face to keep away evil.

She had been told that the four were Arab fugitives who had escaped from Acre Prison during a Jewish terrorist attack and were heading north to join Fawzi el-Kaukji's Arab Liberation Army in Syria. Akiva had to do all the talking.

Shortly after the truck had passed Jenin, dressed in the Arab garb of the attacking party, they left the truck and headed for Saffuryah in a taxi. Surprisingly, the British had not yet set up roadblocks for the missing truck.

They spent two days in the hut, with Akiva keeping them from talking. Jack did not want to talk. He wondered about the radio equipment in his bedroom, he tried to analyze what Naomi's "conflict" could have been that kept her from enrolling in law school, and he had to subdue the fear that was gnawing at him.

At one point, while Akiva had gone to the outhouse, Jack leaned toward Dov and asked him how he was. "Scared," Dov answered. "Me, too," Jack replied.

After two days in the gardener's hut, they were picked up by another taxi and were taken to Mishmar Hayarden, a village in Galilee that was one of the few strongholds of *Irgun* sympathizers.

Akiva got very irritated. "This is too obvious," he said. "Commander Begin has gone crazy. First he tells the British our names; now he puts us in a village that has been raided hundreds of times."

The four men who had been hanged in Acre only a few weeks earlier had also been caught in Mishmar Hayarden.

For a week, the fugitives were hidden under the foundation of a building, lying flat on their backs the entire time. There were no toilet facilities. Their only sustenance was black bread and bottles of a sweet malt beer from the general store in Rosh Pina.

When they were finally let out to shower, Dov began to shave. Akiva stopped him: "Leave the beard; it looks fine on an Arab. Clean your clothes."

With their clothes still soaking wet, they were led through the fields of Mishmar Hayarden, waded across a short stretch of shallow water they realized was the River Jordan, and were picked up by yet another guide, who led them up steeply rising terrain with nothing growing on it until they hit a road. The guide, also dressed in Arab clothing, counted the kilometer markers along the road. When they got to Kilometer 7, they sat down and began to eat the dried figs they had been given.

A truck bearing Hebrew, Arabic, and Latin inscriptions that said "Me'ir Galili Transport, Rosh Pina" stopped near them, loaded full with case upon case of early grapefruit. The driver, an elderly man wearing a gray undershirt, got off and told them to unload the rearmost row of grapefruit crates to make room for them and to carry the fruit out of sight off the road. Weak as they were from spending a week on their backs and hampered by their flowing *gallabiyehs*, they struggled with the heavy grapefruit. Four hundred yards from the truck, they spilled the fruit on the ground, broke up the crates, and brought the wood back to the truck so that the pieces could not be identified. When they secured the load, they climbed on and were driven into Damascus.

In Syria's ancient capital, the driver took the grapefruit to a warehouse while the four fugitives waited on a street comer. All four squatted and spent an hour motionless on their haunches. Middle Eastern squat toilets accustom people to this position and Arabs often squat to relax. For Jack, squatting was painful. He soon lowered his buttocks to the ground and crossed his legs, Turkish style. The three others remained squatting—and silent.

The driver returned and handed Akiva a rolled-up newspaper, muttering "*Mazel tov*," good luck, as he shuffled off. Akiva remained motionless. Minutes later, he opened the newspaper. Without a word, he got up and began to lead them down the street. They maintained some distance behind him and followed, trying not to display any curiosity about this city.

Akiva approached a policeman, who made signs with his arms and let his hands fly in intricate patterns. Akiva nodded repeatedly. When he was done with the policeman, Akiva touched his hand to his forehead and his lips in an Arab "thank you."

They followed Akiva for about ten minutes until he stopped in front of a hotel. He signed for them to wait and went up an external stair to the second-floor lobby. When he emerged, he waved them in and led them up two more flights of stairs. In front of Akiva, a barefoot boy opened a door and grinned as they went in. It was a typical, cheap hotel room. It had one bed. Akiva gave the boy a dried fig.

Then he briefed them. They were not to talk, but to write out what they had to say to each other. "Nothing to write with," Re'uven said.

Akiva passed around the letter he had received in the rolled-up newspaper. After they had all read it, he burned it in the sink, and washed down the residue with water.

Someone knocked. Akiva tried to dispel the last of the smoke from the fire by waving his hands over the sink and signed to them to squat again. The barefoot boy came in with a *finjan* , a brass tea pot, and cups, a short pencil, and some stationery.

Jack was the last to read the letter because they regarded him as an outsider, not a member of their cell and, possibly, not even a member of *Etzel*, even though his name had been mentioned on the air.

> My dear friends,
> Go to the hotel shown to you by the driver. You will be sent important mail, vital to your continued success. As soon as this mail arrives, you must leave Damascus. All but Frumkin go to Paris. Frumkin should go home. His family awaits him. *Abi gezundt.*

"*Abi gezundt,*" which means, "Keep well," was *Etzel's* password.

Jack had to write out an explanation that he was Frumkin while wondering what "home" meant.

They slept in shifts and ate in the room, leaving it only to go to the squat toilet at the end of the hall. They washed in the sink. Re'uven tried to teach them how to play poker, but without anything to use as chips, that did not hold their interest. Dov invented a tournament of solitaire, as three watched while one played. On the third day, they had the boy bring them a backgammon board.

On Day Five, a registered letter arrived for Akiva. The return address on the envelope, sent "On His Majesty's Service," read: "Office of the High Commissioner, Government House, Jerusalem," the office of the highest British official in Palestine. Jack later learned that all the broadcasts of *The Voice of Fighting Zion* were mailed to *Etzel's* American supporters in similar envelopes. He never did learn how that trick was accomplished.

Akiva opened the envelope, cross-hatched with a blue cross to denote registry, and brought out four passports. The one he handed Jack was his blue United States passport, issued by the consulate in Venice, not the brown Palestinian one he received when he was discharged from Athlit. Inside Jack's passport was a chit: "Good luck, darling. Meeting you, Love, N."

Only now realizing that "home" meant Boston, he wondered what would happen next. How would Naomi get out of Jerusalem? How could he get to Boston from this stinking hole? But his faith in the impossible—from an Arab cloister's out-building and a letter from the British high commissioner convinced him that everything would work out. She would meet him, yes she would.

"What now?" Dov asked Akiva, breaking the silence.

"Go to Paris," Akiva said, passing around a letter of credit from World Tours, Ltd., and showing a small wad of assorted currencies and a letter of instructions.

Akiva read the letter aloud: "You will proceed to office of World

Tours. Frumkin is to go in first. He will receive further instructions at that office." The letter was not signed.

"But it's a British firm," Re'uven protested.

"We do what we're ordered to do. Would you prefer to stay in this hole?"

Akiva paid for the room as the Arab boy looked on, still smirking at these four who, he was sure, had had a five-day "*Nablussi*"—homosexual—orgy. Akiva handed him a fifty-piaster note and kissed him on both cheeks. The boy made the Arab "thank-you" sign with his hand.

They walked in their *gallabiyehs* and *keffiyehs*, smoking cigarettes Re'uven bought from a street vendor. It was their first smoke in two weeks.

Akiva led the way, again showing his familiarity with the city. Jack asked: "You know your way around this town. Is this your home?"

"*La*," Akiva answered in Arabic. "Home is in *Al-Kuds*, *Yerushalayim*, Jerusalem. This is merely the filth in which I was unlucky to be born. I left when I was eleven years old. I got a ride from that old man with the grapefruit truck. He smuggled me into our homeland. He, too, is a soldier of *Etzel*."

They turned a corner, and Akiva stopped. He pointed out the not very attractive World Tours office to Jack and slapped him on the buttocks, "Go, *habibi*."

A young woman in western dress greeted Jack in Arabic. He replied in English, showing her his passport. She took one look at the photo inside and then at Jack. She started laughing, closing her eyes in mirth.

In a fine accent that sounded British to Jack although she was a native of Calcutta, she said: "I say, that is frightfully funny: born in Germany, citizen of the United States, looking like an Arab street beggar in Damascus, and not a single visa anywhere in the passport!"

Jack stood in utter silence, feeling extremely uncomfortable.

"Where are the others?" she asked.

He pointed outside.

"Bring them in," she said.

After all were in the storefront office, she motioned to them to follow her into a back room. When they were inside, she left, leaving them with their fears, which Dov voiced: "I hope this is not a trap and she returns with the police."

"Fear not," Akiva muttered in Hebrew. "We will not be led into a trap."

Dov was not satisfied. "Perhaps the clerk who was supposed to see us is out and this one knows nothing, Akiva. . . ."

"Shut up!" Akiva snapped.

"I was just . . . " he stopped as the door opened.

The woman returned with a man, also in western garb. Jack jumped up instantly and threw his arms around the new arrival as though he were a long-lost brother, forgetting his own filthy state.

"Well, kick my fanny, John. Whatcha doing in Damascus? Good to see you. Gee, am I ever glad to see you."

Changing to Hebrew, Jack introduced John Aron to the others.

Aron was silent throughout Jack's outburst, but started to disentangle himself from Jack's bear hug, with something of a grimace. Also speaking Hebrew, he said: "All right, Comrades. You are going to be fine. You are luckier than the last group because you have passports. They are still hiding in Syria. You will go where you are needed. We shall not have time to find you new clothes, so you must travel as you are, I'm afraid. An Air France Dakota is leaving for France this afternoon. When you arrive in Paris, you are to report to the embassy of the Hebrew Committee of National Liberation at 18 Avenue de Messine. Tell them you were sent by World Tours in Damascus. Now, if you will let me have your passports, I shall arrange to have you enter Syria legally."

"How?" Akiva asked.

"Don't be silly," Aron answered. "With dollars you can even buy the use of a rubber stamp or two."

He picked up their passports and said: "Now be dears and take a taxi to the airport. Wait at the Air France sector of the terminal."

* * *

It was as simple as that. They had escaped the Palestine Police and the British army; had been sequestered by Arab nuns in Palestine, stayed at an *Etzel* village, impersonated Arabs in Damascus although only one of them could speak Arabic, and here they were riding a taxi in from Orly Airport. At the "embassy," they were received by Sam Gold, chairman of the Hebrew Committee, who had arranged to have the press there as they walked in. There were floodlights, flashbulbs, and newsreel cameras. They were ushered into a room, where more reporters were waiting for them.

Gold made a short statement in French, saying among other things that he was a colleague of Peter Bergson of the Hebrew Committee in Washington, and that the two of them were the voice of the nascent Hebrew nation while the British illegally occupied the Hebrew homeland. The four fugitives remained silent.

Gold pointed to Jack, and flashbulbs began to pop in his eyes as questions came from all directions in a welter of languages.

"How did you escape from the police?"

"How did you get out of the country?"

"How did you get to France?"

"Do you intend to return?"

Jack waved his hands for silence, then said in English: "I refuse to say anything except my name, rank, and serial number."

There was some laughter, but then Gold took over, freely answering questions that had been addressed to Jack.

The next morning, the story filled the front pages of the French press as wirephotos were sent to newspapers around the world. Their photographs appeared even in the papers that were delivered to Downing Street and the Colonial Office.

Jack saw the results in the Paris edition of the *New York Herald-Tribune* and was furious. He feared that all the publicity would endanger Naomi. He had decided that even if the broadcaster did not sound like Naomi, he was pretty sure she had something to do with *The Voice of Fighting Zion*.

When they were taken shopping by Gold's staff, they were recognized in the streets and a salesperson at Bon Marché even asked for their autographs. When they shed the Arab garb, they melted into the crowd and ceased being celebrities.

GENIA III

Natasha did as she was directed. She met with the ghost writer in Munich and, six months later, "excerpts" from her forthcoming book appeared in *Life*. The full *Life and Death in a Russian Slave Camp* appeared later and was a success, quickly translated into many of the languages of Europe.

As Natasha's ship arrived in Haifa, flying the British flag, she was greeted by most of the officials of the Jewish Agency, the British high commissioner, several foreign consuls, the mayor of Haifa, and Natasha's family. Her escape from Soviet and Nazi terrors and her exposé of life in the Gulag brought her accolades from all except those on the extreme left.

When Genia first saw the tattoo on her mother's forearm, she became hysterical. Soothed by Sabta, she still panicked at each sight of the numbers.

Natasha, for her part, found it difficult to accept this attractive young woman with long black hair as her daughter. When she spoke to Genia, she used the polite, formal form of address, not the intimate, family *tui*.

Moshe, just released from the Jewish Brigade, drove them to Golania in a car the kibbutz borrowed for the occasion. For a week, neither Natasha nor Genia were on the work roster. Miriam moved out to allow Natasha to share the room with Genia. They walked along the Sea of Galilee, visited the church at Capernaum, walked to the archeological site at Hatzor, and talked—endlessly. Finally, Genia asked the question foremost in her mind: "*Ima*, will you join Golania?"

"I cannot, Genia."

"No?"

"No. I am not made for this kind of life. I have a career that I must begin again. I did not study chemistry for so many years for nothing. There is a laboratory in Rehovot where I have been told I might find work. I would like that. I have not lived for myself for so long, Genia; I want to start life again. You do understand that, don't you?"

"But . . . "

"What, darling?"

"But I don't want you to leave Golania."

"You have grown up here. This has become your home. I have no ties to this place. You can understand that, can't you?"

"I suppose so."

"You don't really, do you?"

"I don't know."

* * *

A few weeks later, Natasha wrote that she had found a situation in Rehovot and that she was sure Genia would be proud of her for her contributions to the development of a phosphate fertilizer made entirely from domestic raw materials. Genia, in turn, accepted this and stopped feeling that she had to defend Natasha for turning her back on Golania.

When Natasha came on a visit, driving her own *taxi*, as *kibbutzniks* termed any private car, Genia was full of questions precipitated by Sabta's chance remark that she was unaware that Natasha had ever studied chemistry.

"When did you become a chemist, *Ima*?"

"I worked in a factory before the revolution, Genia. After the Bolsheviks came to power, I was sent to classes. Soon, I became the manager of the factory. That's how I met your father."

"How?"

"Maxim was commissar for light industry before he was made chairman of the Russian Federated Republic's council of ministers. My factory constantly increased its productivity and, even before the New Economic Plan, the commissariat became interested in our methods and techniques. Your father became my friend and, just before he was promoted, we were married."

"When did you stop working?"

"When you were born. I became very, very sick. I was sent to a sanitarium on the Black Sea and, according to the doctors, I was no longer fit to work. Those doctors should only have seen me in Magadan in Siberia and in Ravensbrück! They would have been surprised by how much work I could do—much sicker, starving, and weaker."

As always, Genia tried to direct her mother's conversation away from the years of persecution because she did not want to blurt out what she had come to believe—that because the Jews were unwilling to settle in Palestine, even in the early days of the British mandate when there were no restrictions on immigration, they suffered the punishment of a Europe under Hitler, complete with killing grounds, extermination camps, death marches, and tattoos. But she held it in, not wanting to release another torrent of those recollections from Natasha.

* * *

Genia had always been fascinated by modern history which, for her, began with the writings of early Zionist thinkers like Pinsker and Hess and included only that limited spectrum of history that affected the Jewish people. She had vague notions of Napoleon's Sanhedrin and of the migration of Jews to the United States after the revolutions of 1848. Earlier history was simply "ancient" to her, and this she hated.

Moshe, who really was a historian, became her victim once when she went into a tizzy about "ancient" history. She had just become a member of *Haganah* and was immediately started on a course in Jewish history. Genia cornered Moshe one day because he had been the one who set up the course. He was washing breakfast dishes in the kitchen when she went after him, sticking her finger out at him as she approached.

"I'm so glad you're working, Moshe," she said. "When you aren't working, you're always so busy I can't talk to you. I have a lot of questions to ask you."

"What's the trouble, Genushka?"

"Why don't you teach us to shoot instead of all that nonsense about Rabbi Akiva, Bar Kochba, and the Maccabees?"

"I see," Moshe said, taking off his rubber apron and walking into the dining hall. He extracted a cigarette from his shirt pocket and offered her one as they seated themselves on opposite sides of a table.

"Let me ask you some questions, Genia."

"All right."

"Do you know the Arabs in our neighboring village?"

"Yes."

"Do you know why they fight us?"

"They say we are on their land."

"Are we?"

"No. We bought it from them."

"And whom did they buy it from?"

"I don't know."

"Maybe it was our land before it was taken from us, little one. Maybe if we learn our history, we can understand why we are here in Golania and not in Zanzibar where some early Zionists also proposed we establish a Jewish state."

"I didn't know that!"

"Did you know that Hitter wanted us to have a Jewish state in Madagascar?"

"No."

"OK. Let me ask you this: Why do the Arabs next to us still want to fight us?"

"Because the Grand Mufti and Azzam Pasha tell them to hate us and fight us."

"Is that history?"

"Sure, but that is today. Bar Kochba is two thousand years ago. Who cares?"

"I see," he said, snuffing out his cigarette in the *kolbo.* "Abraham and Moses and King David and King Solomon have no significance. Hitler and Adolf Eichmann do. Is that right?"

"Sort of."

"Do you realize that it was because of Abraham and the others that we are Jews. Had it not been for them, we might be Arabs today."

"But we are not Mohammedans."

"We might have been. The Prophet Mohammed based much of what he taught on the teachings of Abraham and Moses. Have you ever been taught to hate Arabs in the *Haganah*?"

"Not yet."

"And you never will be."

She took a last puff on her cigarette and snuffed it out.

"You can now answer your own question, Genia. The *Haganah* is an army. An army needs to understand why it serves. *Haganah* teaches you that you serve because you love your land and your people. It teaches you the Bible, the valor of Jewish arms, the stories of our brave pioneers. That's why you go to Trumpeldor's tomb at Tel Hai. That's why you have been taken to the early settlements. That's why we teach you history."

"And when will you teach us to shoot?"

"Whom do you want to shoot?"

"No one, but why should I be in *Haganah* if I am not taught to shoot?"

"You will learn all too soon. Meanwhile, learn what we teach you! Now, I must go back to the dishes."

She left the dining hall and went to the cultural center, next to the secretariat. She borrowed Moshe's book on Jewish colonization. After she had read it, she picked out other books, devouring the histories.

One day she asked Moshe what she should read next.

"Can you read English, Genia?"

"A little. I just cannot speak it very well."

"If I lend you a dictionary, do you think you could read a book?"

"I can try."

"Good. I am going to our warehouse in Haifa after Shabbat. I'll bring you a good book from Steimatzky's book store."

"What?"

"The one your mother wrote!"

"But Moshe, that isn't history."

"What do you think it is, a novel?"

"I don't really know."

* * *

Natasha's book became well marked with marginal notes in Hebrew as Genia worked her way through it. When she reached the later chapters, the ones dealing with Natasha's "liberation" by the Wehrmacht from a work camp near Kharkov, Genia was gripped by a compulsion to finish reading it. She sat up an entire night in the library until she reached the last page. With dawn approaching, she ran to the room of the work coordinator and pounded on his door. Without waiting for an answer, she walked in.

"*Nu*, Genia?" Gershon asked sleepily from his side of the room.

"Go back to sleep, Gershon. I want to speak to Monya."

"So early in the morning?" Monya pleaded.

"I am making a puncture," she said, using kibbutz slang for not doing one's job. "Get someone else to work with my class until Sunday. I have to go to Rehovot."

"What's the rush?"

"I can't tell you; but it's important. Please, Monya, I have so many Sabbaths coming to me, that it won't hurt you."

"Everybody has Sabbaths coming to him. Look, go back to

bed. When Moshe goes to town on Sunday in the tender, he can take you."

"I don't want to go next week. I must go on the bus today."

"OK, OK. Ask Eliezer to give you some money."

Gershon sat up and added some advice: "If you can't get money from Eliezer, see Ruth."

Eliezer was the kibbutz treasurer. He was supposed to have money, but never did. Ruth was the new kindergarten teacher who had been hired after a big argument by some mothers. She was not a member of Golania, but had been trained for her work. In emergencies, as Gershon indicated, the members usually found that trying to borrow from Ruth was more likely to be successful than trying with Eliezer.

Genia headed directly for Ruth's room. Sabta was already up, working in her flower garden.

"Good morning, Sabta. My, don't you start the day early."

"Cooler. Aren't you going to work the wrong way?"

"I'm on *Shabbat*. I'm going to borrow money from Ruth."

"How much do you need?"

"For the bus—to Rehovot."

"You don't have to ask Ruth. I'll give it to you."

"Where could you get money, Sabta?"

"I always pick up my spending money, every month. And I saved it all. I have almost ten pounds. I have never needed my money except for that trip to Jerusalem to get your mother her certificate."

Genia next went to the dining hall to get early breakfast. Avner was working the first shift and he brought her the food.

"Hot cereal isn't ready yet," he said.

"That's all right, Avner."

"Where are you going?"

"To my mother."

"I'll pack you a lunch."

He went to the kitchen, sliced some bread, took a hard-cooked egg out of a fisherman's lunch basket, added some black olives and a kohlrabi and a cucumber, wrapped everything in a newspaper, and put it down beside his cousin. When she finished eating, he walked her to the settlement's gate to wait for the bus.

He said he would miss her. She asked why.

"I don't know. We've never been apart before."

* * *

The guard at the laboratories in Rehovot told her where to find her mother. Natasha was wearing a white laboratory coat and working with two men at a bench on which a centrifuge was whirling. After being introduced, Genia was shown what the centrifuge had separated.

"Is this your fertilizer, *Ima*?" she asked.

"No," one of the men explained. "This is what we hope to make the fertilizer from. It is a mixture of potash from the Dead Sea and phosphates from the Negev. It isn't very good yet and costs too much to make; but it's better than what we made two months ago, six months ago, or a year ago."

Some time passed while the contents of the test tubes were decanted into bottles, the bottles were labeled and stacked in a closet already full of hundreds of similar specimens. Genia could see from the dates that the experiments had preceded her mother's arrival in Palestine. One of her mother's colleagues explained that the work had been in progress more than six years.

"Just to make fertilizer?" Genia asked in disbelief

"Yes, just to make fertilizer."

"What's wrong with the fertilizer we use in Golania?"

"Nothing, but we have to buy it in a foreign country and it is expensive. We are attempting to make a fertilizer that is *totzeret haaretz*, a product of our own country."

"Is my mother helping?"

Natasha blushed, but answered the question herself. "Yes, I am helping."

* * *

When Natasha drove Genia to her house in her *taxi*, a small Ford roadster with a rumble seat, Genia asked whose house it was.

"It is my house, Genia."

"You mean you own it?"

"Yes."

"And this *taxi*, you own it, too?"

"Yes."

"And nobody else can drive it?"

"That's right."

"Can all chemists own houses and *taxis*, *Ima*?"

"I wish they could. I earned much money with my book. I am not paid much in the laboratory."

Natasha led her into the house, through a high wall surrounding the garden. The stucco house was painted light tan and one entered into a large living room from a terrace made of flat rocks. Genia looked around in amazement at the furniture, the rugs, the curtains, the lamps. She walked around and found the kitchen, with a refrigerator, an electric range, and an electric hot-water device.

Genia. had never imagined that her mother could be living so well. When a woman in a white uniform came down from upstairs and asked whether she should make supper, Genia could not contain her curiosity.

"*Ima*, is that what is called a servant?"

"Yes."

"And all this is yours?"

"Yes."

"Was it like this in Moscow?"

"Not nearly as nice," Natasha said, smiling proudly as Genia continued to exude astonishment. "Do you like it?"

"Oh yes. It is the most beautiful house I have ever seen. Moshe and Shula have a big room and your kitchen is larger than that. You must be very rich."

"No, Genia. I am not even slightly rich. But I am happy here. For an old woman it is wonderful to start life again after such suffering. Would you like to live here?"

"What could I do?"

"Genia, I could send you to America to attend a university. You could learn something useful and become somebody—not a simple peasant girl."

"You don't understand me, *Ima*, and I don't understand you."

"What do you mean?"

"I belong to Golania and Golania belongs to me. I am happy there. Someday we will also have nice houses and nice furniture, but that is not important. What matters is that we catch fish and produce food for our country and that we make a place for our children."

"Your children?"

"Yes, *Ima*. Gidon from my class is getting married. He will have children and we will have four generations. I like it in Golania, I like all our members. I like Moshe and Shula—and Avner, but he's my cousin. I like Sabta."

"But, Genia, you keep saying 'like'; you don't say 'love.' There is a difference."

"When my man comes into my life, I shall love, too."

"Do you 'like' me, too?"

"Yes."

"Let me show you where you will sleep tonight."

Genia was taken aback. It was a nursery, with a crib next to an adult-sized bed. "Are you expecting more children, *Ima*?"

"I hope so," Natasha said, but Genia's fingers started flying as she counted up the years. Why, her mother had to be older than fifty if she was working before the 1917 revolution. Even the Matriarch Sara was barren at that age, until God intervened! But Genia let it pass, asking instead: "Then you must be thinking of marrying again."

"When I find a man."

The cook called them to supper. Natasha led Genia to the

elaborately laid table and showed her which spoon to use for the grapefruit.

"*Ima*, do you have a boyfriend?"

"Yes, you met him in the laboratory—Dr. Kellerman."

"Will he marry you?"

"No. He is married."

"I see."

"Are you shocked?"

"No. You see, I read your book."

Natasha was flabbergasted, knowing that the Hebrew edition had not yet been published. "In English?"

"Yes," Genia said, smiling as the grapefruit bowl disappeared silently and was replaced by a mixed salad. "Even a peasant can know something!"

Natasha ignored the remark and concentrated on an imagined stain on her knife, wiping it with a napkin.

"*Ima*, what was he like?"

"He was the finest man I've ever met."

"And the child?"

"Beautiful. He had the face of an angel."

"You are lonely for them, aren't you?"

"Of course, to lose two husbands and two children . . . "

Genia kept her seat, but put down her fork. Looking straight at Natasha, she said: "I saw that in your book. That is why I came. Did you really lose me? Didn't you use the wrong word? When you wrote that book, you knew I was in Golania."

"No, Genia. You are dead to me. You are a rough and stupid peasant. My daughter was not. I have truly lost both my children."

"*Ima*, I am sorry for you. I do not understand you, but I am really sorry for you. You are making believe. This house, this servant, that nursery—they are not real. You are living in a make-believe world. You should come to Golania and live with us so that we can show you that your book is wrong, that you have a daughter who could love you if you would not shut her out of your life.

There are doctors who can help you, doctors for people who are sick from worry. Please! I am alive. Don't you understand? I am alive!"

Genia was crying. Natasha signaled to the cook not to bring more food, lit a cigarette, and walked out to the terrace. She began to hum a Russian nursery tune.

"Ima, I don't know what to say to you," Genia said sadly.

"Say nothing, you stupid thing," Natasha shouted. "What do you know of life? You keep saying you are alive. Bah! You are dead and haven't the sense to know it. You call me '*Ima*,' but I hardly know you. You wrote me that you did not want to keep the name of our family. When you changed your name, you lost your last tie to me. I am still a Koganov."

Genia had become angry. She was about to name the second man, a non-Jew and a German, but she checked herself and walked out into the garden. As she neared the gate, Natasha called out to her: "Where are you going?"

"Out of the cemetery," she called back.

* * *

In the street, Genia broke down and wept. She sat down on the running board of an old car parked at the cigarette vendor's kiosk and buried her face in her hands. The owner of the car, who had been drinking *gazoz*, soda pop, came over and tried to comfort her.

"*Adoni*," she said, "can you take me to Tel Aviv?"

"I don't have enough petrol."

"Are the buses still running?"

"No."

"Where can one sleep for the night?"

"You can come to my house, if you wish."

"Thank you."

He drove her to an orange grove south of Rehovot and turned off the road into a lane. As he approached the house, he honked his horn several times. The porch light went on and a woman in bloomer-shorts came out. Seeing Genia, she came over to the car and asked: "Who are you?"

"Genia HaCohen from Golania."

"Moshe HaCohen's daughter?" the man asked.

"Yes," she replied. "I am Moshe HaCohen's daughter."

She was shown to a room where the woman arranged some bedding on a couch. Looking around, Genia could see that the grove owner had been in Palestine a long time. There was a photo of him as a young man wearing the distinctive head-dress of Hashomer, the first Jewish self-defense organization, and a picture of a parade through the streets of London by Britain's Jewish Legion of the First World War. There was also a bookcase filled with volume after volume of Hebrew poetry. Genia picked out a volume of Bialik and took it to bed with her. She fell asleep with the light on.

In the middle of the night, someone shook her awake.

"Shh, we all know it," the woman said.

"Know what?" Genia asked.

"That you are alive. You were talking in your sleep."

"I'm sorry."

"That's all right. Go to sleep."

* * *

In the morning, the man served her breakfast: bread, tea, and vegetables. She did not touch a thing.

"Eat some tomatoes, Genia. They're good. They're our own."

"No thank you. I'm not hungry."

The woman came to the kitchen and asked her: "Would you like a fried egg?"

"No."

"Soured cream?"

"No."

The woman threw a glance at her husband and shrugged.

"I found her crying on the running board of my car," he explained.

"You told me last night."

"It could have been a man without honor," he added. "She would have gone with him, too."

"I wouldn't . . . " Genia began, but stopped when she realized that it was absurd and that the man was right.

"Do you want to take the bus to Tel Aviv?" he asked.

"Yes, but first I must find Dr. Kellerman."

"Who is he?" he asked.

"He works at the chemical laboratory. He's a chemist."

"OK. Come with me. I'm taking the wagon to town. I'll take you."

When the horse was at the gate to the laboratory, Genia approached the guard and asked for Kellerman.

"There is no Kellerman here," she was told.

"I'll know him when I see him," she said. "I'll wait here."

"Suit yourself."

The man who was in the laboratory with her mother and Kellerman arrived on a bicycle. She ran to him and asked after Kellerman,

"Him? You won't find him here. He's at the Technion in Haifa."

"But he was working with you yesterday," she insisted.

"He was just visiting. He is an old friend. Why do you need him?"

"It's about my mother."

"Yes?"

"She's in love with him."

"Nonsense!"

"What do you mean 'Nonsense'?"

"Precisely what I said. She met him yesterday."

"But he said he had been working on the experiment for six years."

"You misunderstood. The work has been in progress for six years. He has not worked on it at all. I have—with my associates."

"And my mother?"

"She asked me to tell you that she is my associate."

"Isn't she?"

"No."

"What was she doing in your laboratory, then?"

"She is my technician. She cleans the equipment and prepares the apparatus."

"That isn't true. My mother is a chemist."

"If you prefer. I have no idea why Natasha wants you to think she is a chemist, but she is as much a chemist as you are Chaim Weizmann."

"And she doesn't really love Dr. Kellerman?"

"I told you. Now look, young lady, I don't know what this is about, but I must begin work. If you will excuse me? *Shalom.*"

Genia stood at the guardhouse, stunned. The guard asked if something was the matter. Then she saw her mother's car approaching and she ran away, away from the institute. She ran all the way to the bus stop.

* * *

Seven hours later, she was marooned in Tiberias. A British policeman led her to the Anglican hospital so she could telephone Golania. An hour or so later, Shula and Moshe arrived on the Fordson tractor, pulling a trailer filled with loose hay and a bale for Genia to sit on. As soon as they were past the town line, Shula pulled up her skirt and untied the folded Sten gun that was fastened to her leg. Moshe came back and undid the bale and pulled out two rifles.

"Now I'm glad we taught you to shoot, Genia. If anything happens, give Shula the Sten and give me one of the rifles. OK?"

"OK," she said as she hid the weapons in the loose hay.

They arrived at Golania safely. The guards had to open the gate for them. Moshe took the tractor back as Shula led Genia to the dining hall.

"I'm sorry you had to come out, Shula. I've had a terrible time. I missed the bus."

"That's all right. It happens."

"Is Moshe annoyed with me?"

"Of course not."

"I'm so glad."

She ate some olives and black bread. Shula watched her. Moshe came in with the Sten over his arm. "I'll be right back," be said, "I'm just going to hide this in the *slick*."

When Moshe returned, he sat down next to Genia as she drank mint tea. Shula got up to get some for Moshe.

"It was bad, wasn't it, Genia?" he said.

"Oh, Moshe, why didn't you warn me?"

"Warn you? About what?"

"My mother is *meshuga*."

"Genia!" Shula exclaimed.

"I mean it. Listen, Moshe. She lives in a house all by herself. She has a servant. She has a *taxi* . . . "

"This does not make her crazy," Shula said, stroking Genia's hair.

"She has a room like our nursery, with a baby bed in it. She called it my room. And she's too old to have a baby."

"That still isn't crazy," Shula said reassuringly.

"And she said, over and over, that I am dead."

"Genia! Genia! You're imagining things," Moshe said. "You must remember that your mother went through terrible times. Now, tell me from the beginning."

They listened to Genia's story until Genia began to choke on her sobs. She sipped more mint tea and said: " . . . and when they asked me if I was Moshe HaCohen's daughter, I said yes."

Shula led Genia to her room and prepared her bed in the dark not to waken Miriam. Then she pulled her out on the verandah and said: "I am very happy that you do not wish to leave Golania and that you like us. We have always treated you and accepted you as our own daughter and as a member of the *meshek*. This is your home and we are your family. Try to forget what happened in Rehovot. I don't know if your mother is sick; but Moshe will get help for her. Don't you worry. Everything will be . . . "

Before she could finish, there was an explosion outside. Shula ran to the light switch and shut off the verandah light. The gong near the dining hall sounded the alarm. There were shots from the sea. The searchlight on the watchtower came on, but was immediately shot out. Genia rummaged under her bed and pulled out her first-aid kit. Then she ran to the watchtower, raised the trap door at its base, and entered the emergency hospital and shelter.

The generator stopped; she lit a kerosene lamp.

The attack came from the Arab village between Golania and Capernaum. Soon, firing began from the opposite direction, from the direction of Syria. The defenders of Golania raced from one edge of their defense enclosure to the other. Genia, alone in her aid station, wondered why Dina had not yet joined her. She climbed out of the bunker and found the nurse sprawled on the ground. Genia helped her into the dugout.

"What happened, Dina?"

"With Dodo in grove . . . infiltrated from the water . . . grenade . . . Dodo dead . . . one of them raped me . . . don't know how they got past mines on beach . . . "

"Tell me what to do, Dina."

"Put tourniquet on leg . . . then we dig out pieces."

They went to work. Genia wanted to give Dina a shot of morphine, but she refused, saying she wanted to dig out the grenade fragments herself.

A half hour later, the shooting stopped and the lights went back on. The British had arrived. Police spread throughout Golania, searching for guns. Following their mine detectors, the police tore up the settlement.

Moshe went to speak to the police inspector, a man he knew from his days in the Eighth Army in North Africa. As Moshe approached, the inspector said: "Now you've done it, HaCohen. Why did you stupid arses have to get caught red-handed with your weapons?"

"We were attacked, Andrews. We were defending ourselves."

"The Arabs say you sent a raiding party into their village."

"Nonsense. They attacked two of our people in the eucalyptus grove. They killed the boy, blew half the girl's leg off, raped her, and then started shooting at the rest of us. Then, another group came at us from the east. We never left Golania."

"Where's the dead boy?"

"We haven't found him yet. Would you help me look for him?"

The two, followed by several constables, went to the grove. There was no sign of Dodo's body.

"Why don't you search them?" Moshe asked. "You might find some weapons to confiscate there, as well."

"Sorry, old boy. I have no warrant to search there. You were caught in the act, so I don't need a warrant. I'll search their village in the morning, after I get a warrant."

"And after they've hidden all the evidence, eh?"

"You're getting terribly cynical, HaCohen."

"Surprised?"

"Not really. When my men complete their search, I'm sure *Haganah* will get more weapons to you. Be more careful not to have me find them next time, won't you?"

"You're a clever bastard, aren't you, Andrews? You know as well as I do that they'll start their attack again the moment you and your men are back in Tiberias. I suppose you'd like us to defend ourselves with slingshots."

"David did it. Bye-bye, we're taking three of your people on charges of weapons possession. Good luck!"

"You dirty bastard!" Moshe yelled at him as he drove off.

Moshe ran to Genia's bunker to inquire after Dina.

"She's unconscious, Moshe," Genia said. "I've treated her for shock."

"I'll send Ruth down to help you. We're in for more attacks. Stay down there."

He and a dozen others ran to the emergency slick built into the drainage pipes under the dairy barn. On top was a large pile of dung. They shoveled manure with all the strength they could muster. When they were down to the concrete floor, they used a hose to wash the floor, then opened the trap door that had been

concealed under the fetid dung. The *slick* had been put there because the drainage system foiled metal detectors.

Each rifle was wrapped in tar paper and heavily greased. There
were twelve ancient rifles in all.

"Shall we take all the rifles out, Moshe?"

"We better leave four to be safe," he said, then started explaining what was happening. "Our neighbors are celebrating UNO's
vote today to partition our country."

Avner came in from the secretariat where he had been man-
ning the radio: "The Arabs are attacking all over Upper Galilee.
The Syrians are firing down from the Golan Heights onto most of
the settlements in the far north, around Dan, Dafne, and Kfar
Szold. Menara is under attack from Lebanon."

The eight rifles were handed to defenders at each of the seven
defense points. Moshe took the last, checked its functioning, and
went back to the top of the watchtower, really a concrete enclosed area
on top of the concrete silo that could be reached either by an outside
steel ladder or, more uncomfortably, by climbing a ladder inside a
chute that was kept free of silage by a reinforced corrugated shield.

As expected, the attack did begin again, but it was curiously
lethargic. The defenders of Golania saved their ammunition. Just
before daybreak, artillery began to hit Golania. Moshe was able to
plot trajectories and concluded that all the firing was from the
Syrian side of the sea, possibly from within Palestine. The Syrian
fire was not accurate and at least one shell hit among Arabs trying
to infiltrate the Golania perimeter from the east.

At noon, the firing stopped. Golania rushed to hide the rifles,
leaving only three in use. Golania had been tricked. When the
Arabs stopped shooting, the defenders concluded that the Arabs
had again seen the English coming. But after ten minutes, the
Arabs resumed their attack, with fifty or sixty men crawling through
the barbed wire north of the settlement. Moshe started sniping
from the watchtower. When the attackers had got well into the
mine field with the wire holding them in as well as keeping them
out, Moshe waved his arm. The crank on a dynamite igniter was

turned and some of the preplaced charges went off, causing severe
casualties among the infiltrators.

When all of Golania's rifles were back in the battle, the Arabs
began a retreat, leaving their wounded behind. This time, the Jews
did not start hiding their weapons, fearing more trickery.

To the south, someone was raising and lowering the Italian
flag over the hospice at Capernaum. Moshe signaled for the weapons to be hidden, and threw his rifle onto the stretched tarpaulin
over the entrance to Genia's dugout.

When the British passed Capernaum, Moshe went down the
outside ladder on the silo and headed for the gate.

"Well, HaCohen, did you sustain more casualties?"

"None, no thanks to you, Andrews."

"We're moving some of our men back into the Tegart fortress
opposite Capernaum. The district commissioner wants to assure
the safety of the Christian hospice. I thought you'd want to know."

Tegart police fortresses, which commanded almost every important road junction in Palestine, are named for Sir Charles Tegart,
the English engineer who designed them and supervised construc-
tion during the 1937–39 Arab riots.

"I hope the Syrian howitzer sends in a long round or two to
upset your teacups, Andrews."

"What Syrian howitzer?"

"The one that was shooting at us all morning. Come up on
the silo, I'll plot it for you."

"If you would be so kind as to open this gate, old chap."

Moshe checked to make sure all the mines had been grounded.
The sapper signaled that everything was in order, and Moshe swung
the gate open. Andrews followed Moshe up the ladder. "Almost
like old times in the army, eh, HaCohen?"

"We're not on the same side this time, Andrews," Moshe said.

"Get off it. You know we're neutral."

"Did you get a warrant to search our cousins? Did you find
Dodo's body?"

"I do have a warrant and my men are searching for the body. If
there really is a field piece over there, we'll get rid of it."

"I'll have to see it to believe it."

"Where's the gun?"

"Use this sighting disk. Look at 1620 mils. It's just beyond that ridge over there and is probably a three-pounder."

"I can't see a thing."

"Obviously! But if one of your planes were to fly out of Rosh Pina, he'd see it. These fellows have not yet learned about camouflage."

"Are you certain it's there?"

"Look at Golania, Andrews. Small arms did not do this."

"Very well. I'll take care of it. Now let me give you some advice—and you can believe me. As long as we are in that Tegart fortress, I want no shooting, from either side. So, if you have some weapons cached, keep them there. I'll warn you of any change in plans."

Moshe thanked him and extended his hand. Andrews looked around before he would shake.

JACK AND NAOMI II

The *Etzel* broadcast was unusually long on the night of Jack's arrest. To reduce the ability of the British to triangulate on the signal as much as possible, there was a fifteen-minute interval between the Hebrew and the English transmissions.

Naomi did the Hebrew tape first. Later, when she finished recording in English, a courier took it to her apartment, removed the spent Hebrew tape, reset the equipment, and hurried away from the house with the Hebrew tape. Before he got to the end of the block, he saw an army van with a revolving directional antenna rounding the comer. He stayed behind to observe. Soon, a second van came from the opposite direction. Then the police came, followed by the army.

The courier threw his Hebrew tape into a rubbish bin and walked away slowly, heading back to Katamon to give the alarm.

He attributed the raid to the length of the transmission, but more that this had been at fault. Usually, *Etzel* used a transmitter mounted on a concealed rack in the back of a panel truck. That evening, because the truck would not start, it was forced to rely on stationary equipment, an extreme expedient that had to be approved by Menachem Begin, the commander in Tel Aviv.

The plan was for the transmitter to stay on only as long as it took to broadcast the Hebrew tape. A timer was supposed to shut everything down at sign-off. That failed; the transmitter stayed on the air and sent a carrier signal for an additional fifteen minutes, giving the British time to track it down.

Naomi and the others in the Katamon studio had ample warning of danger when the English broadcast suddenly stopped; then, without skipping a syllable, it began again.

"Someone has stopped the tape!" Baruch, the engineer, said.

They looked at each other with puzzlement, and quickly began to work out what they would need to do to save Naomi from imminent arrest. But Akiva and his party, who had been sent to recover the transmitter, had no warning and walked into an ambush.

Naomi called her neighbor across the landing and asked her to get Jack to the phone. The old lady went to Naomi's front door, saw that it was open, and walked into the apartment, where a policeman told her to mind her own business. Returning to her telephone, she told Naomi that the police were in her home and that she did not know if Jack was there.

"Call the boss," Baruch told Naomi.

So, for the second time that evening, a trunk call was made from Katamon to the secret hiding place in Tel Aviv where Menachem Begin directed the operations of the *Irgun*. It was a major breach of safety procedures, one of many they made that night.

Begin listened quietly to Baruch's report. But he already knew. He also heard the interruption of the broadcast and had decided on the *Etzel* tactics to limit the damage.

"Send the speaker to the CID," Begin ordered. *"Abi gezundt."* He hung up.

Naomi sat there stunned when Baruch repeated Begin's orders to her. Looking very pale, she took the pistol out of her purse and gave it to Baruch, then left for the Criminal Investigation Division at Police Headquarters. As she walked past English barbed-wire strong points, the word "shitless" kept recurring to her. She wanted to tell Jack she was scared shitless, an emotion she remembered only from the bridge of *Innocent Voyager* as they waited for the Royal Marines to come aboard.

"The police are in my home," she told the English desk sergeant in Hebrew at Police Headquarters.

"And what might you be called?" he replied, also in Hebrew.

"Naomi Ben Horin," she answered, "Number 15 Alfassi Street."

"Ben Horin, you say?" he said, then, with his voice suddenly rising, "You are right! We are in your flat. You'd best speak to the inspector."

An ordinary policeman was summoned to lead the way, and announced her in English to the inspector, who almost choked on his cigar in surprise. He did not rise from his seat as she entered but waved her into a chair at the side of his desk.

"Mrs. Ben Horin, what brings you here?" he asked in English.

"I'm here to complain that your men are in my flat."

"How would you know that?"

"My neighbor told me on the phone."

"Did your neighbor also tell you that the terrorists were using your flat as a wireless station?"

"How could they?" Naomi sputtered, feigning total surprise. "That is impossible."

"We would also like to know how they could, Mrs. Ben Horin. But we do suspect that it is your voice that they were sending out. We now have the original tape of their English-language broadcast, the one they were transmitting. We would like to compare your voice to the one on the tape. Would you be willing to let me record you, Mrs. Ben Horin?"

"As you wish, Inspector," Naomi said, confident that Baruch's techniques for changing her voice would make any such comparison useless. The inspector pressed a button, and a constable entered.

"Would you please bring in the recording dolly?"

Soon, a tea wagon with a suitcase-sized reel-to-reel recorder was wheeled in by a technician, who ran it at the inspector's orders.

Naomi was asked to read a story from *The People*. As she began to read, he moved her hand, which held the microphone, back and forth in front of her mouth.

Naomi did not attempt in any way to alter the way she spoke because she was certain she would not be able to maintain any change. She read clearly in her normal voice.

"That will be enough of that trash, thank you, Mrs. Ben Horin. Now, I wonder if you would be kind enough to read some Hebrew for me. I have some poems of Bialik, a terrorist wall placard, a copy of *Davar*, and a Hebrew Bible. Which would you like?"

"The terrorist placard," she said without hesitation.

"Really?" the inspector replied. "If I were suspected of being a terrorist, I should have chosen to read *Davar*. Isn't that so?"

"Very well, Inspector. I shall read from *Davar* if you wish, only I've read it today and I have not read the terrorist thing. It's really quite the same to me." Naomi noticed that she was using Briticisms, not the Americanisms she had picked up from Jack.

He handed her the leaflet with that night's broadcast.

"Hail to the heroes, glory to the conquerors, for shame . . . "

Naomi read with the stylized eloquence of a Habima actress, a manner she had never used in her broadcasts but one that she was confident she could maintain for hours, if necessary. She manipulated her voice in the best Stanislavsky manner, even trying a slow staccato where it seemed appropriate.

"Thank you, Mrs. Ben Horin. That will do."

"What about the police in my flat? Will you see to it that my home is vacated as soon as possible? I wish to go to my bed without several of your people under it."

"We shall take care that you have a good night's sleep, Madam. I shall place you in protective custody and secure a room for you at the King David. Is that fair enough?"

"I prefer my own lodgings, Inspector."

She asked herself what had happened to "shitless." So far, she surprised herself at how well she had been able to carry it off.

" . . . out of the question," he was saying as she turned off her inner conversation. "We must watch your flat to make certain no other terrorists enter. Of course, if you don't feel safe in the King David, I should be pleased to keep you in one of our ladies' cells."

"I should be pleased to accept your invitation to the King David, Inspector."

"It has been blown up once, you know."

"I am quite aware of that, Inspector. I should have to be blind not to have noticed."

"Might I suggest, Mrs. Ben Horin, that you invite one of my men to watch your door from the outside to assure your absolute safety."

"You would do it whether I invited him or not."

"Quite!"

The two tapes were compared during the night. A military prosecutor had joined the CID people and a Royal Signals officer. They decided that they would be unable to persuade a judge that the voices were the same.

When Naomi was taken back to the inspector's office in the morning, she was told by a civilian whom she had not met before that she was free to go.

Now she followed routine *Etzel* procedure for anyone released from custody. She made no attempt to reach or signal anyone or to do her usual *Etzel* work. Under the special orders given to her, she began procedures to leave the country. The American consulate-general asked for a police good conduct before granting her a visa, and the inspector appeared pleased to provide it.

"I daresay, Mrs. Ben Horin, that I owe you an apology. I have heard two recent terrorist broadcasts and Irgun Irma's voice has not changed. So she and you cannot be one, can you?"

Naomi breathed hard. Although she had recorded several time-less broadcasts to be transmitted in just such an eventuality, the broadcast of the previous evening—in which Jack had even been named—was obviously read by someone else, whose voice Baruch had made to sound as much like Naomi's when it came out of the radio. But Naomi noticed that the substitute speaker's English occasionally showed a Midlands dialect, which should have tipped off the CID that it was a new speaker.

The inspector handed her the good conduct while continuing his apology: "I gather from last night's terrorist broadcast that your husband—who, as you probably know, was named by Irgun Irma—was the culprit behind having the wireless in your flat. You must accept my apologies for suspecting you, but a policeman can never be certain, you know. Why do you need this good conduct?"

"I am going to America, Inspector. Since my husband is in trouble with the police, I feel I should be with his family until this is settled."

"You know, I really admire these people. Your husband has disappeared. Six of our men are dead. We took every precaution, and still . . . "

"I must disagree, Inspector. I have no admiration for those terrorists. They have brought nothing but grief to this country. I am ashamed that my husband was among them."

This, too, was standard procedure. She had been warned: Never let a policeman get you to lower your guard by flattery or admiration.

"Which relatives of your husband are you going to see, Madam?" he asked innocently.

"If you expect me to say 'his parents,' Inspector, you will be disappointed. He has only some aunts and uncles."

He wished her a pleasant voyage and threw in one last gratuitous insult: "If your husband can stay out of jail for a year or so, you may find him still alive when we leave Palestine . . . "

She did not reply.

* * *

She had been instructed to make contact with the Hebrew Committee of National Liberation, the officially sanctioned *Irgun* leadership cell in America under the direction of Hillel Kook, who was known in the United States as Peter Bergson. At LaGuardia Airport, she was met by Shlomo Gabirol, an aide to Kook. Gabirol started giving her orders as soon as they were alone in a taxi to Manhattan. She took an instant dislike to him, not only because he was fat with greased-down hair, but also because he wore a double-breasted blue suit with an *Etzel* pin on the lapel. She was certain he had never been in *Etzel*.

"Please remember, Naomi, that you are still under discipline and that your orders will come through Peter Bergson. Your first task will be to meet the press later today. You will sit behind a sheet with the light behind you so that the press will see you only in silhouette. The name you are to use from now on is the one the British gave you, 'Irgun Irma.' If you should speak to an audience, you will be masked."

Naomi's anger grew as she listened to these instructions, but she waited him out. Then she exploded, screeching at him in Hebrew salted with the most vile Arab obscenities.

"*Een Allah book*, Gabirol. You don't deserve an answer, but I'll give you one: *Kuss emak!* I am not going to have any part in your plan. First, the British are convinced that I am not the broadcaster. Second, they know I am in America. Third, I have no wish to reveal myself merely so that your organization can gain more publicity and make more money. Fourth, and perhaps this should have been first, I do not want to endanger my husband, whom the British know to be a member of *Etzel*. If you wish me to speak against the British—as Naomi Ben Horin—I shall be glad to do it. Mind you, I must continue to play at being the person the British questioned, and I am wholeheartedly against terrorism. I absolutely will not be 'Irgun Irma,' nor reveal myself as a member of *Etzel*."

Gabirol ignored the Arabic insults. "And if you are ordered by the High Command?"

"I should have to assure myself of any order's authenticity. For all I know, Gabirol, you may be a British agent."

The cab took them to the Hotel McAlpin. In the lobby, Naomi told him, "I need to go to the loo. Please leave word with the concierge where I am supposed to go—under my own name, Naomi Ben Horin."

She found a ladies' room out of sight of Gabirol and ran to a pay phone. She had to read the instructions on how to use it, then, because she had no American money, had to go look for a house phone and had to plow through the five New York phone books to find the number she wanted.

"Please let me speak to Joe Kaplan," she said when the Betar office answered. When he answered, she said: "*Tel Hai*, Joe. This is Naomi Ben Horin from Jerusalem. Yes? . . . You did? . . . We must have left the airport just before your people came. I'm at the Hotel McAlpin now and they want me to work for them, but I refuse. . . . No, of course, not. Gabirol claims he is under discipline and his instructions are from the high command. I cannot conceive that I would be ordered to reveal myself to the British just to bring in a few more dollars for these people. Could you have some of your people pick me up and find me a place to sleep? . . . "

When she hung up, she smiled triumphantly. She went to the registration desk and asked for her baggage to be transferred to Betar headquarters on Second Avenue, then went out the revolving doors to await her deliverance. She waited about fifteen minutes for her ride, a car filled with exuberant young people in the emblazoned uniform shirts of Betar. She got in and they drove off.

* * *

She was put up with a Betaria in Long Island City and went to the Betar office daily in search of news of Jack. There had been not one word since he and Akiva's cell had appeared at the "embassy" in Paris. Ten days after Naomi arrived in New York, Joe Kaplan asked her to accompany him to the offices of the American League for a Free Palestine.

"Do I have to go, Joe?"

"No, but they say they have news of your husband."

"I suppose they'll keep him in Paris until I come to work for them."

"I doubt it. Eli, our *Irgun* liaison, has given Gabirol orders to cut the horse shit."

"Is Eli senior to Gabirol?"

"Haven't you heard of him? He was Begin's second-in-command until he was sent off to Gilgil."

"He escaped from Kenya?"

"Yes, with Meridor and Gidon."

"Oh-ho, I think Gabirol is going to do some explaining."

* * *

Eli, a freckled, red-faced man, sat in an easy chair at the side of the office. Next to him was Peter Bergson. Gabirol was at his desk as Naomi and Joe entered. They rose and waited for Naomi to sit down.

Gabirol began deferentially: "Please excuse me for asking you to put your husband in danger."

Naomi was not pleased: "You did not have to bring us across town to tell me this. You could have said that on the phone."

"Eli wanted me to apologize to you in person," he said. "He also wants me to give you this."

He got up, walked to Naomi's chair, and handed her a check for a thousand dollars. "This should pay your expenses while you await your husband. Anything you don't need, we would like back."

Naomi tore the check in two. "I will not accept this, Mr. Gabirol. You have not collected this money to feed me. If you cannot use this money to buy weapons for our people, please be honest enough to give it back to your contributors."

Eli broke into a wide grin. Bergson shifted his weight around and looked uncomfortable. Gabirol retreated to his desk.

"Look, Mr. Gabirol," Naomi said. "Let's get to the point. What news do you have of my husband?"

"Did I forget to tell you? He's arriving tomorrow on the *Queen Mary*."

"You ass hole," she shouted. "That's a British ship!"

"Oh yes," he replied, "but on this voyage she went from Southampton to Le Havre to New York. Your husband boarded in France and was quite safe—and comfortable at our expense."

* * *

When immigration and customs people came aboard at the Narrows, Jack was asked to go to the purser's office and wait there. He sat and wondered what was coming. As soon as the vessel was moored, a United States marshal and a State Department security officer came in. Both carefully examined his passport.

"Mr. Frumkin," the State Department official asked, "have you ever been known by any other name?"

"Sure. I'm called Jack."

"Any other names, such as Ben Horin, for example?"

Jack explained: "My wife is a deserter from the British army. When we entered Palestine illegally, we used that name."

"Why didn't you say that right away?"

"I didn't think it mattered here in the States."

"Are you the Jacob Ben Horin who escaped from British police custody during an ambush near Jerusalem in August?"

"With slight modifications, yes. It was the army; not the police."

"Why the hell did you sail on a British ship? Wasn't that kind of stupid?" the marshal asked.

"Somebody is very free with your life, Mr. Frumkin," the State Department official observed. "If you had not had all that publicity in Paris, neither we nor the British would have known that you were Ben Horin. They have requested your extradition."

"Come again?" Jack asked, startled.

"Under the extradition treaty between the United Kingdom and the United States," the marshal said, "I hereby serve you with this warrant issued by the United States Commissioner for the Southern District of New York. I am sorry to do this, but I have to place you in custody. Please hold out both wrists."

Jack did, and the marshal snapped handcuffs on him.

"May I ask some questions?" Jack asked, turning to the State Department representative.

"Shoot."

"Is your department serious about extraditing me?"

"I don't know. The department will have to review our treaty obligations. In any event, it is standard procedure for the Justice Department to oppose any attempts to extradite a citizen of the United States. The United States attorney's office here in New York will do that for you."

"Wait! Does the United States have an extradition treaty with Palestine or with the League of Nations?"

"I don't know. We made a quick check this morning, and it seems to us that the treaty with the United Kingdom covers that; but you're over my head."

"One more question: May I see my wife?"

"Is she on the pier?"

"I don't know. She may still be in Jerusalem. But she sent me a note saying she was meeting me."

"I'll go and find out, Frank," the security officer said.

"Do you have a lawyer in New York, Mr. Frumkin?" the marshal asked. "If you don't, you better get one."

"If you can bring some books to me in the pokey, I'll handle my own case. You already said the U.S. attorney will oppose extradition on my behalf."

"Hey, this isn't some misdemeanor, mister. They've got you up for murder. You better play it smart and hire a mouthpiece."

"Thanks for the tip."

Through the portholes, they heard the Cunard Line loudspeaker: "Will the friends and relatives of Mr. Jacob Frumkin please report to the second-class purser's office on C-deck. Thank you."

A few minutes later, Naomi and Eli came in, with Naomi running toward him and embracing him, then holding him off to look him over, handcuffs and all. "You have lost five kilos," she said.

"Maybe ten," he said. "I have not been eating regularly or well."

She introduced him to Eli, who shook hands, muttering: "*Abi gezundt.*"

"Mrs. Frumkin," the marshal said, pointing his cigar at a chair, "Won't you sit down? I have some bad news for you."

"Who are you?" she asked bluntly.

"I'm Frank Lawson, United States marshal. I have just taken your husband into custody on the basis of a request for extradition from the United Kingdom."

"Oh my God!" Naomi stammered.

"Darling," Jack said, speaking to her, but looking into Eli's eyes, "can you get me a lawyer?"

The security officer returned and suggested to Lawson that the couple be left alone for a minute.

"OK," said the marshal. "No funny business, Frumkin."

Eli went out with them, and the Ben Horins raced each other to tell what happened since Jack's arrest. It was the first time Jack heard that Naomi was *The Voice of Fighting Zion*. He was amazed, and puzzled.

"It didn't sound like you."

"It wasn't supposed to."

Then Jack asked who Eli was.

"A big time operator pronto," she said, using the GI slang she had picked up in Italy.

"Real big?"

"Very real big."

"Good. Will he get me a lawyer?"

"Ten if necessary."

Jack grabbed Naomi and ran his hands through her hair. They kissed. Then Lawson knocked on the door.

Lawson took Jack to Foley Square. He was fingerprinted, photographed, searched, and locked up. A few hours later, he was taken out of his cell to be brought before the commissioner.

A balding man in a pin-striped, double-breasted suit came forward asking: "Mr. Frumkin?"

"Yes."

"I'm Jonathan Waters. I've been retained to represent you."

"Pleased to meet you. What's up before the commissioner?"

"Motion for bail—requested by me."

"Where will I get the money?"

"Don't worry. It's all arranged."

* * *

The commissioner denied bail. Waters said he would try to have a judge overrule the commissioner and, if that did not work, he would seek a writ of habeas corpus. At three that afternoon, Jack emerged from the courthouse under $50,000 bond ordered by a judge. Waters explained to Jack that the money would be forfeited if Jack did not appear when ordered.

"What are my chances, Mr. Waters?"

"I don't know. I've been too busy getting you out. I haven't started researching your case yet."

"You cannot base your case on precedent," Jack said, self-assured because he had worked on two briefs in Jerusalem that dealt with the citizenship of Palestinian Jews. "You will have to attack Britain's right to extradite me under its treaty with the United States. I'll tell you where to look . . . "

"Whoa, young fellow. I'm the lawyer in the case. Let me worry about all that."

"I was in my second year of law school when I was arrested, and I've been clerking for a firm in Jerusalem," Jack said. "I think you need to examine the status of Britain as to its role in ruling Palestine. In 1939, the League of Nations attacked the fact that England was governing the mandated territory through the Colonial Office instead of through the Foreign Office. The league did not feel that its mandate made Palestine a British colony. That document would establish Palestine's separate treaty-making power, which, of course, was never allowed to be exercised. Then, there was the Order-in-Council of 1922, the so-called 'constitution' for Britain's Palestine mandate. There is a section in it on citizenship. Even though I did it by fraud, I am a citizen of Palestine, not of bloody Britain."

"How would you like to work on your own case?"

"Nothing would make me happier."

Waters handed Jack his card and told him to come to his office. As Waters walked off to the subway, Eli, who had been standing in the courthouse lobby behind a *Wall Street Journal,* came over, saying: "I see you've found a job."

"Uhuh."

"Happy?"

"Sort of," Jack said, "You know, I feel like a foreigner here in the States. I can't explain it, but it isn't my country any more."

"Was it ever? You were from Germany, weren't you?"

"Yes, but even though I belonged to Betar and believed in *aliyah,* I felt totally at home in this country. Now, I can't wait to get home—to Jerusalem."

They took the IRT to Astor Place. The Betar office was a few blocks away, next to an abandoned Yiddish theater. Eli took him into a small room, filled with mimeographed leaflets, a duplicator, and thousands of gummed labels reading "Boycott Bloody Britain."

Naomi was waiting for them. They both started asking questions about what happened on his way to New York, especially his experiences in Paris with Sam Gold.

Eli took it all in, saying nothing to indicate what he thought. Finally, he asked: "Did everything go well while Akiva was in charge?"

"It went like clockwork until Paris."

"Even in Damascus?"

"Yes."

"They did that part, you know," Eli said.

"They?" Jack asked.

"Sam Gold's people."

"I didn't know that. Hey, Naomi, I almost forgot: John Aron was in Damascus working for World Tours. He got us out of there and sent you his love."

Eli put down his notebook, and held up a hand. "This is not

the first time that the Hebrew Committee's need for publicity—
as they did in Paris and wanted to do here—clashed with *Etzel*
security needs. I hate Gold and his friends. We were being held in
Asmara in Eritrea, and before Asmara was secure, three of us escaped. We were quickly recaptured and they transferred us to Gilgil
in Kenya, from which we escaped within a week. Before we could
get out of Kenya, those idiots announced our escape to the world.
Meridor was almost killed. Gidon was recaptured. It turned out
that they were so proud of our escape that they released the news
to the *London Jewish Chronicle*."

"How did you get out of Kenya?" Naomi asked.

"There is a big Betar in South Africa. They sent people to
Kenya to find us and get us out. There's really nothing we can do
about this publicity business. They are very effective in raising
money and spreading our message. In the eyes of the Diaspora,
Ben Hecht, Sam Gold and Peter Bergson are the *Irgun*. We cannot
disown them. Meanwhile, we are all stuck here until statehood.
According to UNO's partition plan."

He pronounced it "You know."

"What UNO partition plan?" Jack asked.

"Two days ago," Naomi explained, "UNO voted to set up two
states in Palestine on fifteenth May next year. The British will
terminate the mandate that day."

"So it will be seven long, useless months here," Jack said.

"Let's hope they don't get you to England before then," Eli
said.

* * *

They moved into a furnished apartment in Washington Heights
and Jack kept busy at the United Nations library, searching for
League of Nations material. But it wasn't needed.

When Jack's extradition hearing took place, Jonathan Waters
sat by and watched as the United States attorney handled the case
for him. The State Department had prepared a brief that closely

matched the one Jack had written for Waters. Neither brief had
been able to corroborate the claim, made by the counselor for the
British Embassy, that mandated territories were covered under the
American extradition treaty with the United Kingdom. The judge
would not even allow the brief to be read in court; instead he
asked the United States attorney to summarize it, then asked the
British to comment. When the gavel came down, extradition had
been denied.

Time dragged. Jack and Naomi tried to keep abreast of devel-
opments in Palestine and found the news disquieting: stories of
Arab invasion; the blockade of Jerusalem; the Arab seizure of the
four settlements in the Etzion block; Jewish attacks against Haifa
and Jaffa and *Haganah* 's fight against *Etzel* in Jaffa, but, more
than anything else, the doom constantly being prophesied for the
Jews by American "experts."

One day in April, Naomi was browsing in a bookstore in midtown Manhattan. Across the table she spotted the lapel insignia of
Haganah, an olive branch entwined around a short sword. In Hebrew, she asked the wearer, a man with curly black hair who had
the erect bearing of a trained athlete, where he was from.

"Rosh Pina," he said. "My name is Yokhanan Galili."

"Ah," she said, "I have heard of you. I am Naomi Ben Horin.
I'm from Jerusalem."

"I can return the compliment. I've heard of you, as well."

"Really? Are you sure it was not my husband you heard about?"

They passed small talk until he asked when she was going
home.

"We are awaiting orders," she said.

"I got mine today," he said, handing her the letter he had
received from Land and Labor for sailing on *Marine Carp*.

"Are they calling everyone?" she asked.

"That is my impression. Why don't you check?"

"I shall. Meanwhile, if you are not busy tonight, would you
care to have supper with us?"

"I'd be delighted"

"Eli Even-Zahav will be there, too."

"Who?"

"He used to be Eli Goldstein. You know, the second-in-command of *Etzel*."

"The 'Iron Man' who escaped from Kenya?"

"Exactly."

"I knew him when we attended Hebrew University together. I'd love to see him again. I hope he will not feel otherwise."

"Why should he?"

"In addition to being the most notorious atheist in Tel Aviv, I am also on David Shaltiel's *Haganah* staff in Jerusalem."

She paused a moment. "Perhaps we can forget our differences thousands of miles from home and enjoy a *Shabbat* dinner, eh, Yokhanan?"

"I shall do my best."

After giving him instructions about getting to their apartment, Naomi went to the Jewish Agency, where pandemonium reigned.

"I am from Jerusalem. Are you calling us home?" she asked someone.

"Yes," she was told. "See Amos—third room on right."

She was told that notices had been mailed and was asked if she and Jack could be at the Jewish Agency first thing Sunday morning for processing.

"Amos, as they say in English, we shall be there with bells on."

Supper that night commemorated the end of their exile. Eli raised a sacramental *kiddush* cup: "Let us drink to the future. Let us drink to victory. Let us drink to a third Jewish state. Let us drink to the brotherhood of all our people as we join the common battle."

"An excellent toast, Eli," Yokhanan said. "May I add to it?"

"Certainly!"

"Let us drink to freedom."

Over coffee, Yokhanan began to question Jack intensely about how he got to Syria.

"We were led. First we went to an Arab village near Nazareth;

then to Mishmar Hayarden. From there, we crossed the Jordan and were driven to Damascus on a grapefruit truck."

"That's the part I want to know about. Tell me about the grapefruit truck and its driver."

Jack described the *Etzel* man in the gray undershirt and noted that he had a "speech impediment. He made all his 'p's into 'f's just like an Arab. He called Rosh Pina 'Rosh Fina.' It was sort of strange."

"And the truck," Yokhanan said, "belonged to Me'ir Galili, correct?"

"Yes.

"That was my father. That 'speech impediment' was a long-forgotten Zionist dream."

"I beg your pardon?" Naomi said, a surprised look and a huge smile on her face.

Yokhanan explained: "In the early days, someone got the idea that if Jews were a nation like all other nations, they should have dialects, like the English and the French. So they made one up. My father was never altogether consistent in the way he applied the 'Galilean' dialect. It is supposed to be much like that of the Arabs. The Egyptian hard 'gh' is supposed to be the Lebanese 'j' and there is no 'v' at all. It either becomes a 'b' as in 'Tel Abib,' or it becomes a 'w' as in '*halawah*.' The dialect idea never caught on, and my father only did the 'p.' But I am very happy, Ya'akov, to learn that my father knew anything other than becoming rich. You have ennobled his memory. I am proud that he worked with *Etzel*, for it is the only contributions he ever made to his people."

"But you make him sound as if he is dead," Eli said.

"Yes, my parents were killed in an ambush in Bab-el-Wad in a food convoy to Jerusalem, but it was for business, not for mercy."

Yokhanan did not hear the expressions of sympathy: "I have at last found a reason to be proud of my father."

"Hey, Yokhanan," Jack said, "he did not just work with *Etzel*, he was one of us. He smuggled Akiva Barzilai into Palestine when Akiva was only eleven years old. From what I gathered later, your father raised Akiva in Rosh Pina while you were in school in Tel Aviv. Surely, you two knew each other."

"Yes, we were brought up together. But I did not know he was in *Etzel*, either."

Yokhanan sailed on *Marine Carp* a few days later, but Eli and the Ben Horins were advised to wait until it was certain that the British were out of Haifa.

GENIA IV

Except for traffic escorted in and out of Golania by Andrews' men, Golania was cut off on its land side. Going by boat seemed an alternative, but when they tried it, Syrian snipers shot at the boats.

They were, however, spared further artillery attack. The RAF attacked and silenced the gun.

Fawzi el-Kaukji's irregulars, joined by local Arabs, were masters of Upper Galilee. Most of the Jewish settlements were surrounded, their people forced inside their defensible areas. Ein Gev was under siege. Degania stopped a tank well inside its outer defense line. But Golania was safe as long as the British were in the Capernaum police fortress, one of many scattered around Palestine by the British.

Toward mid-May, as the British mandate was coming to an end, regular Arab armies poured into Upper Galilee from Syria, Iraq, and Lebanon. Again, Golania was spared, but this time it was because Andrews had allowed Moshe and his men to take over the Tegart fortress on the day the Palestine Police moved out. Raising the Jewish flag atop the fortress cost Haganah one thousand Bank of England notes.

The younger members of Golania reported for infantry training at Rosh Pina. Genia and her companions were put in charge of the defense of Golania when they came back from their training, thus freeing the more experienced Haganah veterans to join fighting elsewhere.

At the end of the first UNO cease-fire, Moshe—who had emerged as the senior *Haganah* commander in Upper Galilee—was planning the unsuccessful attack on Syrian-held Mishmar

Hayarden. One day, Genia found him in his room, sitting at his little writing table with a map unrolled in front of him.

"Moshe, when you are free, can you visit my mother in Rehovot? I know it's a terrible thing to say, but I don't want to see her again. Yitzhak says . . . "

"Who is Yitzhak, little one?"

"Don't you know?"

"No. Should I?"

"But you are brigade commander, aren't you?"

"That doesn't make me omniscient."

"Didn't you appoint our instructors at Rosh Pina?"

"No. Come on, Genushka, who is this boy?"

"He was our instructor in Rosh Pina. Oh, Moshe, he's wonderful. He is a member of Ulpanim. He is—oh, you know!"

Moshe smiled and patted her rear in a mock spanking as he put his arms around her. "Genia, Genia, soon we will lose you to Ulpanim."

"Oh no! Soon we will have a new member from Ulpanim."

"Are you marrying?"

"It's all prepared. We will marry after the fighting ends and he will join our *meshek*."

"Where is he now?"

"He went to Tel Aviv to form our brigade, the Seventh *Haganah* Brigade. We assemble tomorrow." Genia did not see it, but the smile on Moshe's face disappeared and he tensed. He had heard of the levy for the central front and had figured out for himself that the attack was going to be aimed at Latrun, which was defended by a Tegart fortress much like the one in Capernaum. Quickly hiding his fears, he said: "Well, I'm glad you like him."

"Love him, Moshe," she corrected.

"So! Our little Genia loves at last. Have you told Avner and Shula?"

"Shula has given me her blessing. Avner does not like Yitzhak. He says Yitzhak will spend too much time in *Haganah* and not enough in the fishing boats. Avner says we should have no officers in the *meshek*—except you."

"Well," Moshe said with a laugh, "here we have a new army and the men already hate their officers. It's always that way. We're all going to have to spend more time away from work. A country must be defended. Israel cannot afford a big army, so all of us will have to take turns at it. When your Yitzhak takes his turn every year or whatever the interval is going to be, Avner will have to be there, too."

"What about me?"

"You will be there, too, as will all of us."

"Good, I couldn't stand having Yitzhak go without me after we marry."

At dawn the next day, the last day of the first UNO truce, young people from all over the country headed for Tel Aviv in small, innocent-looking groups. Genia and Avner, in their normal, everyday, khaki clothing and sandals, went by bus to fool the United Nations truce inspectors. They had their *Haganah* insignia in their pockets.

By nightfall, the new brigade was formed, partly armed, and on its way to Latrun on Tel Aviv city buses.

Latrun was the only major battle the Israelis lost during the war of independence. True, they had not been able to keep their foothold in the Old City of Jerusalem and had failed to recapture Mishmar Hayarden; but compared to Latrun these were minor skirmishes. The slaughter at Latrun was dreadful. Wave after wave of untested assault troops, of which Genia's brigade was the first, were mowed down from the tower of the Tegart police fortress onto which the Arab Legion had hoisted a small field piece. The Trans-Jordanian gunners from Glubb Pasha's Arab Legion ranked in bravery with the defenders of Bataan and Stalingrad. As one was hit, others rushed to take his place.

The determined stand by this, the most effective Arab fighting force, inflicted casualties upon hundreds of Israelis. Almost all the defenders of the fortress were wounded at Latrun.

Genia was wounded while she was dressing a casualty in a shell hole. The aidman who carried her back to the dressing station was startled by her moans: "I'm alive; I'm alive; I'm alive . . . "

After surgery at the military hospital in Sarafand, her first question as she came out of anesthesia was: "Am I alive?"

Several days later, in a sanitarium in Naharia, Yitzhak visited her on crutches. "How's your leg?" he asked,

"Mending, and yours?"

"Just broken. It's nothing. They tell me that when you were wounded you were crying, 'I'm alive.' "

"Was I? That's the second time I've been told that I was saying that when I did not know it."

"I wonder what I said while I was delirious."

"Delirious with only a broken leg?"

"I was hit in the back, too; probably by one of our own soldiers. We had an American adviser to our brigade, a West Point colonel named Mickey Marcus. He was killed when he was asked for the password. He did not understand Hebrew. So they shot him, also in the back. They were bringing them to Latrun straight from the dock in Haifa and they did not know a word of Hebrew. It was awful!"

When they were both released from the sanitarium, they tried to gold-brick. First, they went to Ulpanim without telling a soul in Golania. The housing committee gave them a room and they spent a week together as Yitzhak's mustering-out holiday. After that week, they tried the same thing at Golania, but Moshe was wise to them and, on the fourth day of their idleness, he sat with them at breakfast and began talking about Golania's labor shortage. That day, Yitzhak and Genia went to see Monya about work. Genia was sent back to her children, but Yitzhak was told to go to the carpentry shop.

"What's with you, Monya?" Yitzhak sneered. "I'm a fisherman, not a carpenter."

"If you can fish without boats or nets, Yitzhak, we would all like to watch you do this miracle. It would be the first miracle on the Sea of Galilee in two thousand years. All our boats have been shot up and all our nets are lost or damaged."

* * *

When Moshe returned from the capture of Eilat, they started preparations for Genia's wedding. Yitzhak's father, a Tel Aviv doctor, put
notices in all the papers. The Histadrut daily, *Davar*, published an
editorial on the marriage of Maxim Koganov's daughter to a
kibbutznik. It could not conceal its pride among all the platitudes
and clichés.

The fanfare brought Natasha, an uninvited guest, to Golania.
Her car had been commandeered by the army, so she arrived by
taxi. Sabta led her to the festive gathering in the dining hall, but
Natasha became hysterical: "How dare they marry my baby off?
She's only a baby. They're taking her from me."

Sabta left Natasha near the gate and scurried to Moshe and
Shula, who were setting the tables, arranged in a horseshoe, for the
wedding feast. Everybody knew this would be the first real meat
since independence, lamb bought from Arabs in Tiberias. Moshe
ran out of the dining hall and found his sister-in-law making a
speech to a few astounded members on the lawn.

"Do you know who this bride is? She is the daughter of one of
the greatest men of our century, Maxim Koganov, one of the plan-
ners of the Great October Revolution. Do you know who this
groom is? A fisherman, a peasant! My daughter could have married Stalin's son. She could have married any man she wanted in
the entire Soviet Union. And here you are—in your ill-fitting rags,
in your abject poverty—trying to take my baby form me. I will
not allow it. This ceremony must not take place."

Moshe put his arm around her and gently led her to his room.
She continued to rave, sometimes in Russian, then in German,
then in a torrent of words Moshe could not follow. When she
started to run out of steam, Moshe sat her on Shula's bed and went
out to get her a drink of water from the cool box on the verandah.
When he handed her the tumbler, she threw it against the wall,
covering Moshe's bed with broken glass.

He slapped her hard on the cheek and spoke sternly in Russian: "Natasha, go back to your *dacha* and forget Genia. You have said for too long that she is dead. As far as you are concerned, she is dead. Go home."

"Oh, you beast. You have kidnapped my baby."

"Come, Natasha, you are leaving Golania."

"No!"

Shula had come in and Moshe made a gesture of shooting a needle into his arm. Shula went out and got Yitzhak's father, who jabbed Natasha's arm with a hypodermic needle. Soon, Natasha was asleep. Yitzhak's elder brother carried her back to the taxi and rode back with her to Rehovot. It was the last time Natasha was seen by her family. A few weeks later, the Weizmann Institute had her committed to a mental hospital after she had gone berserk at work.

The wedding was clouded by the secret that everyone kept from the bride and groom. Yitzhak noticed the absence of his brother and guessed that something was up, but he said nothing to Genia.

On their honeymoon, they spent a week in the Dolphin House, the expensive resort hotel north of Haifa. Then they returned to work.

SCRAPBOOK II

THE VOICE OF FIGHTING ZION

The United Nations has decided to carve up our Homeland.

The Arab State set up by our British enslaver east of the Jordan, is now to be supplemented by a second Arab State west of the Jordan. In Eretz Yisrael there are to be two Arab States while the Jewish State is to be given no more than fourteen percent of the Home Territory—most of it a desert waste. Jerusalem, the eternal capital of David, is handed over to alien rule.

(Broadcast, 30 November 1947)

We are for offensive operations.

(Broadcast, 7 January 1948)

We, the soldiers of Israel, pay our respects to the memory of Mahatma Gandhi. The great son of India was not a friend of the Hebrew freedom movement. . . . Honor to Gandhi, the great fighter for freedom. Honor to Gandhi, the man of personal sacrifice. Honor to Gandhi, the educator of the masses to a proud stand and the desire for freedom.

(Broadcast, 1 February, 1948)

The youth who until recently was in charge of the Haganah unit in the Old City of Jerusalem, Yokhanan Galili, is a courageous youth and a good fighter. He fulfilled his duty faithfully. He stood guard devotedly. He also knew how to maintain decent relations with fighters not of the *Haganah*, with the soldiers of *Irgun Zvai Leumi*, who guard our Jerusalem. The youth is a good Hebrew youth. But what was it that old cynic Shaw said: 'One should not try to be too good.' And our young man wanted to be better than necessary. He appeared at a press conference in America and told of the heroic defense of the Old City. But when asked whether the "dissidents" also participated in that defense, he answered in the negative. A strange answer, which, as polite people say, does not correspond to the facts. There are others who have a different name for that answer, Yokhanan.

(Broadcast, 8 February 1948)

COMMUNIQUÉ

Combat units of *Irgun Zvai Leumi* executed the following attacks on the Arab bands and their points of concentration.

On Friday, 13 February 1948: Arab snipers' nests on the Tel-Aviv Jaffa border were destroyed with mortar fire. Among other objectives, the Jaffa railroad station was bombarded. On the Ramle-Jaffa road, close to Yazur, two Arab vehicles were attacked. Several rioters were killed or wounded. On the Ramle-Jaffa road, near Yehudiyeh, two more Arab vehicles were attacked. Several rioters were killed or wounded.

On Saturday, 14 February, 1948: A combat unit penetrated deep into Ramle. The road blocks were stormed and liquidated. The main concentration of the rioting bands were attacked and destroyed by machine-gun fire and heavy bombs. There ensued a prolonged battle with bands which tried to block the withdrawal of our soldiers. Tens of rioters were killed and wounded. Our soldiers forced a way out for themselves under heavy fire.

(Broadcast, 19 February 1948)

ANNOUNCEMENT

A group of *Irgun* fighters broke into a British military camp in Hedera and seized forty tons of war materiél—arms and ammunition, food supplies and uniforms. Our men disarmed the guard, which consisted of one officer and eight soldiers, and proceeded to load the war materiél on eight big trucks. In the meantime, a group of British soldiers in two cars appeared at the entrance. Our soldiers permitted them to enter, and then seized their arms. The two cars were used to carry part of the war matériel.

Later, three military policemen on bicycles arrived at the camp, obviously for the purpose of finding out what had happened there as they had been unable to contact the camp. They, too, were permitted to enter, after which they were disarmed and their bicycles seized.

Our group returned in full order to their base.

(Broadcast, 15 February 1948)

A large gathering of people last Thursday night in Tel Aviv witnessed a fearful spectacle unprecedented in our country. A young upstart, who had never tasted battle with the enemy, dared to order the throwing of grenades in a crowd of thousands who had come to listen to the words of *Irgun Zvai Leumi*.

(Broadcast, 29 February 1948)

The military court of the occupation army in Jerusalem! Who does not know this Nazo-British nest of war criminals? Our soldiers delivered a frontal attack on this warren of British criminals. They overwhelmed the guards, they penetrated the fortified building and began to carry out their plan-for which the mass of the people has long waited. And the plan would have been carried out to the end, as is usual with our plans, at once calculated and daring. of course, it provided for the safety of the nuns living in the area. The blow was aimed at the heart of the British régime of subjugation and would have inflicted heavy damage.

But the plan did not succeed. Why? Because our soldiers re-treated? Because the enemy was too strong for us? Nothing of the sort! Something else happened. Our soldiers were, in fact, attacked from the rear, but not by enemy forces. They were attacked by Jewish forces, the willing slaves who, even after untold British treach-ery, are prepared to kill (us) and be killed (in fighting against brother Jews) to defend the enslavers of our country and the de-stroyers of their people.

(Broadcast, 29 February 1948)

Citizens of the Hebrew Homeland!

This is the first time, in all our years of struggle, that we call on you, on every one of you, to contribute to a financial campaign to the Iron Fund of *Irgun Zvai Leumi*.

The name of the people's campaign gives its full meaning and goal: To give Iron—to give weapons to the vanguard of the fight-ing nation, to the soldiers of *Irgun Zvai Leumi*.

(Broadcast, 1 March 1948)

We thank the many thousands of citizens in towns and vil-lages for their response to the appeal for contributions to the Iron Fund of *Irgun Zvai Leumi*. The response was widespread, cordial and inspiring. People of all classes and views contributed. It is significant that rank-and-file members of Hashomer Hatzair, a party whose leaders and press incessantly vilify us, contributed to the Iron Fund.

(Broadcast, 3 March 1948)

Moshe HaCohen, the area commander of Haganah in the east-ern Galilee, has refused to extend any assistance to Mishmar Hayarden when it came under Syrian attack (despite the "no re-treat from any Jewish settlement policy" proclaimed by Haganah).

As a result, a fully armed Irgun unit was dispatched to Mishmar Hayarden with the following results:

When our soldiers reached Tiberias, they were met by Haganah men who rule the highways of the Galilee, and were informed that they, our men, could not continue on their way in an ordinary automobile. "We shall put a special armored car at your disposal," said the Haganah men, and our soldiers, in their innocence, believed that the Haganah men were willing to help them reach a besieged Hebrew settlement. Little did they dream that behind this generosity and graciousness there lurked a base craftiness.

After our unit had covered part of the way accompanied by the Haganah men, the automobile was stopped and they were ordered out. They were immediately set upon by nearly two-hundred men armed with Stens and Brens. Without words, the Haganah men began beating our soldiers up until they bled. . . . And, when they had finished their "job," they left our men on the roadside and departed. The arms and ammunition intended to defend Mishmar Hayarden they stole. After many hardships and with the aid of a local farmer, our men finally succeeded in reaching Affula and thence back to their base, their arms shattered, their bodies bleeding and their faces not to be recognized.

(Broadcast, 22 April 1948)

DAVE III

A clutch of officials scurried up *Marine Carp*'s gangplank, led by a Lebanese army major. Loudspeakers ordered all passengers to the purser's office with their passports. None of the Jews reported. When the order was repeated, a few went. The loudspeakers became more insistent. Soon, as the list of missing passengers got shorter, the loudspeakers hailed them by name.

Dave and Amiram went last. The purser took their passports and checked their names off the manifest. He handed the passports to the Lebanese major.

"Mr. Gordon," the Lebanese said in English, "are you Jewish?"

"Yes."

"Mr. Ben Cohen, with that name I assume you are, too."

"Yes, but it does not happen to be any of your business how I pray," Amiram said. "We are not landing in Beirut. We are passengers in transit."

The major ignored him. "Thank you, gentlemen; that is all."

Nothing else happened during the morning. The major and some of his staff left *Carp* and the crew unloaded the freight bound for Beirut. In the afternoon, after the hatches had been sealed and *Carp* was making ready to sail, two six-by-six trucks, once property of the U.S. army, pulled up alongside and fifty or so soldiers took up positions on the ship's stairways and along the companionways.

Passengers were instructed to go to their bunks and to prepare their luggage for inspection. Amiram and Dave, believing that all arms had been turned in, nodded their approval to questioning glances. A pistol was found under one youngster's pillow. He said it was not his, but the Lebanese asked him to come ashore. For good measure, the boy in the bunk above was also instructed to leave *Carp*.

"Nobody leaves the ship," Amiram said, "until the American consul is here and advises us. This ship belongs to the government of the United States and is under the protection of the U.S. flag."

The first mate, who was accompanying the major, said: "The consul has been aboard since this morning. He knows about this."

"Then we demand to see him."

The mate sent a seaman to get the consul, who appeared in a seersucker suit.

The consul greeted Amiram with: "Don't start an argument with me, Jewboy."

Amiram's hands formed into fists, the knuckles white. "I know y'all are in violation of the United States Neutrality Act, and I'm not going to get into a pissing match with these people over a bunch of Jews."

Those gathered around Amiram let out shouts and hisses. The boy under whose pillow the pistol had been found said: "It wasn't my pistol. I haven't got a pistol. I ain't going with these guys. I'm afraid of them."

"Tough titty," said the consul, the Honorable Jefferson Davis Binkle of Spartanburg, South Carolina, who owed his appointment to his townsman, Secretary of State James F. Byrnes.

"I demand," Dave began, "to see . . . "

"You don't demand nothing, mister," Binkle said. "You do what you're told."

Dave turned to the mate. "Can you get the U.S. ambassador? There's no sense talking to this Ku Klux Klansman."

Binkle overheard and started shouting, but the passengers outshouted him, chanting, "We want the ambassador!"

"There is no ambassador," the mate said. "We have a minister in Damascus, and he is on his way here at the captain's request."

"None of our people are going ashore until the minister arrives," Dave said, speaking to the mate. "This pistol was probably planted by the men who did the searching. We protest against this search and the very presence of these soldiers on this ship."

Amiram motioned to Dave to follow him, saying, "Let's go see the captain."

"Yeah," Dave said, "but something tells me that this neutrality game is not working. The American consul is pro-Arab. How about that Luger, did any of your people own a *parabellum*?"

"No. How about yours?"

"Yossi had one, but I turned it in."

Binkle followed them up to the bridge and pre-empted their protest. "Y'all got no right to be traveling in this here area in the first place. So skip the formalities and let's drop the hypocrisy. I cannot protect you individually because you are violating the Neutrality Act. My duty is to protect United States property, this ship, its crew, and those American citizens who can show a valid reason to be here."

The captain, an old-line New Englander, lowered his eyes as Binkle spoke. At one point, he gave Amiram and Dave a sorrowful glance, indicating his disapproval of the consul.

"Now you listen to me," Amiram said, livid with anger. "I do not care what your personal point of view is. I do not even care if your father was a pirate. But you cannot—as the United States consul—stand by during an act of piracy. I insist that you intercede to keep our shipmates aboard and that you protest the seizure of our radios and the two cases of Kotex which the Arabs call 'military bandages.' We are innocent passengers on an American ship and demand protection from the government of the United States."

"Y'all got girls in your army," Binkle said. "I'd call that reason enough to make Kotex a legitimate booty of war. As to those shipmates: Are they American?"

"One is Mexican, the other is Palestinian."

"No skin off my ass, then."

"Oh yes it is," Dave interjected. "We are passengers aboard an American ship. We made a contract with the line, which is under the jurisdiction of the U.S. Maritime Commission, and our contract is for transportation to the destination shown on our tickets. No foreign troops have the right to come aboard this ship and capriciously remove any passengers or their belongings."

"I'd call that piracy, too," the captain said.

"They got no business here, Captain," Binkle said. "They got no business to be toting guns and to be lugging military radios. They took a chance and they lost. Ain't nothing I can do about it. If you feel like these scum, save it for the minister when he gets here. Meantime, I'll tell the major those men ain't getting off until the minister gets here."

"Before you go, Mr. Binkle," Dave said, "let me express my utter disgust with you. I am a decorated veteran of the United States Army Air Forces and I thought consular representatives are supposed to be diplomats who represent the interests of their nationals, not of the country in which they are posted. I see I was mistaken. I find rattlesnakes more diplomatic than you, Sir. They only bite, they do not spit venom."

When Amiram and Dave returned below decks, they found all the passengers herded into the lounge. They waited until late in the afternoon, the monotony relieved only when the stewards came around and served sandwiches and coffee. Eventually the captain entered with a tall, gaunt man who was introduced as Lowell C. Johnson, the American minister to Syria and Lebanon, who was based in Damascus.

Binkle stood by, cleaning his fingernails as Johnson spoke: "Ladies and gentlemen, the Government of the Republic of the Great Lebanon has asked me to convey to you its request that you disembark from this vessel, remaining in the Lebanon until passage can be arranged to return you to the United States. I ask you to honor this request without recourse to violence or resistance. The Government of the Republic of the Great Lebanon has assured me that your stay here will be considered protective custody and that you will be permitted to leave. My staff is conveying to the Department of State the urgency of providing you with transport to the United States. The Lebanon insists that you cannot remain aboard *Marine Carp* because its next stop is the new State of Israel, which President Truman recognized earlier today."

That brought a cheer, immediately drowned out by thunderous protests against Johnson's proposal.

A woman jumped up, "Can't women expect the United States to protect them?"

Binkle left the lounge after a few words from Johnson. When he returned, he said the Lebanese were willing to allow the women to continue to Haifa. But he was unwilling to give any satisfaction to the Jews, so he added: "I guess they figure that your soldier girls can't do them much harm; it might even make the Lebanese army more willing to take prisoners."

A roar of disapproval broke out. Johnson quickly restored order and whispered to Binkle, causing the consul to turn crimson.

"Mr. Johnson," Dave said, "if you and Mr. Binkle will withdraw to allow us to discuss your extraordinary proposal, we'll try to agree on our next step. Should you not bring Mr. Binkle back in with you when you return, you may be spared an embarrassing outburst."

A loud cheer greeted Dave's comment.

As soon as the American officials left the lounge, commotion erupted. The *Irgun* people called for armed resistance. They were hissed down. Amiram climbed on the poker table and hushed them. "We will go. Be prepared to leave the ship when you see me leave."

Just before three o'clock, Amiram led the men off the ship. Of the ninety-two Jews bound for military service in Israel, sixty-one left *Marine Carp*. As they went down the gangplank, the women broke out the flag they had sewn and began to sing the "Song of the Warsaw Ghetto Fighters":

Never say: This is the last road for you.
Leaden skies are masking days of blue.
The hour we yearn for is now drawing near,

One step will beat the signal: We are here!
This song was penned in blood and steel,
Not warbled by a bird in heaven's ceil.
Out from the shambles of a fallen wall,
A folk cried out, to break the thrall!

They sang without harassment until they began the march of the *Palmach*, which the Arabs apparently recognized from hearing it over *Kol Yisrael, Haganah's* illegal radio. They were quickly dispersed from the rail overlooking the loading of the trucks.

But Dave could not resist the chance to needle Amiram a bit over the words of the *Palmach* hymn. "Hey, Amiram. *Palmachniks* sing of an area from Metullah to the Negev and from the sea to the desert. Since you guys believe that the partition of 1922 that took away Trans-Jordan was legal, tell me what that 'from the sea to the desert' refers to."

Amiram, smiled, but did not answer.

After a three-hour ride into the Lebanese mountains, they drove into a large compound that had once been French army barracks. Above them, on a hilltop, stood the ruins of the Temple of Venus.

One at a time, they were searched and led through a barbed-wire maze to a staircase leading to the second floor of a building. A balcony ran along its entire length and several priests were walking up and down, prayer books and rosary beads in their hands. Several Greek Orthodox clerics, wearing stovepipe hats, and a sizable number of well-dressed ordinary people could be seen at the right end of the balcony.

At the top of the stairs, Dave was greeted by a man in a Swiss skiing sweater, who said he was a violinist in the Beirut symphony and was among the hostages taken from the Jewish and Christian communities.

Eventually, the *Marine Carp* hostages were directed into rooms, each with about thirty mismatched cots, straw mattresses, and moth-eaten, olive drab U.S. army blankets. *Pita*, sweetened tea, and a stew made from lentils and lamb were served to each detainee. The Orthodox refused to eat the stew. The bread was soft because it was fresh, but later they were sometimes given bread that had dried out.

For breakfast the next day, they were again served tea and *pita*, but with a hard-cooked egg. The surplus American eggs had been dipped to seal their shells before they were given to Lebanon. If the dip had really sealed the shell, the eggs were edible; but if the dip had missed some part of the shell, the inside was a mass of stench and odor. Most of the eggs were good.

All but a handful of men immediately lay down to get the first night's sleep in two days, but Amiram, Dave, and several others— who had been chosen by the two leaders—met to form prison committees. A kitty was formed to collect cash, American cigarettes, and other exchangeable commodities. Not only was it Amiram's intent to control any bartering, so that not only the rich would be able to get whatever there was to be had, but he also wanted to prevent any contributions to Lebanon's war economy.

Toilet paper, which many of the internees had brought along, was also collected because the barracks' squat toilets provided none.

Doody Gordon, a former medical corpsman in the U.S. navy, and Yehoshua Ben Yeshayah, a barber, were named to a sanitation committee. An escape committee was established under Yokhanan Galili. Two Orthodox men were named to the ritual food committee, which quickly gathered up all supplies of canned kosher meat. Finally, a cultural committee was set up for teaching Hebrew and to help the men pass the time.

A bedraggled Arab boy, Muhamid, brought them their food, offered to buy anything the prisoners wanted, and learned to bring uncooked, raw foodstuffs for those who would only eat kosher food. He set an exchange rate of four Lebanese cigarettes for each American one; and Amiram immediately converted all remaining American cigarettes.

Muhamid was in and out of the area constantly. He offered picture postcards, shoe laces, French movie magazines, a French-language daily newspaper, candy, and a host of other wares that are normally sold on the sidewalks of the Middle East. With the *Carp* prisoners, however, he was out of luck; yet this did not mean they were denied the little luxuries Muhamid had to offer. The delicacies brought in by the families of the other hostages soon spread across the entire second floor, especially after the Jewish community of Beirut got word about the hostages of Baalbek.

The Christian leaders included three Maronite bishops and two Greek Orthodox priests. Leaders of the right-wing Christian youth movement, the Falange, were also held hostage as the Moslem minority in Lebanon tried to make sure that the Christian majority would make its proper contribution to the war.

The bishops quickly befriended Yokhanan, who had met one of them on one of his almost forgotten ski trips to Lebanon.

* * *

It was Yokhanan who started the first internal struggle among the Jewish hostages. On Friday afternoon, he approached the Canadian in charge of the kitty and asked for his cigarette ration. He was told it had been suspended for the Sabbath. Yokhanan argued, but was told to see Amiram or Dave. The kitty-keeper offered him a chocolate bar, instead. Yokhanan stormed off.

He found Dave in line for a haircut. "Dave," he bellowed along the length of the balcony, "you must call a meeting. The kitty has suspended cigarette rations."

"I know, Yokhanan. The committee voted on it."

"You have no right," Yokhanan fumed, "to dictate our religious practices or lack thereof. You are overstepping the authority we have vested in you."

"You better speak to Amiram," Dave said. "I won't call a meeting because I think most of the people would want to honor the Sabbath."

Dave, himself, heard an inner voice saying that he was being a hypocrite, because Dave did not observe religious rules and had always smoked on Saturdays. But he took his stand based only on his concept of the unity of the Jewish people, and in this Arab concentration camp that unity came above his religious beliefs or practices.

"Bah!" Yokhanan replied. "Only twelve eat kosher. The majority wants to smoke."

"This is not a matter to be decided by the majority, Yokhanan. You might go down to the other end and smoke there. I'm sure they'll lend you cigarettes until Sunday. But don't smoke them here."

Yokhanan stormed off and found Amiram at the western end of the balcony playing backgammon with a Christian Arab. A small group stood around and cheered and wailed as the players made good moves or erred. Yokhanan squatted beside the board and began to complain to Amiram, disregarding the other kibitzers. Amiram became visibly annoyed, saying: "This is not the time or place to have this discussion. Leave me in peace."

"You must call a meeting, Amiram. This is dictatorship by the Orthodox. You . . . "

Amiram rose and pulled Yokhanan erect. His fist pulled back. The kibitzers quickly grabbed both men and held them apart until Doody Gordon, the medic, came rushing from the center of the balcony, grabbed both men, and led them into one of the Jewish-occupied rooms.

People gathered quickly to see what all the shouting was about, and Doody started moving bunks to make room. "All right, you jerks, if you want to fight, let's do it right. We'll set up a ring. I'll referee and you guys can provide some entertainment."

Dave came in as everyone was milling around. He asked what was going on and Amiram told him.

"All right," Dave shouted. "Let's everyone sit down. We have to hold a meeting. Would someone please get the people from the other rooms."

When everyone was present, Dave closed the door to the balcony and the windows on either side of it, then faced his shipmates. "We are fighting among ourselves today," he said. "For shame! It is not bad enough that we are sitting here uselessly in an alien land while our people wage a war for their very existence, delighting the enemy with our discord. Some of us believe that all Jews are brothers, don't we all believe that?"

Dave paused for effect. Several heads nodded.

"I see that there are several who agree with me. Is there anyone here who does not believe that all Jews are brothers?" He paused again, and gave Yokhanan a meaningful look. "I see there is no disagreement. Then, we can proceed to the center of the dispute. Is there anyone here who will not allow his fellow Jew religious freedom?" Again he looked at Yokhanan. The latter turned red, but kept quiet.

"I ask you, rabbi," Dave continued, "will you not grant religious freedom to all Jews?"

"It is not in my power to rule over you," the rabbi replied.

"If we, then, grant each other religious freedom in this concentration camp," Dave went on, "let us end our animosities and prevent any actions on our part that will aid the enemy."

Yokhanan had had enough: "If I may, Mr. *Irgun* leader, I should like to remind you that we have not elected you pope. We have not appointed you censor of our thoughts. I would appreciate being heard. Some of you may know that I am the leader in the Association Against Religious Compulsion. Some of you may know that I am an atheist. I doubt that any of you know that I am not opposed to your right to be religious as long as you do not attempt to force your religious practices upon those Jews who do not wish to observe them, including me.

"It happens that I smoke. I choose to smoke when I want to. I also choose to buy my meat at a butcher shop of my choice. I do not force you to do likewise, but when you break my butcher's windows, or when you spit at me for smoking, you are restricting my liberty. And then I act.

"My protest is directed against the halt in giving out cigarettes to everyone, religious or not. Could we not be permissive, to allow the people who wish to smoke to have their pleasure, provided that they promise, and I hereby do so, not to smoke where the religious people are conducting their Sabbath services or are gathered. I would also like to apologize to you, Amiram, for calling you a dictator."

Dave called for a standing vote, certain that Yokhanan's proposal would be rejected. Most of the forty-one Americans and some of the Palestinians sided with Yokhanan. Dave was dismayed to see that all but one of his own people were standing.

"All right, Yokhanan, you may smoke. The kitty will distribute cigarettes to anyone who asks."

* * *

Monotonously, day followed day. The men learned to skip rope, to play solitaire, and to drink from a *jarra*—an earthenware jug with a small spout—by letting water pour into their mouths without getting their shirts wet. A hearts tournament was organized. Several men got together to produce a hand-written newspaper, based, in part on what they could glean from the French-language newspaper that Muhamid sold. But they also had a small portable radio and could hear newscasts from Israel.

During the Lebanese disaster at Malikiyeh, they knew more about the progress of the battle than could be discerned from the Lebanese newspaper. Two days after the battle, the garrison that had been guarding Baalbek camp was replaced by veterans of Malikiyeh while the old Baalbek guard detachment was sent to the front. The new guard unit complained that Malikiyeh had been captured by the Jews, then abandoned. But when the Lebanese went back into the town, Jewish booby traps went off all over the place.

Amiram, and Dave warned everyone to be wary because the new guards had a score to settle.

That was the moment chosen by Jefferson Davis Binkle to visit his countrymen. He was seen coming through the gate leading into the compound, but stayed there as a Lebanese officer came upstairs to order everyone into one of the rooms. Only when they were all assembled, did Binkle enter, with an armed Lebanese soldier at each side: "Well, I hope none of y'all got syphilis, clap, or any of those other diseases. Anyone got cancer? No? Too bad!"

Dave jumped to his feet beside Doody Gordon and they rushed toward Binkle. The Lebanese stepped forward with their rifles held diagonally across their chests, keeping anyone from getting near Binkle.

Both men were shouting at Binkle, as were several others in the room. Doody's voice drowned them all out: "You son of a bitch. You miserable, lousy, Dixiecrat bastard. You get the hell out of here before we throw you into the toilet head first. We don't want you here, and if you need to talk to us in future, send your vice consul."

Binkle, unperturbed, paid no attention.

"Come on, Binkle," Dave shouted, "you heard what the man said."

"What's your name, Jewboy?" Binkle asked.

"David Gordon," Dave said.

"And yours?"

"David Gordon," Doody said.

"Y'all trying to kid me? There's only one David Gordon here and you can't both be him."

Binkle walked out the door with considerable dignity. Then, turning, he yelled: "I've got some packages for y'all from the Kike Red Cross. I'll see that y'all rot in hell before you get them."

The Lebanese commander, however, brought the gift parcels as soon as Binkle's car passed through the gates. They bore the seal of the Lebanese Red Cross and Red Crescent Society, the International Committee of the Red Cross in Geneva, and the *Magen David Adom*, the Red Shield of David. Each was labeled as a prisoner-of-war gift parcel.

The packages contained kosher meat, cigarettes, candy, and sundry other things from playing cards to small chess sets. For the first time, the Jewish hostages were able to reciprocate the kindness of the Lebanese hostages by taking presents to them. For Amiram, it also presented a moment of truth.

"All the kosher meat," he said, "will be given to those who eat kosher."

To most of the *Carp* hostages this was perfectly all right, but Yokhanan protested: "That's more religious discrimination. The rest of us have had hardly any meat for the three weeks we have been here; now meat arrives, and you will not let us have it."

"You don't even like kosher meat," Amiram said, walking off.

Dave grabbed Doody and walked to the far end of the balcony with him, asking what he made of Binkle's comment that there was only one of them.

"Either Binkle or the Lebanese assumed that there is only one of us," Doody said.

"So one of us could take off without being missed," Dave said. "Too bad neither one of us speaks Arabic."

"Hey, Dave," Doody said, "I've got it. We could get rid of Yokhanan. He speaks fluent Arabic."

The two Gordons headed for Amiram with their idea. Amiram agreed to put it to Yokhanan, and, after he agreed, they dressed Yokhanan in a blue business suit and told him to walk out the gate with a group of departing Lebanese visitors.

From then on, Doody became Yokhanan Galili.

* * *

Five weeks after they entered Baalbek camp, Binkle and another man arrived. While Binkle remained downstairs, the other man introduced himself as the vice consul and head of the consulate's visa section. He said he was speaking on Binkle's behalf to save him from "being assaulted again." There was a murmur of dissent from the hostages.

"Yeah," Yehoshua Ben Yeshayah, the barber, shouted, "as if

he's in any danger from any of us now that we all have dysentery, have lost ten to fifteen kilos, and couldn't fight if we had to do so."

The vice consul continued to explain his mission. Each American citizen was to write a statement explaining the purpose of his trip with the proviso that anything he said could be held against him. All hostages were to make separate statements to indicate whether they needed money for return to the United States. The vice consul was authorized to grant repatriation loans to anyone who, under pain of perjury, would sign an affidavit promising not to return to the area of hostilities until the United States revoked its Declaration of Neutrality.

Everyone cheered,

Amiram asked them to sign their statement of purpose in the "library." Dave stood at the door and looked them over before having them sworn to. Some excuses were utterly fantastic, so far from even the remotest possibility that Amiram and Dave would not allow them to be turned in.

One American would not be talked out of telling the truth. He stated that he was going to Palestine to fight in the tradition of the Flying Tigers and the Eagle Squadron.

"I was in the Flying Tigers," Izzy Greenberg said. "It was the right thing, the patriotic thing to do. The Neutrality Act was in force then, too. They gave me a medal. If we believe in America, we must believe in Israel a hell of a lot more than I could ever believe in Chiang Kai-shek. So, I'll take my chances. I'll fight this. I'm going to tell the truth."

Amiram was opposed to the idea, but Dave said: "It might be a good idea to make a test case. If he wants to be the guinea pig, let him."

"See this," Greenberg told them. "This is the Congressional Medal of Honor. I had it hung around my neck by FDR, himself. If they try any funny business about loss of citizenship or any other crap, I've got the answer right here in this little box, and don't think I wouldn't cause a stinkeroo. I may not be very bright, but I can holler. And I'm going to holler so they'll even hear me in the State Department."

Greenberg hung the medal around his neck on its blue-and-white ribbon and led the way to the vice consul as Dave and Amiram followed.

"Here, mister," Greenberg said, "here is my reason for being here. Make something of it." He handed his statement to the vice consul.

"Is this really what you want to say?" he was asked.

"You bet your ass! It's the truth."

"Aren't you aware that you are admitting that you wanted to commit a crime?"

"Mister, if that's a crime, go to Philadelphia and tell them Lafayette was a criminal; go to a Polish-American club and tell them Kosciusko was a criminal. You should know your history. You'd find that most of the big guys in the history books were criminals. Go on, make me a criminal. I like the company I'm keeping."

"Calm down. I'm only trying to advise you that this affidavit is against your own best interests. If this is what you want, fine. I'll let you swear to it."

"You're damn tooting you'll let me swear to it. You wouldn't want to fight this gadget," he said, leaning over to bring the medal right before the harried vice consul's eyes.

"Oh, I'm sorry," he said. "I didn't know . . . "

Greenberg laughed. "What difference does it make? I was a criminal when I got this, too, according to you. You ever hear of the Flying Tigers?"

"Of course."

"Were they criminals?"

"No."

"So why wasn't I a criminal in the Flying Tigers? Why am I a criminal now? Just because I wanted to fight for my own people, that's why. It's all right by you guys in the State Department for me to fight for a bald dictator, or a stuttering king, but God forbid I should fight as a Jew for the Jewish people. Shit on you, mister!"

Dave came over and put his hand on Greenberg's shoulder. "You better swear to that, Izzy. I think you've made your point." The vice consul muttered the formula and Izzy swore.

* * *

United Nations observers in white helmet liners watched as the men boarded *Marine Carp*. She flew no flags, not even the Stars and Stripes at her fantail. It was obvious that either the captain or the American Export Line had decided to enter port bald as a message to Binkle or the Lebanese.

When they were all aboard, they were asked to come to the lounge for a meeting with the captain.

"Gentlemen," he began, "for the first time in my career, I entered port with no flags, not even astern, where Old Glory usually flies. I have been too ashamed. The disgraceful conduct shown to you by an American official was communicated to my line and to his superiors. I am told that the State Department will do nothing about this.

"There is some mail for you in the purser's office. The goods you left aboard were all safely unloaded at Haifa. I should also like to tell you what happened when this vessel entered Haifa the day after you left it. Since my instructions were that Haifa would continue under British control, I flew the Union Jack at starboard. The pilot boat, flying an Israeli ensign, met me outside the breakwater and ordered me to fly the flag of the country, and offered me one. I informed them that I already had one and asked your young women to bring the flag they had sewn. This is, therefore, the first foreign-registry vessel to enter Israeli waters under the Israeli flag. I have that flag with me here and wish to present it to Mr. Ben Cohen. Would you come forward to accept it, sir?"

Amiram thanked the captain, but declined the flag. "Captain, it would please me and, I believe, all my friends, if you would keep this flag as a souvenir of this historic voyage."

* * *

Everyone remained below decks when *Carp* entered the harbor of Alexandria. They had hair cuts and painfully attempted to shave off their Baalbek stubble.

At Palermo in Sicily, ten *Haganah* men, led by Amiram, simply walked ashore. The masters-at-arms looked the other way, and the Italians believed them to be crew. After the ship left Naples, their number decreased by eighteen more. Dave's group intended to jump ship at Ponta del Gada in the Azores, according to cabled instructions.

YOKHANAN I

Rosh Pina is in Upper Galilee. Founded in the 1880s by Baron Rothschild's settlement organization, it was the first Jewish village in the area. The red-tiled roofs of its houses recalled the south of France despite the Hebrew signs, the *felafel* seller along the road to Tiberias, the jackals that cried in the night, and the huge anopheles mosquitoes that came in from the Huleh at dusk. Before the century ended, Rosh Pina was joined by Mahanayim, Mishmar Hayarden, and Yesod Hama'ala.

In the 1930s, Yokhanan Galili and his father used to go skiing in Lebanon. Me'ir Galili, who thought his son was a Paavo Nurmi on skis, sent the boy off to America and Switzerland to race. Yokhanan realized he was outclassed, but insisted that if the ski meets flew any flags at all, then the Jewish flag had to be flown to include his presence. He won no prizes, but his performance in the slalom was praised for a skier from a country where it never snows. The inhabitants of Rosh Pina, on the other hand, who mostly disliked Yokhanan's father, deprecated Me'ir for sending Yokhanan half way around the world just to glide down a snow-covered hill.

Me'ir was the town's richest man and the villagers despised what they called his extravagance. Even before the formation of the Egged bus cooperative, Me'ir was well off because he owned the village restaurant and its general store. When he started to drive the bus from Metulla to Haifa, his wife, Leah, took over the business while his brothers looked after his fields.

Yokhanan was sent off to school at Gymnasia Herzlia in Tel Aviv, the best school in the country, instead of Rosh Pina's two-room structure. The villagers showed their contempt to Leah in the store with sarcasm and mockery. But, in 1937, when Yokhanan entered Hebrew University, their attitude abruptly changed. They were now proud of the village boy who had made good. Leah forgave their slurs; but Me'ir, unable to forget the taunts and jibes, never warmed up to the others again. In return, they managed to get him kicked out of the Egged bus cooperative, which cited his other interests as making him ineligible for the cooperative.

After Egged expelled Me'ir, he was paid back some of the money he had put into the co-op. He used it to build a bar next to the store. English police and Allied troops in Palestine, mostly Poles, filled Me'ir's coffers as they consumed the local malt beer and other drinks.

To the other villagers, it seemed that worship of the Palestine pound took second place only to Me'ir's interest in his son. He hired people, including two Druze and a Christian Arab, to work his fields and he put his brothers to work driving his two trucks—boldly lettered with "Me'ir Galili Trucking" in three languages—around Palestine and the surrounding countries. He built a new house, a modern structure of concrete and stucco for which he hired the world-renowned Tel Aviv architect Erich Mendelsohn.

In 1935, a Jewish orphan from Damascus took up residence in the house and started going to the Rosh Pina school. Yokhanan saw this boy, Akiva Barzilai, only during his own school vacations. At first, they had little to say to each other; later, they became friends, although Akiva always felt awkward around Yokhanan and Yokhanan wondered why his father had brought the boy to their home.

In 1942, a Polish soldier with thick glasses came into the bar and watched Me'ir intently. When the bar was empty, the Pole approached Me'ir and whispered: "I was the leader of Betar in Poland. I need to make contact with the Jabotinsky movement here in *Eretz Yisrael*. Do you know anyone who could help me make such an approach?"

Me'ir looked at the slight figure in front of him and said, "If you are Menachem Begin, I am the man you want to see."

And so, about a week after his arrival in Palestine, Begin deserted the Polish army to join *Irgun Zvai Leumi*. He was driven in Me'ir Galili's truck to the Fortress of Ze'ev, the Betar headquarters on King George Street in Tel Aviv.

As soon as he was inside, Begin asked for David Raziel, commander of the *Irgun*.

"He is dead," he was told. "He led a British force that was sent to topple the pro-Axis regime of Rashid Ali el-Gailani in Iraq. He has been dead almost two years. Where have you been?"

"I was in Soviet camps and just reached the homeland as part of the Polish army. Permit me to introduce myself. I am Menachem Begin, *natziv* of the Polish Betar."

The man he was talking to, stuck out his hand and said, "Tel Hai! Welcome home!"

"Tel Hai," the name of a village in the far north of the country, was the greeting of Betar because it was where Yosef Trumpeldor died during an attack by Arabs.

* * *

While his father poured the drinks, Yokhanan served in the battle of El Alamein, the capture of the Mareth Line, and the storming of the Italian Winter Line, and, eventually, in the occupation of Holland. It was Yokhanan who had the famous encounter with a French general who relieved the German encirclement of the Palestinians at Mechili, southwest of El Alamein.

Yokhanan was then a captain in a company of Jewish engineers attached to the King's West African Rifles who were laying mines around Mechili, the god-forsaken outpost fifty miles from Bir Hakim, where the French were under siege. The British general directing operations in Egypt ordered the Jews to hold Mechili at all costs when the Germans and Italians attacked. The Germans sent in a tank under a white flag and demanded the surrender of the strongpoint.

Yokhanan replied: "We have no white flag! This flag we shall fly. It is the blue-and-white flag of Zion!"

The German officer was surprised, saying in British-accented English, "My God, you are Jews!" He clicked his heels, saluted, and withdrew. And then the siege began. The tanks came first, then the Stukas. Three weeks later, when only forty-five of Yokhanan's original five hundred men were still alive, French tanks broke through to Mechili.

Yokhanan had ordered the Jewish flag run up to mark his position during General Pierre-Marie Koenig's final advance. But when the siege was lifted, Yokhanan ordered it pulled down.

"Why are you lowering your flag?" Koenig asked.

"We are not allowed to fly that flag," Yokhanan replied.

"Leave it up," Koenig ordered. Then, he turned to his own men and ordered: "*Soldats français, le drapeau juif, salut!*"

* * *

After the war, Yokhanan returned to philosophy and religion in the classroom—interests that had been stimulated by two experiences, the first in his youth, the second in the army.

He had never been able to forget the anguish suffered by another boy at Gymnasia Herzlia who was the son of a non-Jewish mother. They became friends and Yokhanan heard other boys taunt Yigael as a bastard. They excluded the uncircumcised Yigael from their games, baited him as a "*goy*" and a "Nazi," and challenged him to innumerable fights.

The rabbis denied Yigael a bar mitzvah, ruling him not to be Jewish, so word spread that if he could not have a bar mitzvah, he must be a girl. Yokhanan was able to rally a small number of friends to Yigael's defense. These boys went out of their way to show the unfortunate boy that he was their equal. By the time they were graduated, all had been forgotten because Yigael and his mother had gone through the humiliating—and for Yigael, painful—rite of conversion to Judaism, including the circumcision.

The pressures that caused those conversions rankled Yokhanan almost as much as the rabbinate's unwillingness to accept the Jewishness of his own group of converts, the Jews of Sannicandro.

It was when the British Eighth Army was just past Bari and while the American Fifth Army had just roared through Naples. It was before the British allowed the Jews of Palestine to have a full-sized unit of their own, despite their heroic efforts at Tobruk and at the French breakout from Bir Hakim. Palestinians in the Eighth Army were scattered around, a few of them in infantry units. They were not allowed to wear a Palestine flash on their uniforms or to fly their own flag. But they wore the patch and, whenever they could, they flew their flag.

Yokhanan's company was attached to a Polish infantry division. No love was lost between the Poles and the Jews. Just before Passover 1944, the company was given a week's leave to observe the Jewish holy days. They were ordered to go to Sannicandro. They were told nothing about the village.

When Yokhanan's company drove into the village aboard the standard Bedfords with Yokhanan leading the way in a jeep, Yokhanan went to the *municipio* to find quarters for his men. He could talk only to a flunky, but the flunky noticed the illegal Palestine flash Yokhanan wore on his sleeve.

"*È questo Palestina?*"—Is that Palestine?—he asked, pointing to the patch.

Yokhanan, whose Italian was limited, said, "*Si.*"

"*Aspettate uno momento!*"—Wait a moment—the clerk said, rushing out of the building.

A few minutes later, he brought in Donato Manduzio, the leader of the Jews of Sannicandro. Manduzio brought along an interpreter. The story was unbelievable and Yokhanan had to run out of the *municipio* to tell his men: "Some Pole has been nice to us. He sent us to a Jewish village for Passover."

When he got back to Manduzio he learned the full story:

"It was right after the Fascist March on Rome in 1923. I had a dream in which I heard Moses, our teacher, say to me that I should have no other gods but the Great God Jehovah, blessed be

He. I went to Bari, to the library and to the library at the university. I found the Old Testament in Italian. I was able to borrow it because, they told me, nobody ever uses it. After I read it, I studied about the Jews, I studied about the history of the Jews, and I became a Jew.

"Twenty-three families in this little town also became Jews. We saved some money, and I was sent to *Palestina*, to the Holy Land, to buy a Torah for our town. I asked the office of the chief rabbi of Rome to send us teachers, so we could learn to read the Torah, so we could learn the Holy Language, so we could become circumcised. We didn't even know what was meant by that. The rabbinate said no. We were not Jews. The Fascists also said we were not Jews—and this was a good thing because they did not turn us over to the Germans.

"So here we are, about a hundred uncircumcised Jews, who have a Torah and cannot read it, who have a synagogue, but don't know how to use it. Can you help us?"

Yokhanan was deeply touched, but he could not help. Only one of his men spoke Italian.

"No," Manduzio said, "I was not expecting your men to circumcise us or anything like that. I was hoping they could take us home with them, to *Palestina*, to the Land Jehovah promised to Moses."

"We cannot help there, either. Our land is occupied by the British. They will not let Jews in. But let us celebrate the Passover together."

"When is it?" Manduzio asked.

"It starts tomorrow. Our cook will bake unleavened bread. Will your people join us for a Seder?"

Yokhanan had to explain what he was talking about. And there was a Seder in the village square, on tables made from saw horses and planks. The women of Sannicandro set the tables, using sheets for tablecloths. Yokhanan's men found all the necessary objects for the Seder except the horseradish, so they ground up carrots and poured vile-tasting *grappa* over them. A child was taught to ask the Four Questions, and he was answered in simple Italian. The age-old answers were all news to the Jews of Sannicandro.

* * *

After Yokhanan's company returned to the front, he thanked the Polish regimental commander for having sent his men to Sannicandro.

"You are welcome," he was told. "I thought it would be amusing for you."

Even after Yokhanan's company was absorbed into the new Jewish Brigade Group, Yokhanan's interest in the Jews of Sannicandro continued. Later, in 1944, they were recognized as Jews by the chief rabbi of Rome, but not by the chief rabbi of the Jewish Brigade, who demanded a full Orthodox conversion, including circumcision. Manduzio agreed to the circumcision, but only if it was to be done by trained surgeons, not by laymen whose only experience was with infants. The brigade's rabbi refused.

The visit by Yokhanan and his men, however, had made the Jews of Sannicandro into Zionists, Zionists who wanted to live nowhere but in the Promised Land.

Yokhanan's interest in "his" Jews never flagged. In his final year at the university, he wrote a thesis on the development of their beliefs. His correspondence with Manduzio and other elders continued until the Jews of Sannicandro settled into their own village in the Galilee after the Israeli War of Independence. Yokhanan was the guest of honor at their consecration of their house.

"We have all been circumcised," Manduzio's son told him. "My father would have been so proud. But he died before we left Italy."

"Who circumcised you?" Yokhanan asked.

"Tel Hashomer Hospital. It was still very painful, but there was no damage to anyone. We were so afraid of ritual circumcision."

* * *

Soon after Yokhanan finished his studies, he founded the Association Against Religious Compulsion. Its objective was to promote a change in the mandatory regime's laws on religious status. The British had merely retained all the rules and regulations of Ottoman Turkish *irades*, permitting religious courts of the three great faiths to control marriage, adoption, divorce, and inheritance. The association campaigned for civil jurisdiction and, in addition, sought to foster resistance to the two Orthodox Jewish hierarchies, Ashkenazic and Sephardic, which banned any other form of Jewish worship in Palestine, effectively halting the introduction of the Reform and Conservative movements. Not that Yokhanan wanted to join a Reform synagogue, but he wanted one to exist so that if he ever did want to join, he would have been able to.

The association, however, made no impression on anyone during the bloody days at the end of the British mandate. Everyone had more important things to think about, including Yokhanan, who was on the *Haganah* staff in Jerusalem. His job was to plan the defense of the Old City, but he never had to carry out that project, which ended with the complete victory of John Bagot Glubb's Arab Legion. Yokhanan had been sent to America to join the arms buyers for the *Haganah*.

Before leaving Jerusalem, Yokhanan marched at the head of a slowly moving funeral procession in which eighteen shrouded corpses were carried on horse-drawn wagons to save gasoline in the encircled city. The dead had been in a convoy bringing water and food to the City of David. Two of the trucks had signs saying they belonged to Me'ir Galili of Rosh Pina. Thus, Yokhanan helped bury his father, his mother, and his Uncle Gabriel, victims of the stretch of death at Bab el-Wad.

* * *

After escaping from Lebanese captivity in Baalbek, Yokhanan hid in the daytime and walked all night. Fearing far better police work in Lebanon than was actually the case, he dared not visit any of his acquaintances. It took ten slow nights to reach Marjayoun, a village on the Israeli—Lebanese frontier. But the entire area in front of him was sealed off by Arab troops, so he backtracked until he reached another part of the border. He went around Taibe until he reached Wadi Doubbe, then followed it to the Jebel Haroun. Crossing a ridge line near dawn, he saw the Valley of the Upper Jordan in front of him. He awaited full daylight and started creeping and crawling toward the road that crossed his path toward Israel. A barbed-wire entanglement projected out into the Lebanon from the village on the Israeli side of the road, the kibbutz of Menara. He crawled under the first strands of wire, and was fired upon. He took off his *keffiyeh* and shouted. The firing stopped.

"Stay where you are. Do not move," he was told in Arabic through a megaphone.

A small group of men, each armed with a rifle, came out of Menara toward him. They went around the defense perimeter and brought him out as he had entered. That way they did not reveal the path through their own mine field.

Yokhanan was led to the dining hall, several rifles constantly pointed at him. A man who did not identify himself questioned him, at first in Arabic, then in Hebrew.

"Who are you?"

"Yokhanan Galili from Rosh Pina."

"Me'ir Galili's son?"

"Yes."

"Are you a thief like your father?"

"I honor my father and my mother. If you will not, you should be ashamed. They died in the defense of Jerusalem!"

"What are the names of your uncles?" he went on, ignoring Yokhanan's previous answer.

"Gabriel, Moshe and Menachem. Gabriel also died at Bab el-Wad."

"What is a *sitzmark*?"

"The mark you would make if you attempted to ski."

"Welcome home, Yokhanan. I must say you found an unusual way to arrive. What were you doing in Lebanon?"

"I was imprisoned in Baalbek by an act of piracy in which our 'friends,' the Americans, sided with the Arabs. I escaped and spent more than a week to get here on foot. Let's cut the pleasantries. I would like to get to my unit in Jerusalem. How do I get there from Menara?"

"Very funny! You cannot get there from here. The entire Upper Galilee is cut off. Jerusalem is also cut off. Between here and Tiberias, you will find units of Fawzi el-Ka'ukji's Arab Liberation Army, Glubb Pasha's Arab Legion, and several brigades of Syrians. As you go south, the Iraqis are almost at Herzliya. And here, we are cut off from the rest of Galilee except from Kfar Giladi, from which we are separated by an impassable cliff. We are up; they are down."

"How did you reach them before the war?" Yokhanan asked.

"That road you crossed is on our side of the border. We could take it north and south and could descend at the Nebi Yusha police fortress, which the *Palmach* captured last week. But we cannot use that road now."

"Can I get to Jerusalem if I can get down to Giladi?"

"Not easily," he was told. "There are Pipers that land in Metulla, but we do not want them to take chances. They are still forced to fly where Arab rifles can shoot at them. Let me show you on the map. These are Ka'ukji's positions. We can push a force past Ayelet, but getting to Rosh Pina is not yet possible."

"Can you inform the *Haganah* commander in Jerusalem that I'm stuck up here?"

"Why tell Shaltiel? I'll report you in up here. We're expecting to open the whole area the minute this goddamned U.N. cease-fire ends, so you'll have plenty to do right here. Meanwhile," he said, looking at Yokhanan's suit, "you better get some clothes in the *makhsan*."

"Thanks. Who are you, by the way?"

"Gidon. I'm a member of Menara."

When Yokhanan had changed into the standard kibbutz garb of khaki shorts and a short-sleeved blue shirt that may have belonged to a woman because its buttons went the wrong way, they went to a communications trench and followed it into a bunker overlooking the plain east of the kibbutz. A home-made telephone switchboard and a knapsack-type military radio of British origin indicated that this was Menara's command post. The switchboard was hooked to each of the defensive positions on the perimeter and to the other bunkers by wires that were buried only inches under the ground. The radio was part of *Haganah*'s net. There was no one in the bunker.

"Where is everyone?" Yokhanan asked.

"We evacuated the women and children to the Valley of Jezreel and we are only twenty-two people. In the daytime, one man is on watch on the silo and one in each defense point. The rest of us try to do the work. At night, we all man the defenses. Now, let me call you in."

He inserted a wire into a snap bracket and turned a crank. "Gidon here. Shmuel? Yes . . . Listen, Yokhanan Galili, Me'ir Galili's son, just turned up in the *meshek*. Yes . . . Well . . . he wanted to tell Shaltiel in Jerusalem that he's here. Can you do anything? . . . What? . . . What? . . . Wait a minute. Here, he wants to talk to you."

Yokhanan took the phone as Gidon pulled a crushed pack of cigarettes from his pocket. He lit one for Yokhanan and handed it to him.

"Hello; hello, Shmuel? . . . I'll try, but Gidon says we are cut off. I'll ask him. . . . What? . . . Sure, here he is."

Gidon listened, then scratched his chin pensively as he turned the crank to end the call. "I think he's *meshuga*, Yokhanan."

"Why? It sounds perfectly reasonable. Can you get me to Giladi?"

"Now is a poor time. It is late."

"I don't see what the time has to do with it," Yokhanan said.

"It is best to leave Menara at dawn to keep the sun in the Arabs' eyes. Do you think he can wait until tomorrow?"

"It sounds like he wants me right now."

"Then you must go down the cliff to Khalsa. We are between you and the Arabs in Lebanon, and we have captured Khalsa. In honor of the men who died in the defense of Tel Hai with Trumpeldor, it is now called Kiryat Shmone, the village of the eight. It would be too dangerous to try to get to Giladi."

"Very well, can you get me a pick, some rope, and a rifle?"

"Sure. Leave them with Shmuel when you get down there."

* * *

Using the pick as an alpenstock and with the rope tied around his waist, Yokhanan made his way down the cliff. Several hours later, he walked into the Khalsa police station, asking for Shmuel.

"Shmuel who?"

"I don't know his last name. He's the *Haganah* commander here."

"Oh, you mean Shmuel Hasbani. I'll take you."

Shmuel was the Egged bus driver who had taken over Me'ir's route. He was a member of Ayelet and knew Yokhanan well.

"When did you become Hasbani?"

"On Independence Day. Like it?"

"It's geographical like mine. Why not?" The Hasbani is one of the three sources of the River Jordan and flows through Tel Hai.

"I like it better than Ginsburg. But I didn't ask you to break your neck coming down here for pleasantries. The cease-fire ended this morning. We are in combat all over the north. Come, let me show you the situation map."

Areas held by Jews were marked in blue on an acetate overlay; those held by Arabs were in different hatchings of red to designate Syrians, Ka'ukji's men, Glubb Pasha's Legion, and local Arabs.

Shmuel took a pointer and quickly sketched out his plan for clearing all Arabs out of Upper Galilee. To hear Shmuel tell it, it would be simple.

The campaign was called Operation *Barosh*, Operation Uppercut. It was intended to prevent a Syrian attack to link up with the Lebanese at Malikiyeh, the Lebanese town the Israelis had booby trapped as they withdrew. Other objectives included lifting the siege of Mishmar Hayarden, now occupied by Syrians, and clearing the road from Rosh Pina to the north. Then they would turn south and go after Ka'ukji.

The Jewish attack on Mishmar Hayarden was already in progress. Four separate columns were moving toward the Syrian bridgeheads across the Jordan. Shmuel's task was to clear the road to the south and, after getting past Ka'ukji, to connect the Upper Galilee with the rest of Israel.

But several days earlier, a terrible thing had happened when a group of *Irgun* soldiers came north from Tiberias on their way toward Mishmar Hayarden. At Rosh Pina, they were stopped by *Haganah* forces, who beat them into bloody pulps and confiscated their arms and equipment. The *Irgun* men made their way back to Affula, where they told their story. On the next night, it was broadcast over *The Voice of Fighting Zion*, the broadcasting station of the *Irgun*.

"Right now," Shmuel told Yokhanan, "we are assembling a column of armored cars and men at Ayelet. They are going to move out in about an hour. Our people are also coming down from Safed and, when the two groups make contact, they push Ka'ukji into the Lebanon. When he is running, the hilltop settlements are to cut off his retreat."

"How do I fit in?"

"Come to Ayelet with me. You should report to Danny and take over one of his units. Its commander is a youngster who hasn't even been through leadership school."

"What does Danny have, a battalion?"

"Yes, but without the artillery or any of the other stuff we had in the Eighth Army."

"OK," Yokhanan said, but in truth he did not like it. All the way to Ayelet he wrestled with the problem of taking command of a unit without knowing its men, the training they had had, or the level of their equipment. He knew he could not make any command decisions without knowing more about the unit or its mission. At Ayelet, Danny had the same misgivings. He asked Yokhanan to stay with the youngster and to help him only when needed.

What Yokhanan saw in Ayelet was also not encouraging, The "armored cars" were trucks with varying amounts of sheet metal attached. The best mobile weapons were two jeeps with machine guns mounted on unipods; so they could fire across the hood.

At one thirty—late in this war in which most attacks began before dawn—the column moved out of Ayelet. Firing from Mishmar was drowned out by the noise of their engines.

The battle never developed. Ka'ukji had withdrawn during the truce and the road to Rosh Pina was clear. Joined by the small column that came down from Safed, the battalion turned north toward the Lebanese frontier. Shmuel recalled them after they were well inside Lebanon without having met any resistance. They were rerouted to Mishmar, where the fighting had gone badly and the Syrians had broken out of their bridgehead.

During the next ten days, before another cease-fire was ordered by the United Nations, Israel captured Ramle and Lydda, most of the Galilee, including Nazareth, opened the roads to Upper Galilee and stopped two Egyptian attacks in the south. Their only setbacks were at Mishmar, where the four-pronged Israeli assault was badly botched, and at Latrun, where Genia HaCohen had been wounded.

While the second cease-fire was in effect, Yokhanan reported to Jerusalem. He was told to remain where he was, holding the command he had taken from the youngster during the Syrian attack on Ulpanim.

When the war ended, Yokhanan and his unit were in Eilat, spearheading what was now called the Golani Brigade. Meanwhile, Shmuel had gone to the general staff, Danny had been killed during Ka'ukji's full-force attack on Menara, and Yokhanan had been given command of Shmuel's battalion.

The army had assumed ranks, and saluting had been instituted. Girls were taken out of combat units, the dissident *Irgun* (which had captured Ramle by mounting a blitz with stolen British jeeps) had been disbanded, the air force had bombed Cairo and Damascus, and the navy had raided Tyre and had sunk the flagship of King Farouk's Egyptian fleet.

On the Golani Brigade's last operation, Moshe HaCohen of Golania had been named brigade commander and the staff work began to function in the best tradition of the British Eighth Army, the new army's godfather.

The Golanis scored Israel's most illustrious victory of the War of Independence when they crossed the southern wilderness, without water, to capture Eilat on the deep blue Gulf of Aqaba. The men were restrained from diving in and going swimming. Only after a defense perimeter had been set up and the guns sighted on positions in Trans-Jordan was the command given: "Go swimming."

Arab Legion troops could be seen on their side of the Israel—Trans-Jordan border. A British destroyer lay at anchor at Aqaba, its guns ominously pointed toward Eilat.

The gulf was paradise. The water was warm and crystal clear. Yokhanan swam over to Moshe HaCohen, hollering: "What now, Moshe?"

"Me, I hope to go back to Golania. What about you?"

"I don't know."

"Two wars in one man's lifetime is too much for a man to take. What a waste!" Moshe said.

"An American once said, 'War is hell,' Moshe."

"He was right; he was so right. Not to change the subject, though, isn't it beautiful here? I have visions of a marvelous winter resort if UNO doesn't make us give it up."

"They will. Then the Arabs can let it go to hell for another two thousand years. Did you know that this was King Solomon's port?"

"Yes. In my signal, I flashed: 'Bay of Solomon is ours!' "

DAVE IV

As they sailed into the Portuguese islands, Dave borrowed binoculars from the first mate. He sighted *Carp*'s sister ship, another converted troop-carrying C-4, tied up on its eastward trip. There were two other ships in port a British frigate and, near it but away from the quay, a small fishing boat flying the Colombian flag.

From starboard, Dave scanned the passengers aboard *Marine Perch*, giving up the other two as a lost cause. Spotting no one he knew, he became irritated for not having taken his men ashore in Palermo with Amiram Ben Cohen. He also noticed that the U.S. government had not honored the promise of its minister to get them out of Lebanon as fast as it could. *Marine Carp* and *Marine Perch* made the voyage every two weeks. That meant *Perch* reached Beirut only two weeks after they had been seized on the *Carp*. Instead, they had spent five and a half weeks in Baalbek until *Carp* came back to Beirut on its next voyage.

For the first time on their westward voyage, the captain authorized shore leave. But Dave and his people, without funds and without hope of making contact with their movement, decided to stay on board.

Dave watched without much interest as pineapple brandy was hauled aboard *Carp* from bumboats tied up to starboard. He returned to portside and again searched the faces on the *Perch*.

"Hey, Dave," someone yelled from his rear. "You are wanted over here."

He went to the starboard rail and looked down. In one of the bumboats, two young boys were waving furiously to get his attention. "Come ashore, Dave. Bring two more."

"OK," he answered, without recognizing the youngsters.

His group gathered and drew lots. Those chosen to go with Dave put on layer after layer of underwear, put their toilet articles in their jacket pockets, and took up a collection from those remaining on *Carp*.

Sweating profusely in the July heat and all that underwear, they left their passports with a Portuguese inspector and bounded happily down the gangplank.

The bumboat tied up and its occupants ran to meet them. "Tel Hai, Dave, Mike and Uri," one of the boys shouted.

Uri jabbed Dave and whispered, "They're Betarim."

One of the boys approached Dave, came to attention, and saluted. "I'm Phil Kantor of the Bronx Brigade. Welcome to Ponta."

Dave returned the salute, sloppily, hoping that no one had noticed. "I'll be damned," he said, "I never would have recognized you, not even in a Betar uniform. Where did you lose all the weight?"

"At sea, but you lost a lot more than me. This is Misha Kirsch from Frisco. He was in Betar in China."

After the introductions, they all climbed into the bumboat and Phil rowed toward the Colombian fishing boat, the *Sally Jane*. She was forty-five feet long and looked like a river boat; not an ocean-going merchantman. Yet she had crossed the Atlantic with a crew of amateurs. Phil was captain because he bad spent eighteen months in the navy after the war. He was, however, the most experienced seaman aboard *Sally Jane*. Misha was the radioman and cook. The third crewman was from the American League for a Free Palestine and the owner of the fishing boat, Manny Cardozo. Manny was the ship's engineer and navigator.

They were shown around the ship, which was loaded with steel helmets, helmet liners, boots, several cases of Garand rifles, an old Maxim water-cooled machine gun, and their pride and joy, a case of 67mm recoilless rifles with three cases of shells.

Manny served a nondescript meal and outlined the plan: "I have been handed the problem of getting you aboard legally. You need not agree with me, but unless you have a better idea, I suggest you do it my way. This is it: Go ashore and take a taxi up into the hills to go sightseeing. Way up on top, you'll find a U.S. Air Force rest center. Go in there, have a good meal, and, if you like, get loaded. Your real reason for being there is so you can watch the harbor. Kill time until you see *Carp* sail. Make sure you do not start back until she is safely out of the harbor, and do not confuse her with that other ship. To tell them apart, watch the starboard flag. *Carp* is flying a Canadian red ensign; *Perch* has an Italian flag.

"Then, go dashing back into town and approach the first cop you see and jabber away at him about missing your ship. If you're not drunk, you had best spill some liquor on yourselves to smell drunk. After you are left high and dry, this is what should happen: American Export Line will have to post an illegal-entry bond for you before *Carp* can leave. The line will want its money back. So, you tell them that we'll hire you on as crew. See? It's quite simple."

"Can they throw us in the pokey, Manny?" Uri asked.

"Sure they can; they won't though."

"I'm game," Dave said. The others concurred.

"You might want to know that the U.S. consul here is a Sephardic Jew, distantly related to me. He may be of help if anything goes wrong."

"Thanks, Manny," Dave said. "Tell me, why did you guys tie up under this Limey frigate?"

"To watch their movies," Manny said.

"Don't let him kid you," Phil threw in. "They hauled us into Ponta when we were adrift."

"Adrift?"

"Yes," Manny said. "We drifted three days without power. I couldn't repair the engine. The frigate took us in tow in response to our SOS. The Portuguese impounded us until we get spare parts, and we talked some fly-boys into bringing them back on a training flight. They should be here today or tomorrow."

This did not sound very reassuring, but Dave let it pass.

They followed Manny's plan. When they were sure *Carp* was out of the harbor, they returned to town in varying degrees of drunkenness. Dave was stone-cold sober, but smelled like a pineapple-brandy factory. Even so, the plan backfired. The police took them to the U.S. consulate, not to American Export Line.

The consul was decidedly unfriendly: "What are you boys trying to do? I've heard all about the ever-decreasing passenger list of *Marine Carp*. The State Department warned me to keep an eye on this ship. But, knowing that you had had a rough time, I permitted you shore leave so you could booze and wench. It never occurred to me that any of you would be nutty enough to jump ship in the middle of the Atlantic.

"What sort of gratitude do I get? Three more take off. Didn't you sign an affidavit under oath in Lebanon that you would return to the United States?"

"Sure," Dave said, trying to feign drunkenness. "You know how it is. We had a coupla drinks. We didn't know we missed the boat. We just wanted to have fun."

"I don't buy it, boys. I won't buy it. I know what you had in mind. You heard that the consul here is Jewish and you thought you could pull a fast one. You figured I'd do nothing about it. But you were wrong. You are returning to the United States and it will not be on that broken-down heap in the harbor. Sure, I know all about it. I even know what its cargo is. That bunch will never leave Ponta, but you will. You're getting aboard *Marine Perch* and I'll see to it that you stay on her."

Two Marines escorted them out of the consulate. Together with the consul, they were driven to the dock where *Perch* was still tied up. On the bridge, the consul handed their passports to the captain with instructions to take them to New York with maximum precautions to keep them from jumping ship again.

Then, they were led to the stern by a master-at-arms, down several ladders, and into the paint locker. They were well below the water line. Here, a barred door, with hands and faces protruding between the bars, greeted them. The master-at-arms opened the door, pushed them in, and locked the door after them.

* * *

The trip lasted four weeks, all the way back to Lebanon. In the beginning, until the ship arrived at Genoa on its eastward leg, they were together with four Maltese who were being deported from the United States. The tiny brig, situated below the ship's screw, was crowded, hot, and unpleasant. There was only one toilet, and it had no seat. There was only one sink, and it had only cold, undrinkable seawater.

Their food was brought by a master-at-arms twice a day, along with a two gallon jugs of water for all seven of them.

After the Maltese were taken ashore, the three Betarim were allowed out of the brig until three hours before the vessel put into port. Then they remained locked up until the ship was out to sea again. But there was one exception even to that. When *Marine Perch* neared Gibraltar on its westward leg, they were locked up again. "We don't want any diving," the mate said as he escorted them below deck.

In New York harbor, after their release from the brig, they planned to split up so that no pictures could be taken of them together. An FBI agent came aboard at the Narrows and took away the passports that the purser had just returned to them. Dave had looked in his and found it stamped: "Valid for travel only to the United States of America."

At Betar headquarters on Second Avenue, they walked into a press conference. Dave was furious and walked out. He telephoned the national commander from a pay station and swore at him: "Joe, you should have your head examined. There should have been a lawyer up there instead of those reporters. Have you lost your marbles, you bastard? What the hell are you trying to do, keep us from ever getting to Israel?"

"Relax, Dave," Joe Kaplan answered calmly. "You can't leave even if you want to. The Betarim who returned on *Marine Carp* can't get out of the country and they didn't jump ship. Relax and sweat it out. Come back here and talk to the press. One of your

Haganah friends in Baalbek charged that the *Etzel* people had been holding target practice on the poop deck and you better straighten that out."

"Didn't he tell you how we threw Arab babies up in the air to use as targets? OK, Joe, I'll be right up."

MANNY I

The Cardozos came to America from Curacao before the Boston Tea Party, even before New Amsterdam became New York. The cemetery of the Spanish and Portuguese Jews in Lower Manhattan bears testimony to their lineage. An 1837 gravestone records the last burial of a Cardozo in the East.

During that fourth decade of the nineteenth century, the United States headed into one of its worst depressions and, with the expanding frontier, the family moved west. Uriah, youngest of three brothers, founded a small general store in Oklahoma; Joel became a homesteader, and Ezra, after several false starts, opened a bank in Colorado.

By the time Manny was born, the Cardozo name had taken on the aura that surrounds America's great—and wealthy—families. The family fortune, shared by the three brothers, stemmed from a foreclosure by Ezra's bank on a mortgage on a prospector's stake that had turned out to be silverless wasteland. In an effort to save the bank's equity, Ezra brought in a mining engineer from Pennsylvania to see if anything could be salvaged from the property. The gamble was sound; the Cardozo Lode bore its gold in the form of copper. Expeditious buying of adjoining tracts, in which the other brothers joined, consolidated the holding into a unified property. Their activities spread into other fields and the Cardozo Empire was born.

In 1917, young Henry Cardozo was appointed to the Advisory Commission of the Council for National Defense by President Wilson. Three other Jews were on the panel: Lessing J. Rosenwald, Bernard Baruch, and Samuel Gompers. Henry became the advisor on mineral resources.

Henry's son, Emanuel, matriculated to his father's alma mater, the Colorado School of Mines. However, Manny was more interested in machinery than in mining, and turned to diesels at Caltech, from which he was graduated in 1936. After his graduation, he spent a year in the Dutch East Indies and a year in Belgium, working in diesel repair shops, factories, and electrical generating plants. Returning to America, he joined a firm that manufactured tractors, generators, and locomotives. But not for long. When a controlling interest in that firm was gained by Henry and his cousins, it was absorbed into the Cardozo Empire and Manny was made a director. Manny quit. He wanted to make his way in life on his own merits and resented the family's interference.

His feud with his family had hardly begun when it came to a halt because of the mobilization that began a year before Pearl Harbor. Manny tried to enlist in the navy, but was rejected because of the malaria he had picked up in Sumatra, even though he had had very few relapses after treatment by Belgian doctors. The family asked him to take over Cardozo Diesel as president and chief operating officer and he agreed, but only because the company was now part of the war effort, turning out bulldozers, tanks, and engines for PT boats.

After the war, Cardozo Diesel moved its headquarters to New York's Park Avenue, bringing Manny to the city of his ancestors for the first time. He now found a purpose in life for which he had been searching: his roots.

From his Central Park West penthouse, he went into the ghettos of Williamsburg and the lower East Side where he observed his co-religionists as though he were a sociologist. He joined his family's old synagogue near Wall Street and became active in Zionism—a Zionism that to him meant the creation of a Hebrew state for those Jews who had no other place on Earth. His interest was quite impersonal. He, as an American Jew, would never live in such a state; the Hebrews in the displaced persons' camps would achieve their national destiny—if only they could escape their bondage in

Europe. As he was an American Jew, they would become Hebrew Jews.

Manny spent increasingly more time and money on the projects of the American League for a Free Palestine and the Hebrew Committee for National Liberation, both the creations of Hillel Kook, who called himself Peter Bergson to protect his family in British-occupied Palestine. Bergson and his *Irgun* colleagues quickly cashed in on the Cardozo name by making him national chairman of their fund-raising drive, the Palestine Freedom Appeal, Inc.

Manny was one of the few prominent Jews Bergson had been able to attract. Playwright and columnist Ben Hecht was another. There were a few other prominences, among them a few actors and actresses, but on the whole, most of the leading figures of Bergson's front organizations were not Jewish, including Senators Guy Gillette and Dennis Chavez and the Reverend Pierre van Passen.

Henry Cardozo was so annoyed at his son's cause that he spoke at a B'nai B'rith convention to attack his son's views publicly. All other Cardozos simply avoided Manny.

But the name of Manny Cardozo at the bottom of so many full-page newspaper ads became associated with their name despite all their disclaimers.

The most notorious of these ads was Ben Hecht's letter to the *Irgun*, in which he said the Jews of America "make a little holiday in their hearts" every time the *Irgun* attacked the British. It came at a time when Britain had turned over the future of its mandate to the United Nations after simply refusing to accept the recommendations of an Anglo-American commission of inquiry that Britain, itself, had asked for.

* * *

That year, 1948, the Arab invasion of Palestine began from the east and north. Manny bought a fishing trawler to run arms to the *Irgun* and—such was the nature of his enthusiasm—to lay claim to the first Hebrew merchant ship's run to North America.

The two-man crew of *Sally Jane* (named after Manny's secretary) was furnished by Betar with which the League was friendly, at least at that moment. With Manny as ship's engineer, they made preparations for the long voyage. Unexpectedly, Manny's naïve Zionism, especially the Hebrew–Jew controversy, led to friction after they put to sea. The two Betarim made his life miserable.

Over and over again, Manny heard the definition of an American Zionist as a Jew who collects money from a second Jew to send a third Jew to Palestine.

Manny, however, took pride in knowing that except for the controversy about Zionism, they accepted him as a peer and that his family name did not make any difference to them. It was the first time he had been able to forget his origins since he had sailed for the Indies.

* * *

After they had failed to add Dave and his companions to their crew, they faced permanent anchorage in the Azores. The Portuguese would not allow them to sail.

Henry Cardozo pounded on desks and acted in his "talking-to-the-union" manner at the offices of the League to learn where his son was. When he found out, he immediately called the State Department, thus getting the word from Washington to the hapless Jewish consul in Ponta del Gada, who had to act against his own beliefs by informing the Portuguese that *Sally Jane* was a smuggler.

Misha and Phil then advocated going to Palestine on a commercial vessel. Manny talked them out of it.

"I'll get the company plane over here from Paris and will take you there. As for myself. That's it! I don't want to join a foreign army and jeopardize my citizenship. Personally, Phil, I'd give you the same advice, but Misha is a Hebrew and can join the army. What do you say?"

For the first time, the two Betarim let him get away with his Hebrew–Jew business. They agreed.

Three days later, they circled the small airport at Tel Aviv in a Cardozo Diesel Stimson four-seater. Israel's Air Defense Command sent up a Messerschmitt, which intercepted them and signaled them to land. The fighter swooped back into the air when Manny's pilot touched down.

Phil got out and faced the soldiers who drove out to the plane, their Sten guns at the ready.

"We are Jews," he yelled over the noise of the prop. "We have come to join your army. Turn those guns around."

The others were ordered to come out of the plane with their hands up and were led to a hut that served the tiny airfield as an operations center. Their passports were inspected and stamped; then they were turned over to a khaki-clad policeman. They were driven to the former German Templar colony in Sarona where Manny was told to go into a building while the others waited outside with the policeman.

A bespectacled man in an open-collar white shirt and khaki shorts greeted Manny across a desk. "Welcome to Israel, Mr. Cardozo. I am Me'ir Shatir of the North American Section of the Ministry of Foreign Affairs. It is my duty to tell you that you have become a *cause celèbre* and an enigma. Perhaps you and I can cope with the difficulty.

"Your well-publicized voyage has caused your illustrious father to exert a great deal of pressure in America. The Department of State has requested that we not grant you the right to land because American passports are not valid for travel in this area under the American neutrality law. We, of course, reject any diminution of our sovereign right to welcome any Jew who wishes to come. But we are not sure of your purpose in coming here and we have delayed our reply to the American *aide mémoire*."

Manny, who had taken a seat without an invitation from Shatir, surprised even himself when he reacted against his father's meddling: "I have come here, provided I can do so as a civilian. I am a diesel engineer, Mr. Shatir, and I am certain you can use my skills here. But I have heard that you take all men into your army. If that is true, I shall leave immediately. My traveling companions, on the other hand, have come to enlist."

Shatir got up, came around his desk, and put his hand on Manny's shoulder. "You are under a misapprehension, Mr. Cardozo. We welcome you as a respected American guest. You are under no military-service obligation whatsoever."

Manny was given an immigrant's visa and driven to the Gat Rimon Hotel along the beach in Tel Aviv. Phil and Misha said good-bye to him and stayed in Sarona, now renamed Hakirya.

Manny discovered that the Jewish settlements of Israel that were not served by the grid of the Palestine Electric Company made their own electricity in generating plants of their own. It was suggested that he help keep those plants running. The army made a similar proposal. Many was not interested.

Manny wanted to set up a Cardozo Diesel plant to assemble tractors and generators where Israelis—whom he still called Hebrews—would learn to service and use diesels. He so insisted on this that he was sent back to Hakirya to talk to the prime minister.

David Ben Gurion welcomed the proposal: "As you know, Mr. Cardozo, in this country we of the labor movement first had to create the jobs before we could organize the workers into labor unions. We had to have means of production before there were workers to organize. We had to reclaim the land before the farmers could work the fields and sow their crops. Thus, the Jewish state was fashioned—long before the fourteenth May. But I would be happier if your company would enter a partnership with our labor movement, the Histadrut."

"Mr. Prime Minister," Manny replied, remembering some of the anti-Histadrut views of Peter Bergson's people, "that's totally out of the question. I am not certain I can convince my board of directors of the wisdom of making an investment here in view of the many unanswered questions about your economy; but I could never convince those very pragmatic people to accept any sort of partnership. You may very well get no plant at all."

Ben Gurion clucked his tongue, realizing that Manny's brand

of Zionism had no use for the Histadrut, a labor union that owned almost all the industries in Israel, thus making Histadrut the owner of the means of production that classical Marxism reserved to the people. But Ben Gurion stayed silent.

"If you are opposed to a Cardozo Diesel plant, perhaps you have ideas of other means by which I can help the Hebrew state?"

"Yes, I think so. We need your experience. If you could speak Hebrew, you could teach our youth. If you could speak Hebrew, you could teach our army and our navy. If you could speak Hebrew, you could teach at the Technion. But you will learn Hebrew. You will easily find work as an engineer, but I fear you will reject our wage scales."

"I have not come here to get richer, Mr. Prime Minister. I will accept no pay. But I do want to plan for the future. To get back to the plant . . . it would provide a splendid opportunity to train your people. I do know the problems of teaching young people about machines. I learned this in the Dutch East Indies. I still believe that, in the long view, making the machines will prove a greater asset than using me as a teacher."

"I agree," Ben Gurion said. "But you would lose money. Only by a partnership with labor, which can afford to absorb some of your losses, would you overcome the cost of importing the parts and bringing in technicians. Please, do me a favor. I do not wish to have you listen only to an old labor organizer. We have a manufacturers' association. I would be happy to arrange a meeting for you. Why not talk to them?"

"That's fine," Manny said. "Agreed."

"When you have decided, I assure you, you will need no appointment to see me. My staff will be instructed that my door is always open to you."

* * *

Manny did talk to manufacturers, entrepreneurs, and bankers. They told him the tax picture was unclear; the labor partnership was a kiss of death; costs of production would be phenomenally high compared to his American experience, especially because Israel's productivity was low in manufacturing; electricity was expensive, and technical skills were abysmally low. But, they told him, by all means he should open his plant.

His stubborn streak got the better of him. He decided that the odds being so hugely stacked against him, the challenge was worth going back to his board and putting on a good fight to set up the plant.

Knowing he would lose his passport for violating the neutrality act if he returned to New York, he decided to arrange things by teletype. But Israel's teletype connections had not been restored, so he ordered the Cardozo Diesel pilot to fly him to Rome where he had a teletype machine installed in his hotel room.

The wires buzzed, but he could get no decision. His secretary, Sally Jane, reported that his family's representatives on the board were stalling while the independent directors had split on going along with Manny.

"WHAT TIME IS IT IN DENVER?" he typed.

Sally Jane replied: "FOUR ANTE MERIDIAN."

"WILL CALL DAD AT SEVEN THIRTY."

"GOOD LUCK, BUT IT WON'T WORK."

When Manny called Henry Cardozo, he was going right to the top, knowing that his cousins and his uncles took their cues from the family's emperor. Hanging up, he knew he had lost. The family would oppose his every move.

Henry's anger over Manny's Israeli adventure and his shame because of Manny's role as a showpiece of an extremist ideology made him adamant. He wanted nothing whatsoever to do with Israel.

To Manny, his father's rebuff was a signal to break away.

"Father," he said, "I shall show you how a free man can exist without need of Cardozo money. I am tendering my resignation at Cardozo Diesel. From now on, I shall stand on my own two feet and I expect you to stop interfering. Wish me luck."

Henry thundered, almost without need of the transatlantic cable: "I'll be damned if I will."

Manny quit the firm and ordered his lawyers to sell his belongings and to transfer his funds to a Swiss bank. Then he bought a jeep and set sail for Israel. On his return, he called Ben Gurion from Haifa.

"What do you propose to do now, Mr. Cardozo?" the prime minister asked.

"I think I'll get busy learning Hebrew. Meanwhile, I'll try to repair some of those generators out in the villages. I'll let you know when I'm ready to work in a more responsible capacity."

"I am glad, Mr. Cardozo," he was told. "I hope you will become an inspiration to many, many other Americans to come to build with us a home for our people. I wish you the very best of luck."

Manny noticed that the good wishes he bad sought from his father came from this Socialist politician whom Manny did not quite trust.

JACK AND NAOMI III

They both volunteered for the army right after disembarking from *Marine Perch*. Jack was assigned to an artillery unit training in Pardess Katz; Naomi was assigned to the *Chen*, the women's army. Her first assignment was in the adjutant's department at army headquarters. When ranks were instituted, she became an officer as the adjutant for *Chen*. She was tied to a desk until she was discharged to the reserves. Jack was not as lucky.

The army had only a few pieces of artillery and had to use its few guns both for operations and for training. On one of the journeys between the artillery school in Pardess Katz and the front lines near Latrun, Jack was injured as a gun carriage broke off the trailer hook of a truck to which he and others were attempting to attach it. The gun carriage landed on top of him, breaking several ribs and his pelvis. When he was discharged from the military hospital at Sarafand, he was judged medically unfit for duty and faced his future dependent on two canes or, years later, aluminum crutches.

Naomi was given leave to help him get established in Jerusalem. Their apartment had been shelled and, being unable to find other lodging, they moved in with Naomi's parents. The Hebrew University, driven off its Mount Scopus campus, allowed Jack to restart classes at its substitute campus in the New City.

Naomi came out of the army with the three *felafels* of a captain. Still in uniform, she went to the Hebrew University to meet him as he left classes.

"Ya'akov," she said, as she took him by the arm to help him to the bus stop, "I am relieved of my vow. We have a state. Now I can start to live for myself. I shall apply at the university and also read law. We shall have a joint practice: 'Ben Horin and Ben Horin.' "

* * *

During her second year of study, they used Jack's disability preference to obtain an apartment. They exchanged presents. Jack gave Naomi a photomontage he had cooked up in a friend's darkroom. He tied it up like a diploma with a blue-and-white ribbon.

"As we move into our very own home, Naomi, I want to present you with this new wedding contract. If you accept it, you must obey my every wish, be my total slave, forget about being a leader among our people, and dedicate your life completely to me, even before Jabotinsky, Menachem Begin, or anyone else. Do you agree?"

"No, you stinker. Even if you are jesting, my country will always come first. Gimme that!"

She grabbed it and pulled off the ribbon. When she had carefully unrolled it, she shrieked with laughter. She kissed him and thanked him, then said: "For this marriage contract, I'll agree to anything."

The photomontage showed, among other things English sergeant's stripes, Israeli captain's pips, an old-fashioned spider microphone, a tape recorder, a *Chen* kepi, a headline about Irgun Irma from an English newspaper, a pair of high-heeled shoes, a glimpse of black lace, Jack's flag flying on the Funkturm, the Tower of David as seen from their old apartment, and a sign saying "Ben Horin and Ben Horin, barristers and solicitors."

"When we open our office, Ya'akov," she said, "it will be on the wall next to our diplomas."

* * *

In 1953, they were called to the bar. Now it was Naomi's turn to give him a gift. it was an oil painting by the *Irgun*'s most celebrated artist, Zippora Brenner, who usually worked in watercolors. Zippora made an exception for Naomi , saying, "I hung on your every word on every broadcast, so if you want oil, what can I do? I'll paint in oil."

Zippora painted a man in an American uniform and a *keffiyeh* in front of the Arch of Titus. The man had his back to the bas relief showing the removal of the Temple treasures and was walking away from the arch. The top of the arch was covered in the sheets Jack had hoisted, and the inscription now read "IUDEA RESURRECTA!" Naomi had thought "ROMA CAPTA!" was irrelevant.

The wall of their office thus recorded a goodly part of their lives with their pictures, their Israeli army discharge papers, their diplomas, and a portrait of Ze'ev Jabotinsky.

On Jack's desk stood a photo of Naomi holding their first-born, Ruth, named for Jack's mother's Hebrew name.

For the first nine months of their joint practice, hardly able to pay the office rent, they stood on principle. They would accept no cases arising out of the agreement with West Germany for the payment of reparations to Israelis. Their Herut Party termed the entire deal "blood money."

But then they got a case rising out of Stalin's charges against a group of Jewish doctors who, Stalin claimed, were conspiring to kill him and overthrow the Soviet régime. It became known as the Doctors' Plot.

Veterans of *Etzel* and their allies in the Fighters for the Freedom of Israel, called *Lechi*, watched and listened in horror as Stalin's anti-Semitism grew and as the two English speaking announcers on Radio Moscow—Olga Danilova and Sergei Rubin—fumed about "cosmopolitans," the new codeword for Jews. Every listener in Israel felt sorry for Rubin, who was assumed to be a Jew himself.

And then three *Lechi* veterans decided to teach Josef Stalin a lesson, just like the one they had taught John Bull when their organization killed Lord Moyne in Cairo in 1946. Singly and dressed in Arab clothing they approached the Soviet Embassy on the comer of Shadall Street and Rothschild Boulevard in Tel Aviv.

They were shown to seats in a consular waiting room. One of them was wearing the Arab pantaloons that include a pouch dangling down between the legs that is intended to receive the Prophet, who, it is written, is to be reborn of man. A Soviet official sat at a desk in the waiting room. One of the "Arabs" approached him and started asking questions in machine-gun Arabic, which resulted in the Russian's brief departure from the room, leading the "Arab" to an interpreter.

As soon as they were gone, the pouch in the pantaloons was cut open and the bomb was placed under the Russian's desk. They returned to their seats and waited for their companion to return. When he did, they started a loud discussion with him. He made a sign of disgust and left the embassy. Soon, the other two followed.

In proper *Lechi* tradecraft, a phone call alerted the Russians that their embassy would blow up in fifteen minutes and urged them to evacuate. The three watched the Russians pouring out a few minutes later from the villa across the street in which they changed back into khaki shorts and sandals.

But *Lechi* wasn't *Lechi* any more. They were apprehended and charged within days by the Tel Aviv police. The Herut Party hired a battery of lawyers to defend them, including the unknown firm of Ben Horin and Ben Horin.

Naomi, in what she called her first "starring role" since *The Voice of Fighting Zion*, represented Rafael, the man who had worn the pantaloons. She positively established that Rafi was in Haifa on the day of the bombing. This was not *Lechi* tradecraft; it was simple perjury.

The other two were convicted; Rafi was acquitted.

And then the cases came more easily. Their bylines began to appear in the party newspaper, *Herut*, with legal arguments supporting Herut policy in favor of a written constitution, opposing the government's retention of Britain's emergency laws, and opposing German reparations. Ben Gurion's government was the target of all their attacks.

One day, while Jack was in court, Sha'ul Nachmani, general

secretary of the Israel Communist Party, came to the office and confronted Naomi: "Mrs. Ben Horin, I know you are not in sympathy with my party or its aims. Nevertheless, your husband and you have been championing civil liberties and appear to believe in freedom of the press. I hope you will take my case."

"Just a minute, Mr. Nachmani. I have not heard of a case in which you are involved," Naomi said, rising from behind her desk and shaking his hand. When she had seated him and returned to her chair, he went on.

"It has not yet started. You see, last night in the Knesset I made a speech on the secret defense budget. It will be printed in this afternoon's *Kol Ha'am*, I am shopping for a lawyer in advance because I know I will be charged with violations of national security laws."

"Mr. Nachmani. As you know very well, I am an Israeli nationalist, a follower of Jabotinsky." She pointed to his photograph on the wall, and he followed her gaze. "I believe you have come to the wrong lawyer. I also believe that when the very existence of the state is threatened, civil rights do not take precedence."

"Wait, Mrs. Ben Horin. Read my speech. It divulges no secrets. I only point out that the defense budget, which is secret, is used to cover expenditures that have no connection with defense. The defense budget has become a Mapai grab-bag. Most Knesset members do not question anything which the cabinet hides under a secrecy label. These money bills are seldom discussed. Go ahead, read it."

Sha'ul walked around the office looking at its framed objects. Then he sat down and picked up *Herut*, leafing through it with evident distaste.

"Mr. Nachmani," Naomi said, holding her new horn-rimmed glasses in front of her, "if what you say is true, I shall accept your case. How can you substantiate your charges?"

"That's the trouble. The defense budget bill contains these items. But my party does not have access to the version that will become law. We are barred from the Defense Committee, as you know." Naomi accepted this as a dig, since even her tiny Herut Party was represented on the committee although it held only seven seats in the 120-seat Knesset.

"However," he went on, "I had lunch the other day with a young party member who works at the Government Printer. He told me what it says, and I tabled a question on the defense budget that the defense minister refused to answer."

"And then you made your speech?"

"Not quite. I went to your friend Eli Even-Zahav, and asked him, as a member of the Defense Committee. He was, understandably, most cautious in speaking to me, but he did say that I was correct on some of my charges. He refused to tell me which were true and which were not. I was grateful that a Fascist would help a Communist even to that extent. Then, I made my speech."

"How was it received?" she answered, ignoring the pejorative.

"Strangely. When I began, Mr. Speaker cleared the house. Then he warned me that I was not to continue until the sergeants-at-arms had reported the security of the house. When I was through, he ordered that the record be stricken. I challenged this and all but the Mapai and the Orthodox joined me. The Orthodox abstained, leaving Mapai all alone and in the minority. The speech would appear in the record. Mr. Speaker then ruled that the defense minister could censor the record of the proceedings of the Knesset. Whatever appears in the published record of debates will be printed in our party newspaper. The record is a public document. Thus, if my paper prints the speech as the defense minister permits, the document is privileged. Despite that, I am certain that the paper will be confiscated and that I will be charged with violation of the State Secrets Act. Now, will you take my case?"

* * *

Late that afternoon, *Kol Ha'am*'s entire press run was seized by the government. Sha'ul Nachmani's speech had been on its front page under a banner headline: "What is Secret in Mapai's Defense Budget?"

Nachmani was arrested at his seat in the Knesset, a violation of his parliamentary immunity. A Communist Knesset member called Naomi at home, and she quickly called the police to inquire. She got no answer. She next called the attorney general: "Chanan, this is Naomi Ben Horin. I have been retained to represent Sha'ul Nachmani . . . "

She could hear him sputtering as if he had swallowed the telephone.

"Are you kidding?"

"No, Chanan, I am not. Now listen to me. I want to know where my client has been taken and I want to know the charge. I want him freed on bail immediately. I am prepared to post bail."

"You're crazy, Naomi. I thought you were an old *Etzelnik*."

"I am, but I am also sworn to the defense of the law."

"I still don't believe it."

"Stop stalling, Chanan. Where is Sha'ul?"

"I am not at liberty to say."

"All right, Chanan. I know we still don't have a constitution. But I do know that *habeas corpus* is an implied right, even of Israeli citizens. The instant I hang up, I shall go to the chief justice and demand a writ of *habeas corpus*."

"Listen, Naomi. You are going too far. The man is a Communist. Remember?"

"Yes. And he is an MK and an Israeli citizen. Remember?"

"What has that got to do with it?"

"Do we have two laws in Israel, Chanan? One for Zionists and one for anti-Zionists?"

"You know better than to ask that, God damn it. Go ahead! Call the fucking chief justice. I don't think that will get you very far with him, either."

"We shall fucking well see," she answered, slamming the receiver.

The chief justice came to the phone, and Naomi explained her purpose. She volunteered to come to his house to get a writ.

"For whom, Mrs. Ben Horin?"

"Member of the Knesset Sha'ul Nachmani."

"Really? I hadn't expected your practice to be doing so poorly that you would stoop to his defense."

"I take it, Sir, that you do not feel that my first responsibility is to the law?"

"Of course it is," he agreed. "What makes you say that?"

"My client's legal rights have been seduced, Sir. As a member of the bar it is my privilege and my duty to defend the rights and privileges of my clients—and to defend the law."

"Yes, of course, but he is a Communist and . . . "

" . . . and I am a member of Herut!"

"Precisely!"

"So much the more reason for me to make sure that I have no reason to be ashamed of my country, Chief Justice."

"Very well," he said, after they went through legal niceties for a few minutes. "Come to my house. I shall issue a writ."

Naomi got to Katamon a half hour later, taking the same bus she had taken to make her *Voice of Fighting Zion* broadcasts. She got off at the same stop. It was the same house!

He came to the living room from upstairs in a purple silk dressing gown over his black trousers. He went directly to a Biedermeier version of a Governor Winthrop desk, opened it, and sat himself down, leaving Naomi standing. He signed a paper and turned to her, "I wish I could understand what made you accept this case."

"Am I acting in violation of the best traditions of the bar, Sir?"

"I would not want to say that. But right after you hung up, the attorney general called me and asked if I thought your behavior might not be worthy of study by my ethical practices collegium."

"Would you want me to take that as a threat?"

"Nooooo! But the attorney general sounded concerned. He may wish to have you suspended from the right to appear until the collegium has informed itself about your motives."

"I deeply regret to hear that, Chief Justice. If you will excuse me now? I must go. Before I do, though, permit me to ask you to take me into your pantry."

"My pantry? What on earth for?"

"I know this house quite well. I broadcast from it for nearly two years. This house was *The Voice of Fighting Zion*. I'd like to see your pantry, please."

He took her there. Without asking his permission, she opened a cupboard and used her fingernails to pry at a piece of wood. It came off, revealing an empty space behind it.

"I was just making sure we took away the booby trap with which we would have made this into our Masada in the event of discovery."

She put the panel back, smiled, and said, "You are safe, Chief Justice. You will not be blown up in the cause of Hebrew freedom. Well, I'm off to find Sha'ul."

"I am able to help you on that. He has been placed in confinement by the Israel Defense Force at Camp Marcus."

"By the army?"

"Yes, I questioned that, too. Chanan assured me that it was a mistake. He will be transferred to civilian authority."

"So where shall I present your writ?"

"Try Camp Marcus. If he is not there, I am sure the attorney general will advise you further."

For the next three hours, Naomi rushed around Jerusalem, mostly by taxi. At two o'clock, she called home: "Ya'akov, our phone is tapped. Come to where Akiva was seized."

He drove to Rehavia in a roar and stopped in front of their old apartment house. Naomi was seated on the curb, her elbows on her knees.

"What on earth?" he asked.

"*Yakh, Yakoub*, I am in trouble."

"What's up?"

"The Nachmani case broke."

"So?"

"They have him incommunicado someplace. I cannot find him

to serve this *habeas corpus*. And they're bringing me up on charges before the ethics collegium and may suspend me."

"I didn't think they would stoop so low. Where have you been?"

"First, to Camp Marcus. They had him transferred to Chanan's office. Chanan had him taken to the central police station. I felt like I was turning myself back into Irgun Irma going there, especially after I learned that the chief justice lives in the house from which I used to broadcast. The police said Sha'ul had not arrived. So I went back to Chanan's house. It was empty. Can you drive me awhile?"

"Sure. Where to?"

"Let's try hotels. Chanan is hiding so I cannot serve him. Let's find him."

At the third hotel, Jack noticed three policemen drowsing in the lobby. He whispered to her: "This is it."

"OK, Ya'akov. Go serve Chanan with the writ. You are an officer of the court, too."

"Why me?"

"So Chanan will not think that I am all alone in this, against your wishes."

He agreed. He extricated himself from the driver's seat and, while leaning on the car, worked his way to its trunk. Naomi came around and helped pull out his lightweight wheelchair, opened it, shut the trunk, and wheeled him into the lobby.

She asked for Chanan at the desk and was handed a house phone and told to dial a room. When Naomi walked over to a house phone, he turned and wheeled his way to the elevator. After his knock, Chanan came to the door in his pajamas, startled to see Jack. "Chanan Aharoni, I hereby serve you with a writ of *habeas corpus* for Sha'ul Nachmani."

Without another word, Chanan picked up the phone, called another room, and ordered that Sha'ul be brought to his room.

* * *

Getting Sha'ul out of custody was only the beginning of a complex legal battle. Chanan's first move, as he had indicated to the chief justice, was to have Naomi suspended during an investigation of her ethics. Jack dropped his cases, to take on hers.

With the exception of newspapers on the far left, most Israeli papers started to take an interest in the academic discussion of freedom of the press. The nearly independent *Ha'aretz* editorialized against the harassment of Sha'ul's attorneys as well as the violation of his immunities as a member of the Knesset, including his arrest inside the chamber and his detention by the army.

The press campaign put pressure on Chanan, but his bag of tricks was still full. His crucial blow came on the eve of trial, after Naomi's suspension was lifted and she had been completely exonerated by the ethics collegium. That evening, she was called out on an army alert. The secret word came over the radio at the six o'clock newscast. She did not get home until eight the following morning and arrived in court in uniform, now with the single insignia of a major.

"My apologies to the Court, Your Honor, that I appear in uniform. I have not had time to change. Since I do not wish another continuance, may I ask the Court to allow me to proceed?"

She was asked to borrow a judge's robe from an attendant.

The trial lasted five days. Sha'ul was fined one thousand pounds for violation of the State Secrets Act and an additional five hundred each for publishing a slander against the minister of defense and for unauthorized use of a classified document, the published record of the proceedings of the Knesset.

Naomi appealed immediately.

The Supreme Court, sitting as a court of appeals, reversed all three verdicts, making a point to note that *Divrei Ha-Knesset*, the public record of debate, was not and could not be considered a classified document.

As a result of public reaction to the case, Sha'ul Nachmani, the Communist general-secretary, won for all members of the Knesset the right of sanctuary inside the precincts of the Knesset under the Members of the Knesset (Rights and Immunities) Law.

YOKHANAN II

On his last leave, Yokhanan met a classmate from the Hebrew University who worked on *Ha'aretz*. Before the leave was up, Yokhanan had also joined the staff of the newspaper.

With money borrowed from his uncles he bought an apartment on Tel Aviv's Bialik Street, right across the street from an Erich Mendelsohn house that reminded him of home in Rosh Pina.

Slowly, he settled down to the chore of earning a living. Since he had never been greatly interested in politics, except where politics affected his anti-Orthodox campaign, Yokhanan's affiliation with the almost nonpartisan *Ha'aretz* was fortunate. The paper was the most impartial in Israel even though it had some links to the General Zionist Party.

Yokhanan's writing won no prizes, but several of his articles on religious issues brought him into prominence. At the first parliamentary elections, the General Zionists placed Yokhanan's name near the bottom of their full list of 120 candidates, only a handful of whom had any chance of winning a seat in the Knesset. It was more an honor than anything, but Yokhanan campaigned as if he was sure that the whole list would be elected under Israel's complex system of proportional representation.

He even found himself agreeing with a member of the Herut Party, a party he really disliked, but right is right and this was such a case.

Eri Jabotinsky, son of the party's founder, had got up in the Constituent Assembly that preceded the Knesset elections. He began to speak in French. The speaker, Joseph Sprinzak, ruled him out of order.

"How can I be out of order, Mr. Speaker, if we have no Constitution that says I cannot speak Pushtu or Urdu here?"

Sprinzak, a veteran member of Ben Gurion's Mapai Party, ruled him out of order just the same.

So Jabotinsky tried speaking English.

Again he was ruled out of order.

So Jabotinsky began to read the Declaration of Independence, in Hebrew:

"We hereby declare that, as from the termination of the mandate at midnight, the 14th-15th May, 1948, and pending the setting up of duly elected bodies of the State in accordance with a Constitution to be drawn up by the Constituent Assembly not later than the 1st October, 1948, the National Council shall act as the Provisional State Council, and that the National Administration shall constitute the Provisional Government of the Jewish State, which shall be known as Israel."

Sprinzak pounded his gavel as Jabotinsky ignored him and kept reading from the document which was on the desk of every member of the Constituent Assembly. The speaker signaled to the sergeant-at-arms and Jabotinsky was dragged off the floor.

Yokhanan, of course, wanted a constitution as much as Jabotinsky, if for different reasons. He wanted definitions of "Who is a Jew?" and a spelling-out of what the British feared to do in 1922 in their Order in Council that served as the mandate's constitution. The British simply left things as they had been under the Turks. Israel was doing likewise, thus giving immense power to religious establishments and no power at all to those who were not included in those communities.

This left religious courts in charge of marriage, divorce, inheritance, and other aspects of life that Yokhanan wanted to fall under the rule of civil—and secular—law. In his mind, the same laws should apply to Jewish, Arab, Christian, and atheist citizens of Israel.

When Yokhanan wrote a signed opinion piece in Ha'aretz backing Jabotinsky's stand, General Zionist leaders called him to ask if he had gone crazy. He was threatened with having his name struck from the electoral list. He told them to go to hell. His name, however, was taken off. One of the party's leaders called on Yokhanan at the *Ha'aretz* office to tell him that he was being "watched" and should clear some of his more controversial points of view with the party.

The General Zionists fared poorly in the national elections, but Yokhanan was appointed to a seat on the Tel Aviv City Council when a General Zionist councilman died. Yokhanan reasoned that his appointment had to be because there was a split in the party.

* * *

At one City Council session he was attacked by Moshe Korb, a member of an extreme religious party, because of his paper's alleged anti-religious bias. The issue was an innocuous item favoring the playing of football on Saturdays, the only day Israelis were free from work.

Yokhanan went to the files of *Ha'aretz* to look up Korb's background and found that he had been one of the key troublemakers in the debates ten years earlier about the Teheran orphans.

He started writing an article:

> It has been almost ten years since a judgment of Solomon dictated whether the 700 orphans brought here from Iran would be brought up as secular or religious Jews.
>
> The orphans were among the last Polish children to escape the Holocaust and were delivered to Iran by the Russians. And then Zionist leaders fought over them.
>
> When they arrived here, the younger children were given a catechism: Did your mother light candles for the Sabbath? Did your father say morning prayers?
>
> The answers determined whether they would go to religious or secular schools.
>
> One of those braying for sending all of the orphans to religious schools was Moshe Korb . . .

But he got no further. Was it fair to reopen the wounds of 1943? Was he using his position on the newspaper to advance his own goals? He had found a *Ha'aretz* editorial backing his views, but all that was way back then and not now. For now, Yokhanan felt he had to stick to the issues of today.

At the Tel Aviv municipal elections a year later, Yokhanan ran as a General Zionist. He won. In the City Council chamber, he surprised everyone by becoming an outspoken opponent of the left—the Mapai and Mapam parties, the Histadrut labor federation, and the most extreme of the three kibbutz movements. It really did not seem to matter in that chamber, but the city did business with the Histadrut's sick fund, contracted with Koor Industries, the large conglomerate owned by the Histadrut, and negotiated labor contracts with its employees, most of whom belonged to the Histadrut.

On the council floor, he charged Histadrut with being the unelected government of Israel and said that Prime Minister David Ben Gurion was exceeding his authority and power by pulling Histadrut strings that affected every person in Israel.

The General Zionists thought he was more trouble than he was worth and asked him to vacate the seat in favor of a party regular.

He wrote in the newsweekly *Ha'olam Hazeh* that began:

> I am not giving up my seat in the Tel Aviv City Council. I won it by campaigning for it under my own name, not because I was put on a party list. I promised the voters where I would stand; I stand on my principles. Let the General Zionists kick me out of the party, but if they want my seat, they will have to run someone to replace me who will gladly promote the welfare of Histadrut against the welfare of the people of this city . . .

In addition to his work on *Ha'aretz*, he wrote often for *Ha'olam Hazeh* and read a fortnightly English-language segment on *Kol Zion LaGola*, the international broadcasting station that still called itself "The Voice of Zion to the Diaspora."

After Yokhanan made fun of that exclusive name in *Ha'aretz*—charging that its meaning was that non-Jews were not welcome as listeners—the name of the broadcasting service was changed to *Kol Yisrael*, "The Voice of Israel," which had been the name of *Haganah*'s broadcasting station.

His personal life, however, did not unfold so successfully. He quarreled with his uncles who, over his objection, wanted to sell out his inherited share in the business to collect the money he owed them for his Tel Aviv apartment. He argued with Moshe HaCohen during reserve maneuvers, best of friends though they had become. He acquired and lost girlfriends in rapid succession.

His interests were varied and the number of his acquaintances read like a *Who's Anybody in Israel?* He had a season ticket to the Israel Philharmonic Orchestra, was on the committee to build a new concert hall to be called the Mann Auditorium, belonged to an amateur dramatic group, drank the finest liquor to be found in the finest homes in Tel Aviv, and slept with some undeniably beautiful girls. But he was dissatisfied.

He found that he was learning to respect many of the people he met, regardless of party, movement, or religious considerations. This decreased the fervor in his anti-religious campaign as he became convinced that there should be tolerance for all viewpoints. Still, he insisted that Orthodoxy be disestablished and that the Law of Return, which guaranteed every Jew the right to enter Israel, should apply to Jews who drew their Judaism from their fathers despite non-Jewish mothers, should include Jews from the Soviet Union whether they were circumcised or not and no matter how little Jewishness they observed, provided that either the Soviets of they themselves considered them Jewish.

Ha'aretz, which realized that he was attracting readers, wanted to muzzle him just a bit because he was embarrassing its General Zionist owners. He was made military editor and was told that he could write opinion pieces only if they fell in the field of his new assignment.

* * *

In 1953, Yokhanan met a girl whose views somewhat paralleled his. She did not like the Mapai—Histadrut—kibbutz movement steamroller; she believed in disestablishmentarianism, and she was a writer. There was just one little hitch. Mary was a Baptist who had attended the recently opened Brandeis University and had become a Zionist there. She was in Israel under an immigrant's visa and as a Christian.

Yokhanan and Mary traveled all over the country. They spent two weeks together at the Dolphin House. He took her to Rosh Pina and took her through the Erich Mendelsohn house there, now the home of his uncle Menachem. He took her to Golania to meet Moshe HaCohen, the commander of his reserve unit. From there, they went to Eilat to go swimming and he said, "I captured this place. I did it so I could bring you here on our honeymoon. Will you marry me?"

She said yes, but they had no idea how hard it would be to do that.

The rabbinate refused to perform the ceremony unless Mary converted to Judaism. The U.S. embassy would not marry them because it obeys all local law, and marriages across religious lines are illegal in Israel. There was no way to obtain a civil marriage and Mary's minister in Jerusalem said his hands were tied by Israeli law. He suggested they leave the country to marry.

That was also impossible. Israel at that time issued exit visas sparingly to those whom it trusted when they wandered into the big, wide, non-Jewish world. The visas were ostensibly required to conserve hard currency during a period of national austerity and such visas were granted or withheld in accordance with the purpose of the intended journey. In this case, the visa would not be granted because the reason for Yokhanan's desire to get out of the country was too well known. Ben Gurion was quoted as saying that a trip abroad, during a time when there was extreme shortage of hard currency, only for the purpose of performing a marriage, was out of the question.

"Jon," Mary said. "I don't care if we marry or not. Why make a fuss? Let's continue as we are and the hell with them all. I'll even be able to bring you legal bread during Passover from the French hospital in Jaffa. The hell with all of them."

So, Mary and Jon, as she preferred to call him, lived on Bialik Street. The tax collector permitted Yokhanan to file as a married man; the army refused to allow him married pay during his annual call-up.

They collaborated on an English-language novel, *Convert*, about an assimilated American Jew's conversion to the Episcopalian faith. When it was published in New York, it caused hardly a murmur in Israel, but Steimatzky's chain of foreign-language bookstores refused to sell it.

When his elected term was up on City Council, he ran as an independent, something that had never been done before either in pre-independence *Yishuv* elections or in any election since statehood. In her Brandeis-accented Hebrew, Mary climbed the soapbox in front of the Mograbi Theater when Yokhanan finished haranguing the crowd:

"Fellow citizens, and you are my fellow citizens: My husband and I are fighting for the right to have the religious freedom that has been the goal of all Jews throughout the centuries. We oppose the very idea of a Russian Pale of Settlement or a German Schutzjude, a protected Jew who may only marry with the permission of the government. We think every Jew everywhere should be able to do what he or she wants when it comes to faith and have all rights and privileges of life. And we don't just want these freedoms for Jews. We want them for every man, woman, and child in Tel Aviv, even for the *goyishe* wife of an Israeli war hero, the man who conquered Sinai and took Eilat.

"We don't believe that butcher shops need armor-plated windows to protect them from religious fanatics. We believe it is wrong for children in the Tel Aviv public schools to be forced to take religious instruction that is against the wishes of their parents in schools that are supported by taxes from the religious as well as the irreligious.

"We believe that freedom to abstain from religion, to go see a soccer game on the Sabbath—the only day off from work most of us have—is as sacred a right as having the right to attend any synagogue, Orthodox, Conservative, or Reform.

"But that choice is not available here, either. You are Orthodox, or you are a nothing, a piece of dirt, a mote in the eye of the chief rabbi!

"We believe women should have the right to ask for and obtain a divorce. She should never have to beg her husband for her freedom. It is not his to give. We believe in freedom for everyone. We deny no one the right to practice as he or she pleases provided only that he or she allows others the same rights and privileges.

"Vote for Yokhanan Galili. A vote for Yokhanan is a vote for freedom . . . "

* * *

Yokhanan was re-elected—and as an independent. His apartment house was soon picketed by ringleted Orthodox youths. His mail box was stuffed with poison-pen letters which the authorities at Israel Post were unwilling to investigate. When Yokhanan charged that the Orthodox minister of posts was responsible for the inertia, he was sued for libel.

He became a national figure. His pro-Americanism—predicated on the American separation of church and state—made him a popular speaker for an odd assortment of groups, although he was shunned by the entire center and right.

Inside City Council, Yokhanan introduced a flurry of motions to memorialize the Knesset for religious freedom and of bills on the licensing of butcher shops and Sabbath transport. His jibes and comments were ignored in Jerusalem by a government forced to keep together a precarious coalition of Orthodox and left-wing parties, even though leading members of all three Socialist parties told him repeatedly—but privately—that they agreed with his every word.

* * *

Mary's pregnancy precipitated a crisis. An exit visa was now an absolute necessity. Yokhanan asked Ya'akov Ben Horin for help. Following Jack's instructions, Yokhanan and Mary went to the chief rabbinate of Tel Aviv and sought permission to marry. As usual, it was refused because Mary would not convert. Yokhanan asked for the ruling in writing.

With the ruling in his hand, Yokhanan went to the Ministry of the Interior to seek an exit visa so he could marry and give his child a name. The minister got tough:

"Galili, I would not be surprised if you got your wife in a family way only so you could embarrass the government and create a cabinet crisis. I would be willing to believe that this is all part of your continuing campaign to damage the State of Israel in the eyes of the world. Thank God, your book has not yet appeared in a Hebrew translation, but I am certain you are working on that too.

"I have had to act on your exit visa three times. You are very persistent, and I know you are a ranking officer in the Israel Defense Force. We all know you are basically a good Zionist. We know you are not an anti-Semite, a Communist, or an Arab agent, although you have been called all these things by the Orthodox members of the government coalition. You have become the darling of the Communists and now appear to have picked up some support on the right. If we would allow this to come to a vote, we might have to go before the Knesset without allies. The government would fall, all because you had to go and get your wife pregnant."

Yokhanan's fists clenched. He bit his lip, but said nothing, following Jack's advice to await a wiggle or a wriggle from Ben Gurion.

The minister asked if he couldn't have waited until there was an all-labor government.

"No, goddamn it, I cannot wait," Yokhanan exploded. "The baby is due in six months. An all-labor government may not happen in my lifetime. Besides, as a small child I learned what our beautiful Jewish children do to a half-Jew. I can't imagine what they would do to one who is a bastard, as well."

"Under the law, the child would be a Christian—after its mother."

"And what name would you propose to give this child?" he asked, noting that the taking of religion from the mother was only true under rabbinic law.

"Yours."

"That's very expedient, but it does not meet the needs of the moment. Have you actually discussed the exit visa with the prime minister?" Jack had told him that this was an absolute certainty.

"You may rest assured."

"And?"

"He is on your side, but wants to avoid a cabinet crisis."

"The son-of-a-bitch," Yokhanan swore, in English.

"Stop it, Galili. You see that my hands are tied."

"No, they are not," he said, smoothly sliding over into the deal Jack had proposed. "You can give me an exit visa. If I prepare recordings of my broadcasts and write my articles in advance, no one needs to know that I am out of the country."

"Except the Orthodox members of the Tel Aviv City Council, eh?"

"OK. You win. But let me tell you something. Every Protestant pastor in America, every Reformed rabbi in America, every Catholic priest in America is going to hear about this, as will all Christian Zionists. Neither Mary nor I will remain silent."

"Yes, I was expecting your threat. That's why I am prepared to offer an alternative."

Yokhanan came out of his seat to lean over the minister's desk.

He knew that Jack had been right, that Ben Gurion would make some sort of underhanded offer.

"Ben Gurion has agreed to call you back to the colors in his capacity as minister of defense. He will second you as a military attaché in an embassy that calls for a colonel in that role. That means you will be sent to Washington, London, Paris, or Cape Town. That should get around the bottleneck, shouldn't it?"

"Oh if you Mapainiks would only stop ducking the issues and write a constitution! I'll talk it over with Mary. If I don't miss my guess, she'd prefer the bastard to such a piece of political chicanery. But let me tell you this: You cannot conceal this expediency, either. The story will go to the press. It will leap the walls of your censorship like a cat over a fence and the world will hear of it. I warn you: If Mary does not agree with your sneaky proposal, you'd better be prepared to give me an exit visa."

"As you wish. We expected you to yell about our offer. You cannot threaten or push me. If our well-meaning attempt to solve your personal difficulties does not meet with your approval, go ahead. Proclaim to the world that your child is a bastard. If you relish such notoriety it will only amuse the voters and perhaps cause your regretted loss from the Tel Aviv City Council. We are also sure it would just delight your wife's family."

Yokhanan walked out in an ugly mood, pleased that Jack had sensed a deal but certain that Mary would have none of it. Mary, however, surprised him. She accepted the idea immediately: "You know, Jon, that I don't really care if the child is a bastard or not. In my eyes and in the eyes of God, we are married. I shall have the child properly baptized. My church will forgive the lack of a wedding certificate when I explain. But I cannot do this to my parents. The publicity would hurt them. Yes, I was willing to flaunt my independence when I chose Brandeis over·Bryn Mawr; yes, I was willing to fight for my freedom from them, too, but this I could not do to them. We shall report to any embassy they pick for you, even on a desert island."

JACK AND NAOMI IV

A few months after the Nachmani case, Naomi was called out on another practice alert. When she came home, she found Jack reading the *Jerusalem Post*.

"Thanks for waiting up," she said, starting to get out of uniform. "I really wanted to talk to you. I have the strangest feeling: I think I'm getting too old for soldiering."

"You don't have to stay in reserve. It was your choice after Ruthie was born."

"I know, Ya'akov; but I thought it was my duty, taking my place where I belong and taking your place, too, I suppose."

She went to look at Ruth and returned, tying the sash of her dressing gown around her.

"Have you seen the paper yet?" Jack asked as she slouched into an arm chair.

"No. Anything worthwhile?"

"Have a look at this."

He rolled his wheelchair toward her and handed her the paper.

INFANT REFUSED BURIAL IN TEL AVIV

A four-week old infant, son of Tel Aviv Councilman Yokhanan Galili and his Christian wife, Mary, was refused burial yesterday by the Tel Aviv Burial Society, who ruled that the child was not Jewish. A spokesman for the society explained that interment in sanctified ground cannot be granted to a non-Jew.

Mr. Galili, a controversial figure in the recent butchers'

case and the co-author of *Convert*, is unavailable for comment. Mrs. Galili is in Hadassah Hospital under sedation.

It is expected the incident may spark a major struggle among the government parties. Seven Members of the Knesset, all from parties of the far left and outside the coalition, said they would introduce a civil burial bill. The coalition, which is committed to preserving the status quo on religious matters, is expected to oppose the idea.

* * *

Naomi put down the paper and looked at Jack with some indignation. "Our party will back the Burial Society, Ya'akov," she said.

"I know. I have already resigned from the party. I have been on the telephone since Yokhanan called me. I am volunteering to help him—*pro bono*—because I cannot countenance taking money over a dead child."

"I agree, but why did you quit the party?"

"I called up two of our MKs and told them I was going to represent Yokhanan. I asked them to support the burial bill."

"You're going too fast for me. Start at the beginning."

"All right. Yokhanan called from Sarafand after the alert began. He thinks it was called for political reasons—to make him unavailable for comment, just as they once did to you. Anyway— I started calling MKs. I have fifteen pledges of support, even one from a Christian Arab. But all of them were on the left. I got nobody in the coalition. Our people raised hell with me. Eli Even-Zahav charged me with having turned Communist and told me to call Sha'ul Nachmani for help. I resigned to Eli on the spot."

"But they knew all about Sha'ul, Ya'akov. They even helped him, and me."

"I know, but they're playing dirty. All of a sudden, the Herut Party has become the one and only guardian of Judaism."

* * *

Yokhanan's baby became a cause celèbre. American Zionists protested against Israeli "theocracy"; the Reform movement did the same; the small Brandeis alumni association (including the "alumni" who had paid to be called alumni but had never set foot on campus) asked their university to send an official protest without specifying to whom such a protest should be addressed. Even the Israeli rabbinate debated the point, but never from the point of view of allowing non-Jewish burials. Their only concern was this: If Yokhanan's baby had lived, what would have been its inheritance rights since Me'ir Galili had been a man of property. The prime minister, however, was firm. He said that henceforth anyone claiming to be a Jew would be considered a Jew under the Law of Return as long as he practiced no other religion. The rabbinate immediately challenged him, vociferously pointing out that the minister of religion was from one of their parties and he would follow rabbinical law, not "Ben Gurion law."

Jack and Naomi were unable to help Yokhanan. Burial in Tel Aviv was out of the question. Yokhanan, on principle, refused to bury his unbaptized infant in a Christian cemetery. There were dozens of offers from kibbutzim for use of their cemeteries, but Mary decided that she should thumb her nose at the rabbinate just one more time, by donating the remains for dissection to the medical faculty at the Hebrew University, since corpses were scarce because of the Orthodox prohibition of autopsies.

When Naomi found out that the baby was in Jerusalem, she checked Jerusalem's ordinances on burial societies and found one dating back to Ottoman days that permitted any twenty-eight adults to form such a society. She quickly persuaded many more than that number of her friends and found a small plot for sale near the outer walls of the monastery of N've Sha'anan.

When the hospital released the remains in a plastic container, Naomi and Yokhanan dug a grave as Mary stood by, dressed not in Christian black but in Jewish white. Jack sat in his wheelchair holding Ruth Ben Horin in his lap. When the grave was filled and covered, Jack wheeled his chair so his back was to the grave—his old flag from the Arch of Titus draped around him as a prayer shawl. He began to read a burial service he had written:

"Take this, Lord, as a sin offering from Your guilty people. Take this, Lord, as penance from those whom You chose to spread Your commandments but for whom Your commandments did not say 'This one is worthy' and 'This one is not.'

"Take this innocent child, a pure and unsullied soul who did not know that he would cause rumblings among the mighty and bloodshed among the poor in wisdom.

"Take this, the offering of Your servant, Yokhanan Ben Me'ir Galili and Your servant Mary Weldon Galili, and make from it a lesson that You can teach Your unseeing and unknowing followers: those who care more for words than for meanings, those who respect the dead more than the living, those who learned nothing from their two-thousand-year exile, those who will not permit their brothers to serve You according to their own conscience . . . "

"Stop, Ya'akov!" Yokhanan exclaimed. "He never listens to the voices of reason, if He listens at all, considering that He never heard a murmur from Auschwitz. You are wasting your breath. Only the black ones have His ear, to fill with mumbled formulas and meaningless nothings. Thus goes our firstborn! So be it."

"No, Jon," Mary said quietly. "I asked Jack to say a few words. Please allow me this comfort. It is fitting to note that the Lord giveth and the Lord taketh away, blessed be the name of the Lord. Ashes to ashes and dust to dust . . . "

She wept softly as she prayed and Jack folded the paper he had not finished reading because he was not sure whether he should honor Mary's or Yokhanan's wishes. He handed it to Yokhanan, "Here! Mary may want to read this sometime."

"No," Yokhanan said. "Mary should not be reminded of this. Perhaps one day, when we can place a marker on my son's grave, we will look back on this gloomy day and reflect on the theocratic dictatorship in our country as a thing of the past."

"Yokhanan and Mary," Naomi said. "I intend to have a garden planted here. No one needs to know what the garden is for, but our burial society may be called upon again to offer a grave to someone in need."

She went to Jack's wheelchair. He folded up his flag and picked up Ruth and held her in his lap as Naomi pushed the chair toward the highway where the cars were parked.

Yokhanan helped her put the wheelchair in the trunk and thanked her for helping him dig the grave, kissing her on both cheeks. And then he saw the tears in Naomi's eyes.

"I never cried as a child," she said. "I did not cry for my brother when he died on the *Struma*.. I did not cry when I was broadcasting *The Voice of Fighting Zion* or even when I was having Ruthie. And now I am sobbing. Tell me, Yokhanan: Why?"

DAVE V

Three years passed without a thought of Betar or Israel or *Etzel*. He had only three goals: to earn his master's degree from MIT, to get the State Department to return his passport, and to find a wife who would accompany him to Israel after he accomplished the first two goals.

MIT was rough. His GI Bill benefits ran out while he was still an undergraduate because tuition at MIT was higher than the six hundred dollars a year that the law allowed. He was docked one day of benefits for every dollar over the limit on tuition. He applied for a scholarship and got it. He worked in the student cafeteria for spending money. For three years at the start of spring break, he hitchhiked to Washington to pound on the desk of Ruth Shipley, the despotic head of the Passport Office, who was a law unto herself.

She was polite enough to have him ushered in, but each year the demand was the same:

"Mr. Gordon, the department would be pleased to return your passport instantly after it has your sworn explanation of what you were doing in Lebanon in 1948 in violation of the United States Neutrality Act and why you jumped ship in the Azores during your repatriation at the cost and expense of the United States Treasury. Once we have those sworn documents, I can assure you, we shall process your case."

Dave had asked a Boston civil rights lawyer, Larry Shubow, nephew of an *Etzel* rabbi, what to do. Shubow told him not to supply the requested documents. "They just want to get you for perjury, Dave."

With the gray hairs beginning to show at his temples, Dave

stood in line as the master's degrees were being handed out. He got a handshake, a rolled up piece of paper, and kisses from his family, who had tried to help him through school with occasional gifts of twenty dollars here and ten dollars there.

"Do you have any debts, Dovidl?" His mother asked as they posed for snapshots on the lawn.

"No, Mom. I owe nothing to anybody. But America owes me. I am a colonel in the U.S. Air Force Reserve, hold a Distinguished Service Cross and a bunch of other worthless medals, and cannot even take a vacation in Cuba or Mexico. I'm a prisoner in my own country. So I'm going to change that. I'm going to change countries!"

"Dovidl," his father said, trying to be the voice of reason. "You shouldn't be angry. You did make all that trouble with Betar and with Lebanon. Now you have your degrees, you can get a good job making airplanes. I understand they pay very good. *Soll sein shah* already with that passport!"

"This is not the day to fight with you, Dad. Just give me your blessings and wish me well."

"I always wish you well, son, but I won't give my blessings if you do what you just said. America has been good to us. Don't turn your back on it."

He rode back to New York with his parents, all his belongings packed in the back of their 1946 Hudson. But he never unpacked when he got to what everyone wanted him to call "home."

He took the subway down to Second Avenue and climbed the stairs to Betar headquarters. A young boy sat at the president's desk under a photograph of the retreat parade held on the day Jabotinsky died. Dave spotted himself in the picture. Eleven years, he thought, what a long time eleven years is!

Dave did not know the youngster. "Who is the president?" he asked.

"I am," the youngster said.

"Where's Joe Kaplan?"

"In Israel, at Mavo Betar."

"How about Abe Slotkin?"

"At Ramat Raziel."

"And Judy Steiner?"

"Married and living in Bensonhurst." The boy looked irritated. "So who are you, already?"

"Dave Gordon."

"From Boston?"

"Yes."

"I've heard of you. What can I do for you?"

"I want the movement to finance my trip to Israel. I have no passport. I have no money. I'll pay it back, but I need help."

"Oh," said the young man, "all you want is an arm and a leg. But I better tell you, we don't have shit in the bank. Neither do the United Zionist Revisionists. I don't know where you could get the help, so I think you've come to the wrong place. I think you would do better if you went to the Israeli consulate and talked to them. I believe they have a lawyer there who would know about the passport thing. And I think they might be able to arrange things."

Dave said thanks and left. And then the pickle he was in became clearer to him.

He could wangle a flight on the Military Air Transport Service if he got into uniform and went to McGuire Air Force Base near Fort Dix. But he'd have to take pot luck on whether he could find a way from Rhein-Main in Frankfurt to Israel. Also, he wasn't sure he could do it as a Reservist without having orders or a passport.

He knew that there is no way for an American to give up his citizenship inside the United States, so he though of sneaking into Canada using identification other than a passport, going to a U.S. consulate, and doing it there. But he had to be sure Israel would help after that. But he wasn't sure Israel would help an *Etzel*nik.

He took the advice of the Betar president and went to the Israeli consulate. It was the sort of place where you spend hours waiting for someone you must talk to and are then told you have to talk to someone else, with another long wait ahead. But he did

get the message: The consulate in New York would not do anything that was unfriendly to the United States, so it would not
offer him any help.

"Can the consulate in Montreal help me?" he asked.

"Maybe," was the most commitment he could obtain. It was
said by a woman with red hair who was wearing high heels and a
home-sewn dress. He asked her out on a date; she accepted.

"Spare me the Sabra nightclub," she said. "The one place in
New York I don't want to go to is a nightclub where they sing
'Hava Nagillah.' "

"How about a ballgame at the Polo Grounds?"

"You're on. I've never seen a baseball game."

It was a time when baseball was still played in the afternoon and
when the Giants were still in New York. She couldn't go when she
had to work. But she agreed to go on Saturday, despite the Sabbath.

They arranged a meeting place—she lived in Forest Hills—at
the end of the shuttle in Times Square and jabbered away at each
other all the way to the Polo Grounds. That's where Dave found
out how to go to Israel.

The Jewish Agency in New York could help with his immigration, give him a physical, and lend him money; but the Israeli
entry visa had to come from a consulate. The visa had to be placed
inside a travel document, such as a passport. An Israeli consulate
could, at his request, supply him with a *laissez passer* to serve in
lieu of a passport. He would be able to immigrate to Israel from
Toronto or Montreal, but he would face trouble on returning to
New York, where they looked at visas and demanded proof of U.S.
citizenship.

"Do I have to renounce my citizenship?" he asked her.

"No. But you had best do something about your reserve obligations. In the event of a call-up, you may not be able to report to
your unit . . . "

"How come you know so much about the reserves?"

"Everybody in Israel is in the reserves. We serve one month
every year."

So what he did was to take a train to Montreal, where the Israelis gave him a travel document. From there, he flew to Rome, took a bus to Naples, and boarded an Israeli ship, the *Negba*. He had no passport.

* * *

"WELCOME TO ISRAEL" was repeated in many languages on banners throughout the port of Haifa. The gay bunting belied the tedious bureaucracy of customs and immigration officials. From the *Negba,* he could see the greetings, but had to wait his turn on the ship.

Leaving his suitcase in the customs locker and carrying only a small gladstone, Dave left the port area through Palmer's Gate and went directly to the central bus terminal. A few hours later he was at Tel Aviv's central bus depot. Somehow he managed to find his way by bus to the "Anglo-Saxon" Section of the Jewish Agency.

"Hello," he said, as he entered the one-woman office. "My name is David Gordon. I was told in New York to report here. It's all right to speak English, isn't it?"

"Quite all right," she said, rising and extending her hand across the desk. "My name is Hannah and I'm happy to welcome you to Israel."

Hannah gave him a handful of papers to fill out. Then she answered his questions about finding a job and a place to live. As he was leaving, he asked her where she had learned her American English.

"Everyone asks me that. I grew up on the lower East Side of Manhattan, Avenue C to be exact. My parents took me on a visit to my grandparents in Poland just before the war. We were not yet American citizens and could not get out of Poland when the war started. I survived."

"So I see," Dave said, looking at her tattoo. It read *"Feldhure."*

"It's all right, Dave," she said. "I am no longer embarrassed by it. I survived in the only manner I could. I lost my entire family, but I am here. To be a survivor is to be honored in Israel."

* * *

Walking toward a hotel that had been recommended, Dave wondered about Hannah's unattractive face and wondered why she had been chosen to be a soldiers' whore by the Nazis. It never occurred to him that she might have been much more attractive before her ordeal or that she was, in fact, three years his junior. He also wondered how she had managed to become a Nazi whore when German law prohibited "race defilement," any sexual contact with Jews. He decided that Hannah had voluntarily become a sex slave.

In the afternoon and evening, Dave explored Tel Aviv. He found *Metzudat Ze'ev*, the Betar fortress on King George Street for which he had collected funds; the mosque in Jaffa where *Etzel* had raised the Jewish flag after wiping out the sniper's nest on the minaret only to be attacked from the rear by *Haganah* ; the hulk of the *Etzel* ship *Altalena* which had been sunk just off the beach by *Haganah* with large loss of Jewish life, and the police Tegart fortress in Ramat Gan that had been attacked by Dov Gruner and his men. Opposite the police station stood the Dov Gruner monument, portraying him as a lion because Orthodoxy does not permit statues depicting humans.

After much walking and bus riding, he sat down in a cafe near his hotel. It was a time of austere rations and meager portions. There was chicory in the coffee and the ice cream tasted like sherbet.

Hearing English spoken at a nearby table, he could not help but listen.

"If we do not find a way to automate the plant so we can run it on the Sabbath, you'll have to hire a non-Jewish crew to take over. I don't think it makes business sense to hire more workers, not even part time. Why don't you go to America and see if you can find equipment so we can just run it and leave it?"

"No, Fritz. Out of the question. We won't automate. The whole idea is to industrialize this country and use Hebrew labor. Hasn't it got through that thick Prussian head of yours yet that I want to employ as many people as possible?"

"But you are violating every economic principle of industrialization."

"Those principles are not true if the worker who makes the machine is in another country and outside your economy. Let me tell you this, Fritz: This country can adopt mass-production techniques economically. That would lower costs of production, spur efficiency, and reduce the rate of inflation. The pound would become stable. In theory, then, everything would be better. But there is a catch, Fritz. This country's main economic principle is not what the economists say. Instead, it is the heart that dictates economic policy, and the heart says absorption and more absorption. We must make jobs for Hebrews from North Africa who don't know what a sit-down toilet looks like. We must make jobs for Hebrews from Romania for whom Israel is the several thousand dollars apiece it costs Israel in bribes to bring them here from Anna Pauker's paradise. We have to be ready to bring in Hebrews from Russia if Stalin ever lets them out."

Fritz was smoking furiously. The man talking to him appeared to be his boss and Fritz listened attentively.

"The keys to Israel's future are immigration and more economic employment of the people who are already here but are only marginally employed. We have to make jobs so we don't have beggars and peddlers in the streets. We have to become more efficient so we don't need three people to run a bus. I was told the other day that only a quarter of our nonfarm work force is in production. God only knows how many of them are actually producing economically. I'd be willing to guess that half are redundant. But that's not our immediate problem. We've got to get around the bastardly rabbinate. Even if we automate, the rabbinate might still blackball our tires. Anyway, there is nobody in the country who could set it up and maintain it. We cannot afford to bring in someone from America to program this. He'd cost more than a non-Jewish part-time crew."

Dave had heard enough. He walked over to their table and said: "I couldn't help overhearing . . . Hey, holy cow, aren't you the guy who was on the *Sally Jane* in the Azores?"

"Well, isn't it a small world?" Manny Cardozo said. "Fritz, I found this fellow out in the middle of the Atlantic in forty-eight, or should I say he found me. What was your name again? Dave, Dave . . . "

"Gordon."

"Yes, stupid of me to forget. How long have you been in Israel?"

"Since this morning. But I did not come over because I recognized you—I only saw your back until I came over. I came over to tell you that I can automate your plant. I have a master's in aeronautical engineering from MIT and my minor was cybernetics."

Fritz had sat through the exchange silently, still unused to the informality of Tel Aviv, even though he had lived there since he fled Dortmund in 1934. Now he came to life: "An engineer who can program? Miracles don't happen any more!"

"I spent a lot of time in the computation labs. It looks as if you fellows have a job for me."

"*Ach*, no experience!" Fritz sneered.

"That all depends on what you need. I helped set up the Univac that CBS used in the 1952 elections and I've worked on Raytheon's radar-guidance computer for use with anti-aircraft direction finding."

"Have you done anything in manufacturing?" Manny asked. "Hot rubber? Timing devices? Relays?"

"I've worked with relays. I wired an electronic organ with over a thousand of them. I also own a patent on a duodecimal computer I worked out for British currency. I haven't been able to do anything with it, though."

"Where have you tried to market it?" Fritz asked.

"I tried the London stock exchange. My patent agent in England is still trying to sell it for me."

"Any other patents, Mr. Gordon?" Fritz asked

"Some minor ones, but I do have my Rube Goldberg."

"Your what?"

"Rube Goldberg," Manny explained, "is an American cartoonist. He draws crazy inventions. Almost all American engineers try to patent an absurd idea before they graduate from college. What's yours, Dave?"

"It's a gadget for teaching your dog to lick postage stamps."

"They give patents for that in America?"

"No, Fritz. It's all in fun. The 'patents' are given by fraternities; but you wouldn't understand. You haven't got a sense of humor." Turning back to Dave, he asked: "Working on anything now, Dave?"

"I'm job hunting."

"Would you come up to our plant and have a look to see what you could do?" Manny suggested.

"Sure. Where is it?"

"In Ramat Gan. The Cardozo Tire Company. Ask anyone, but I can't promise you anything. Even if we could get the tires past the rabbis, we might still not get import licenses for the equipment you would require. It's been touch and go for us since we broke ground. The rabbis pulled the plug on us this week about closing on the Sabbath and about employing Jews on the Sabbath. We have to mark our Sabbath tires so that, God forbid, they cannot be sold to the army or the government and we have to make them without Jewish labor. They've been quite decent about it and gave us a month to figure out a way before they go public."

"And you can't close down from Friday to Sunday, Manny?" Dave asked.

"Sure, but it would cost a fortune. You can't play games with hot rubber. Do you have those figures, Fritz?"

Fritz took out a notebook and began analyzing the cost of a Sabbath shutdown. It would eat up all of Friday's production and waste half of Sunday's. It also entailed replacing some equipment blocked by hardened rubber.

"Are you running the plant, Manny?"

"No. Fritz runs it. I'm in and out of there all the time, but I'm a diesel engineer—Colorado School of Mines and Caltech—and they've made me into a diesel repairman here. I go around from kibbutz to moshav to army base and repair diesels. It brings me a living, helps teach Israelis to take care of diesels on their own—and to put oil in the crankcase—and lays the foundation for starting a diesel industry in Israel."

"You shouldn't have to worry about making a living, Manny."

"Cardozo money, Dave?"

"I thought . . . "

"Forget it. I'm the black sheep of the family because I'm a Zionist. My father tied up whatever I might inherit in an irrevocable trust and, even though I still have a little money in Switzerland, I'm basically living on what I can earn. But when the tires start rolling, I expect no more trouble on that score."

"You must have had money to build the plant."

"In Israel," Manny said with a huge smile, "one can work wonders on credit, Dave. Actually, the plant is a fifty-fifty deal. I only did some fancy financial footwork. Fifty percent is owned by South African investors. I put up the other half with the last of my own resources. I'm going for broke on it, and that's probably what we can expect next—going broke. If only we could have started production before this happened."

"How far along are you?"

Fritz pulled out copy for an advertisement he was placing:

THE CARDOZO TYRE COMPANY, B.M.
is pleased to announce
that it will commence production
of all standard-sized
TYRES
and TUBES
in its ultra-modern Ramat Gan plant
this Sunday
SHOP THE FLYING "C"
WHEN BUYING TYRES AND TUBES.
LOOK FOR THE "MADE IN ISRAEL" LABEL

Dave looked at it, then asked: "Why this? Why not diesels right away?"

"This tire thing is only an investment. If I can make a go of it, I'll go back to diesels full time, with a diesel plant in the Haifa bay area. I couldn't get any backing for that because nobody believes we could compete with the rest of the world. I think we can, but it'll have to wait until I can capitalize myself. The tire plant is the next best thing. It has taken two years, mainly because of the hard time they gave us when we needed to import machinery. A lot hangs on our ability to sell these tires."

"I see," Dave said, impressed by Manny's zeal.

"We have a barter arrangement worked out with Finland for prefab houses which the South African investors will put up all over Israel, and we have a cash-and-carry deal set up with Denmark. There is hope we may sign deals with Burma and Turkey. We are not yet assured that the Israel Defense Force will buy our tires, at least not until the rabbis put a 'kosher' seal of approval on them."

"Doesn't sound too bad," Dave offered.

"It is not enough," Fritz muttered. "Our tires will cost more than Continentals, Pirellis, Goodyears, Firestones, or Michelins. To sell, we must price them competitively, meaning that our profit margins are less. Mr. Cardozo will have to wait a very long time before he has enough profit to build a diesel plant in Haifa."

Manny waved him into silence. "You forget the profit we make with domestic sales, Fritz. We can't compete abroad in price with foreign tires, but Israel's duties will allow us to make a healthy profit here provided we can keep the rabbinate from shutting us down every weekend. The rabbis may prefer doing business with gentile firms abroad to doing business with a blue-law-violating Hebrew firm here."

"I wish I had your faith in the rabbis, Mr. Cardozo," Fritz said.

"You're a pessimist, my friend. Why Israel could have one of the highest living standards in the world if we would get busy producing things we can make—even without begging from Jews in the rest of the world.

* * *

That night, Dave dreamed of an economic powerhouse. He saw watches being made in an Israeli Switzerland by dark-skinned Yemenite women. He found himself in an RCA laboratory as amazed technicians uncrated an Israeli computer and heard them comment, "Why didn't we think of that?" as they disassembled it. He watched Israeli textile machinery being sent off to mills in all parts of the world on Israeli ships built in Haifa with Manny's turbines providing the power. He even saw an Italian prostitute taking off her Israeli raincoat, lay down her Israeli purse, and put an Israeli condom on her client.

He woke up in the morning with a ravenous appetite.

Manny and Fritz met him when he arrived at Cardozo Tire. Manny did not wear his ever-optimistic grin. Fritz looked even glummer than last night.

"I'm terribly sorry, Dave," Manny said. "I've wasted your time. I've decided not to automate at the expense of Israel's job-creating ability."

"God damn the rabbinate!" Fritz said.

"No, Fritz. All thanks to the rabbinate. We shall be the first Israeli industry with a five-day workweek for all our employees. We'll stagger the shifts so half work a half day on Friday to shut us down and the other half on Saturday night or Sunday morning to open us up again. I think it will work out. I think it's going to be just great!"

Manny's ability to find good in desperate situations had been why he had been able to adjust to Israel. That, at least, is what he told Dave as he drove him back to Tel Aviv in his jeep.

"I'm a new Zionist, Dave. I hardly knew I was a Jew until I was a grown man. Now, I think what we're doing in this country is just wonderful. Fritz is a manager; he can't see farther than his balance sheet. People like Fritz wouldn't have a Hebrew state even now. It takes dreamers like me and the prime minister. No, I'm not being conceited; he told me that himself."

* * *

A few days later, Dave was hired by the Ministry of Defense to work out a Hebrew data-processing system for the personnel section of the Israel Defense Force. Since Ben Gurion was also minister of defense, Dave suspected that Manny had greased the skids for him. The new system was to use punch cards into which women soldiers would punch information for Israel's complex emergency call-up system. Each soldier's state of readiness and training, military specialties, call-up time factors, and family status were punched in and the printouts from the cards were in Hebrew. In the old system, only payroll and other numerical data could be automated, but the system lacked a program for Hebrew printouts and Hebrew data cards.

Hardly had Dave finished with that project—with quite a bit of help from IBM personnel—than the Ministry of Posts and Telecommunications was after him to design a system for it. Dave was kept busy, and was able to pay off his Jewish Agency immigration loans. Because of currency controls, he could not send any money to his parents, but he decided to "organize" a way to do that. He went to Manny and asked him, without any courtesies about such an intrusion into his privacy: "Hey, you got any money in the bank outside Israel?"

Manny was not upset, but his answer was useless to Dave: "You know that's illegal. Every cent I had went into Cardozo Tire and Cardozo Diesel. And I'm in debt up to my ears. Why do you ask?"

"I want to send some money to my parents. I tried at the bank and they told me it was impossible."

"I've got a way I can help you. Sally Jane still works for me as my American secretary. When I liquidated my own Swiss bank accounts, I set up one for Sally Jane. She has complete authority over it and she is outside the reach of the Israeli tax people. I can wire her instructions and she can cut a check."

"But I'll never be able to pay you back!"

"Never say 'never,' " Manny said with a wide grin. "Just think how far we have come since we first met in the Azores. There have been miracles. Maybe there'll be another miracle and you'll strike it rich in dollars instead of in Israeli pounds. I'm able to wait."

* * *

He joined an "Anglo-Saxon" housing cooperative and waited to move into its new apartment house in north Tel Aviv. It was going to be built according to American standards, with large refrigerators, dish washers, and freezers.

In 1954, the Israel-American Chamber of Commerce named him one of the "Ten Outstanding Men of the Year" and invited him to an awards ceremony at the ZOA House in Tel Aviv. Arriving early, he went to the handsome cocktail lounge and ordered a whisky sour while surveying the crowd, who apparently had been told that dress was black tie. Someone tapped him on the shoulder of his sports jacket.

"Remember me?" she said, arching her body backwards for him to admire.

"Miriam?"

"That's right. I did not know you were in Israel until they gave you this award. Why didn't you look me up as you promised?"

"Still waiting for that real American date, Miriam? In all honesty, I would have been delighted to find you. But things got all screwed up in Baalbek. I lost your address and even forgot your last name. But, honest! I have never forgotten you. Have a drink?"

"Please. May I have what you have?"

"Another whisky sour," he told the barman.

"Why are you receiving an award, Dave?"

"Engineering. I'm converting Israel to automatic data processing. What are you doing here?"

"I'm getting an award, too. They think I'm a man. They will have a little surprise that I'm not a tuxedo."

"You look pretty damn good in what you are wearing," he said, looking her over again.

"I designed it," she said.

"Holy shit! Are you Mirco, the big fashion designer?"

"Yes. Miriam Cohen and Company. But the word is couturière."

"OK. I didn't know we had anything like that here in Israel. I thought we only make khakis here."

"Didn't you read about the prizes I won in Paris and Cannes?"

"Frankly, no. It probably would not have been the kind of story I would read in the paper."

"I suppose not. How long have you been here?"

"Two, going on three years."

"I still do not understand why you are getting an award. Tell me in Hebrew."

After they killed their drinks, they entered the auditorium. While not embarrassed to find almost all other men in evening clothes, Dave considered himself fortunate that he had even put on a necktie. The speeches, mostly in English, were abysmally dull. As each recipient was called forward, there was polite clapping of hands until the master of ceremonies called out, "Mr. Mirco."

Loud guffaws, laughter, and applause started when Miriam rose from her chair and started on her way to the stage, purposely undulating the lower part of her anatomy as she came down the aisle, her floor-length, lime green gown accentuating every step. Dave noticed that she was probably not wearing panties because no panty line showed on her buttocks.

The master of ceremonies quickly recovered his composure and announced: "From now on, ladies and gentlemen, our award will be called 'Ten Outstanding Israelis of the Year.' "

Laughter and more applause greeted the about-face.

When Dave resumed his seat after his award, Miriam pressed a paper into his hand: "Here, this is my address and phone number. Please do not lose it again. And, anyway, Cohen is not so hard a name to remember."

"May I escort you home?"

"Can you drive?" she asked.

"Sure."

"Here are the keys to my car. It's a green Hillman Minx. You may come up for a nightcap if you wish."

* * *

For the next few weeks, Dave and Miriam were inseparable. Through her, he discovered a whole new life in Tel Aviv that included dancing, partying, and sex. Through Miriam, Dave met Yokhanan and Mary Galili. Through Yokhanan, he regained his interest in politics, this time real politics. His vote in the election for the Second Knesset had gone to Herut by instinct rather than conviction. But Yokhanan's perpetual crusade against Orthodoxy opened his eyes to real problems not so easily apparent while designing data systems.

Yokhanan's living room, a reminder of Billy's studio, helped erase his guilty conscience about Billy. He unburdened himself about it to Miriam; she dismissed the whole thing as puppy love with a snap of her fingers.

Then, one day, he was invited to a Cardozo party. The invitation said "Israeli attire" so he wore khaki shorts and a white shirt. Miriam, however, said, "I always wear my latest design," and was in a sleek orange cocktail dress.

There were servants bringing around hors d'oeuvres. There were servants pouring drinks. There was a small combo on the verandah playing American dance music. And there was Billy.

"What are you doing here, for God's sake?" a surprised Dave asked.

Billy, in a khaki skirt and yellow T-shirt on which she had pinned a tiny *Etzel* insignia, looked Miriam over and said, "We've known each other an awful long time."

"I know," Miriam said in a perfect put-down. "Dave told me all about it."

"All?"

Miriam shrugged.

Billy did not pursue it, saying: "The answer, Dave, is quite simple. I have a commercial art studio on Hadar HaCarmel in Haifa. I designed the Cardozo Tire logos and do all their other art. I've been in Israel since 1948. When did you finally manage to get here?"

Dave sensed that she was about to make a scene, and excused himself to go speak to Manny. "Jesus, Manny. What an embarrassment. My new girlfriend just met my old girlfriend."

"Take me over, maybe I can help."

And Manny apparently liked what he found. He asked Billy to dance with him. As the evening progressed, Miriam pointed out to Dave that Billy was doing a number on Manny.

"What do you mean?" he asked.

"See the way she is rubbing her body against him. I bet she never leaves here after the party."

"I hope she doesn't think that Manny is one of the rich Cardozos," he said.

"I tend to think he is," Miriam said, waving her arm around the large living room and pointing at the servants.

"Gee," Dave said, "maybe he is doing all right with his tire plant after all."

When Manny and Billy sat one out, Manny commented about her pin.

"When I ran the American arm of the *Irgun*, Billy, I was given a pin like yours. Were you in *Etzel*?"

"No, Manny," she said. "This is Dave's pin. He couldn't take it when he sailed for Israel and so he gave it to me. I have kept it ever since."

Turning to Dave, she asked: "Perhaps you want it back, Dave. It's not too popular here in Israel. Want it?"

"No thanks. I've left the movement."

He thought he saw a smile on Miriam's face.

Golania, 1953
Rehovot, 1954—55

GENIA V

Golania's peace after the War of Independence was sporadic.

Syria was unstable. It changed leaders often. One of them, Colonel Husni Zayeem, dubbed himself a field marshal and had a diamond-encrusted baton made by a Paris jeweler. Another thought of himself as the reincarnation of Lenin.

But whenever the political situation in Syria required that attention be diverted from Syrian problems, the big guns on the Golan Heights fired on places like Golania. Aside from that, Gamal Abdel Nasser in Egypt was sending *fedayeen* into Israel to kill, maim, and destroy. Golania, because of its proximity to one of the few places where Syria was near the level of the Sea of Galilee, became a target to the *fedayeen*. Fishing boats were fired upon, flocks were slaughtered, irrigation pipe was dismantled and carted off, fields were put to the torch.

The Syrian-Israeli Mixed Armistice Commission debated and haggled while the children of Golania, Ulpanim, and Shamir learned to play new games with shell fragments and slept in bomb shelters.

Inside Golania, members continued to have passionate ideological disagreements. They argued a lot about the children with issues ranging from how long they should be kept in children's houses, whether they should be sent to schools outside the kibbutz, and to a host of other things. But some members thought these arguments petty. They had more weighty concerns, about hiring outsiders to work in the kibbutz, about the split in the party—which, fortunately did not affect Golania because they all stayed with the Mapai faction.

The first huge ideological debate was not a tempest in a teapot, it was a tempest about a tea kettle: Should members be allowed to have tea kettles in their rooms? The compromise that was worked out was much like the one adopted years earlier about pocket money. Those who wanted it could have it.

But that was nothing compared to the dispute about changing the way members ate. It started when the wife of Moshe "Gimmel" said she felt she was being subjected to a degrading form of master-servant relationship when Monya assigned her to waiting in the dining hall. "I am a farmer, Monya," she said. "I don't work the dining hall."

And she did not. Monya backed down, but he raised the issue at a meeting by suggesting that this "degrading" of the members who brought the food to the tables could be ended by eating cafeteria style, with each member carrying his or her own tray to the table.

"It would also save manpower," he said.

Poor Monya! He was subjected to abuse from all sides, even from Moshe "Gimmel," who wasn't aware that his own wife had started this dispute. And some members said very unsocialist things, such as: "When I sit down to eat, I want to feel like a man."

Some of the women took offense at that one.

But the cafeteria idea died when the purchasing committee noted the high cost of buying serving trays and converting the dining room.

Throughout its existence Golania had had one or two specialized employees. For many years they hired a nurse, until Dina was trained. They hired Ruth for the kindergarten, until Shoshana was trained. But they were all against having employees, which, they felt, undermined their socialist ideals.

Yet the problem that started with the wife of Moshe "Gimmel" and her view of working in the dining hall soon spread, slowly at first, to the de facto sexual role-playing that the work coordinators proclaimed daily. Women worked in the chickens, in the laundry, in the kitchen, or with the children; men fished, drove the tractors, and worked the fields. And some of the women did not like it. Hava, one of the twins from Genia's class, argued with Monya one day because she felt she was as good a carpenter as Avner so why was she never given that work? Aviva complained about the laundry.

Similar debates were going on in other kibbutzim, so much so that a hit play. *Hedva and I*, was being performed in one kibbutz after another. The play dealt with women who wanted to leave their kibbutz.

And then, one day, Nurit got up at a meeting and made a speech: "I did not join a kibbutz to tend children and do 'women's work.' The very idea of collective care for our children was to free parents for other work. Here, it has only freed the fathers. I have yet to see any of you men working in the laundry or in the chickens. When it comes to stoop labor in the vegetables, we sometimes have the pleasure of a man's company—to drive the vegetables off. But this is not the way it should be. If we are truly equals here, women should also be in the boats and in the fields and men should be in the kitchen and the laundry."

Some women went along with Nurit's proposal because they always felt uneasy when they had to deal with a group of children that included their own. But most appeared to take no side. The dispute just kept on simmering without a compromise, but also without change.

* * *

The worst disruption ever to hit Golania fell squarely on Genia. All of Golania, from its beginnings, had belonged to a small left-wing part of Mapai called "The Second Part." After that faction merged with two other parties to form Mapam, people who had once belonged to those parties were now welcome in Golania. And so Yitzhak—who was from Ulpanim and was not a member of the Second Part—could become a member after he married Genia.

The merged Mapam party was very far to the left. It could see no wrong in the Soviet Union. But this was Israel, a Jewish state in which people were sensitive to Soviet anti-Semitism, to the word "cosmopolitan," to charges against Jewish doctors, to the closing of Yiddish theaters, and to the sarcasm constantly directed at Israel by the Soviet delegate at the United Nations. Worst of all, everyone noticed that the Soviet Union was aligned with Israel's enemies, including Syria, which frequently shelled Golania. The right wing of the merged Mapam party—the ones who had belonged to the Second Part—could no longer be quite as chummy with the Soviets as the left, who bad come out of Hashomer Hatzair and Achdut Avodah. The left talked in favor of the Stockholm Peace Appeal, praised the "people's democracies," and denounced the "Nazo-Fascist military revanchists" in the Pentagon. But they kept quiet about Uncle Joe in the Kremlin.

All over Israel, kibbutzim waged internal combat over such things. International affairs became as important as the chickens and the laundry. And then Mapam split again. Golania went back into Mapai.

This made no difference in Golania where everybody had been in the Second Part from the start. But in some kibbutzim, barbed-wire partitions went up in the middle of the dining halls so that the right wing and the left wing would not have to eat at the same table. Husbands and wives moved out of their common rooms. Several kibbutzim arranged for exchanges of population, much like the one between Greece and Turkey after World War I. Sometimes the wife stayed and the husband left; sometimes it was the other way around.

And so it happened with Genia and Yitzhak. Yitzhak disagreed with much of the "right-wing rhetoric" that he heard in Golania, but to preserve his marriage, he kept quiet. At the elections to the second Knesset, one person in Golania voted for Mapam; the rest for Mapai. Yitzhak was questioned and admitted casting the solitary vote. In a normal society, such independence would hardly matter; in a kibbutz it did. The members voted to expel Yitzhak.

"What are you going to do, Genushka?" he asked after the vote.

"Go!" she said, using the singular imperative.

"And you?"

"I'll stay."

Pointing to her maternity smock, he asked, "And it?"

"Would you want me to bring it to Ulpanim?"

"No. Come with me to Ulpanim."

"I can't. I belong here."

"Don't you love me enough to come with me?"

"Didn't you love me enough to vote so you could stay?"

"I have a right to vote as a free man any way I wish."

"Not in a kibbutz. Maybe because your father is a doctor in the city and you were not brought up on a kibbutz, you don't understand this. Suppose you had voted for Herut? Or for the Communists? Wouldn't you yourself agree that we should expel you? It's just a question of degree between your party and one of the others. Had it been someone else, you would have voted to expel. I did not vote against you; but Moshe and Shula did. Had you not been my husband, I would have voted with them."

"Then it's hopeless."

"Yes. Go!"

Yitzhak gazed at her awhile. "Genia, do you remember what you once told me? You said you were not really sure you were alive until I came to the sanitarium. How can you be like this now?"

"I don't know. Maybe I'm *meshuga* like my mother."

"Don't."

"It's hereditary, you know."

"Not her kind; she got that way in the camps."

"Who knows? Maybe it was already there before. Anyway, I am not leaving Golania. This is where I belong. This is where I stay."

He kissed her good-bye and said: "I don't have a choice."

* * *

When her baby was born, named Michael after Maxim Koganov's Hebrew name, Genia asked Moshe to invite Yitzhak for the circumcision. Yitzhak did not come.

Sabta had a solution: Natasha's house in Rehovot was Genia's for the asking. Sabta asked Genia if she would consider moving into her mother's place after she had secretly gained Yitzhak's agreement.

"And what do I do in such a house? With what shall I buy food for Michael?" Genia asked.

"Hush, Genia," Sabta said, "your husband will find the means to provide for you. Think of it, you will have a home of your own. Michael will have his father. If you wish, I'll come to help with the baby until he is older. Yitzhak has agreed."

"You already asked my man?"

"Yes."

"And he agreed?"

"Yes."

"He wants to leave Ulpanim?"

"He wants to be with you and with his son."

"Is that what he said? I mean, are those his actual words?"

"Yes," Sabta said. "He said he would even live in a foreign country if it meant that you would return to him."

"You are making it sound as if it was I who left him. Yitzhak voted with Stalin, the man who killed my father. By doing that, he left me and all of Golania. We don't like Stalin here!"

"Genushka, Genushka. Do you think this makes any difference to Michael?"

"You want me to say yes, don't you, Sabta?"

"Of course I do. Michael needs his father and you need him, too."

"You are right. Tell him I said yes."

"No, Genia. I shall not be a mailman. Go to the dining hall and telephone him."

"Thank you, Sabta. Will you come with us?"

"If you so desire."

* * *

Sabta and Yitzhak were driven to Rehovot in Ulpanim's pickup truck, hauling their few belongings in the back. Genia and Michael followed in a taxi.

"I feel uncomfortable and strange in this house," Genia said at the dinner table.

"Don't worry, Genia," Yitzhak reassured her. "At least the nursery will now be used for its intended purpose."

"That's not what I mean, Yitzhak. It's the ghost of my mother being here, telling me that I am a dead peasant, telling me I should have married Stalin's son, saying you're not good enough for me. It is a hard thing to be reminded of all the time. I can actually see her where Sabta is sitting. I can hear her inside my head. It makes me feel weird."

Yitzhak came over to her and took her in his arms, and changed the subject. "Here, let me read you something Ben Gurion wrote: 'With the split in the labor movement, particularly affecting labor kibbutzim, many kibbutzim sided with what they call revolutionary socialism; I call that the Communist world. They pay lip service to people's democracy; I call it totalitarianism. They caused a breach in the kibbutz movement. Members of the same kibbutz, who based their lives on labor, agriculture, and pioneer values erected walls and refused to send their children to the schools in their own kibbutz.'

"It looks, Genia, as if he was talking about us. The split in the movement broke up our marriage. If I can give up living in a kibbutz to be with you and Michael, you can learn to live with your ghost."

"I, too, have given up the kibbutz, Yitzhak. Since I was eight years old, it is the only life I've known. I don't know how to use that kitchen. I don't know how to manage here. And I do worry about money. We have to pay bills here. And my mother may come back at any time to torment me again."

"Shh, Genia," Sabta said. "Natasha will not come back. She is in a special hospital and, poor thing, she has deteriorated even more since we last saw her. Moshe had a report about two months ago. She cannot even tell who or where she is. I feel very, very sorry for her. When she first came to us, she was full of life and laughter and love. She was fun to be with. I could not recognize the original Natasha in the woman who came here from Ravensbrück. And as to money, Natasha still receives some money from her book and it will help pay your bills. Anyway, Yitzhak will find work and you will manage."

"Not quite, Sabta," he said. "This house is more than a fisherman can afford."

"So," she answered with a shrug, "you'll find something else."

In a few days, Yitzhak found work in an orange grove, saying sarcastically that he was the best-housed farmer in Israel. But then he got a break. A rich American was opening a radio factory in Rehovot to make Israel's first radios since Philips of the Netherlands closed its factory under pressure from the Arab boycott. Yitzhak sensed that this might be an opportunity for him and applied for a job.

The "rich" American was Dave Gordon, who was using his own funds as well as some from Yokhanan Galili, Manny Cardozo, and Miriam Cohen, to reopen the Philips plant. When Yitzhak went for his interview, he was startled to see a portrait of a fascist, Ze'ev Jabotinsky, behind the factory owner's desk.

"Is this a Herut factory?" he asked belligerently when he sat down.

"No," Dave said. "This is an Israeli plant. Jabotinsky happens to be my hero, but my fellow investors come from Hashomer Hatzair and from the General Zionists. Does it matter? We're going to build radios here, not run a country."

"I, myself, am from Achdut Avodah," Yitzhak said. "I had to leave my kibbutz after the split."

Dave ignored the comment and got back to the point: "What can you do for us? I am hiring people who will make money for this firm. How can you be useful?"

Yitzhak showed his school grades, said he was a lieutenant in the army, and noted that physics had been something he was good at in school.

"OK, Yitzhak," Dave said. "I'll give you a try, but you must promise to take correspondence courses in radio and electronics. I expect you to submit your grades in those courses to the personnel department. Your pay will be adjusted in accordance with what you learn. The more you train yourself to be useful to the company, the more you will be worth to the company. Do you understand?"

This was not the way things were done in Israel. Wages were determined by membership in Histadrut and by Histadrut pressure on job-givers. Dave had not even made contact yet with Histadrut and had no plan to do so. His hiring criterion was not Histadrut membership but usefulness to the company. And he was going to hire no Arabs.

* * *

Genia asked Yitzhak about the job interview when he came home. She was weeding in the garden and he squatted next to her.

"They're *meshuga* at the factory," Yitzhak said, explaining the revolutionary concepts Dave had outlined to him.

"I don't think that sounds so *meshuga*," she said.

"Nor me," Sabta shouted from the dining room. "That's the way things should be. That's what Genia's father never understood. He kept talking about 'From each according to ability; to each according to need.' So commissars had very big needs and had to have a *dacha* and a car. Workers did not have big needs and could get by squeezed into abysmal shacks with a promise that someday, when the gold rains from the sky, there would be apartments. When the first apartments came, they were so tiny that my room in Golania was big by comparison, and I only had to share that with one woman."

Sabta had wiped her hands on her apron and had come out in the garden. She was on her favorite anti-Bolshevik crusade, and she was not going to let her grandchildren off easy: "No, Yitzhak. This man's idea of how to pay his workers is much better than Comrade Maxim's. He is saying 'From each according to ability; to each according to performance.' That's what was missing in Golania and Ulpanim, too. Moshe could be a history professor, instead he runs the secretariat; Shula could be a talented actress, instead she works in the laundry. All socialism levels people to their lowest possible forms of life. This man has the right idea. Go work for him, Yitzhak!"

Genia finished what she was doing, and they all adjourned to the kitchen, taking Michael's crib along. Genia got cleaned up and started lunch. Yitzhak grabbed a handful out of a bowl of pitted olives.

"Stop eating the olives, Yitzhak," Sabta said, "they're for the salad."

He obeyed—for a while, then began *noshing* again.

"There's something I was wondering about," he said. "That man said he had a partner from Hashomer Hatzair. I really would like to talk to him."

"So ask," Sabta said, "who he is and how to find him. Invite him here for dinner."

"Can one really invite a factory owner to the home of a worker?" Genia asked.

Sabta, who was tasting something, spit it out into the sink, and laughed loudly. "What's this, Genushka? Are you fighting the class conflict? We have in Israel maybe a boss class and a working class? The two shall forever be on opposite sides of the barricades as the workers sing that the 'International Soviet shall be the human race'? Don't make me laugh. Of course you can invite the boss—and I won't even mention that this is probably one of the finest private homes in all of Israel and that the boss may be impressed. And of course the boss will be glad to come. He'll bring his wife and they'll love the fancy dinner you serve. For God's sake stop looking at the world through the eyes of your movement; see it as it is."

* * *

It was not long after this outburst from Sabta that Yitzhak went to Dave's office to inquire about the Hashomer Hatzair partner. Dave was not there. The secretary said this was only a part-time job for Dave. Right now he was working at Cardozo Diesel in Haifa. Yitzhak could not believe his ears. "But he has a job here!" he sputtered.

"Each of Isradio's directors has a full-time career outside Isradio. One is a newspaperman and an army colonel, another is a couturière, two are lawyers, and one owns Cardozo Diesel."

"Which one was Hashomer Hatzair?" Yitzhak asked.

"Miriam Cohen, the couturière."

"How does one find her?"

"You could leave a message with me. By the way, my name is Mary Galili; who are you?"

"I am Yitzhak Brueckman. My father never believed in changing our name."

That night, Mary said to Yokhanan: "You know, it's really odd. Israelis always tell you much, much more than you asked them." She told him of Yitzhak Brueckman, who was ashamed of his family name.

"I know him. He was under my command in Upper Galilee. Where did you meet him?"

She told him.

"Invite him for dinner," Yokhanan said. "He's a kibbutznik. I'm dying to find out why he's working for Isradio."

* * *

"What do we do? Do we call to say that two of us are coming?" Genia asked.

"I went to the office and said you were coming. I thanked her for the invitation and asked how come."

" 'My husband is Yokhanan Galili,' she replied. 'He says he knows you and would like to renew old acquaintances.' Maybe we should also take Sabta to tell them about the class conflict . . . "

"Or lack thereof," Genia said.

Yitzhak drove Natasha's car to Tel Aviv. When they got to Bialik Street, Genia noticed the Erich Mendelsohn house across the street from Yokhanan's apartment house. She insisted on walking past it to look more closely, then offered the opinion that Natasha's house looked very much like it.

"Maybe they're by the same architect" Yitzhak offered.

"Can we ask?"

"No, we'll be late for dinner."

Genia had brought a bouquet from her garden. They went to the walk-up third floor apartment, looking at each name on every door as they climbed. They knew none of the names. When they came to the one marked "Galili," Yitzhak pointed at the door post. Genia made a questioning gesture with her hands and he whispered, "No *mezuzah*."

Genia had not noticed. None of the doors at Golania had a *mezuzah*, either. Neither did Natasha's house.

Yitzhak rang the bell, and Mary opened it. She held out her hand for Genia as Yitzhak introduced her. Yokhanan followed Mary to the door and threw his arms around Yitzhak.

The two kibbutzniks were totally unsure of how they should act, what to say, how much to stare at the surroundings. But there was one object that drew all attention of anyone who entered that living room. It was a large oil painting that startled the Brueckmans because it showed a gray-black Romanesque church with a cross on top of its square steeple. Underneath was the caption, "H. H. Richardson's Church of the Holy Bean Counters."

Mary, as always, noticed the amazement and calmly said, "That is my church on Commonwealth Avenue in Boston. I am a Baptist."

"Oh," was the only thing Genia could answer. She said to herself that she must find out what a Baptist is.

Yokhanan, who was used to having this little scene played each time new people came to the apartment, introduced several other people in the room.

"Genia and Yitzhak, I'd like you to meet Miss Billy Stone and her escort, Manny Cardozo. You, Yitzhak, have already met Dave Gordon and this is his date, Miriam Cohen, alias Mirco. Finally, I'd like you to meet Cynthia Bond, a friend of Mary's. If I have counted right, we have three people from Boston; small world isn't it? And we are all, except Cynthia, linked to Isradio. Cynthia does not yet speak Hebrew, so do you mind if we speak English? Can you understand English, Genia and Yitzhak?"

They both nodded, but Yitzhak said he did not understand how they were all linked to Isradio.

"Simple, we own it and you work there. So we are all in the Isradio family," Dave said.

Manny took over and outlined his ideas for industrializing Israel—briefly.

A servant in a white apron brought cocktails. Yitzhak and Genia refused the drinks. They thought they were being targeted for an ideological harangue as Miriam picked up where Manny left off. "I used to be in Hashomer Hatzair. I do not have to explain what my opinion then was of capitalists who exploit the proletariat. Now I am a capitalist like everyone else in this room. And, you know, I am dating a man who used to be in *Etzel*, Dave here. And we don't need to build a barbed-wire fence in our dining hall and can even sleep in the same bed . . . "

"Oh, Miriam! How could you?" Mary exclaimed. "Why you two are not even married!"

"Billy and Manny aren't, either," Miriam said, pretending to take her seriously. "If you ask them nicely, I think they will confess to sharing a bed, too."

They gathered around the dining table, where Mary had prepared what she called a "down-home" dinner. The first

course was a pink soup and Mary announced that it was shrimp
bisque.

"Manny found us a supply of shrimp with some fishermen
whose diesels he fixes. They can't sell their shrimp in Israel, so now
Manny gets them and freezes them and shares them with his grateful
unkosher friends," Mary said.

Yitzhak plowed into the soup without hesitation, Genia noticed. But she was a bit hesitant. "Go ahead, Genushka," he assured her. "You'll like it."

She took a tentative taste off a partly filled soup spoon and was
surprised that she did.

The main course, was what Mary called Boston baked beans,
which were served with boiled sausages. When the servant brought
out the beans, each in its little beanpot, Billy shrieked: "Baked
beans and hot dogs! Wow."

Genia watched how Billy ate hers, how she cut up the sausage
and dipped it into mustard. She followed her example.

Again, she liked what she ate, although she found the sweet-
ness of the beans surprising.

Manny asked Mary if she had any hot-dog buns.

Mary turned to the servant and she brought one out to Manny,
who broke open the bun, placed the sausage inside, slathered it
with mustard and piccalilli, and proceeded to eat it in his fingers.

Genia would have liked to try that too, but was afraid to ask.
But then she blurted out something that made Yitzhak shove his
elbow into her side: "Is this how rich capitalists eat all the time?"

"So who's rich?" Yokhanan said.

Miriam immediately recognized what was happening on the
other side of the table and asked: "How long have you two been off
the kibbutz?"

"Less than two weeks," Genia said.

"OK," Miriam said. "Let me tell you about the world outside
the kibbutz. As you can see, we are all friends in this room. Manny
feels comfortable enough to ask the hostess for something that she
did not serve on the table. I feel comfortable enough to tell you

aloud that it is no sin to fear strange, new foods that you never saw on your *meshek*. But please, never be afraid to ask what you want to know; never feel that you are 'out of place.' If Yokhanan and Mary had not wanted you here, they would not have invited you. Now that you are here, make yourself at home just as you would feel at a general meeting of the members. You may say anything. Mary won't even mind if you ask her what a Baptist is, will you?"

"Not at all, but if I do, Cynthia will say I'm all wet. She was my roommate at Brandeis and she's Catholic. We used to argue all the time at Brandeis."

"What made two Christian women go to Brandeis?" Dave asked.

"Mary and I went for different reasons," Cynthia said. "Mary was rebelling against her family; I wanted to go because I wanted to learn about my origins. My father always concealed the fact that he was a Jew who converted to the Roman Catholic Church. He was born Berkowitz. When I found out, I wanted to know what the Jewish part of me was, so I went to Brandeis."

"I sincerely hope you were not too disappointed," Yokhanan said.

"Let's not get into that now, Jon," Mary admonished.

After dinner, they all turned their attention to Genia. Yokhanan had started it by saying: "Genia, do you know anything about the religious beliefs your father held?"

"How do you know about my father?" she asked,

"Come, now, this is Israel. Everybody knows everything about everybody. When Mary told me Yitzhak worked in our factory, I recognized his name immediately, remembered your wedding, re-called who your father was, and said, 'Invite them.' Surely you read in that rag that serves as a newspaper in your *meshek* that I have been at great odds with the rabbinates and that I take a great interest in religion."

"Yes," Genia answered, "but I really know very little about my father's views except what he wrote, and my grandmother says not to believe anything he wrote. My grandmother is his mother. She hates Stalin."

Cynthia was lost: "Can someone fill me in? Or did I miss something?"

Yokhanan quickly explained: "Genia is the daughter of Maxim Koganov, one of the great leaders of the Bolshevik Revolution. He was purged by Stalin in the 1930s."

Then he turned back to Genia. "Tell me, Genia. When you were a little girl, was there a *mezuzah* on the doorpost of your home?"

"No, the first I ever saw was at my grandmother's in Leningrad."

"Did your father eat pork, Genia?"

"I think so. My mother's book said something about pork being served at a Kremlin dinner and both my parents ate it."

"So they were conscious that it was pork when they ate it at the Kremlin," Yokhanan said. "That means they probably did not eat it regularly."

"Maybe," Genia said.

"How about you, Genia, would you have eaten a pork chop if Mary had served it at dinner tonight?"

"Sure. During the austerity period, Golania ate pork several times. We bought the pigs from Christian Arabs. Most of the members ate the meat."

"OK, Genia, one more question. I notice that both your parents are Jewish. Were they married before or after the revolution?"

"Much after."

"Would either of them have married a Russian?"

"You mean a Russian who wasn't Jewish?"

"Obviously."

"From what I read in my mother's book, she would have married Adolf Hitler if he had asked her. She lived with a Nazi a long time. My father, on the other hand, would probably not have married anyone who wasn't Jewish."

"That proves my point," said Manny. "You must all admit that Maxim Koganov was not a Jew in the religious sense. He was a Bolshevik. Religion was the opiate of the people. He bad nothing but contempt for the religion of his ancestors. But he was still a member of the Hebrew nation, a Russian Hebrew, who would only marry another Hebrew."

"Jesus," Dave said. "Are you still on that tack, Manny? He drove us crazy in the Azores with that stupid theory."

"Dave, I'll thank you not to call my legitimate point of view a 'stupid theory.' In Yokhanan's home, my views are as welcome as yours. That is why we are friends. I have a right to my opinions and you to yours. And I am an American Jew—who has just become an Israeli citizen, making me an Israeli Hebrew."

"I heard that debate in Brandeis," Cynthia said. "It's the age old argument whether Jews are just a religion or whether they constitute a nationality. Mary and I sort of prove Manny's viewpoint. I am a Catholic American Hebrew. Mary is a Baptist American Baptist. Yokhanan, just for the record, is an atheist Israeli Hebrew. Does that settle it?"

"Cynthia," Yokhanan said, "you have just simplified my series of questions to Genia to the quick. I think you should be named chief rabbi of Israel. You're much wiser than the current ones."

"Plural, Jon?" Cynthia asked.

"Sure, Sephardic and Ashkenazic."

"You mean you have separate establishments for European and Oriental Jews?"

"Hey, Cynthia," Manny said. "I'm not exactly Oriental. I'm from Colorado and that isn't even half way to China, but I am definitely Sephardic."

* * *

The conversation lasted until late in the night. On the drive home, Genia said, "I have never had such a wonderful time. We talked about everything. We disagreed, agreed, and nobody got angry. We disagreed and agreed and nobody said 'anti-Semite, Communist, Fascist.' And we ate some really strange things. How did you like that 'Pie à la mode?' "

"Very good," Yitzhak said. "I liked the other food, too, and I was amazed at the conversations. You know, those were the first Christians I ever talked with. And Manny was the first Sephardi who was not from Yemen or North Africa. But let me ask you, what is Brandeis?"

"I don't know. It sounds like a university, but I don't know."

A few days later, Yitzhak went to the office during his lunch hour. He found Cynthia behind the secretary's desk. He asked her.

"Oh," she said, "I am so sorry. I could not imagine that there was anyone in that room who had never heard of it. It is a university near Boston sponsored by Jews. They say it is not a Jewish university, and there are many non-Jews and Negroes who attend, but just between you and me, it is a Jewish university."

"Tell me about Negroes, Cynthia."

"Awmygawd," she said. "You better arrange to get invited to another dinner party. That would take a lot of talking."

"If Genia and I gave a dinner party, would you and Mary come?" Yitzhak asked.

"Of course, silly. You set the time, and we'll be there. But don't forget to ask Yokhanan, too."

"Of course."

* * *

It was through dinner parties—once at Natasha's house, once at Dave's "Anglo-Saxon" apartment in north Tel Aviv where Miriam seemed to be at home, and once at Manny's—that Genia realized that Golania had failed to educate her properly. Yes, she knew four languages, and knew her numbers, her history, and how to read music. She knew about Jewish history, but she did not know anyone else's history or their beliefs and ideas.

Yitzhak, who had gone to the very good Reali School in Haifa, agreed with her. "But when I was taught some of that stuff, I couldn't imagine why."

When they ate at Manny's Rothschild Boulevard villa, there were two new people at dinner, a husband and wife who were both lawyers. He was in a wheelchair. And the conversation that night turned to Jewish intolerance.

"When I took on the case of Sha'ul Nachmani," Naomi Ben Horin said, "I was called a Fascist, a Communist, and an anti-Semite. I am none of those things and never have been."

Cynthia Bond chimed in: "You should have heard the stink I caused at the Ministry of Interior when I applied to be listed as a Jew under the Law of Return, based on my father's Jewishness."

"What happened?" Dave asked.

"First they were quite polite and explained that Jewishness carries through the mother, not the father. But then one of them asked me what my religion was, and I told him the truth. He just about exploded. 'So why does a *shiksa* like you want to come under the Law of the Return?' I told him I knew the exact meaning of the derogatory term he had just used, that he was calling me the scum of the earth, and I objected to being called names. So then he really went berserk. He wouldn't have the Pope in Rome telling him how to speak and a *shiksa* is a *shiksa*. In the end, I was refused. But I cannot imagine such intolerance from an American official."

"I can," Dave said. "When I was a prisoner in Lebanon, the American consul called me and all the other Jews every anti-Semitic term I had ever heard. Intolerance probably exists among all people, possibly in varying degrees."

"I always believed," Genia said, "that Russians are the most intolerant people, and that the Swiss, the Swedes, the Dutch, and the Danes the least."

"I wonder who measures the degrees of intolerance," Mary mused.

"OK, everybody," Jack said. "Let us all resolve here and now to put Israel on Genia's list with the Swiss and the Swedes. I like that company better."

Manny chimed in with, "I hear they're pretty nice in New Zealand and Costa Rica, too."

"Yeah, but only Rafael Trujillo opened the doors of his country, the Dominican Republic, to Jews after Hitler came to power," Yitzhak said.

"Yitzhak, where did you learn that?" Genia asked.

"In the Reali School!"

"That settles it," Genia said. "You are all so much smarter than I am, so better educated, what with Brandeis and MIT and the Colorado School of Mines, not to mention the Hebrew University. I have decided, if Yitzhak will permit, to go to university myself. I am so stupid, so unlettered. I think you will all like me better if I can say things I learned, too."

Mary put her arm around Genia's shoulder. "By all means, my dear, go back to school and absorb the wisdom of the ages. But never believe for a moment that we like you less if you don't or more if you do. You came into this *kaffeeklatsch* because you are Yitzhak's wife. We all adore you. We like your fresh viewpoint and your resistance to phoniness. You don't have to go to school to remain the friend of Yokhanan and Mary Galili, or of anybody else in this room."

They all chimed in with similar viewpoints.

"You mean, you think of me as a friend?" Genia asked. "The Hebrew word for 'friend' and for 'comrade,' *haver*, is the same. Comrades all think alike and are in the same movement and party. Can friends think differently, to believe in opposite tendencies?"

"Of course. All of us are friends," Manny said. "Isn't that clear to one and all?"

"But I do not always agree with what you say," Genia said. "So how can we be friends?"

"That's OK, Genia," Naomi said, "even Ya'akov and I don't always agree. Do you and Yitzhak always agree?"

She said "yes" very quietly.

They all raised their glasses as Manny proposed a toast to the only married couple that is never in disagreement.

"I will not drink to that," Yitzhak said. "We did disagree after the Mapai-Mapam split. We compromised by moving into town."

"I'll bet you haven't regretted it for a moment," Miriam said.

"Yes," Genia. said. "Sometimes I feel sorry for Sabta. She isn't a servant, you know. She is my grandmother. And she helps me with Michael and when we invited all of you to dinner. She should not have to work so hard any more. She is old. In the *meshek* , she did not have to work."

"Ask her sometime," Jack said, "if she would rather be in the *meshek* or be with you and your son."

JACK AND NAOMI V

Israel's biggest libel case was a precursor to the trial of Adolf Eichmann and included many of the same witnesses.

With a loan from Mary's family, Yokhanan had struck out on his own and began to publish a liberal fortnightly called *Ha-Liberali*, a "journal of lost causes" as Yokhanan called it and a "red-ink factory" as Mary termed it.

In 1953, Yokhanan met Joel Brand, the tragic figure who was imprisoned by the British when he carried Adolf Eichmann's offer to exchange the Jews of Hungary, the last million Jews of Europe, for trucks. After hearing the bare outline of Brand's story, Yokhanan decided to write a new book. He spent two or three hours a day questioning Brand. Then, one day, he saw the name of Dr. Yehuda Kahn in *Ha'aretz*.

"Is this the man you have been talking about?" Yokhanan asked Brand.

Brand broke into tears, and said: "Yes. He lives. He is in Israel. The Nazis spared him—and you know why."

The next issue of *Ha-Liberali* broke the story. Other survivors of Budapest—whose lives had been saved by the Christian Raoul Wallenberg, not by the Zionist Kahn—then came forward to fill in parts of the story that Brand did not know.

Kahn, the Jewish executioner of Hungary's Jews had been the head of the Hungarian Zionist Federation and the Jewish Agency's man in charge of "rescuing" Jews in Hungary. He selected which Jews to turn over to Eichmann. Selection meant a train ride to Auschwitz.

But Kahn also rescued some Jews, who left Hungary aboard a special train dubbed the Kahn Limited. It carried to safety in Switzerland some 400 prominent members of Kahn's own Zionist party and about 200 of Kahn's friends and relatives.

Other Israeli newspapers picked up the story from *Ha-Liberali*, but they were careful. They stayed well inside the boundaries of libel or slander, but Yokhanan was not made of such stuff. He let go with full force in an extra edition after questioning survivors, Israeli officials, and the director of the Jewish Documentation Center in Vienna, Simon Wiesenthal. He also spent days on end at Yad Vashem, the Israeli archive on the Holocaust, and found corroboration for what he had been told by Brand.

And so *Ha-Liberali* appeared with an expanded press run for an extra that Yokhanan dubbed "Eichmann Walks Among Us."

It was a sixteen-page affair with a two-column editorial on its front page. Fifteen-and-a-half pages were thoroughly documented facts. But the half-page editorial brought a million-pound libel suit from Kahn.

Who really runs Israel?

The moral leaders of the world sit in their Dome of Depression along New York's East River, and tell us whether we may live. They have a high UNO ethical code, but it is written in two ways: one way for them, another way for us.

They sat by and watched six million Jews get slaughtered. The Pope did not raise hell then as he does now over the miserable holy places when he perceives the slightest danger that, God forbid, a Jew should control the territory that contains them. When was the last time you heard the Pope lament the fact that Moslems administer the Christian holy places? When did he cry out that Jews are denied their holiest of holies, the Western Wall of the Temple or the Tomb of the Patriarchs?

They sat by and watched the six million get killed, but they would not allow those who escaped that fate to enter their lands. And now they bemoan and bewail that we have had the *chutzpah* to say "That's enough" when our children are killed at their desks by *fedayeen*, when our farms are made into battlefields, and when our ships are denied the freedom of the seas.

In speaking of the six million, Israelis often ask, "Why didn't they resist? Why didn't they fight?" One always perceives the undercurrent that remains unspoken, that something was perhaps not so noble in the deaths of these millions. One knows that Lodz had an "Elder of the Jews" who chose the names of the Jews who were to report for "labor service." One knew that in Vilna the young Jewish leader of the resistance was asked by the Jewish community to give himself up to the Nazis to prevent the execution of hundreds of hostages—who were shot anyway. But this did not answer the question.

One knows that when the leader of the Jewish resistance in Kovno wanted to warn the Jews about the killing grounds at Ponary, the Jewish leadership muzzled him.

One knew that brave Palestinian parachutists were dropped into Hungary to lead the Jewish resistance to Nazism, but one only knew that they died, including heroes and heroines whose names we still honor today: Hannah Szenes, Aviva Reich, and Enzo Sereni.

• One did not know that they were yielded to the Hungarian fascists by the leader of the Hungarian Zionist Federation, Dr. Laszlo Kahn.

• One did not know that Kahn and his family survived the Holocaust only by cooperating with the man who invented "The Final Solution to the Jewish Problem," Adolf Eichmann.

• One did not know that Kahn testified to the War Crimes tribunal in Nuremberg to save the life of SS Col. Kurt Becher, the man in charge of pulling Jews' gold teeth and of collecting every pfennig he could squeeze out of the dead Jews of Europe and the man who was in overall charge of all the extermination camps?

• One certainly did not know that Kahn showed up in Bergen Belsen with Becher, and both were in the uniform of the SS.

• One did not know that Kahn was the only Jew in Budapest allowed to drive a car, to have a telephone, and to wear suits that did not display the yellow star.

• One did not know that Zionist leaders, like Kahn, sent letters to the Jews of Hungary urging them to volunteer for "labor service" even when they knew that this was a synonym for death.

• One did not know that for motives of personal gain, one Jew could sell another Jew into the gas chamber. But Kahn did all these things and lives—here, in Israel.

Can one honestly keep any faith in the term "Zionism" when it meant organizing a Jewish police force that would do for the Nazis what would have taken precious manpower from the Nazi war effort? Yet Jewish police were organized by Kahn to round up Jews for the deportation trains.

And all this time, Kahn knew what "labor service" meant. He knew because the record shows that he was told by the Yishuv's heroic parachutist, Hannah Szenes, brave Hannah Szenes, whom Kahn turned over to the Nazis. The Nazis murdered Hannah Szenes.

Kahn knew the alternatives when he sent Joel Brand to Istanbul with Eichmann's infamous trucks-for-Jews offer. Not only had Eichmann told him, he even gave him a timetable. Britain was to deliver ten thousand trucks starting in two weeks to save a million Jews. After that the trains were to start rolling to Auschwitz carrying twelve thousand Jews a day until only Kahn and his "Zionist" aides remained.

But let no one think that Kahn is the murderer of Hungary's Jews. No, the Germans played that role. But

what does one call a man who ties the hands of another,
places a blindfold over his head, leads him to the trapdoor,
and then turns to the executioner and says: "Go ahead!"

* * *

Kahn is not guilty all alone. The world is guilty. Joel Brand
told the Allies and the Jewish Agency exactly what would
happen if the trucks were not delivered. The Jewish Agency
asked Winston Churchill and Franklin Roosevelt to bomb
the gas chambers, to slow down the efficiency of the death
machinery. But those good, humanitarian men were afraid
their bombs might hit innocent prisoners in the adjoining
concentration camps and kill a few! They would not even
order bombing the railroads out of Budapest because that
was in the area of their great Soviet ally and they had to leave
those tracks alone so they could be used by the Red Army.

So now we know. The six million did not resist because
they were led so well-by a man who would sell them into
death to save his own skin, to live well, to drink champagne
with Eichmann, to profit by their deaths.

* * *

Kahn's lawyers listed a half a dozen separate counts of libel in their
suit. To Jack and Naomi it became clear immediately that the truth
defense—showing that what had been called libel was really true—
would be tested most on the issue of whether Kahn had "profited."

If Brand was telling the truth, the truth defense was airtight,
but how could they prove "profited"? Yokhanan insisted that the
matter was really quite simple: "He is alive; he survived; *quod erat
demonstrandum!*"

Naomi agreed that Kahn's survival was sufficient proof that he
profited. Kahn's lawyers, however, insisted that Naomi had to prove
that Kahn had received money or other valuables from the Nazis

while Kahn, in fact, could prove that he had lost all his worldly goods when the Red Army eventually saved him from the last deportation train.

The trial was in Tel Aviv and the first witness for the defense was Joel Brand. Naomi led him gently and skillfully to keep him from breaking down in the witness box. When Naomi got near the end of her questions, Brand began to sob as he told of his imprisonment by the British in Egypt as a Nazi agent.

But Brand had not been the only one to offer the British a million Jews for ten thousand trucks. The next witness was the director general of the Ministry of the Interior, Amnon Hadani, who was an official of the Jewish Agency Executive at the time Brand arrived for his brief encounter with emissaries sent by Jewish Palestine.

"After Brand was brought to meet us on the Turkish-Syrian frontier," Hadani testified, "I flew to Cairo to plead with Lord Moyne. I never reached Lord Moyne. The British arrested me on charges that I was attempting to obtain matériel for the enemy. Jews, you see, do not count in the larger balance of the world. They are expendable. But trucks, now that is another matter! Trucks carry soldiers and some poor Tommy might get shot. One simply could not entertain such a suggestion. 'We are at war, you know,' they told me."

And then there was Ira Hirschman, President Roosevelt's special envoy on refugees, to whose office in Istanbul Brand had been sent. Jack was doing the questioning.

JACK: How did you know the offer was genuine, that Eichmann was not bluffing, that he intended to carry out his side of the deal?

HIRSCHMAN: Twelve thousand of the people who were to be traded were taken to a special camp in Hungary where the International Committee of the Red Cross duly found them. This was exactly what Eichmann had told Kahn to tell Brand. When Brand reached me, the Red Cross informed me that the Jews had arrived.

JACK: What assurances did you have that Eichmann would

not double cross you?

HIRSCHMAN: The German collapse on the Russian front. They needed those trucks, although they still would not have had fuel for them.

When the verdict was about to be announced, the sidewalks in front of the Tel Aviv courthouse were filled with people who had been unable to get in. Some wore their striped concentration camp uniforms. Many carried signs supporting Yokhanan and denouncing Kahn.

The judge ordered Yokhanan to rise as he began to read the verdict. Each count was ruled on separately. "Not guilty, not guilty, not guilty" five times. And then "Guilty!"

The audience, silent until now, stirred. There was a sigh here, a moan there, and then sobs.

The one count on which Yokhanan was found guilty was the allegation of profit. But Dr. Kahn's victory was pyrrhic. Yokhanan was fined one pound. The judge ordered that court costs be borne by the plaintiff, Kahn.

Kahn appealed to the Supreme Court.

Still, that did not end things for Kahn. His attempt to clear his name by suing Yokhanan made him a symbol of everything the native-born Israelis hated:

• Here was a "Zionist," a man dedicated to ending the Jewish Diaspora; yet he had stayed in Hungary.

• Here was a man who did help Eichmann's "Final Solution of the Jewish Problem" by choosing the candidates for death. An Israeli law made collaboration with the Nazis in the killing of Jews the only offense for which the death penalty could be invoked. Why had Kahn not been charged?

• Here was a man who, instead of leading a Jewish resistance to the Nazis, collaborated with the enemy of his people.

All over Israel—in cafés and in kibbutz *kumsitzes*, in cocktail lounges and in classrooms—the question of Jewish resistance was on everyone's lips. Why did they walk meekly to their deaths?

Why did they not take a few Nazis with them? Why hadn't Kahn pulled a gun on Eichmann to kill him?

And then the news came from Germany: Becher had somehow managed to keep all that gold from Jewish teeth for himself and was now the richest man in Germany.

Nor did the end of Yokhanan's trial end the case for Jack and Naomi. Before the Supreme Court could rule on Kahn's appeal, Kahn was shot on a Tel Aviv street by a young man whose father and mother had been put aboard an Auschwitz train on Kahn's diktat. They, too, had been Zionists. They sent their boy to Palestine for a summer in 1939, saving his life.

No defense was possible for the young man. He admitted the deed proudly. He even boasted of it, gloated in it. To many Israelis he was a hero, a *gibor*.

Naomi suggested that he should plead guilty by reason of insanity. He refused: "I knew exactly what I was doing. I was avenging my parents. Make *Shabbat* with it!"

Eventually, the young man was able to address the judge: "As God is my judge, I have done it. I am guilty of killing the murderer of my parents. I am proud of it. But this is not a crime. You cannot charge me with murder. One cannot murder the likes of Kahn; one can only execute them. I am the executioner. I plead guilty. I don't care what you do with me. 'An eye for an eye; a tooth for a tooth, justice is mine, sayeth the Lord.' "

Naomi tried to silence him. When he sat down, she asked that his plea not be entered until psychiatric examination could determine whether the youth was sane.

"I am not insane," he shouted.

The opposing lawyers were asked into chambers and the district attorney backed Naomi's request saying: "By every law of man, this man is guilty; but what court in Israel can sentence him? What court in Israel can punish him? Please, Your Honor, do not accept his plea and direct that a plea of not guilty by reason of insanity be entered on the court record."

"We cannot allow," the judge replied, "that Israelis take the law into their own hands. This boy deserves sympathy, but he does not have a license to act as an executioner. I will enter no plea pending a report from a psychiatrist. I hope counsel can agree on one medical expert because this is not the kind of case I want to see dragged out."

Two weeks later, trial resumed and the guilty plea was accepted. The psychiatrist had ruled him sane.

"Under the law," the judge declared, "I find you guilty of premeditated murder. The law carries a penalty of from twenty years to life in prison. In view of the circumstances in this case, I hereby impose the minimum penalty and hereby suspend sentence on good behavior."

The anti-climax came too late for the dead Kahn. The Supreme Court reversed the original judgment and overturned the ruling that Kahn was to pay Yokhanan's legal costs.

* * *

The libel trial and the murder trial that followed (Yokhanan's case was always referred to as the "Kahn trial" even though Kahn was the plaintiff, not the defendant) had taken Jack and Naomi to Tel Aviv for almost a year. They had sent Ruth off to Naomi's mother. They liked being in Tel Aviv for the company of Yokhanan and his friends, not to mention that Jack had known Dave Gordon in Betar.

"Do you realize, Ya'akov, that Ruthie has hardly seen us for a year?" Naomi asked as she was driving their new two-door Plymouth back to Jerusalem.

"Uhum."

"Let's take a trip, the three of us, and have a little fun," she said.

"I'm way ahead of you," Jack said. "I got the idea at Genia's house last week when I realized how much those people travel. I've got exit visas for all three of us for a trip to Europe. How about Italy?"

"Why Italy?"

"Because I never really saw what was worth seeing there. No Florence, no Pisa, no lakes, no art treasures, no historical sites."

"I would certainly call the Arch of Titus a historical site."

"Yeah, but you know what I mean."

"Sure. When do we leave?"

* * *

When they got back home. Israel had changed. There was a report every day about attacks by *fedayeen. The Voice of the Arabs* in Cairo broadcast a speech by a cabinet minister in which he said: "There is no reason why the *fedayeen . . .* should not penetrate deep into Israel and turn the lives of her people into a living hell." And hell it was. A school was blown up, killing twenty-four children. A bus to Eilat was attacked at Ma'alei Akrabim, and all its passengers machine-gunned. The highway to Jerusalem was unsafe and was impassable at night. The train to Jerusalem came under fire whenever it came close to the Jordanian frontier, and sometimes the tracks were mined. Settlements were attacked. Pipelines were cut.

"At least we in *Etzel* did not kill civilians and children!" Naomi said.

In the Knesset, David Ben Gurion said: "The government of Israel will not allow the country to be turned into a living hell, and the assassins and their masters will not go unpunished."

It was 1936 and 1939 all over again. People traveled in convoy and vehicles were armor plated. Israelis carried arms. But the *fedayeen* raids continued. Occasionally, the Israeli government—always worried about world public opinion, as if the world gave a tinker's damn whether one Jew or six million Jews were killed—would take action against the bases of operations from which the *fedayeen* launched their attacks. But the Arabs soon learned that Israel struck back only at police stations and army bases and learned to antici-pate where the reprisal raids would be because they knew where the *fedayeen* came from. So reprisal targets were defended and the raiders had to muster ever-greater force, using air power and armor. Thus, the situation slowly escalated from armistice to non-peace to near-war.

Land warfare was only part of the growing crisis. Egypt barred the use of the Suez Canal to Israeli vessels from the beginning, even under King Farouk. The republican coup led by Colonel Mohammed Naguib continued it. The Soviet Union vetoed condemnation of the blockade in the Security Council.

First, cargoes to or from Israel were banned. Next, under Colonel Gamal Abdel Nasser, ships that had docked in Israel within the past year were barred.

Israel continued to appeal to world public opinion. It wanted to show the world that Nasser wasn't nice. So an Israeli vessel, the *Bat Galim*, was sent into the canal. Nasser promptly confiscated it and jailed the crew for three months.

World public opinion didn't say boo or lift a finger, and Nasser noticed. He put guns on Ras Nasrani and announced that the Strait of Tiran leading to Israel's port of Eilat was closed to vessels except with approval of Egypt. Again world public opinion, so valued by the government of Israel and its leaders, did nothing. Nasser hiked the odds one more notch: He closed the air space over the Gulf of Aqaba to Israeli traffic, effectively stopping El Al from flying to East or South Africa because the only alternative routes passed over hostile Arab land.

Israel was choking. Its trade routes to the south and east were cut. Its balance of international payments, always in the red, plunged. And the *fedayeen* continued to maim and kill as *The Voice of the Arabs* chortled about the day the "government in Tel Abib" would be crushed, the Jews pushed into the sea, and David Ben Gurion and Chief of Staff Moshe Dayan hanged.

Growing ever bolder, Nasser nationalized the Suez Canal. Those Israelis who always depended on world public opinion smiled at each other like Cheshire cats. Nasser had finally gone too far, they said. England and France would never stand for it. Israel would finally have allies.

On the surface, it seemed that Israel was doing nothing about her commercial strangulation and the murder and mayhem of her people, but only on the surface. Early in October, Naomi found a red notice on her desk—secret and selective mobilization. Similar notices went to Major General Moshe HaCohen, Brigadier Amiram Ben Cohen, Colonel Yokhanan Galili, Major Akiva Barzilai, Captain Yitzhak Brueckman, Captain Miriam Cohen-Gordon, Air Force Brigadier David Gordon, Sergeant Major Mary Galili, Staff Sergeant Yevgenia Brueckman, Lieutenant Yohevet Stone, and Corporal Cynthia Bond. Manny Cardozo was not called up but learned of the mobilization from Billy Stone. He called the army and demanded to be called, too; he was.

It was the call-up for Operation Kadesh. According to the Book of Numbers, Kadesh was the place where Moses wrote a letter to the king of Edom: "You know all the troubles that have befallen Israel . . . and how the Egyptians have vexed us and vexed our fathers."

Operation Kadesh was to be the answer. Its goal was to kick Egypt out of the Sinai, to take one bank of the Suez Canal, to clear the entrance to the Gulf of Aqaba, and to end all harassment from the Gaza Strip by capturing it.

What Israeli soldiers won in the Hundred-Hour War Israeli diplomats, forever worried about world public opinion, lost even before the first shot was fired. Israel's secret alliance with Britain and France left Nasser stronger than ever, for it had not been the Israelis who had humbled Egypt's armies, it had been the "neo-colonialist" powers. Israelis could not even negotiate with Nasser; they had to work through go-betweens from the U.N.

The Suez war bore bitter fruit for Israel.

Moshe HaCohen, conqueror of Eilat, opened the Gulf of Aqaba by capturing Sharm el-Sheikh and Ras Nasrani. Moshe's Golani Brigade, now the Ninth Reserve Infantry Brigade, was given the hardest job of the three columns that raced into Sinai. Where the others had roads, the Golanis had sand dunes. Where the others had flat land, the Golanis had the worst terrain on the face of God's earth, starting at the Dead Sea, lowest point on earth. They

pushed and pulled their vehicles and their guns between the gran-
ite cliffs and over the quicksand, getting unleavened bread and
rationed water for the entire two hundred and fifty miles.

During briefings for Operation Kadesh, Moshe had been told
that he could not ask for reinforcements; there were none. But the
general staff's timetable for the capture of Sharm el-Sheikh was D-
Day Plus Five while the Golanis were held back until D-Day Plus
Two to make sure Israel had air superiority to protect Moshe's
column, the most valuable of the three attacking forces. As Moshe
reported his slow progress, the general staff dropped an airborne
brigade at the tip of Sinai to help in the final assault on Sharm el-
Sheikh.

When they reached Ras Nasrani—on what was called the Strait
of Yotvath in Hebrew—the Golanis found that the Egyptians had
fled, abandoning their workable guns to the Golanis. Intelligence
said the troops had been moved to Sharm for a last-ditch defense.

The Airborne Brigade, fresh from the capture of El Tur on the
Red Sea, joined the Golani attack, but they all had to withdraw
because of Egyptian mine fields and a fierce defense. Moshe was
desolate. The navy had not delivered the tanks that had been
shipped around Africa and the paratroopers possessed no armor.

At that exact moment, as the battle was paused, Dayan—who
had dreamed up Operation Kadesh, complete with the failed Anglo-
French attacks on Suez and Kantara—arrived on the scene and
took command. Moshe wanted to attack at night, recalling his
experience without armor and without air cover in 1948. The para-
trooper commander wanted to await direct air support from the
air force. Moshe got his way and the Golanis attacked at 3 a.m. They
failed. The most elite unit of the Israeli military was thrown back.

Though Egypt had not expected an overland attack on Sharm
el-Sheikh, it had anticipated an airborne assault. Therefore, Sharm
el-Sheikh had a fine perimeter defense that the Golanis simply
could not pierce.

At dawn, Dave Gordon's fighter-bombers came over the hori-
zon, followed by fighters that strafed and shelled the fortifications.

The Egyptians retreated to their final resistance lines with the half-tracks and the combat jeeps of the Golanis in pursuit. By noon, Sharm el-Sheikh was flying the blue-white flag of Israel.

Moshe called Operation Kadesh "Exodus in Reverse." Here were Israelis marching through Sinai on five liters of water per man per day, including washing and cooking water, eating unleavened bread. But they were not trudging toward Israel like Moses; they were marching out of it,

At the parade on the Sharm el-Sheikh airfield the following day, Moshe said: "Moses our teacher led our people through this desert for forty years to kill off one generation of slaves and to breed one generation of free men. It took you only one hundred hours to prove that this generation of free men is made of the same stuff from which was made the generation of Joshua Bin Nun."

* * *

But what the Golanis and the paratroopers and the air force won in one hundred hours was already lost. The French and British landings in the Suez Canal Zone were disguised as an attempt to keep the Israelis and Egyptians from interfering with the canal. London and Paris sent Egypt—as well as their secret ally, Israel— an ultimatum to stay ten miles from the canal. Then they took their sweet time before landing their first troops at Port Said, long after Israel had seized most of Sinai. By now world public opinion had taken over.

While Soviet tanks were shooting up civilians in Budapest, the Russians at the United Nations joined the Americans in proclaiming their love of peace. They demanded that Israel pull its forces back to the 1948 armistice lines. They pledged nothing in return. At the very same time, the Russians went merrily about their slaughter in Hungary, totally unconcerned about world public opinion.

Cynics noted that what a small country (Israel) does is subject to moralizing; but what big powers do is nobody's business.

Yokhanan did a piece on it for *Ha-Liberali*:

Pioneers and Sabras

The basic contradiction of Israeli politics, even before statehood, has been that we have an élite, a generation of so-called pioneers who came here with the Bilu and the First Aliyah and has held power ever since. You know who they are. Give them a cabinet portfolio and they are instant experts on any subject because they belong to that élite. They are, oh, so clever at diplomacy that they can lose a war even before our army has taken the field. They are equally clever at making fine speeches at the United Nations, in flawless and cultured English. They make us ordinary *sabras* look like so many peasants, like boors, like country bumpkins who have not yet mastered the ways of high society.

These distinguished gentlemen are now showing us their greatest talent in making the impossible look easy. Their problem is how a victorious army can be asked to withdraw from the lands it has conquered while it gets nothing in return: No security; no freedom of navigation through the Suez Canal; no guarantee that the Strait of Yotvath is not blocked again. But they will bring off this miracle because we are going to have Lester Pearson's "peacekeepers" guarding our frontier.

Oh certainly, the UNO peacekeepers will not be stationed on our territory, we couldn't possibly permit that! They will be on Nasser's side of the line and they will keep us secure even though Nasser is free at any time to tell them to leave. But our able diplomatists do not need to concern themselves about that. After all, the Israel Defense Force crushed Nasser's army and it will be a very long time before he can mount another attack.

And what of the *sabras*? How many cabinet ministers were born in this country? How many of them are under the age of forty? How many are from Morocco? From Iraq? From the Yemen?

None.

Oh, no, they would not be cultivated enough to run this country. But then, who ever heard of a Moroccan Jew who walked into a gas chamber without a murmur of protest? Who can forget that the Yemen was once a Jewish kingdom? Who can forget that these "black" Jews never made deals with the Eichmanns of their lands?

Ah yes, it's wonderful. UNO's secretary-general, U Thant, will be Israel's first line of defense as troops from Indonesia and from India—two countries that do not even recognize the existence of our country—stand guard over our border. This is what the élite has wrought. Some élite!

But we have friends, too. Rule Britannia and Vive la France! They "rescued" us at Port Said. They wanted desperately to put Compagnie Maritime de Suez back into business so oil tankers would pay their tolls to them and not to that evil Gamal Abdel Nasser, who looks Semitic enough to be a Jew. But we should not complain. These wonderful allies sold us planes with which to defend ourselves while they also sold them at the very same time to the Arab states. Business as usual, it's real John Bull.

And what of our good friends in America? Let's talk about the Christian ones first. They cannot bear to have their embassy in Jerusalem because we "grabbed" the city illegally. They cannot tolerate our "aggression" against Gamal Abdel Nasser, but do you ever recall them demanding that the *fedayeen* raids stop?

These holier than holy people sent their broadcasts daily to the people of East Europe over their *Radio Free Europe* and actually promised those poor slaves of Soviet imperialism that if they were to revolt, America—big strong America—would join them on the barricades. So where were the Americans on June 17, 1953, when East Berlin revolted? Where were the Yanks in Budapest? Sailing up and down our coast in their Sixth Fleet to blockade us, that's where they were; getting ready to land their Marines in Tel Aviv, that's where they were.

And what of our faithful Jews of America, the ones who give all that money and then like to come over here to ask: "Where's the plaque with my name on it? I gave $1,000."

Were they in our army? No.

Were they in our kibbutzim or in our factories? No.

They bought themselves a clear conscience, but God forbid their children should even think of coming here to live. No! That's not the American way of life.

And what of our Marxist-Leninist friends in the Kremlin? They recognized Israel hours after its birth-to embarrass the capitalist states. Damned decent of them.

But what have they done for us since? They had a "doctors' plot," and Jews went to jail.

They closed down synagogues, and Jews went to jail.

They pressured their puppets in Hungary and Czechoslovakia, and Jews were executed.

And then, demonstrating the superior logic of Marxist dialectics, they refer to Israel, tiny little Israel, as a "neocolonialist power" and send planes and tanks to Gamal Abdel Nasser, good old Nasser, their ally, who puts Communists in jail. But he also puts Jews in jail, so they have something in common.

Yet all these people, together with their friends from dictatorships like Soekarno's Indonesia, Trujillo's Dominican Republic, Batista's Cuba, Salazar's Portugal, Tito's Yugoslavia, and Chiang Kai-shek's Formosa sit in their multinational palace in New York and decide for us how we should behave. After all, history has taught them that the only good Jew is a dead Jew. They hope to let it come to pass. They will defend us. They will protect us.

God forbid!

* * *

Naomi returned from the underground headquarters of the general staff in Ramat Gan to find that their firm had become identified with "big" and difficult cases. They were still known as Herut lawyers, despite the fact that they had publicly left the party during the fight over Yokhanan's baby. While they gained a few cases from people outside their former movement, their defenses of Yokhanan drove off Orthodox clients needing help with secular law.

Both started writing pieces for Yokhanan's journal. But then the second half of Kahn vs. Galili hit. The Mossad had found Eichmann in Argentina and had brought him to Israel. World public opinion, always ready to condemn Israel, did so again for not observing the niceties of international relations. The world, which had remained so silent when six million Jews were transported to the killing pits and the gas chambers while Eichmann was solving the "Jewish problem" once and for all, now howled because Israeli agents had transported Eichmann to Israel. They charged that Eichmann had been kidnapped.

For the Israeli bar, Eichmann was a dilemma. Should Israel assuage world public opinion by permitting his trial by an international tribunal patterned after the one at Nuremberg? Should Israel apply its laws against genocide to Eichmann, who had committed his crimes before the very existence of Israel, thus raising the specter of *ex-post-facto* law in his defense?

Jack noted in *Ha-Liberali* that the International Convention on Genocide, which had been passed many years before by the General Assembly, had yet to be ratified by such bastions of enlightenment as the United States of America. "There is no international tribunal that can or could try Eichmann," he wrote. "There is no law to bring him to justice, except in West Germany, where he would get a slap on the wrist and receive a pension as a veteran or, even more likely, be exonerated because he 'only obeyed orders from the Führer.' "

The government determined that it would try Eichmann, world

public opinion be damned! But it needed defense lawyers, lawyers to appear on behalf of Eichmann.

One Israel lawyer after another turned down the attorney general's request. Chanan did not ask Jack and Naomi—at first. Not only were they former members of *Etzel*, but he remembered how Naomi had got the best of him in the Nachmani case and how, in the Kahn trial, they did not hesitate to embarrass the Mapai government by forcing Amnon Hadani to testify.

Finally, Chanan invited them to "join" Eichmann's defense.

"Whom are we joining, Chanan?" Naomi asked him over the phone.

"I don't know yet, Naomi. We have many invitations out."

"Why don't you invite some of those American lawyers in the State Department who so deplored bringing Eichmann here?" Naomi asked.

"You know very well we must have local counsel."

"Did Eichmann allow Jews to defend themselves, Chanan?"

"Naomi, I do not wish to argue the merits of the case now. We'll do that in court. All I ask is that you join the defense."

"And all I'm telling you is that you can keep looking. Neither Ya'akov, who lost his entire family to the Nazis, nor I would lift a finger to defend Eichmann."

"That is not what you preached when you defended Sha'ul Nachmani, Naomi."

"Sha'ul Nachmani never killed a Jew, or need I remind you of that?"

When no Israeli lawyer could be found for Eichmann, a German lawyer was brought in. Again Chanan called on the Ben Horins, this time only to assist the German chief counsel on points of Israeli law. Chanan added that since Jack and Naomi had built their practice by defending unpopular causes, their practice would not be damaged by adding one more.

When she told Jack what Chanan had said, Jack turned his wheelchair toward her desk and blew up: "Fuck him, Naomi. This is no 'unpopular cause.' This is the devil himself. I'd just as soon shoot the bastard as try him. After the Kahn cases it's pretty obvious he'll hang, and the sooner the better. Let Chanan find another patsy. Chanan can run his show trial any way he wants, but without me."

Naomi told him not to get upset.

He was shaking: "God damn it, why shouldn't I get upset? Just because I don't make it a practice to talk about the murder of my family day and night the way some people do around here, that has not brought them back to life. Ruthie and I are the only Frumkins or Apfelbaums remaining in this world and you tell me not to get upset over the thought of defending the man who killed my family. Tell Chanan he can go to hell."

"I have not suggested that we accept, Ya'akov, but . . . "

"No buts! No anything. Just no!"

There was a short silence. Jack sat brooding. He turned the chair around and began fiddling with a file on his desk.

"Naomi, I've been thinking that just for once I wish I were a *Mapainik* so I could join the prosecution."

"But that's the 'but' I've been trying to tell you. We would be on Chanan's staff, not of defense counsel. Our task would be to advise the Kraut lawyer on matters of Israeli law."

She was proud of her continuing use of GI slang from Italy. But Jack paid no attention.

"Where did you get that brilliant idea? That isn't what Chanan said. And besides, I wouldn't trust myself to do even that. The net result would still be that we would be helping Eichmann. Forget it, Naomi. Without me!"

"Perhaps with me, Ya'akov," she said softly.

"What?" he screamed. "*The Voice of Fighting Zion* defending Eichmann. Irgun Irma defending that? Are you kidding? And besides, I thought we were agreed on the matter of accepting or refusing cases. I have let you accept or refuse, aren't you going to do the same for me, especially in this instance?"

"Stop it, Ya'akov. Someone must do it. If the State of Israel we of *Etzel* helped create is to become a real democracy, we must have justice and the rule of law. Democracy cannot exist without them. If it will make you feel any better, I have a solution. I shall go on active duty and have Moshe HaCohen, the new chief of staff, order me to work in Eichmann's defense on my army pay and in the service of the nation."

"Naomi, have you gone mad?"

"No, Ya'akov, not mad. Not mad at all. I have thought it over very carefully. I know you will think that because I am a fourth-generation *sabra* I do not feel for the Jews of the Holocaust what you do. I know you will think I am not being considerate to your father's murder by the storm troopers or the murder of your grand-mothers. Believe me, I bleed for them. I do not relish this case, but Israel cannot be permitted to lynch Eichmann. 'It must be seen that justice is done,' as one of your justices in America said."

"Aha. The *sabra* speaks! 'You Americans,' eh? Next you'll be saying 'You *yeckes*' because I am a German Jew."

"Hush, Ya'akov. Surely you know me better than that. Let us not quarrel. I am indeed sorry I said that. You are Israeli. You have become what you said to me in Gorizia you would like to become, 'a Jewish Jew from Palestine.' "

"All right. I accept your apology. But let's get something straight. Have you already made your deal with Chanan?"

"No, Ya'akov. I would never do that without your consent. I did call him this afternoon. That's when he told me I would work for the prosecution, not for the defense. But I would need you. You speak German; I do not."

"How are you going to get me back into uniform? After all, I was invalided out."

"Chanan said that would be taken care of. You would be given a brevet commission in the legal branch, and I would be trans-ferred from the general staff. Are you changing your mind?"

"Let me think about it a few days."

Three days later, Jack went to *Ha-Liberali* in Tel Aviv to ask Yokhanan's advice.

"Mary and I have been talking about this," Yokhanan said.

"We suspected you might be asked."

"And what did you decide?"

"Mary hoped you could bring yourself to do it. She quoted some American judge who said, 'Justice must not only be done, it . . . '"

" ' . . . must be seen to be done,' " Jack chimed in, smiling. "Do you agree with that, Yokhanan?"

"Yes, Jack. I agree. But I could not bring myself to do it even though I suffered no losses from Hitler. I would not think less of you if you rejected the offer."

"Naomi wants to do it."

"Really?" Yokhanan asked, his brow rising.

"Hey, for Christ's sake, Jon," Jack screeched, suddenly remembering whom he was talking to. "Don't you dare print a word about this!"

"Relax. I wouldn't. If nothing else, I know how to keep a confidence, and I still owe Naomi for inviting a *Palmachnik* to a *Shabbat* dinner in Washington Heights. You know, that was the first step toward making me a political liberal."

"Thanks."

* * *

It was Ruthie who ended Jack's battle with his demons. At supper she asked: "*Aba*, I know *Ima*'s parents. Why don't I know yours? Where are they?"

"*Aba*'s parents died in the Holocaust, Ruthie," Naomi said.

The child merely said, "Oh!"

" . . . and you want me to defend him?" Jack said, looking at Naomi.

"So your answer is no?"

"Yes. My answer is no."

"Then my answer shall be no, as well, Ya'akov. I too have thought about it, from your point of view. I understand. I cannot ask you to act against your conscience. Believe me, I did not relish the idea of doing this, but someone has to do it, even if we do not."

"I know," Jack said, "and it won't be us. I don't know why, but a phrase keeps running through my head: 'Masada shall not fall again.' It's like your flashbacks on the word 'shitless.' It doesn't even relate to Eichmann and it doesn't have anything to do with us, but when we teach Ruthie about the Holocaust, we have to start in Fusine Laghi, with that inscription I showed Rabbi Morris Goldberg, of blessed memory be he. 'In blood and fire, Judea fell; in blood and fire, Judea shall rise.' Through that, I came to you. And, damn it, that's where the Masada thing comes in. Helping some Kraut lawyer defend Eichmann is like helping to build the ramp up to the battlements at Masada. And that leads to the Arch of Titus, with the bas-relief of the Romans carrying the sacred objects from the Temple to Rome. Suddenly Jacob Frumkin is on the edge of the stage of history, but this stage I shall not climb. Fuck Eichmann!"

She got up and kissed him.

EPILOGUE

Of course the story does not end here.

In 1966, Golania was shelled from the Golan Heights, destroying the middle children's house. Twelve children were killed.

Gamal Abdel Nasser asked United Nations Secretary General U Thant to remove the "peacekeepers" from Egypt, and the *fedayeen* again started attacking Israelis. The Gulf of Aqaba was again closed to Israeli shipping and *The Voice of the Arabs* again predicted the annihilation of Israel's Jews.

Before Israel struck back in what has become known as the Six-Day War in 1967, Jordan's King Hussein was warned that if Jordan stayed out of the coming fray, Israel would not attack Jordan. The Jordanians answered by shelling the New City of Jerusalem. Jack was killed instantly when a shell hit the Ben Horin apartment; Naomi and Ruthie were seriously injured. While Ruthie recovered fully, Naomi lost two fingers on her left hand. When Menachem Begin led his party to victory in 1977, Naomi became Israel's ambassador to the United Nations.

In the 1967 war, Israel took the entire area of the original mandate west of the Jordan River, including the Old City of Jerusalem. Jews could, once again, worship at the Western Wall of the Temple and in the Tomb of the Patriarchs in Hebron. By taking the Golan Heights, Israel guaranteed that the intermittent shelling of the Upper Galilee would never recur. But while the war raged high above Golania, Golania's Moshe HaCohen opened Israel's sea lanes to the east for the third time since independence, this time as chief of staff.

Genia and Yitzhak were with the Golanis when they crossed the Suez Canal into Egypt.

Yokhanan was among those who were wounded in the climb to the top of the Golan.

Mary served in an evacuation hospital in the Sinai, Cynthia at an air base near Afula.

Dave reported to the air base at Ramat David before the general call-up and led the attacks on Egyptian airfields, destroying the entire Egyptian air force on the ground. Isradio eventually was listed on the New York Stock Exchange and was making computer chips, memory, and hand-held message pads. But Dave sold his stock and joined Israel Aircraft Industries, returning to his first love, aeronautics.

Miriam was sent to Rosh Hanikra to join an artillery battery guarding Israel's sea lanes to the north. Her Mirco Fashions firm also won a listing on the New York Stock Exchange, but was eventually bought out by an American conglomerate.

Manny's Cardozo Diesel did not quite meet Manny's hopes and dreams, but Cardozo Tyre was listed on the American Stock Exchange while the diesels traded over the counter. Manny and Billy were married in the great Sephardic synagogue on Shadall Street in Tel Aviv. No American Cardozos attended, although Sally Jane had carefully sent engraved invitations to all of them. Dave and Miriam were in the wedding party, as were all the people who met regularly at the Galilis' apartment.

When the Galilis had their second baby, they named her Naomi. Had it been a boy, he would have been Ya'akov.

Yokhanan and Mary were aware that naming children after the living was anathema to most Ashkenazic Jews, which is what Yokhanan was; but he realized that it was completely acceptable in the Sephardic tradition. Yokhanan felt that in Israel, where all Jews are brothers, one could take from either or both traditions. Anyway, Mary wanted those names, and Yokhanan, who had won many battles, did not want a battle with her.

Menachem Begin met with Yokhanan while he was forming his first cabinet. He offered Yokhanan the defense portfolio; Yokhanan turned him down, saying he wanted to be minister of religion. Begin, a very pious Jew, laughed in his face, saying: "No, My Dear. That is out of the question. Most of those who voted for Herut came to us from the National Religious Front. I shall not chase them back by humoring you. It's up to you, defense—where even the Orthodox will recognize you as an able holder of that portfolio—or nothing."

Yokhanan accepted.

Yitzhak Brueckman earned a study-by-mail bachelor of science degree from Pennsylvania State University, and became general manager and chief operating officer of Isradio. On the day he was made CEO, he came home with flowers. When he gave them to Genia, he said: "At last we can afford to live in this house." The Brueckmans changed their name to Ben Ha-Bricha and Genia's second child was named Yokhanan.

Manny and Billy fought over a name for their firstborn, but Manny won out: the boy was named Ben—for Ben Hecht, not for Benjamin Cardozo.

Needless to say, the characters in this novel are fictitious, but many of the events are real.